SUN KINGS

Noel R. Byrne

Copyright © 2015 by Noel R. Byrne

Published in 2015 by
CompletelyNovel.com

The right of Noel R. Byrne to be identified as the Author of the Work has been asserted by him in accordance with the Copyright, Designs and Patents Act 1988.

All rights reserved. No part of this publication may be reproduced, stored in a retrieval system, or transmitted, in any form or by any means, electronic, mechanical, photocopying, recording or otherwise, without the prior permission of the author, nor be otherwise circulated in any form of binding or cover other than that in which it is published and without a similar condition, including this condition, being imposed on the subsequent purchaser.

This book is a work of fiction and as such all events and characters are products of the author's imagination. Any resemblance of characters to actual persons, living or dead, is purely coincidental.

ISBN 978-1-849-14614-2

This book is dedicated to my wife, Antonia, whose patience and encouragement made it possible.

Special thanks also to:

Corinne, Gareth and Knuckles who convinced me I might be able to tell a story.

The Scribblers, whose constructive criticism and humorous derision kept me thinking and refining.

Prologue

Somewhere in the ground, buried in the bosom of the earth, a thought flutters and flits, a butterfly uncertain where to land. A mind, clouded with the comfortable touch of a long and restful sleep, flickers back into existence, into awareness.

Pushing gently into the waking world, this mind begins to wonder. How long have I slept? Where is this that I rest? Doubt does not last long, and memory begins its welcome return, gently rolling back the fog that slows the stirring thoughts, like a winter sun easing past the morning frost.

While it ponders what the future might hold and how like the past it may be, the mind settles down, somewhere in the ground, buried in the bosom of the earth, and waits.

oOo

The birds were quiet in the evening. There was no noise from the wolves and wild creatures of the surrounding woods either, for animals have a sixth sense about such things, and tonight, they could smell the blood and fire on the wind.

When he heard the crash, Kip Tildry awoke as though he had been plunged in ice water, heart galloping in his chest. He swung himself out of bed and onto his feet, grabbing his old sword from its place on the wall. He leapt back across the bed and scrambled for the door, but even as he did, the door exploded.

Great chunks, pieces and splinters whistled into the room,

flying forth in all directions, filling the air with wood. The door handle itself spun across the bed, shattering the small window on the opposite wall.

Framed in the jagged doorway, a huge figure filled the tiny space. It stooped to leer wildly in, thick blood streaked across its face and on the pointed teeth. An animal bulk of taut muscle rippled and flexed beneath the pale skin, dark hair crested its head and broad shoulders. From somewhere deep in the cavernous chest, came a low, rumbling growl, and what seemed a grotesque imitation of a smile split the vicious mouth.

Kip's feet slid uselessly against the floor, pedalling vainly backwards. As his legs gave way, he crashed down heavily on to his back, and his sword clattered from his hand. He half-slid, half-crawled clumsily away, hands and feet thrashing on the wooden boards.

The creature reached in. Arms like tree trunks stretched forward into the room. Kip narrowly avoided the thick, grasping fingers, pulling his legs desperately up to his chest as he continued to scramble away.

The creature gazed around the room, until it lighted on a set of skulls, cleaned and mounted like trophies on the far wall. Familiar shapes, though smaller and more delicate than the creature's own heavy brow, its jutting jaw, were mirrored in the grim display. For the briefest of moments, Kip's eyes met the creature's, sparkling black, and hateful.

Kip rolled, wailing madly, and dragged himself to the window. Clumsily, he flung himself outside, thinking of nothing, instinct alone guiding him, urging him to survive. He struggled to his feet in the mud and dirt beneath the window, blinking in the night air, and staggered on. He ran wildly down the slope towards the rest of the village, didn't look back as a furious roar erupted from the window behind him. But after a few steps, his pace slowed and he came to a stop. He stood open-mouthed, tears streaking his face, a warm, orange light dancing in the wet trails on his cheeks.

Before him, the village burned, brightening the night sky with a hazy glow. Kip dropped to the ground and sat, gagging and crying in the mud, unable to do anything else. When he heard footsteps in the earth behind he turned, looking up with round, red eyes. For an instant he saw the creature from his house, a crude, wide sword raised high in its hands. He screwed up his eyes and raised his arms uselessly to protect himself, before the broad blade split his skull in two.

In the silence, another man stepped out from the shadows behind the creature, slowly clapping his gloved hands in approval. Most of his tall frame was hidden by a long cloak and hood, stout leathers and light mail just visible beneath.
"Well done," he said, softly, "But make sure you leave one or two alive. There must be witnesses for the word to spread."

The creature turned slowly to look down at the newcomer, lips pulled back across its sharp teeth in a disdainful snarl. But after a few moments it gave a careful nod.

The man gave a broad and easy smile, green eyes flashing in the firelight.
"Don't worry. You and the others will have everything you were promised. Just do as we agreed."

Chapter One

Deep in the Empire's western reaches, not far from the vast Furrindoun Woods, the village of Lerncos stands. Perhaps half a day's ride from its nearest neighbour, small, timber-framed houses huddled protectively around the village square, where the squat Council hall stands facing the Cooksharp Inn.

Lerncos wasn't the sort of village where one could easily get into trouble, but Joseera Mayweather had always been a troublesome sort of girl. It wasn't that she deliberately courted it, but her natural curiosity and outspoken observations often landed her in what her father would call 'unfortunate situations'. She had been a uniquely imaginative child, her mother said, suffering from violent dreams and nightmares from a young age. This mightn't have been quite such a problem had Joseera not then insisted on terrifying the rest of the village children with her stories of a monstrous creature, bewildering the adults with dark tales and wild ideas. Her parents often despaired of her inquisitive nature, mostly when the village council were once again reprimanding them for their daughter's behaviour. Today was no different.

"The girl simply has no respect!" declared Elder Vithru, a look of bottled frustration on his thin face, "She must learn! I mean honestly, to suggest one's senior, let alone a member of the council, is a common thief without so much as a by-your-leave! It is simply unacceptable! Especially when the member in question is trying to teach the girl a craft!"
"I understand, Elder Vithru," replied Joseera's father quietly, head bowed, "I have tried to speak to her about

these things, but she simply won't be told..."
"Then it seems we will have to take responsibility for instilling the girl with some manners, and perhaps a little sense." rumbled the deep voice of Elder Jarry, head of the council, "She cannot be allowed to continue in this manner. It is poor example to the other youngers, and yet another black mark in Joseera's behaviour. She has yet to choose a path, has been unable to stick at any apprenticeship for more than a week, and appears to believe that she can simply do as she pleases! Since you do not seem capable..."
"Excuse me!" Joseera's mother could restrain herself no longer, "I'll have you know I've raised two perfectly-"
"Juna, please," cut in Mr. Mayweather, "Let the Elders finish."
"Oh for Ancient's sake Parvel," she replied, "They're accusing us of being poor parents! I'd like to see this stuffy lot do a finer job with her!"
"Then you shall Mrs. Mayweather!" boomed Elder Jarry angrily.
"Well," responded Juna, a little cowed, "I'm sorry for speaking out of turn Elder, but we have tried our best! And have you even thought to check whether there was any sense in what Joseera said, I mean she's often-"
"Enough!" thundered Jarry, his dark eyebrows a furious arch, "It is one thing to speak of your daughter's failings, Mrs. Mayweather, for she is young and can still be forgiven childish mistakes. It will be another thing entirely if you choose to repeat her accusation in full knowledge of what you do!"

Elder Jarry stood slowly, and leant forward toward the couple on his smooth wooden walking stick.
"The members of this Council give their time and life to the safe running of our village, and each of them is known

well to me. As such, they are certainly beyond the reproach and hearsay of a younger tailor girl! This is not the first time we have had such words with you, Parvel, Juna, but I am determined it will be the last. Joseera will forgo all other work or schooling to come study with us each day, until I am satisfied that her behaviour is fitting for one of her age and station, until she learns the meaning of responsibility and respect, and that she cannot simply give up at the first sign of difficulty or boredom!"

Jarry softened slightly, and for the first time since he started speaking seemed to show his great age with a weary sigh, "You are good people, and I do believe Joseera is a good child. But she must learn sometime, Juna, we all must learn."

Elder Jarry sat slowly back into his chair of office, as Joseera's mother quietly nodded her assent.

"Thank you members of the Council," said Parvel, calmly, "We will see to it that Joseera attends you. And Councillor Grace – I hope there is no ill will born of Joseera's imaginings... you have my apologies for her foolish words."

Councillor Grace, a pale skinned woman with a friendly manner, and the youngest member of the Council, laughed graciously, "I accept your apologies gladly Mr. Mayweather, I bear no ill will. Your daughter is young and surely has a fine imagination-"

This drew a laugh from several of the Council.

"-so just be sure you get her here to study what she must with us, and I will speak no more of it."

Joseera's parents made their thanks, the members of the Council sounded their agreement, and everyone began to make their way slowly out of the musty meeting hall.

oOo

A little way outside the village, in the quickly dimming evening light, a small and lonely figure wandered purposefully along the path that led off and away to the edge of the Furrindoun Woods, and if one had drawn close enough, they might have heard the figure muttering and mumbling to itself as it went.

"Teach them to call me a liar... not even look at the place... see how what they think now... don't need them at any rate..."

The figure wore a fine cloak and hood of animal skin, dyed a pale blue, well made and suited for the cold weather of the day, and carried a small bundle wrapped in cloth slung over one shoulder. A moment's further observation would have revealed that the figure was a young girl of about sixteen or seventeen years, with pale white skin, cheeks redded by the crisp air or her swift pace, perhaps a little of both. Here and there a few fine strands of red-golden hair escaped her hood and fell about her shoulders, and her delicate face might have been called pretty, were it not scrumpled with frustration and annoyance. She was dressed in simple dark cloth and hides, but well crafted, and wore a stout pair of boots. About her waist was slung a wide leather belt, and an old but serviceable sword hung from one side. An indignant frown sat in contrast above soft blue eyes, and she walked angrily, scuffing her feet, kicking up dirt as she went.

"Call me up to the Council *again*! I mean really! As if Councillor Grace had done nothing at all, and before they even checked!"

A sudden cold rush of wind cut short the girl's complaints,

and for a moment she stopped, silent, and turned to look back at the village in the distance. She stood, as if privately contemplating, then abruptly turned away and continued on her path, silent now, jaw set in youthful determination.

oOo

Back in the village there was uproar. The soldiers of Bantha had arrived shortly after the meeting of the Council had finished, and went directly to the inn, demanding to see the Elders in charge, and the village tailor also. The landlord, Tutty Cooksharp, a great mountain of a man, slow and simple but warm and welcoming with it, well suited to his profession, had tried to calm the men and offer them refreshment and rest while they waited for the word to be passed to the Elders, but the soldiers refused flatly. The matter was of great urgency, they told him, in no uncertain terms, please send word immediately, we will await the Elders outside.

Elder Jarry was quietly preparing for a little time to himself, well earned, and almost knocked the pan from his stove when the hammering at his door began. It continued unabated until he pulled open the heavy door, and found a young man panting on his doorstep, breath steaming in the cold air.
"Yes, young Lallow? What is so desperate a cause as to have you a-hammering through my door at this hour?" asked the Elder.
The young man looked up at the imposing form of the Elder silhouetted in the doorway. Jarry was far from young, that was true, but even the most impetuous and fool-hardy of the village's young men would have thought twice before tangling with the Elder. Jarry had the look of

one who had been carved from rough wood, by just as rough a craftsman.

"I-I'm sorry to trouble you Elder," panted Lallow, hands planted on his knees, "There's soldiers... soldiers in the inn... says they needs to speak with the Council, and a tailor, although they don't say why... but I figure they can't just need a tunic mending!"

Jarry chuckled, a warm and rolling sound. Thom Lallow was not the most respectful of the village's youngers, but he was a likeable lad, with a manner of putting things that never failed to amuse the Elder.

"Soldiers? From where Lallow? Of the Fold?"

"Oh yes Elder, most certainly. They come straight from the courts of Bantha itself to look at 'em, I never seen no soldiers in so fine a get up."

"Very well, Thom. Tell Tutty to fix a drink for me, and I'll be over as quickly as I may."

The lad nodded and made an undecided attempt at a little bow of departure, then ran off across the frozen square toward the inn.

"Hmm." said the Elder quietly, to the night outside. "I doubt this will be good news."

And then, with a longing look at his supper, cooling on the stove, he pulled on his boots and robes of office, and set out after Thom Lallow.

oOo

The girl first noticed them just as the path began to skirt the woodlands. A party, several men it seemed, was following her, of that she was now certain. At first she had thought it a trick of the light and her mind, a little fear setting in as the evening grew darker, but then she had heard a man's voice in the distance behind her, and another sharply silencing him. Now she was certain she could see figures in the frosted trees at the side of the path a little way back behind her, and although her pursuers did not plainly show themselves, it seemed they did not worry that she had noticed them, sliding from tree to tree at the edge of her vision, growing slowly closer.

She began to feel very foolish, and more than a little scared. She had thought she might travel to the next village, perhaps trade a little, and travel home when she was ready, prove to those who doubted her that she was capable of taking care of herself. But that was in the full light of the afternoon, when tales of other villages, friendly towns and inns, music, story and song ran through her head. Now the light had almost gone, those stories too seemed a little less bright, and in the shadows now were eclipsed by tales of mercenary bands and robbers, cruel and unforgiving folk who lived a life in the gaps between the light, on the roads and lands outside. She gripped the hilt of the sword at her waist tightly, more for comfort than protection, and wished that she had set out earlier, or perhaps that she had not set out at all. She quickened her pace, then slowed again, worried that speed might make her fear plain to those who followed, then quickened once more on hearing the crack of undergrowth close behind. Then she stopped, quite suddenly, and turned.

"I know you're there!" she shouted to the darkness, defiantly.

There was no response.

"Why don't you just stop all this? You can see that I'm alone," she regretted stating this aloud even as she said it, "so... so why don't you just come out and stop being so cowardly! Just come out and tell me what it is you want from me and let me be on my way!"

There was a muffled laugh from somewhere in the trees to

the left, and another rustle of brush from the right. She bit her lip, and turned back walking swiftly, swiftly along the path now, trying to stop the tears from running down her frozen cheeks.

oOo

Elder Jarry was at the end of his patience, and this was not helped by his rumbling stomach.
"Tutty, good fellow, would you be kind enough to fix something to quiet my hunger?" he asked the still-smiling innkeeper.
"Oh, certainly Elder, certainly – you should have said earlier! No trouble, Elder, no trouble at all." replied Cooksharp, glad of an excuse to escape the tension in the room for a spell.
"Can I fix anything for you gentlemen?" he asked awkwardly of the remaining two soldiers.
"No. Thank you." responded the younger of the two, a clear-eyed, blonde haired fellow, with a serious, fervent way about him that seemed ill-suited to his age. "Once we have concluded our business here we will be on our way directly."
The older of the two, a sharp faced man with dark black hair and a gaze that made you feel he would uncover all manner of secrets given time, even if you had none, nodded curtly at his companion.
"We simply wish to be sure, Elder Jarry, Mr. Mayweather, that you will waste no time in informing us by the channels we have outlined if your daughter, Mr. Mayweather, should be found. My men will be searching for her as we speak, but we believe she may be in danger, and if she has indeed left the safety of the village as it seems, this threat is increased by so many unknown factors. Therefore I cannot impress upon you strongly

enough the urgency with which I wish you to contact us."

"Yes, yes!" shouted Parvel Mayweather, his face a knot as he tried to reconcile his good manners with his concern and frustration, "We have already said we will be glad to co-operate, especially if it is for my daughter's safety! But you must tell me, please, Commander, what is this danger? What could possibly be so serious to demand the attention of your forces, and why my daughter? I am her father, Commander, please, I have a right to know!"

"The man is right, Commander Gensu," added Elder Jarry, wearily, "You cannot simply turn up here and put such a concern to a man whose child is already missing without telling him what it is that he should fear!"

Gensu sat back calmly in his chair.

"I'm sorry gentlemen, but that is beyond my authority. I'm to find your daughter and ensure her safety, and I cannot tell you any more or less than this. But take comfort in the fact at least, that wherever she may be, you have extra eyes to help search for her, and my men to protect her if they find her."

The Commander nodded once more to his young companion, and both men stood, raising their hands to their chests in salute.

"And now, we must leave you gentlemen. Thank you for your time."

Elder Jarry raised a hand to gently silence Parvel's protestations as the officers made their way towards the door. The earnest blond man left first, followed by Commander Gensu, who turned just as he stepped through the door.

"Don't forget. We will be looking for her, but should you find her first, you let us know right away. Don't forget."

And with that, the soldiers were gone.

Outside the inn, Commander Gensu breathed in the cold

night air deeply, and stood for a moment, looking up at the stars.

"Sir?" said his companion quietly.

The Commander made no reply, nor indication that he heard the other man.

"Sir." repeated the young officer, a little more insistently

"Yes Lieutenant?" replied Gensu after a moment, eyes to the heavens.

"What is our course of action? If I may, sir, I believe these foolish folk when they say the girl is gone."

"Yes, Ripfer." said Gensu with a sigh, turning to face the younger man, "They have no idea where she is. If you hear nothing by morning, you know what to do."

"Yes, sir." replied Ripfer, with a slight smile. The young man enjoyed his work thoroughly, but some aspects more than others.

"Hm. Try not to look so happy about it man." said Gensu, turning to leave, "We don't even know if this is the one."

"Yes, sir." replied Ripfer, but the Commander was already gone.

oOo

The girl had thought she was already frightened before she noticed the figure on the path ahead. In the manner of such things, time seemed to slow and remove her from herself, giving her ample opportunity to reflect on the fact that she had been merely *afraid* of the noises in the darkness before, a simple *fear* of men who meant no good. Now however, she considered in her moment of calm and collected clarity, now was *terror*, a primal shaking upon seeing that which meant no good, but was no man.

The creature had stepped out on to the path a way ahead of her, and made no attempt to hide itself in the bright moonlight. It stood an easy eight feet tall, and was at least half again as broad. Its huge hands hung low, at the end of long and thickly corded arms, ropes of muscle and sinew creeping and twisting under the leathery skin, and in one massive fist it held a rough and weighty looking axe, a blade on each side, bound to a thick wooden haft. Dark tufts of hair sprouted from its head and heavy shoulders, and a little spread down onto its face, framing the wide mouth, filled with rows of curved and pointed teeth that seemed impossibly clear in the white light. Clearest of all, she saw its eyes. Small and sparkling, fixing her to the spot with a powerful intensity. Focused. Intelligent.

Behind her, Joseera heard more movement in the trees. Try as she might, she could not stop the tears this time.

Chapter Two

The fertile farmlands of the Fold, heart of the Empire, nestle in the protection of the mountain range known to most as the Long Hills. The mountains shelter the Fold to the north and west, with only a few narrow passes and the wider plain of Vas Aloron in the north east leading to the lands beyond. Along its southern and eastern edges, a great river, called the Pulchren, runs fiercely by, giving life to the Fold as it does. On the banks of this river, at the foot of the Long Hills, the walled city of Bantha stands, seat of the Empire.

Bantha is, in the manner of such places, a strange construction to look upon – architecture, buildings and styles from every age, new and fashionable next to the ancient and traditional. The city has stood in some form as the capital of the land for as long as anyone cares to remember, and its vast and sprawling borders, rebuilt and expanded many times, are the living proof of this. In the south, overlooking the Pulchren river, stands Bantha's great Keep, traditional home and stronghold of the Empire's leaders. A broad, castle-like building of dark stone, adorned with odd additions and extensions over the years in all manner of styles and materials, its imposing shape is undermined by its patchwork appearance. To the east, climbing high above even its tallest neighbours, rises the narrow tower of the Order of Keepers, like a pale finger pointing off into the sky. At the city's centre lies a wide, open square, in odd contrast to every other part, which is taken up with an explosion of structures clamouring for space, crowding the narrow streets one atop another, without method or design. In spite of its apparent disorganisation however, Bantha is, by nature of its position and its mighty walls, eminently defensible, and has seen many enemies and would be attackers fall at its feet. Today however, this was scant comfort to its leaders.

"How is this possible?" exclaimed one, a lean, athletic man with a kind face and pale grey eyes. He was simply dressed, in pale wool and leather tunic, and one hand rested easily on the sword at his belt. Despite his aggravation, he moved with an assured ease and confidence. "How can this be happening so soon, and so sudden? They have never attacked in such numbers without provocation before, what drives them to it now?"
"Patience Duma," replied another, a small, owlish woman in voluminous robes, with a wildly disobedient shock of red hair. She pushed her battered gold-rimmed spectacles to the top of her nose with one finger, only to have them slip back to half-mast a moment later, "There must be more to this, and we must wait until we have all the facts before we jump to any conclusions, eh?"
"He is right though Sofya," said the third calmly, turning her face into the light streaming through the window of the chamber. She wore a long dress of deep blue cotton, open at the neck, and she stood for a moment feeling the sun's warmth on her smooth skin. "Although it seems impossible on such a beautiful day, there are villages on the edge of our lands who have already fallen victim to the raiders. There is little time for contemplation, these forces are at our doorstep and beyond." She turned back toward the others, twisting the dark brown curls of her hair thoughtfully in one hand.
"I have asked the Scribe to join us," she continued, "in the hope that he and his Keepers may shed some light on these developments for us."
"I hope so, Loulouthi." replied the grey-eyed man with a

smile, "I hope so. Especially if you have had him climb down from his tower and travel all the way over here. But if neither my eyes nor Sofya's art can tell us more, I have little hope for the Keepers."

Around their neck each of the three wore a delicate chain, at the end of which hung a fine shape of shimmering gold and dark metal decorated with intricate lines and carvings, ancient symbols of their office and authority, passed down through Bantha's history. The Triumvirate were considered unusual, as rulers went, but unquestionably effective. This, it was suggested over many a tavern table and shop counter, was due in no small part to the fact that each member of the Triumvir was expert in their fields of interest and concern, and bowed entirely to the wisdom of the others in their own areas of expertise. Their rise to power had been meteoric, after the chaos of the last wars with the Savage tribes these three had been plucked from obscurity quite suddenly. Stories were told of their miraculous return after being cut off deep within enemy lands, and how they had brought back a child, heroically rescued from the clutches of the Savages. It was rumoured that they had seized control of a scattered battalion in the north, and even that they had played some part in reaching peaceful terms with the Savages. Quickly they were promoted to office by officials short on candidates and keen to capitalise on any good news. When the previous Lord Emperor, a greedy, warmongering man, had disappeared, the common vote had shown overwhelming support for the Triumvir to replace him and they were swept unexpectedly into the highest office before the aristocracy had time to suggest otherwise. They had official titles, each of the three, but the people had ceased using them almost altogether in favour of simpler nicknames, and once these names had caught on almost everyone referred to the members of the Triumvir this way. So it came to be, in spite of any other names or titles they may have held, that the three were known throughout the lands as the Heart, the Book and the Sword.

oOo

On the cobbled square outside in the centre of the city, there was a considerable commotion. Of course, there was a commotion there almost every day, since the large square was home to dozens of market stalls and traders, and was bordered by several taverns and hostelries. Today though, even through the usual chorus of bargaining and conversation, the crisp air hummed with whispers and rumours flitting back and forth. Some spun stories from the villages they said had fallen foul to the Savage enemy, others muttered conspiratorially that the Scribe himself would be visiting the Keep that day, and with a laugh suggesting perhaps he might even stop for a bite or to browse their wares. Then suddenly the noise and hubbub dropped, and apart from the unfortunate few who had already committed to some loud expostulation, drawing sniggers and raised eyebrows from their now silent friends, the crowd almost as one noticed the approach of the figures in white from the far end of the main street. A few daring individuals made quiet comment to their companions under their breath, although they would never admit it if they were caught out, while others attempted to continue discreetly with their transactions, all nods and business. All fell hushed though, when the Order arrived.

For generations, the Order of Keepers had continued quietly, autonomous and objective, recording and storing the stories of the world. They governed themselves, not subject to the common law, but sworn to serve the interests of man's progress and improvement. It had always been considered an honour if your son or daughter were invited to join the Order, and while the life of a Keeper was not always glamorous or adventurous, it was secure and respected, your needs and the needs of your family would always be met. There were, of course, posts and roles within the Order, of greater importance or significance. The Order maintained that it was just as important to record food production for the month, or sale of wine, as it was to record political and historical events, providing in this way a reference for the future, a template against which comparisons could be made, and judgements reached. And so it was that some Keepers, the many ranks of Actuaries and Reckoners, had most mundane lives, meeting with the same farmers or officials day after day, week after week, while others, most notably the mysterious Seekers, met and travelled with scouts, soldiers and spies loyal to the Order, with details of events and happenings from far afield. Ultimately though, the life of a Keeper altered little, and the flow of information was relentless.

At the head of the Order sat the Scribe, always chosen from the most talented in the Order's ranks, charged with personally recording in the Great Tome, with writing penned in the Keeper's Ink, which prevented the writer from setting down anything they knew to be false. Most Keepers would only see bits and pieces of information from here and there as they went about their daily business, but the Scribe and his most senior Keepers had access to it all, and the unenviable task of deciding exactly what, and in how much detail, should be transferred into the Great Tome. Although all Keeper's records were stored, it was only for a time, the parchment and ink eventually degraded and faded, trying to find single pieces of information would have been a long and laborious task. But the Great Tome was crafted of the highest quality, and the Keeper's Ink never faded, so those who governed the Empire had come to rely on the lengthy entries made to see overall what had taken place, to reflect on what had happened in the past, and to consider what the future might hold.

The ghostly figures travelled down the street in slow procession, the white robes of their Order brushing the ground as they went, and fetching up a cloud of dust that surrounded them, only adding to their wraith-like appearance. There were not only Scriveners and Notaries however, although these men and women numbered most in the group, heads bowed and hoods pulled forward. The Order also counted soldiers and swordsmen among its ranks, carefully chosen, zealously loyal, and tasked with the protection of the Order and its interests. They skirted the edges of the crowd now, swords sheathed but at the ready, ensuring that people cleared a path and did not interfere. And at the centre of this procession, seeming to float on the sea of white figures surrounding him, sat the Scribe, born aloft on a litter by his personal guard.

From beneath the thick hood of his robes, the Scribe looked out at the crowd and the chaos of the city beyond with a typically inscrutable expression. Stern, blue eyes peered intently out at the crowd over the sharp curve of his nose, jaw tensing beneath the short, white hair of his immaculate beard. The people in the square jostled and craned for a better view of the Order's enigmatic leader, but their efforts would gain them little insight. The Scribe's office led him to deal with all walks of life, from lords and merchants to beggars and thieves, and he had learned long ago the value of concealment. As his gaze drifted across the sea of faces, the Scribe wore a studied look, taking in all around him, betraying nothing to would-be observers. The gilt and silver detail of his robes of office glittered against the white, and the crimson crest of the Order emblazoned on his shoulders seemed to glow in the bright sunlight. His left hand clutched an ornate sceptre, ceremonial symbol of the Order, and in his right he held the lodestone, source of the Keeper's Ink, secured by chains about his waist. Just ahead of the litter, walking slowly before it, two curious figures moved, conspicuous among the white clad Keepers by their jet black clothing, well fitted and unusual. The better informed among the crowd knew the pompous, bald headed man to be Mr. Glower, and the dark-haired, sharp-eyed woman to be Miss Glass. In recent times the pair had become closest aides and advisors to the Scribe himself and were always at his side, although they held no official office.

As the crowd parted around it, the strange procession gradually made its way to the centre of the square and there paused for a moment. The Scribe rose slowly to his feet. He was not a young man, but his tall frame and a life of discipline gave him a stately bearing, an imposing figure. He lifted the sceptre high in the air and looked steadily around at the people gathered there.

"People of Bantha!" he said quite suddenly, with a voice that seemed to carry effortlessly to the furtherest ear. "May the blessings of the past and the fortune of the future be upon you!"
The crowd shuffled reverentially, murmured words of approval floating on the breeze.
"Some of you may have heard of the troubles that befall our countrymen beyond the Fold, in the north, in the west. But do not fear. Your leaders are even now acting to

resolve this problem, and it is about this matter that I visit them today. Be at peace, but vigilant. Let us not fall victim to idle gossip, but rather steadfastly see to our duty, and our great country will stand as firm as ever!"

The Scribe lowered the sceptre and gestured for his guardsmen to continue. The procession slowly travelled along the wide path that led out of the square, towards the outer walls of Bantha's Keep. When they drew near, the heavy gates swung slowly outward to admit them, providing the people in the square with a furtive glimpse into the gardens beyond. Once the last of the Order had passed, the gates closed with an ominous boom.

As the noise and chatter began to rise again, one could almost hear the remonstrations and recriminations tumbling from the mouths of those who, minutes before, had been holding court with half-heard rumours from the border villages. Now those very same were declaiming such malicious talk, and explaining vigorously how such calumny is bad for the spirits and leads to all sorts of mistaken ideas.

Inside the grounds of the Keep the Scribe sighed as his guardsmen lowered his chair to allow him out. A few choice words, he thought to himself, a few choice words and they will swear that up is down.
Mister Glower and Miss Glass were waiting for him. "Please excuse us, if you will, Your Eminence," said Mister Glower, with a low bow, "we will be unable to accompany you to the Council chambers. There is an urgent matter requiring our attention."
The Scribe glanced down at Glower's bald head with a distracted expression, and nodded absently.
"Oh, of course, Mister Glower, of course. Do as you must,

I doubt you will be missing a great deal."

"Very good, Your Eminence, thank you," replied Glower.

"We will return as soon as possible, Your Eminence," added Miss Glass in her sharp, clipped tone.

The pair gave another slight bow, then turned and headed away.

"Are you ready, your Eminence?"

"Hm?" the Scribe gathered himself and turned to the young Scrivener addressing him, "Yes, yes, Parfort, quite ready. Let's go and see what our esteemed leaders make of all this shall we?"

He smiled warmly at the lad, not the brightest of his Order, but loyal and dependable and not too prone to question, which counted for a great deal as far as the Scribe was concerned.

"Yes Sir, very good." replied Parfort awkwardly, and the Scribe and his attendants began their ascent into the Keep.

oOo

Elsewhere in the city, far from the noise and bustle of the market square, a group of rough and unseemly individuals waited impatiently in the back room of a dark and dusty house. None seemed able to stay entirely still, and as a result the room was filled with quiet shufflings, sighs and shifts of weight, until someone finally broke the ruffled silence.

"For the Ancients sake, what are we waiting for? What's with all the cloak and dagger stuff, eh? Are they just trying to wind us up or what? 'Cause I for one have got better things to do than stand around waiting for some swingeing toffs who think they-"

"That's enough!" hissed another of the men, "If you want

your cut, then shut up and wait. It's me as makes the deal, so it's me as decides how long is too long." He turned to face the first man, who was already clearly regretting having opened his mouth.

"And right now, Pash, I feel I've been listening to your whining voice for too long, and one way or another, I've heard enough, if you follow my meaning."

The first man, despite his broad build and rough appearance, stammered an apology, "R-right, right, course Cullen, s-sorry Cullen, it's just-"

The second held up his hand for silence, as the others in the room tried desperately to look interested in anything else they could lay eyes on.

"I said.. I've heard.. enough, Pash."

Much to the general relief of his companions, Pash caught on, and simply nodded his acquiescence meekly.

"Good." said Cullen quietly. "Good."

Jen Cullen was not a big man, neither the tallest or the broadest waiting in that dim room, but this only lent further to his intimidating air. Judging by his size, and the network of both fresh and faded scars that crossed his face and arms, there could be no doubt that Jen Cullen had fought hard to get where he was, and would fight just as fierce before he gave it up.

Pash and the others in the room were grateful when, a few moments later, their lookout, an ambitious young lad known as Swipe, popped his head round the door.

"They're here Mr. Cullen – two of 'em, and alone as well according to Tip and Walker outside. Shall I show 'em in Mr. Cullen? Only they seemed pretty narked at 'aving to wait while I just checked it out with you Mr. Cullen, if you know what I mean."

For a moment Pash had an indignant look on his face and seemed about to say something, but Cullen caught his eye

and he immediately thought better of it.
"Alright Swipe, good work, send 'em in, and have Tip and Walker fetch the merchandise." said Cullen, calmly.
Swipe's head bobbed quickly, and disappeared behind the door.
"Now then gents, stay easy, but keep your eyes open." added Cullen quietly.
His men nodded softly to each other, as the door re-opened. A well-groomed couple entered, a woman with short, sharp edged black hair, and a bald man with a friendly expression. Both were clad in well cut black clothes.

"Mr. Cullen," said the bald man, smiling warmly, "How good to see you here. I apologise for the delay, but we had a few other last minute errands, did we not Miss Glass?"
He turned to the woman at his side, who in contrast with her companion, looked thoroughly bored.
"We did, Mr. Glower" she replied gently, "We did."
"Mmm. Indeed." Mr. Glower's smile did not flicker despite his associate's lack of enthusiasm. "So Mr. Cullen, given the delay, shall we dispense with small talk and get straight to business?" He didn't wait for a reply.
"Marvellous. We have the agreed sum. Miss Glass?" he gestured to the woman, who pulled aside her jacket to reveal a tightly bound cloth parcel, "And I am assuming, although I do not see such present in the room at this time, that you have what we require, hmm?"
Mr Glower gave one final obsequious grin and raised his eyebrows expectantly.

Cullen said nothing, but gave a whistle, and the door swung open again, young Swipe leading Tip and Walker through, as they carried a small wooden chest between them. At Cullen's signal they placed it on the floor in the middle of the room and cautiously opened it, revealing a curious looking carving of dark metal and stone, the size of a balled fist, nestled on a bed of straw.

Mr. Glower's smile became painfully wider. "Ahh, yes... excellent, excellent, good man, good man indeed!"

Mr. Glower began to step towards the case, but on another signal from Cullen his way was barred by Pash and several others, who stepped silently into his path.

Mr. Glower's smile faded only a little. "Mr. Cullen?" he enquired, "Is there a problem of some description?"

"No Glower, no problem," replied Cullen, gruffly, "But the, ah, acquisition of this particular item was a little more troublesome than we expected, see. And we was thinking, seeing as there was a little trouble for us, and a couple of good lads got caught out, we was thinking we might need to re-negotiate, if you follow my meaning."

Pash and the other men rested their hands casually on their weapons, and spread a little further around their visitors.

Mr. Glower seemed taken aback, but only for a moment. His face showed disappointment briefly, then a sad smile took its place.

"Very well, Mr. Cullen. As you wish. Miss Glass, as the bearer of said fee, will be the one to deal with such negotiations. Ah, Miss Glass?" He turned to his companion, who raised her eyebrows expectantly.

"Mr. Glower?" she replied.

"If you wouldn't mind Miss Glass."

"Of course Mr. Glower, of course."

oOo

In the Council chambers of Bantha's keep, the Scribe was finishing his address to the assembled dignitaries and leaders of the city.

"To conclude, my lords and ladies, our Order has found no precedent for such an attack, in either magnitude or reason, but early suggestions from our intelligence abroad indicate a unified organisation across the Savage races, and some shared and singular objective. We have also received reports of uncommon weapons and techniques employed against our forces. If this information is borne out, we advise the Council to prepare swiftly and completely, for we may face an assault such as we have never seen from these creatures. Further details will be presented to you by our Scriveners as you require them, I thank the council and our esteemed leaders for their time." The Scribe bowed slightly before taking his seat, and was met with supportive cries and applause from his audience.

"Aye, crush 'em for good before they get any more ideas!" called one.
"We've done it before and we'll do it again," cried another, "Teach 'em where they belong!"
"But what do they want? Why all at once?" shouted yet another.

The woman known as the Heart stood to address the room before order was lost altogether.
"My lords," she called in a strong but gentle voice, "my lords, my ladies, please."

The room fell quiet again. Duma Angsen, whom people called the Sword, looked up at his friend in wonder, and out at the attentive faces of the council. Loulouthi was beautiful, it was true, and looked younger than her years, but there was more to it than that. She inspired trust and faith in others, and brought a peace within her gaze – this was some subtle part of her strength. Even after all this time, Duma thought, it was still remarkable to see. Despite all his skill or speed with a blade, he could never silence a room as quickly as Loulouthi.

Peering across behind her, Sofya, known as the Book, chuckled quietly at Duma. "Heh, don't you start Duma, for the Ancients sake, or we'll never get anything done!"
"Oh don't worry witch," the Sword whispered back, with a smile, "sometimes I think she wields more magick than you!"
"Magick's just a word for that you don't understand Duma," sniffed the Book, "so in your case, I think you may be right, eh?"

The Heart spoke to the room, looking about as she did so, seeking understanding in the eyes of each member of the council.

"My lords and ladies, I understand your concerns and the desire for action. But we must proceed with caution. We can ill afford to enter into such a war on all fronts, and cannot commit to such a serious action until we are certain there is no alternative. We have scarcely begun to recover from the last struggle. While we must, of course, protect our people, we should also try to discover what it is that provokes our neighbours, and whether we may resolve their grievances peacefully. We must not forget, in our ire and eagerness, the cost that comes with any conflict."

The Sword stood, and spoke to support his colleague.
"Our past engagements, however large or successful, have been with no more than three identified clans or tribes of Savages. If we have to fight them all at once, it'll be a disaster. Put simply, we don't have the resources right now to deal with something of that scale. Like it or not, Emperor Dray left a great deal of confusion, and very

little else."
This was met with a low grumbling from several areas of the chamber, as the old establishment's supporters voiced their disapproval at what the Sword implied.

Finally the Book rose from her seat.
"At this moment I have no better idea than anyone else as to what led to these fresh attacks. But I urge you, all of you, don't fall foul of panic and rumour! The enemy, if indeed they are organised, will have no need to fight us at all if we pull ourselves apart before they ever have the chance! And if they are not united, we do not wish to *encourage* them to band together through our show of strength! So be calm, eh? Do not speculate. The Keepers are hard at work even as we speak, I'm sure, and we'll discover the cause of all this trouble. Until then, we do best by standing firm – we must be certain of what we know."

The wind taken from their sails somewhat, the council members began to file out of the meeting room. The Book stopped the Scribe before he could drift out with the others.
"A few moments, if you would Your Eminence."
"Of course, Madam Sofya, whatever our leaders require."

They waited quietly until the rest of the council was empty before they continued. As the door swung shut, it was the Sword who broke the silence.
"Thank you for coming, Your Eminence, and for your report. But we need to make sure the rumours don't run out of control before we know what we're dealing with."
"Indeed Lord Duma, and thank you for hearing me," replied the Scribe, bowing his head.
"In the meantime, Your Eminence, you've still got a good

number of men in the field, trying to figure this out?" asked the Sword.

"Of course, Lord Duma, of course – it is our highest priority at this time, have no doubt!"

"Hm. Good – I have sent a few choice men of my own to the front lines also. I hope your Seekers will be good enough to co-operate should they encounter one another." the Sword went on.

"I... well, of course, Lord Duma... but... if I may enquire... Do you not trust our Order to complete their task... Have we somehow-" the Scribe spluttered his response.

"No, nothing of the sort, Your Eminence, nothing of the sort. But given the gravity of our situation, I thought we could use as many hands as possible. Your Seekers do fine work, and I hope they continue to do so."

"Ah, I see." the Scribe replied quietly. "Very good, Lord Duma. If there is nothing else?"

The Sword looked at his companions briefly, then, with a wave of his hand, "No, Your Eminence, thank you for your time and trouble."

"Thank you my Lord, my Ladies."

The Scribe bowed before the Triumvirate, turned and left.

Alone in the chamber, the three rulers sat, and looked at each other gravely. The Heart smiled slightly, and put her hands on the shoulders of her two companions.

"I hope he can understand. We cannot afford to leave any stone unturned. If we can't resolve this situation, I'm not sure how we'll cope... and think of those out on the very edges of our land, those who face these dangers every day – what can we tell them to do? Leave their homes, and lands behind that we may consolidate our defences? I hope it does not come to that my friends, I truly do..."

The Sword lent forward with a sigh.

"I'm doing what I can – I have forces in place to defend

the most vulnerable areas, try to protect people from the raiding parties. But we're thinly spread, very thinly spread. One big push from them at any point might well break through, and I can only hope they don't know that yet."

The Book nodded her agreement, "Yes, at least their uncertainty may buy us a little time... You said you had sent men out to investigate though, Duma? You think this will yield an answer more quickly than the Keepers?"

"I don't know Sofya." shrugged the Sword, "The Keepers aren't obliged to answer to us. They're a secretive lot, and fond of bureaucracy – you know, everything checked, re-checked and checked again. By the time they tell us something, chances are it'll already be on top of us. I just thought it might be wise to send one of our own out to have a look, someone who can use their common sense, and get back to us as quick as they can..."

The Sword stood, and paced over to the windows of the chamber.

"Besides, he and his men volunteered."

The Heart and the Book exchanged glances.

"Who did you send, Duma?" asked the Heart, softly.

"Gaven." replied the Sword flatly. "I sent Gaven and his men from our personal guard. I just... I hope they come back with something useful. Perhaps I should have gone myself."

"Heh, those days are over Duma," smiled the Book, "We need you here, eh? Gaven and his company are good men. If they volunteered they must believe they can help. The best we can do is send them our blessing and ask the Ancients do the same."

The Sword turned back to face his friends, and nodded solemnly.

"Well," said the Heart, as much to herself as to the others, "Good luck to them then. Good luck to Gaven and his men, wherever they may be."

oOo

Down below, the Scribe seemed displeased as he returned to his men.

"Everything all right, your Eminence?" asked Scrivener Parfort, keeping cautiously out of arms reach.

"Eh? Oh, yes Parfort, yes, fine, fine. Just... interference, that's all, interference." muttered the Scribe, in response. "All my life, I've given to the Order, all my life, and years in office as the chosen Scribe, and every newcomer with a season under their belt thinks they know better... no respect, I tell you, no respect..."

Parfort was uncertain what to make of this, so went what he considered to be a safe bet.

"Ah yes, your Eminence, quite right, quite right."

For a moment he thought he had chosen poorly as the Scribe suddenly seemed to focus, and snapped his head round to face the young Scrivener straight on.

"You're a good lad Parfort. A good lad." said the Scribe slowly, "Now go and fetch me some parchment and a sending slate... I need to get a message to Aleph and his Seekers..."

Chapter Three

As it happened, Captain Gaven Mayweather was, at that moment, lying in a ditch beside a cart-trail. His thick, brown hair was matted by the pouring rain, and his broad features knotted as he tried desperately to remember just why it was that he had volunteered himself and his men for such a task as this.

It hadn't been entirely his fault, he thought to himself, as the cold mud seemed to work its way into every space in his clothing. It was Thurro, his sergeant, who had come up with the idea. When Gaven had approached Lord Duma with the suggestion, it had seemed very much the right thing to do, he told himself, a very good plan indeed. His reverie was interrupted by Grays, one of his men flopping down heavily at his side.

"Grays."
"Sir." replied the soldier, curtly.
"Any development? Can we move?" asked Gaven.
"Not yet I'm afraid, sir, still a large party of 'em not more than a hundred yards of us." said Grays in reply.
"At any rate, sir, even if they don't find and butcher us, with all due respect of course," continued Grays in a conspiratorial tone, "I might, sir, should we ever get out of this bloody ditch, consider killing us both for coming here in the first place. With respect, sir."
"Very good Grays," replied Gaven, nodding, "If we get out of this ditch, I might give you the order myself."
The two men looked at each other, streaked with rain and mud, shivering in the ditch, and tried not to laugh loud enough to alert their nearby foe.

Gaven was a young man, for an officer, and had worked his way up through the ranks from the very bottom, having travelled to Bantha to join the Guards when he was just fourteen. He was well liked by his men, and although some of his fellow officers considered his familiarity with his subordinates unbecoming, Gaven believed it brought out the best in them. This was borne out, much to his peers frustration, by the fact that his unit had consistently out-performed all others, whether in action or manoeuvres. Consequently he and his men had been posted to the Keep of Bantha itself, under the direct command of Lord Duma, and considered themselves fortunate to be among the trusted staff of the Triumvirate, whom they may even have called friends, had their military nature and respect not prevented them from doing so.

Right now, however, Gaven and his men were wishing they were back in the warmth and safety of Bantha's Keep. Their journey across to the borders of the land had been swift and easy, fun even, but almost as soon as they drew near to enemy territory, the weather had abruptly worsened, as if reflecting the peril of their situation. Their job, to discover what they could about their enemies movements, tactics, motives, would have been hard enough as it was, but it had been compounded by hour after hour of freezing rain, turning the hard land into marsh, and bringing visibility down to a hundred yards or less.

The day before they had met with a raid by the Savages as they passed through one of the border villages. They had done what they could to help the handful of soldiers stationed there, giving the villagers a chance to escape, leaving behind their goods and their homes. They spent several desperate hours fighting alongside the other soldiers and local militia, until together they finally hacked down the last of the monstrous creatures. They left the others counting up the dead, caked in mud and blood. Since then, the mood of the men had been grim but determined, and they had pressed deeper into the enemy's territory, till they had come across another, larger group a few hours earlier.

"Do you have any idea what they're doing Grays?" asked Gaven, shivering as the icy raindrops ran down his face and dripped from his nose.
"Not really, sir," replied Grays, "They've pitched up one small tent, and a couple of the important ones keep ducking in and out of it, but we don't know what for or what they've got in there. At any rate, they're not making camp, the rest of 'em are just taking the chance for a breather but that's about it."
Gaven sighed and stared up into the pouring rain.
"Dammit Grays, what do they want?" he asked, "This isn't like them, it doesn't-"
He was interrupted by two more of the company ducking into the muddy ditch alongside him.
He nodded a greeting, "Thurro, Brackley."
"Alright Sarge, Brackley," said Grays, "anything happenin'?"
"Somethin', not sure what," replied Thurro. The Sergeant was a squat, barrel of a man, with low, gentle voice almost entirely at odds with his bristly, brash appearance.
"There's some new arrivals, sir," he continued, "Top brass, so to speak, from the look of 'em."
"So they were hanging on for orders, is that it?" said Grays, with a frown, "But why not just send a runner? Why would their brass come all the way out 'ere?"
"Well that's just it," said Brackley, leaning in

conspiratorially across the Sergeant, "They ain't *their* brass! I dunno much about their markings and colours and what 'ave you, but they ain't from this tribe, an' that's for certain! Totally different gear, totally different. And that's not all-"

"Alright Brackley, alright," interrupted Sergeant Thurro, pushing the man back to one side, "Let's 'ave a little order, shall we?"

The Sergeant turned his attention back to Captain Gaven and Grays.

"That's not all, sir." he continued, "Not only do they look different, sir, but there's a man with 'em. Not a pris'ner, not a captive, not a slave. Some fella all wrapped up in decent cloth and leathers, no markings mind, arrived with the other newcomers, and walkin' and talkin' with 'em, sir, as if he were right among 'is own. I can't be sure, but some of 'em even seemed to be doin' what he told 'em."

Once the amazement had fallen from Grays' face, it was replaced almost instantly by a dark cloud of anger.

"Bloody traitor! Traitor! Ancients damn them, I bloody knew it!" His knuckles whitened on the hilt of his sword as he spoke. "All them people, all them people back there! Sold out, died because of one of their bloody *own* is a greedy, gutless little wretch! Sir, we can't leave 'em be here. We've got to *do* something! We should slit the bugger's throat!"

Gaven grabbed hold of Grays firmly by the shoulders, and pulled him back down low into the ditch.

"Ancient's sake man, alright!" he said, as Grays struggled to push up out of their sodden shelter.

"I agree, we need to do something, but I can't say I see how getting ourselves torn to pieces will be a valuable contribution. Get a hold of yourself!"

Grays met his Captain's eye, and calmed a little.

"Well, we have to do something, sir, lads, right?" Grays

looked across at Brackley and Thurro, who looked at each other in turn, and then back to Gaven.

Gaven sighed quietly to himself. He had hoped that he and his men could discover something that might be of use to Bantha, but he had not expected this.

"Alright," he said, gathering himself. "Sergeant, if you're right, then this is something Lord Duma and the others need to know. If nothing else, we must find out all we can, and make sure we get whatever we can find out back to Bantha as quickly as possible. For now, let's see if we can discover anything else about their new friend out there."

The others nodded their assent, and the four men quietly made their way out of their hide and along the marshy ground, circling closer to their enemy.

oOo

Life in the armies of Bantha was considered a respectable career for any young man of the Empire, and for most it was a good one, especially since the arrival of the Triumvirate, and Lord Duma's appointment as High Command. There were, of course, many young men who had grown up in Bantha, and had aspired to be a part of its army since they were boys. Then there were those who had made their way from elsewhere in the Empire, always with the dream of reaching a post in Bantha's forces, such a far cry from the poorly organised militias and mobs that passed for military in most of their home towns. Discipline was tight, and training rigorous, but the Sword ensured that their life was a fair one, and that they were treated well. He also insisted on being personally involved in their education whenever his duties allowed it, and as a result, many of Bantha's soldiers considered themselves honoured to be amongst those coached in swordsmanship, or schooled in tactics by Lord Duma himself.

Gaven had been fortunate enough to be in such a class himself upon his arrival in Bantha, full of nervous excitement, tempered with a measure of doubt. Tales of the Sword's prowess with a blade were rife, and as they stood awaiting his arrival in the courtyard, with a smith preparing weapons in the corner, there were already bets and wagers being made as to who could last longest in sparring with the Sword, or bold claims as to who might unseat the Lord's weapon from his hand. Gaven had kept quiet, unsure what to expect, but certain that no-one could live up to the wild rumours he had heard. He glanced over to the plain looking man sat, stripped to the waist, working a whetstone methodically on the swords lined up in the rack beside him. Not a big fellow, by any account, thought Gaven, but with the look of one who does such work, as if the metal and wood had seeped through the skin, and grown into the muscle below.

"Here, smith!" called one of Gaven's more outspoken companions, an arrogant lad from the great port-city of Pife, fresh from their officer training and, as Gaven had already discovered, fiercely competitive. "When can we get started? Do we have to just wait around looking at the likes of you all day, or can we grab a sword and get cracking?"

The man in the corner stopped his work for a moment, and looked up with a smile. "All things in good time, sir," he replied calmly, then returned his attention to the whetstone. "Might I ask who I am speaking with?"

"I beg your pardon man? Who am I?" the young man looked round at his friends with a snort, "I am Junior Lieutenant Boughton, Pife Officers Academy, and I'm certain you can spare a blade or two for my friends and I to warm up with, polished or not!"

The man raised his head from the stone again, and smiled.
"Well, Junior Lieutenant Boughton of the Pife Officers Academy, I'm almost finished here, then I'll be sure everyone gets a decent weapon in a fit state, sir."
"Oh don't be difficult man," blustered Boughton, "We're not chopping wood here, just a bit of a knock-about! Now give me a sword before I come over there and take one!"
The man stopped in his work, motionless, and looked thoughtfully at the stone for a moment or two. Then he lifted his head once more, and unsmiling this time, simply raised an eyebrow.
"Well? Come on man, for Ancients sake, get about it and give me a sword!"
The man sat back, and looked around the courtyard. "Anybody else think they're ready for a sword?" he asked.
Some of the local lads were nudging each other, whispering things Gaven couldn't make out as they studiously inspected their boots or the clouds. The man's gaze drifted over to Gaven, who met his eye, and, uncertain of quite what else to do, smiled awkwardly and made an apologetic gesture in the direction of Boughton. The man laughed, and winked one twinkling grey eye.
"Oh very well!" exclaimed Boughton, his patience exhausted, "I'll get my o-"
"Wait, Master Boughton!" said the man, getting to his feet. He took a sword from the rack and held it loosely in his left hand. "If you desire a sword quite so badly, then come and take this one from me."
"What?" replied Boughton, "Take it?" He looked back at his friends from Pife again, flushed with anger at the cheek of this smith. "Very well man, on your own head be it!"

Boughton started furiously forward, and snatched out at the sword with his right hand, but the smith casually turned away, his shoulder fending Boughton off, and using his own momentum to send him stumbling into the rack behind. The smith stood waiting as Boughton struggled angrily to his feet, and flashed a conspiratorial smile in Gaven's direction. Boughton, positively incandescent now, charged forward again, both hands grasping at the smith, but the smith was effortlessly quicker again, and as Boughton gripped at his arm he dropped the sword to the floor, took hold of Boughton by wrist and elbow and quickly turned against him, dropping low on his knees at the same moment. Boughton sailed gracelessly over the smith, a look of confused indignation on his face, before landing heavily on his back at the feet of his friends. Breath knocked from his lungs, this time it took him considerably longer to find his feet.

No-one, it transpired that morning, could unseat the Sword's weapon from his hand, much less last more than a few seconds in sparring with him, least of all Junior Lieutenant Boughton. In fact, the young soldiers did not cross blades at all that afternoon, learning instead to disarm one another, or keep hold of their sword without using its blade. They learnt the importance of maintaining and caring for their weapon, and to see employing it as a last resort. In addition, and of great interest to Gaven, they learnt a little of Lord Duma himself, son of a blacksmith, brought up in a village not unlike the one Gaven called home.

The Sword earned Gaven's respect that day, and in the months that followed, that respect became mutual, as Gaven's attitude and diligence in his training and duties were noted, and he began his steady climb through the ranks of Bantha's Guard.

oOo

Although there were men and women among the Empire who had learnt the rudiments of the languages of one or other of the Savage tribes, there were none who could claim to have mastered any of the tongues, and certainly none who could manage more than a handful of the wild range of dialects and variations.

The figure who stood among the Savages now, however, seemed to have no such difficulty. He spoke with ease and fluency, seeming perfectly relaxed amongst the brutes surrounding him. Gaven and his men watched as the figure pointed and gestured, seeming to give out orders and organise matters without any question from his unusual companions. Gaven wondered, from his position in the mud, just how someone could turn against his own, cause such suffering, yet seem so comfortable in their skin.

Before he could give the matter any further thought however, two of the Savage creatures emerged from the tent and rushed over to the man, gesturing and exclaiming urgently as they did so. As they reached him a few hurried words were exchanged, then the figure raised a hand to silence them. He reached inside his tunic and removed an object that Gaven could not quite make out, then, twisting it in his hands, the figure brought it close to his face, murmuring something as he did so. The Savages looked at each other expectantly, and one of those who had hurried over before seemed ready to interrupt the man, but was silenced by his companion. A few moments later, the figure placed the object back into the folds of his tunic. He straightened up, seemed to look off into the distance for a moment, ignoring the open mouths and wide eyes of the creatures around him, then calmly, coolly, he turned and looked directly into Gaven's eyes.

For a moment none of the four huddled together moved, as realisation took precious seconds to reach their frozen limbs. Gaven was the first to respond.
"Go." he said simply, softly, and launched himself backwards and onto his feet with a lurch, "Go, go!" he cried.
Gaven turned to move off, but saw Thurro looking at him, bewildered, and the other two still staring in disbelief at the figures approaching them. Sliding and staggering in the mud, he lunged back toward them, grabbing at their tunics.
"Don't you hear me?! Go! We're made, they see us! Sergeant, get your men moving, NOW!"
The order seemed to snap Thurro out of his daze. His mouth flapped noiselessly for a second, then he rose and joined Gaven in hauling Grays and Brackley to their feet.
"Didn't you hear the Captain?! 'E gave you an order, now on your feet! Let's go!"
Brackley stumbled backwards as Thurro and the Captain pulled him up, still staring at the dark figure.
"How did 'e do that? 'E just knew... 'e never even looked, 'e just knew we was 'ere..."
"Some kind of dirty magic! Treacherous swine! Some kind of witch!" shouted Grays, eyes wild.
"Never mind that," yelled the Sergeant in response, "Do yer job and MOVE!"
The four plunged headlong into the driving rain, calling out desperately to the rest of their unit as they went, pursued by their Savage enemy. As they ran, they wished once again for their home.

Chapter Four

As the high moon cast a shimmer on the dusting of frost on the woodland path, time seemed to Joseera to stand still for a moment. She found herself able to appreciate every tiny detail laid before her. Each glittering speck of ice, clinging to the grass and tangled branches all around, reflected in the cold, clear sky above as a hundred stars cast down their chilly light. The sharp wind, burning her cheeks, and grasping at her clothes. The pressure of unseen eyes, boring into her from the woods behind. And ahead, the moonlit giant, unmoving, watching her intently.

Although her senses told her she had all the time in the world to escape, to run away, she found her body disobedient, rooting her to the spot as firmly as the grasping trees that surrounded her. In that frozen moment, she had time, it seemed, to reflect on how foolish she had been, how thoughtless and rash in her reaction. She thought of her home, her village, her friends. She thought of her family. She saw her parents faces before her, and wondered, as the moment stretched out, if she would ever see them again.

oOo

Just a few days earlier Joseera had been stood in the kitchen of her parents home, half-listening to her mother's voice as she once again reprimanded her for speaking out of turn.

"...the fact is Joseera, you're not a child any more! People aren't going to make excuses for you much longer, and you have to realise that eventually someone is going to react badly!"

Joseera sighed her resignation. "I know mother, I'm sorry. I should have waited, but -"
"No buts, young lady! Thankfully Mister Fossley wasn't paying a close ear to what you were wittering about, but that isn't the point! Whether you like the work or not, you have to find *something*, Joseera, make yourself useful... You can't just give up! Your father and I have enough troubles as it is, without having to defend you to half the village."
"Yes, but I thought about it this time! And I just don't know what I want to do, how can I without trying things?! Don't you want me to be happy?"
"Oh, for Ancients sake, Joseera, of course I do, don't say such a terrible thing! But we *all* have to *work*, Joseera, and not everyone has the luxury of picking and choosing!"

Parvel Mayweather pushed through the kitchen door having finished his days work and took stock of the familiar situation. With a deep breath, today he chose to ignore the exasperated looks on the faces of his wife and his daughter, instead attempting a cheerful greeting in the hope of defusing the problem without learning any of the details.
"Hello, my beautiful girls! How are my two favourite ladies this afternoon? Enjoying the fresh day?"
He kissed them each in turn on the cheek and raised his eyebrows optimistically.
"Hello father," started Joseera, arms around his neck, "You're just in time, mother doesn't want me to be happy!"
Juna Mayweather turned angrily from the stove. "Oh Joseera, you spiteful thing! I did not say that!"
She looked to her husband, "For Ancients sake, Parvel, will you tell her?"
All hopes deflated, Parvel looked at his daughter.

"What is it this time Joseera? Who have you upset now?"

"It's not like that father," replied Joseera insistently, "I'm certain this time! Councillor Grace was up to something, I know it! I went down to help in the hall when people were taking their donations for Wintersfest, I was doing as Mister Fossley told me to, and I saw her, standing at the door! She was staring at me all funny, and whispering to herself, but when she saw me looking she gave me this big smile and acted all friendly. Then she came over and was asking how everything was going, and Mister Fossley said I had to be polite, and I said-"

"Joseera, that's enough!" Her father's sharp tone shocked her into silence. She was used to arguing with her parents, but something in her father's tired face seemed more threatening than usual, a dark cloud hidden just behind the furrows of his brow. He pointed stiffly at her.

"Now you listen to me, young lady, and listen close. Your mother and I have tried, Ancients help us, to be patient with you, to encourage you to think for yourself, and use that imagination. But whatever you've seen, or think you've seen – I will not let you drag this family into trouble! You're grown now Joseera, an adult so I'm told – so why can't you use that fanciful mind of yours! Think of someone else for a change Joseera, think of your family! Whether we believe what you say or not, what do you think will happen to us if you keep this up, eh? If no-one is willing to offer you work, to give you yet another chance? Have you thought of that girl?"

Joseera looked from her father's flushed face to her frowning mother and back again.

"But father-" she started softly.

"No, Joseera, no." said Parvel, firmly. "I said that's enough, and I meant it. Now go clean yourself up for supper, and we'll have no more of this today." He ushered his daughter gently out of the kitchen.

"She was up to something, father," Joseera's voice drifted back through the door, "I know it."

Juna leant wearily on the stove, and looked at her husband with a frayed expression. He ran his hand along the side of her face, smoothing her forehead with his thumb, then stood behind her, arms wrapped around her waist and kissed her cheek.
"Don't worry so, Juna," he said gently, "She'll learn. She has to learn."
"I know, Parvel, I know," she replied. "I just... She gets so upset. If we'd known what we're getting into when we took her in... I wish her brother were here to talk some sense into her. At least she listens to him!"
Parvel laughed. "Yes, she always did. Perhaps we should write and ask him what his secret is."
Now Juna laughed too, and smiling again, they began to lay out the evening's food.

oOo

Time caught up.

Joseera heard a sudden rustling commotion behind her, a whistling growing quickly close, but before she could think to move or turn around, the creature thundered forward at a pace she would have thought impossible for something of such size. She had no time to move before it reached her, terror freezing her limbs in any case. As if in slow motion, one of the creature's gnarled claws flew towards her face.

The next thing she knew, she was yanked powerfully to the side, the creature pulling her round behind it, turning as it did so. As she looked up, an arrow thudded solidly

into the back of the creature's shoulder, where her head had been just seconds before. The creature dropped her against its other arm and reached back to throw up its heavy cloak, shielding them both. Several more arrows struck against it uselessly. Suddenly, and quite unexpectedly, the creature threw back its head and let loose a sharp, piercing whistle. In response, she heard screams of pain and fear from the trees, men's voices shouting out in terror and confusion.
"What the blazes is that!"
"Where did it come from?!"
"Get out the way, get out the way!"
A group of uniformed men tumbled raggedly onto the path, and with a snapping of branches and brush, they were closely followed by the body of another, propelled by a barrelling ball of fur, tusks and muscle. As the archer landed limply on the cold ground, the huge boar slowed, and skirted round behind the men, eyeing them carefully as they formed rank and drew swords. Then an arrow shot out from the trees on the other side of path, striking the boar's flank. It let forth a rasping squeal, then with another sharp whistle from the creature, crashed into the undergrowth in pursuit of its assailant.

The three men remaining on the path turned to face Joseera and the creature.
"Let them deal with that beast, let's get the job done while we've got the chance!" shouted one, advancing.
"Yeah, looks like we'll have to take down another one of these things in the bargain, eh?"
"Heh, too bad," growled another.
They were interrupted by a torrent of furious shouts and squealing from within the woods again, then gradually four more men emerged from the trees, heaving and cursing at the corners of a thick net, in which the great

boar was thoroughly entangled. To Joseera's surprise, the creature loosed its hold on her and stood, axe at its side, facing the struggling men. It let out a low trill and the boar seemed to calm itself and lay still.

Joseera saw her chance.
"Help me! Help me, please!" she cried, darting around the creature, in a panicked run towards the soldiers.
Before she could go any further, however, the creature's massive left hand leapt out and caught a handful of her cloak, stopping her short, pulling her off her feet.
She scrambled up and was about to grab for her sword, but the creature flicked her cloak about her and pulled her tight against its side, preventing her from moving her arms at all.
She cried out again to the men on the path, "Please! Please help me! Don't let it take me! Please!"
She managed no more, as her sobs stole her voice.

One of the men, a thin red and white sash about his arm that distinguished his uniform from the dark colours of his companions, stepped forward calmly.
"Don't you worry missy," he said, without taking his eyes off the creature for a moment. "We'll have this all sorted out no problem, then we'll take special care of you, don't you worry."
This prompted a low laugh from some of the other men. Joseera reined in her tears with an uneasy breath. These men, she recalled, had been following her.
"Yes, special care, that's for sure..." The man had a gristly look to him, with a face that seemed to have spent so long twisted in contempt that it could not recall any other expression.
"Now listen here monster," he continued. "I'm given to believe you can understand me well enough, isn't that

right?"

Joseera twisted her head to look up at the creature. If it did understand, it made no response nor indication.

"Hff." sniffed the man. "Well the way I sees it, you got something we want, and we got your little... friend back here."

Eyes still fixed firmly on the creature, the man gestured behind him with his sword, in the direction of the helpless boar.

"Now I suggest you hands over what we want... before we have ourselves an accident – eh, boys?"

He waved his other hand, and one of the soldiers walked over to the boar, and raised his sword in both hands, point hovering above the animals belly.

"Well monster?" asked the man, an ugly look of pleasure on his face, "From what I hear you an' your animals are as good as family..."

The creature remained impassive, still.

The man waited for a second or two. "Huh. Have it your way then." He raised his hand and turned to the man standing over the boar. As he did so he felt a faint rush of air. There was just enough time for a blank look of surprise as the creature's rough axe spun past him and buried itself forcefully in the would-be slaughterman's chest, carrying the body a further six feet back with the weight of the blow.

The men stood in stunned silence for a second. The boar grunted appreciatively.

The gristle faced leader turned back to face Joseera and the creature, venom rising in his stare.

"Fine. Fine." he spat, tightly. "Kill them both."

With a palpable release of tension, the men charged forward, screaming and roaring, swords swinging. Before the first two could reach them, the creature pulled at

Joseera's cloak, revealing her sword, and deftly drew it from the scabbard. It was little more than a dagger in the creature's huge fist, but nonetheless it swept the blade in front of it, turning as it did so and pushing Joseera behind. The blade met the first man's sword, knocking it into his companion's, and as the two men stumbled together the creature turned its shoulder into them and drove forward, hurling them bodily into the men behind. One approached, bellowing, from the right, sword raised above his head, but the creature swung out a long arm and launched the man violently into the trees, where he struck a frosty trunk with a dull and final thud. While the others found their feet, the creature swept Joseera up and in long, powerful strides rushed over to retrieve the axe from the slaughterman's chest. Then it stood and drew Joseera behind it again, great axe in its right hand, Joseera's sword in its left, stepping in front of her and the still tangled boar.

The five remaining soldiers faced them cautiously, keeping their distance. They muttered a few words to each other, then split, three charging straight at the them, the other two circling round to the left. As they came, the creature drew back the huge axe and Joseera stumbled backwards in fear. Then the axe rushed forth in a wide arc, battering aside the men's weapons and barely slowing as it ripped through each of their chests. Joseera screamed as the leader of the men lunged at her from the side, roughly grabbing her arm and raising his blade, but the creature swiftly turned and launched Joseera's own sword with a flick of its sinewy wrist, impaling the man at the base of the neck. The gristly face twisted in one more look of contorted surprise, then finally stopped moving for good. The last man charged at the creature brandishing his sword before him like a lance, eyes wild with anger and terror, and the creature dropped its axe to the ground and caught the man's arm, turning and redirecting the blow until they stopped still, face to face, the soldier's own sword planted in his stomach. Silently, the creature let the man fall to the earth, then pulled a short knife from its belt and set about freeing the boar.

Joseera felt numb. Suddenly in the silence following all the confusion, her legs didn't seem quite strong enough to bear her weight any more. She sank slowly on to the ground and sat there, watching the creature, open-mouthed. The creature stopped what it was doing and glanced up at her. Then it nodded its head curtly at her sword, still resting in her attacker's neck. When she didn't move, it reached over and drew the blade out, forcing Joseera to turn her head away in revulsion. It turned the sword about and offered it, pommel first, to Joseera. Gingerly, she took it.

"Th-thankyou." she said, meekly. "It was my father's."

The creature grunted and rolled its eyes, then gestured with its own knife to the ropes entangling the boar.

"Oh... oh, you want me to help?" asked Joseera, "Oh, of course, I'm sorry."

They set about sawing through the tough ropes and between them had the boar free in a matter of minutes, only hindered by its enthusiastic squeals and attempts to lick them in encouragement. The creature checked it carefully for injuries while the boar snuffled happily against it.

Satisfied that it had the measure of the damage, the creature sat and took a pouch from a loop on its belt. It scooped out a thick salve and began applying it liberally to its own injuries and those of the boar.

In the calm, Joseera began to cry.

The creature looked quizzically at Joseera and gestured to her cheek. Choking back her tears, she raised her hand and felt a long scratch on the side of her face, dried blood on her skin. Very slowly, very gently, the creature reached out and with one gnarled finger, smeared a little of the paste on to the cut. She smiled, and very much to her surprise, the creature smiled back. The boar contributed by happily attempting to lick off the medicine with its rough tongue. Joseera laughed awkwardly.

What happened next surprised her even more. The creature spoke. It pointed a finger at the boar, and with a voice like a soft roll of far-off thunder, it said, "Jubal."
Joseera wasn't sure whether to respond, or what this meant, but before she had chance to consider it any further, the creature turned its finger to point at itself.
"Fulza." it said.
Finally the creature said something that, despite the awful events of the evening, shocked her more than anything else.
It looked her steadily in the eye and pointed at her.
"Joseera." it said.

Chapter Five

Jen Cullen lifted the torch higher as Pash worked at the old stone with the point of an axe. With his other hand he scratched absent-mindedly around the patch covering his right eye. The skin surrounding it looked red and angry. Another man ducked in through the tunnel leading back outside.

"Is it done? Are we in yet?" asked the newcomer.
"Almost." replied Jen quietly, without looking round.
As if on cue, the remaining stonework gave way beneath Pash's axe and fell back into the chamber beyond, leaving a rough, dark hole. Jen's hand went to his eye again. Pash laid his axe gently on the rocky floor and pushed away the last of the loose pieces of stone, then turned to Jen and raised his eyebrows questioningly. Jen nodded, then turned to the other man.

"Wait here." he said, simply, then he and Pash disappeared through the opening, and into the darkness beyond.

oOo

High in the main building of Bantha's great Keep, The Heart pushed open a heavy wooden door cautiously and peered inside.
"Sofya? Are you in here? I knocked, but..."
She heard a sound that she took to be shattering glass followed by a delighted laugh and smiled to herself. Stepping into the large but cluttered chamber and negotiating stacks of odd looking furniture and glassware, piles of parchment, feathers, leafy branches, and various other items that had no business being in the Keep, she

called again.
"Sofya?"
"Loulouthi? Is that you?" a voice called back from somewhere round the corner within, "Come and see this Loulouthi, fabulous stuff!"

The Heart slowly picked her way deeper into the chaos, until she found the Book by the room's huge windows, at a heavy bench laden with glasses and beakers of all shapes and sizes, tubes of copper and rods of iron. As Loulouthi approached, the Book turned to greet her, with a wild smile framed by rampant red hair, looking for all the world like a mischievous flame escaped from the fire that burned in the great stone hearth by the far wall.
"Look at this, look at this!" she cried, and bustled the taller woman over to the table.
The Heart laughed happily, feeling Sofya's excitement.
"Ancients, what is it Sofya? Have you discovered a way to clean this study of yours with a charm?" she smiled, as the Book fussed at the various containers and mixtures.
The Book stopped in her tracks for a moment and glanced back at the Heart over her shoulder, eyebrows raised in indignation.
"Just because you don't understand the system, Loulouthi, doesn't mean it isn't there," she said with a scoff, turning back to her instruments, "Everything in this room is quite precisely organised, thank you very much, I know the place of every speck and splinter."
She turned again and gave the Heart a wicked grin, "At least, I know they're in here somewhere."
The Heart smiled back. She didn't share her friend's understanding of magicks, of the arts and sciences of the world, but she felt her passion and inspiration just as keenly when she was nearby. The chamber seemed outwardly to mirror its occupant, but Loulouthi never

ceased to be surprised at the crystal sharp focus and clarity that could be achieved by such a seemingly disorganised mind.

"It wouldn't surprise me if you had discovered such a charm, Sofya, it would only surprise me if you chose to use it."

The Book finished her preparations and turned to face the Heart with two glasses, half full of coloured liquid, in her hands.

"If you're quite finished insulting my housekeeping, Loulouthi, I'd very much like to show you this. Look here-" she held out the containers, "-what do we have in here, eh?"

The Heart took one of the glasses and inspected the light, straw coloured fluid within. She took the other, and looked closely at the rich, burgundy contents. She sniffed at each. She paused.

"Sofya, you do know that people have been making wine for some years now?"

The Book chuckled excitedly.

"Yes, Loulouthi, I am aware that I am not the first to such a discovery... but... taste it! Just one though mind, very important, taste only one!"

The Heart looked uncertainly at the two glasses. Then she took a small sip from the golden wine.

"Mmm. Yes, it's wine Sofya," she said after a moments thought, "And not particularly good wine at that, I might add."

The Book gasped, eyes wide, a look of mortal insult on her face for a second or two, then suddenly relaxed, grinning again.

"No, the quality is not the finest, I'll grant you, and believe me, you can say the same for the red!" she pushed her gold-rimmed eyeglasses high on her nose as if to emphasise her point, "However, taste is not the quality I am interested in here Loulouthi, not at all..."

Sofya took the glasses gently from the Heart's hands, and very carefully poured a small measure of each into an empty beaker sitting on the bench. She turned, and placed the glasses steadily on another table a safe distance away, then retreated herself, pulling the Heart along with her.

"Watch..."

The Book took a small pebble from one of the many pockets in her robe and tossed it gently at the glass, where it hit the side with a delicate tink. The glass promptly exploded, much to the Heart's surprise and the Book's delight.

"Hah!" exclaimed the Book, triumphantly, "Tremendous, eh? Every time! I wasn't sure, but it seems so..."

"Ancients, Sofya!" gasped the Heart, "What is this? Exploding wine? I'm not sure I see the purpose, save perhaps a few less brawls in the taverns of an evening... Although I have to say, I shouldn't think the landlords will be best pleased with the mess!"

"No, no, no, Loulouthi," replied the smaller woman, sweeping away the broken glass, "It's not the wine itself. It's what I've added – two powders, one to each glass, entirely inert and completely harmless on their own, but once properly mixed, extremely unstable as you see! This is the future Loulouthi, an understanding of our minerals and raw materials that we have never known! A world of untapped potential – ah... but I'm sorry Loulouthi. You didn't come here to listen to my ramblings. What was it you needed?"

The Heart smiled warmly at her friend. "Actually, Sofya, it does me good to hear someone talk about something other than conflict and politics. I know, I know it needs to be discussed, but these last few days I have longed for just an hour to pass without some councillor, official or officer demanding an answer or decision."

The Book peered over her glasses at Loulouthi for a moment, then ushered her gently over to a somewhat less cluttered part of the chamber at the fireside, where several battered chairs sat, for the most part covered with parchment and papers, next to a wooden side-table, curiously clear save for a bottle and few glasses. The smaller woman swept a few stray sheets from two of the more lightly burdened chairs and set her friend down in one of them, while she poured them both a glass of dark wine from the bottle atop the small table. She handed one to the Heart, then took at seat herself.
"Just wine this time, I promise – and a particularly good one at that, eh?" she said with a wink.
The Heart smiled once more and took a little of the wine. She reached for the chain at her neck and pulled forth the shape that hung from it, shimmering gold and dark metal, ancient symbol of her office.
"What do we do Sofya?" she sighed, staring at the fire's reflection on the etched gold surface. "We have been fortunate this far, but now... what if we cannot do enough? We were given a warning, Sofya, I know you can't have forgotten. What if this is the moment? What if something is coming, and we are not ready?"
The Book thought for a moment, then took a deep draught from her glass and smacked her lips appreciatively.
"I may be a little older than you, Loulouthi, and perhaps even a little wiser in some matters, but I'm afraid even I can't predict what comes next. Duma believes we must convince the council to wait, gather more information before we commit our forces in any number, and I am inclined to agree with him," she smiled conspiratorially, "as much as that pains me. But as for doubting us, Loulouthi, as for doubting yourself – do you wish harm

upon our people?"

The Heart looked at her friend with a frown. "Of course not."

"Do you want the best for them?"

"Of course."

"And will you do as much as you may to achieve it?"

"Yes. Of course."

The Book went to drink from her glass but found it disappointingly empty, so reached over to refill it from the bottle.

"Dear Loulouthi," she said softly, "You always were a sensitive soul, even before... what happened. Perhaps we were lucky, perhaps cursed for all I know, eh? But what does it matter now? Right or wrong, we are the leaders of this land, chosen and accepted by its people, and as long as we give the best of ourselves while we can, I for one will not look back with doubt or regret."

The Heart nodded, then smiled, looking back to the fire.

"Yes, Sofya, you're right, of course. There's nothing to be gained from doubting ourselves now. We must do the best we can. I only hope we can stop all of this," she turned back to her friend, "before its too late."

oOo

Cam Blowgrip stamped his feet and cursed his poor employment choices as the torch he held flickered and threatened to give up altogether. Barely twenty, he was a skinny young man, and where some fat or muscle might have lessened the cold a shade, Cam had little of either. He thrust his head briefly into the tunnel that led back through the entrance to the ruins and outside, and listened for a moment. Still raining. A small mercy, he thought, but at least he was not stood waiting in the rain like the others, even if it did feel colder in here than out. As he tried to coax a little more warmth from the tired torch, he wondered what it was that Cullen wanted from this musty old place anyway, since Cam himself certainly hadn't seen anything he'd consider to be of use or value so far. But, nevertheless, Cullen had paid good coin, half up front too, for doing little more than standing around so far. Still, Cam thought, he was a miserable swine, yet to crack a smile. And then there was his stone faced friend! Big fellow, never uttered so much as a word, even to say 'hello'! Cam sniffed, and was toying with the idea of popping outside to see what the others were up to, at least they had company, when he heard a noise within the dark hole.

A few moments later Jen Cullen and Pash appeared, covered in dust and dirt, awkwardly carrying a dark object of smooth stone and metal between them. Cullen's one eye seemed to shine, surrounding by the filthy darkness of his face, as it fixed on Cam.
"Come on Blowgrip, what am I payin' you for, eh?" Cullen growled. "Get over here and give us a hand!"
Cam hurriedly laid down his torch and rushed over to take the object from them and lift it out of the narrow hole. About the size of a small jug, the thing was deathly cold to the touch and made Cam gasp as he grasped it. Although it was too dark to see any real detail, Cam could make out odd carvings on both the stone and the metal that wove across it. Once Cullen and Pash had managed to clamber clear of the hole themselves, they quickly took the object from Cam and carefully placed it in the small wooden crate they had waiting. The thing seemed to draw the warmth and light out of the air around it as it lay heavily on its bed of straw packing, and Cam was very grateful when Cullen and Pash finally sealed the lid on top. The three men stood for a moment in the flickering

torch light, staring down at the plain wooden box.

"What is it?" asked Cam, in a hushed voice.
"If you've any sense at all about you lad, although I can't say I'm sure about that, you won't ask again." said Cullen quietly. "Believe me, you're best just taking the rest of your pay and forgetting all about it."
Cullen scratched again at the red raw skin around his patch.
"There's those that won't take kindly to anything else."

About half an hour later they had managed, with the help of the two other young men who had been standing guard outside the ruins, to carry the crate outside. They had set torches in the ground to work by, then Cullen had instructed them to wrap the crate in cloth, before it was placed on the back of the cart they had used to travel out.
"Be a bit slower going back I'm afraid," Cullen had said, once they were done, "Someone'll have to walk ahead of the cart with a torch 'stead of riding in it, now the light's gone. But keep quiet and get the job done, and you'll all get the rest of your moneys the minute we're back in town, understood?"
The others, most not much older or wiser than Cam, shuffled, nodded and murmured their assent, and Cullen nodded back, glad of their simplicity and lack of imagination.
"Good." he growled. "Good. Now we'll be ready to leave in just a few minutes. You wait here with Pash, I have one more thing to attend to." He turned and, to Cam's surprise, seemed to glance nervously at the silent Pash, who nodded and patted Cullen's shoulder firmly. Cullen set his jaw, and walked a little way off, back towards the entrance to the ruins.

They stood in awkward silence for a minute or two, shivering in the rain, Cam and the other boys, while the torches spat and sputtered in protest at the clouds. Pash ignored them, staring impassively after Cullen, until it became too much for one lad, who blurted a question.

"So, how'd you two come to be in Purren then? Don't get too many people passin' through, that's for sure, specially now with them Savages venturin' out again."

Pash's head turned slowly round until his eyes rested heavily on the speaker, but he made no offer of an answer, or so much as opened his mouth. Uncertain what to do, and too young to know when to shut up, the speaker continued uncomfortably.

"Ah... uh.. you know, most people are worried about the trouble spreadin' again... you know. Should kill 'em all, my old man reckons!" He laughed, loud and inappropriate. "Head into their lands, round 'em up, and get rid of 'em, eh? You know... eh..."

Gradually the voice tailed off. Cam's curiosity got the better of him.

"Uh, Mister Pash," he started, as politely as he could manage, "No offence or nothin', but I was wonderin', have you taken vows or somethin' like that? I mean to say, is that why you never say nothin'?"

The young man who had spoken first was deeply grateful to see Pash's head turn slowly to face Cam. Then Pash's brow creased for a moment, droplets of rain tracing his frown, and he strode forward, scattering the others away from Cam as he gripped the boy's face firmly and leaned in close to him. Cam struggled for a moment, then stopped as Pash opened his mouth and revealed a fat, blackened stump where his tongue should have been, wet and shiny in the light of the flames. Pash released his grip, letting Cam fall to the floor, before walking slowly back to the edge of the torchlight and staring off into the darkness after Cullen.

By the dark of the stone arch that marked the entrance to the ruins, Jen Cullen was oblivious to the disturbance behind him. His mind was focused on one thing only and he was trying as hard as he might to maintain his composure. Hand shaking, he reached into the deep pocket in the lining of his jacket and drew out the little package he had been given. His fingers were numb and cold, and he told himself that was why he struggled to unwrap the soft cloth, that was why his fingers trembled so. Finally he revealed the contents, a smooth ball of blue glass, small enough to sit comfortably in the palm of the hand, wrapped by two thin bands of iron, each with a single point jutting out from its edge. Nervously, Cullen pushed at the bands with his thumbs, until the two points lined up, then he waited, breath jerking noisily through his teeth.

After a moment, a soft, cool light appeared within the blue glass, sparkling in the raindrops on its surface. Cullen stood there in silence, as if listening intently, although anyone stood nearby would not have heard a thing.
Cullen swallowed hard and gathered himself.
"Yes, Mr. Glower sir, yes. I hope you'll be pleased sir, we've done as you asked to the letter, Mr. Glower sir."
He stood in silence again, staring into the pale light flickering within the glass sphere.
"Yes, Mr. Glower sir." Cullen replied softly. "We have it."

Chapter Six

Gaven lay, for the second time that day, shivering in the mud at the bottom of a ditch, damp clothes clinging to his skin. He wasn't sure how long he'd been there. He'd run as hard and fast as he could to evade his pursuers, and when he'd collapsed into the welcoming trench, it had been because his lungs and legs burned, and he could run no further. Now he felt nothing, legs and all numb with the cold, and though his lungs drew breath more easily, it was still ragged. He wondered what had become of the others. Whether the rest of the unit had also been discovered he did not know. He had seen Brackley fall, brought down by a thick crossbow bolt before the Savages caught up to him, and although he and Thurro had run on together, another group of Savages had joined the chase, forcing them to cut through thick brush, where Gaven had lost the sergeant. As for Grays, Gaven had no idea what had happened to him.

Like any good soldier, it was his duty that stopped him from simply lying there. If nothing else, he knew he must get word to Bantha.

He pushed himself up, aching muscles protesting, to sit against the wet earth of the ditch wall, and looked above, to the sky. It had grown dark. At least it had stopped raining, he thought, and this brought forth a humourless laugh that quickly became a rasping cough. Eyes watering, Gaven sat back for a moment to recover, then with a sigh forced himself onto his feet. He almost fell, in the first instant, as his frozen legs betrayed him, two thick, unfeeling weights threatening to drop him back into the mud. Then, gradually, warm blood found its way into the icy flesh, pricking life into it with an almost pleasant tingle. Eventually Gaven stood, leaning on the grassy earth at the edge of his shelter, and surveyed the scene.

Not that there was much to see. Although he believed he had lost the Savages some distance back, he had continued on apace for some time, knowing their reputation for persistence and their skill as trackers. He had crossed and re-crossed a narrow river, passed through some unexpected woodland, and kept on moving through the hills until he no longer could. Unfortunately, he realised, this had been more effective than he might have hoped. Gaven had no idea where he was.

He looked blankly at the landscape around him, hoping to pick out in the darkness some landmark or feature that would seem familiar, ignite some spark of recognition. Instead he found little more than rugged hills covered in patchy, windswept grass, here and there worn so thin as to reveal the rock beneath. Each way he turned, he was faced with the same view, or if not quite the same, then at least as close as made no difference. The clouds above were thick, hiding the stars from view. Without the sun, he couldn't even tell which way home lay.

Gaven closed his eyes, placed his head in his hands. Higher ground, he thought. That's what I need. Higher ground, a point where I may see a little further. Then, when the sun rises again, I will know which way to travel. He looked over to his right, to the nearest hill.

He drew a deep, jagged breath, put his thoughts of warmth and rest aside, dismissed the complaints and carping of his limbs, and set out, slowly upwards.

oOo

Fulza looked at the girl with equal measure of concern and irritation. Jubal snuffled at his hand, seeking his attention, and Fulza turned to scratch the great boar between the ears, while it grunted happily.

Of course, he understood the girl's surprise, and had been prepared for her reaction when he spoke her name, which alternated seemingly at random between 'You can speak!', 'You know my name!' and 'How?!'. Once she fell silent, he had spent the next few minutes patiently attempting to explain and answer her questions, until it became clear to him that she was no longer listening, but rather staring slack-jawed at or maybe through him, with a glassy look in her eyes.

At first he had been glad of the silence, and she had sat there quite quietly while he began, business-like, to clear up the scene, hiding the bodies in the woods and removing any evidence of the confrontation or their presence. Now he was finished, however, and the girl had neither moved nor made a sound. Fulza had been hoping she just needed a little time to recover, collect her thoughts. Now he was uncertain what to do, an unfamiliar feeling for him, and not one he enjoyed.

He sighed heavily and looked from the girl to Jubal. The boar met his gaze with a blank expression and snorted quizzically. Fulza gave a look of sarcastic thanks, but this was met with another, more emphatic snort in Joseera's direction. Fulza wearily looked back at the girl and nodded, resigned.

He walked slowly over to where Joseera sat and stood a

few feet away, facing her.

"Girl?" he tried, as softly as he could manage, "Girl?"

There was no response.

"Joseera."

Nothing. Fulza heard an encouraging grunt behind him.

"Joseera, must go. Must travel my home-"

Abruptly Joseera jumped into life with a squawk, loud and sudden enough to surprise even Fulza, who stepped back in alarm.

"Home!" she cried, "Oh Ancients, home! I have to go home! My family, my parents, they'll be- Ancients, what time is it? I have to go home!"

Fulza gathered himself and shook his head firmly.

"No, Joseera." he said "Men hunt you, not I. Others will look your home."

This was not met with the response Fulza hoped for.

"What?!" Joseera screamed, almost forcefully enough to make Fulza back away once more, "My home? My parents? They'll go there? Well... we have to go! We have to, I have to make sure they're okay!"

A low growl started in Fulza's throat, then he stepped toward her, one thick finger jabbing in her direction. "No!" he barked, harshly, teeth bared, and now it was Joseera's turn to jump. Wide-eyed, the colour gradually drained from her face as he drew nearer. "Foolish! I save you! You safe! No! No time for this!"

He turned abruptly away, whistled sharply to Jubal and began to gather his things. As he strapped his great axe across his back, he cast an eye back at her over his shoulder.

"Come. Must leave now." he said.

Joseera stared fiercely at him. Her eyebrows knotted and her lips, pressed tightly together, began to tremble. Once the first tear grew fat enough to tumble on to her cheek she lost her composure and began to cry.

"I won't, I won't go with you!" she sobbed, "I don't know what's going on, I don't know what you are, but I won't leave them, I won't!"

She grabbed at her breath to continue, "I don't care, I can't leave them like this, I won't go with you! And you can.. you can probably drag me and make me come, but that's what you'll have to do, because I won't go..." she fell forward, shaking and gasping through her tears, "I have to go home... I want to go home."

Fulza stood, impassive, looking at the pathetic figure on the ground. For a moment he did not move at all. Then he hooked his thumbs into the belt about his waist and leaned back, looking straight up, into the violet sky. He took a long, deep and weary breath. Eventually his gaze dropped back to earth and he rubbed roughly at his temples. He looked to Jubal. The boar tipped its head to one side, then trotted over to where Joseera sat and began licking and nuzzling at her face.

Fulza shook his head, defeated.

oOo

Gaven chewed hungrily at the strips of dried meat. The salt interrupted his eating with the occasional cough, but he continued regardless. Although units such as his were encouraged to travel light, each man carried as a bare minimum a small pack containing a few simple tools for survival – hunting knife, flint, thin cloth that might be used as a makeshift blanket or torn up for dressing wounds, and a little dried food, anything that would keep. When Gaven had neared the top of the hill, he had found some shelter from the biting wind at the roots of an old tree. He had gratefully wrapped his thick cloak about him, a fine thing of dark woodland green gifted to him by his father, and slept, fitfully, for a little while. When he awoke, he was happy to see the first light of day pushing back the darkness, and as he sat, watching the dawn's arrival, he realised how ravenously hungry he was. Swiftly he had dug through his pack and pulled out the little bundle of jerky with some suspicion - he didn't remember it tasting so good, but right now he was struggling to recall a more satisfying meal.

A short while later, Gaven stood on the hillside, stretching a little life back into his exhausted muscles. The wind had dropped a little now, and he was enjoying the warmth of the sun's first rays. Last night he had pushed on blindly, hopelessly, close to giving in to fatigue and despair, but now, with the daylight on his face and the sun to guide him, he felt a little spark of optimism. Yes, he was alone, and yes, he was lost, but now he knew which way home lay and at the top of the hill, he thought, he may see the path to get there.

Legs aching, wooden, he slowly made his way the last short distance to the highest point of the hill, and looked out, over the rough country. Craggy hills much like the one he stood upon stretched out behind him, patched here and there with woodland, and ahead a twisting valley, crossed with worn paths and trails. For a moment, his heart sank, as he saw no landmark or feature that was familiar to him, but it leapt again a second later, as he made out several figures heading away from him on the path below. He staggered forward, shielding his eyes from the bright morning sun, and squinted at them, trying desperately to see more clearly. With a smile, he saw they were no Savages. They were like him, soldiers, although simply attired – perhaps from a small border town or village riding out against a Savage party? Maybe twenty men or more, on horseback and travelling at speed.

Quickly, Gaven began to hurry down the hillside, limbs suddenly refreshed, calling out to them as he went, desperate that they should see him before they rode out of sight around the valley, disappeared behind the hills and were gone. Could he? - yes, he could hear their voices now, shouting urgently to one another in the cold air, hear the sound of the horses hooves faintly drumming the hard earth!

As he leapt and crashed his way down the hill, legs jarring and shuddering, yelling out, "Ho! Wait! For Ancients sake, wait!", one of the horsemen turned and peered back at him. The horseman called something, shouted out to Gaven, but he was too far off, and Gaven could not make it out. Once again Gaven ran, as hard and as fast as he could.

oOo

In the early light, Fulza and Joseera saw the fires long before they could make out the village itself. Although it had been grimly obvious to Fulza just what the flickering lights were, he was uncertain what to say, and it had taken Joseera just a little longer to realise. As soon as she understood, her eyes had widened, horrified, and Fulza was forced to physically restrain her in order to prevent her from simply running down the path towards her home. Eventually he had been able to calm her a little, not enough to convince her to turn back it seemed, but at least enough that she could see sense, and when he suggested they should stay off the path, use the trees to get a little closer, she quickly agreed.

The fires were rampant, and it seemed to Joseera that no building was untouched. They crept as close to the village as Fulza would allow, but it was all Joseera could do to prevent herself from rushing forward and trying to save the places that she knew so well. Then she saw movement, and against the bright backdrop of the flames, Joseera watched several men in dark uniforms gather in the square in front of what had been the council hall. The light flashed and flickered on their bright metal buttons as they turned to and fro, then they waved, as if to signal someone further down the street, beyond Joseera's view.

Joseera watched, horrified, as the people she knew, villagers, Elders, friends, shuffled into the square, bound together with rope and twine. The uniformed men pushed and harried them as they came, forcing them into a ragged line. Then Joseera saw her parents. She gasped, and clasped her hand over her mouth to keep from crying out, although this did not stop her eyes from welling up, tears spilling silently forth.

"Girl..." started Fulza, at a whisper. She did not take her eyes away from the group of people in the square, but raised her other hand to him for silence.

One of the soldiers, an arrogant looking young man with blonde hair, was shouting something at the first of the prisoners – Elder Vithru, Joseera realised, narrowing her eyes against the glow of the flames – although she couldn't hear the words from here, not over the roar and crackle of the fire. The blonde soldier stabbed at poor Elder Vithru with his finger, then stood back, hands clasped behind him as if waiting for an answer.

Joseera felt an odd wave of guilt. She had never liked the bossy old man, and had sometimes dreamt up awful fates for him, most often when he had been telling her off for one reason or another. Now he looked rather helpless, and Joseera simply wished there was something she could do to help.

As the young man paced back and forth before him, the Elder appeared to be speaking desperately, but his words seemed to displease his interrogator, who turned and nodded coldly to someone out of sight. Then, to Joseera's horror, Councillor Grace stepped into view, spoke briefly with the blonde soldier, and approached Elder Vithru. Before she could say anything to the Elder, however, Vithru spat angrily at her. Councillor Grace shook her head, and beckoned to the blonde man, who stepped forward, drew his sword, and struck the Elder savagely about the head with the hilt, knocking him heavily to the ground.

Joseera watched, transfixed, as several carts were brought in, and the villagers were loaded unceremoniously on to them. Joseera's mother and father went on to the last cart, bound together and comforting each other. Just before they were pushed out of sight, her father seemed to look round, and if she hadn't known better, Joseera would have sworn he caught her eye. She kept her hand firmly pressed over her mouth, forcing herself to stay silent.

Then, her parents were gone. Under the blonde soldier's supervision, the carts began to move out of the village, each one flanked by mounted men. Once they had gone, the blonde and his remaining troops began hurriedly unwrapping several odd looking packages, rushing here and there about the village, but Joseera had seen enough. Not daring to speak, lest she let loose the cries she had worked so hard to silence, she simply turned and waved to Fulza that they should move away.

They went in silence. When Fulza was satisfied they were at a safe distance from the village, he stopped. Jubal set about digging for something amongst the maze of roots at their feet, and Fulza turned to Joseera, and knelt before her, although even then his head was level with hers.
"Sit." he said, simply.
Dazed, numb, Joseera slumped down to the ground, feeling almost as though she was watching the scene from a distance.
Fulza breathed out heavily. "Girl. I am... sorry...what you see."
Joseera said nothing.
"Must have questions." said Fulza.
Joseera laughed awkwardly, then bit her lip and frowned up at him.
"No. Just one." she said, weakly. Her eyes welled up again, and her voice cracked and rasped as she spoke. "Where are they taking my family?"

Fulza sighed, and looked down at the earth. "Don't know, girl. But, what I see, know this – family will be alive, wherever men take them."
He lifted his head and looked into her eyes.
"I know... must be hard. Must trust me. Best you do for family, is stay safe. I am here, keep you safe. Perhaps... find them in time. But cannot do that dead. Trust me. Must travel my home. On way, I answer questions, tell you all I can."
Joseera sniffed, and half-laughed again. Then she stood, and composed herself.

She shrugged, and smiled a sad half smile at the great creature before her. "Perhaps I will wake up soon, in my own bed, in my own house," she said quietly. "But till then, what choice do I have?"

oOo

Gaven's legs ached and shook, and with each bounding step he feared they might give way, send him spinning helplessly down the hillside. He shouted out to the horsemen again and again, even though his voice cracked and wavered with exhaustion. He was sure they'd seen him, certain that one of the men had called to him. So why didn't they stop?

As he reached the flat of the path, his momentum proved too much for him, and sent him sprawling on to the hard packed earth, scraping his hands and arms. He scrambled desperately to his feet just in time to see one of the riders turn again and call, and with the hill behind him Gaven could hear the words this time.
"Stay back man! For Ancients sake, stay back! Stay back!"
Gaven shook his head, raised his arms in confusion, and was about to call back in question, when he spotted more men, up on the high cliffs and hills each side of the path ahead, archers and crossbowmen, others with staff-slings and spears.

Realisation washed over him. This was an attack, an ambush of some kind, they were waiting for someone coming into the valley, a narrow point where they could surprise them. Small wonder they had been telling him to stay back – he was running towards a battle.

He stood uncertainly for a moment, wondering whether these men faced Savages, whether the very same Savages might be out looking for him, when he heard an odd noise, above the sound of horses and men shouting orders ahead.

Thung. Thung. Thung.

Steady it came, rhythmic, a curious, metallic sound, cutting through the curses and commotion, low and heavy like the ringing of a deep, dull bell.

Thung. Thung. Thung.

Gaven listened intently, unable to fathom what might be the source of the noise, hypnotised as it rang around the valley. The harsh scream of a man's voice snapped him out of his trance.

"Stand fast!"

Thung.

"Stand fast I say!"

Thung.

"Archers, loose, loose now! We must stop it here!"

Thung.

Gaven watched the men on the cliffs as they let go every arrow, every bolt, stone and shaft that they had onto whoever it was down below, although he still had no sight of them yet around the sharp bend of the valley, and he watched the same men try to escape and run clear as the ground at the edge of the cliffs suddenly shook and gave way, sliding into the valley below. And still, steady and slow, that strange sound persisted.

Thung. Thung. Thung.

He watched as the horses, wild-eyed, reared and struggled against the wills of their riders, and as their captain cried out again and again for his men to stand their ground.

Then he saw it. How tall it was, he couldn't be sure, perhaps twenty, thirty feet or more, a colossal figure of glittering gold, sparkling and shimmering in the sunlight as if lit from within. As its great feet struck the earth, the steps rang out, filling the air with that sound...

Thung. Thung. Thung.

...and yet, despite its huge size, like some vast suit of armour, it was etched and engraved on every surface, ornate designs adorning the edge of each plate, and atop its head a burnished circlet of twisting golden bands, like a burning crown.

Gaven watched the battle unfold in what felt like slow-motion. Swords, spears, all fell against the giant's metal hide unheeded, leaving not even a scratch. Horses wheeled and jumped, hooves clattered uselessly against the great armour, and man and beast alike were trampled either by their own panicked allies or the ringing steps of the giant. The monstrous thing seemed irritated at their interference, as a man might be by a fly, and swatted at those who drew near with its terrible blade, but it did not stop even for a moment, did not pause or break its pace, and even as its feet swung through the melee of men and horses, sending them flying this way and that, as its steps fell, cracking and crushing bone and blade alike, still it kept its steady, solemn pace, rhythmic, heavy and low.

Thung. Thung. Thung.

As it came along the path towards Gaven, a soldiers sense of self-preservation kicked in, and almost without thinking, he half-ran, half-crawled to the scraggy brush nearby, and concealed himself within. He did not move then, but watched, and listened, terrified, transfixed, until he could neither hear nor see the giant at all.

Chapter Seven

The Keepers tower stood in a small, walled compound, separating it from the chaos of the city beyond. The compound contained a modest, but well-tended garden, and several simple outbuildings also used by the Order. Within the wall, the Order governed itself and answered to no-one but its own, allowed to undertake its mission of observing and recording without interference. Nonetheless, the Order was sworn to serve the interests of the Empire, and so to provide such aid and information as it could to the Empire's leaders. The great tower, its pale grey stone rising above all else, afforded its inhabitants with an unrivalled view from which to watch the world, a pinnacle of quiet contemplation among the clamour and din of the city below.

Despite the early hour, the Scribe walked purposefully down one of the tower's many twisting corridors, long strides covering the cold stone floor easily while his robes swept swirling patterns in the dust behind. He did not look up as he travelled the familiar route, fierce attention focused instead on the thick sheaf of notes and papers in his hands. The few Keepers he passed along the way recognised his mood at once, and knew full well enough to step aside, staying well out of the Scribe's way. As he reached the two great oak doors of the tower's receiving room, set aside for official business and visitors, he looked up from his stack of pages and for a moment stared silently at the fine carvings and brass furniture of the huge doors in contemplation. He took a deep breath and raised a hand to pinch firmly at the bridge of his nose. Then, with a sigh, he set a smile upon his face and plunged through the heavy doors.

The room beyond was a colourful contrast to the plain stone corridor without. The morning light flooded in through wide, leaded windows overlooking the courtyard and gardens below, illuminating the rich reds and golds of the fine carpets, shimmering blue on the silk-clad walls and gleaming on the polished wood of the large table in the centre of the room. Here the wealth and influence of the Order of Keepers was on display.

The Sword stood at the far end of the room, studying one of the many portraits of the Order's leaders and luminaries. As the doors swung open, he turned to greet the tall figure that entered.

"Scribe." he nodded.

"Ah, my Lord Duma," smiled the Scribe broadly, "What an unexpected pleasure to see you, my Lord, and to have you grace our chambers."

The Sword looked blankly at him for a moment.

"Have we got company, your Eminence?" he asked, flatly, as he sat in one of the sturdy wooden chairs around the table.

"My Lord?" replied the Scribe, eyebrows raised.

The Sword sighed and sat back.

"We're alone, Scribe, aren't we? In which case," he sat forward and looked squarely at the other man, "perhaps we could get to the point."

The Scribe pursed his lips and stood, sharp blue eyes quietly studying the other man until the Sword shifted uneasily in his seat. After a moment he stepped forward, dropped his papers unceremoniously onto the table and sat at the corner nearest the Sword.

"Thank you." For a second an uncertain look flashed across the Sword's face, then he continued, "You know my name, Scribe. Might I ask yours?"

The Scribe's face was a mask, unreadable as ever, but an answer came, soft and quiet.

"Prow." he said gently, "Gideon Prow." The Scribe's eyes studied the tabletop. "Though I have little call for it these days."

"Prow?" replied the Sword, "A southerner then? From the coasts?"

"My family, yes."

"Hah!" the Sword smiled, "Well you'd never guess it from the sound of you!" he exclaimed.

"I'll take that as a compliment, my Lord."

"As you will, as you will," said the Sword, still smiling. Then he continued, with a serious tone. "I feel I owe you an apology, Gideon Prow. When I told you the other day that I had sent men out to investigate – believe me, I meant no disrespect to you or your Order. We all, Loulouthi, Sofya and I, all of us value your experience and insight a great deal. I just..."

The Sword paused for a moment and looked up to the ceiling as if searching for inspiration.

"We're on the same side, Gideon. I know the Order may not agree with everything the Triumvir does, and I know you were a supporter of Dray. But I was placed in this office, chosen by the people we both serve, and I hope you wouldn't hold it against me if I use every resource I can to protect them."

The Scribe nodded slowly.

"I understand, my Lord. In fact, I too must apologise – please forgive my reaction at the time, I'm afraid I must confess to being a little surprised, that is all. Such things have ever been the domain and duty of the Keepers. However, I am glad that you felt able to inform us of your actions – I was able in turn to inform Aleph, the Seeker Prime, and so ensure that he and his men are aware of your forces. In future I hope we may... co-ordinate our efforts in a manner which best serves you, my Lord."

The Sword sighed.
"Thank you Gideon." he said warmly, "Good to hear. I must be certain we all stand together, or I'm afraid we won't stand at all."
As the Scribe nodded his agreement once more, the Sword leant forward, a grave look upon his face.
"And that brings me to the other reason I came to see you today. As if what we face isn't enough, I've had some... worrying reports. Mostly nonsense I'm hoping, a lot of garbled ramblings, impossible things, but... I have several such reports. Different sources, different fronts. Too similar to be coincidence. Wild stories of great... giants, huge creatures clad in golden armour!"

The Scribe frowned. "Yes, my Lord. We have similar reports. When we heard you were coming, we began to collect any such information we had acquired, and to check and verify the sources as thoroughly as possible. I have collated what I could for you here." he gestured to the pile of papers sat before him.
"However, I'm afraid the news is not good. We cannot be as certain as we would like, but many strange things have been happening, many concerning sights. It would seem they are a weapon of the enemy. They strike against our forces, my Lord. And they are moving."

The Sword slammed his fist upon the table.
"Curse it!" he rose suddenly from his chair, and paced tersely to the window. "Ancients be damned! I had hoped... hah, foolish perhaps, I'd hoped there might be some other explanation, some... some other reason! And you're sure?! They move against us?"

The Scribe raised his hands, gestured to the pile in front of him on the table. "My Lord, you may read for yourself. The Empire must prepare for a serious assault, and we must do it now."

The Sword sighed. "Very well. Thank you Gideon. I'll take these reports back with me for now. In the meantime, please, get us as much information on these... weapons as you can."

"Yes, my Lord, rest assured, Aleph and his Seekers are working to discover more even as we speak."

The Scribe stood, and straightened his robes. "If that is all for now, my Lord? I have duties to attend to, and a class waiting for me"

The Sword nodded. "Of course, Thank you Gideon. And please, in future, you know my name, feel free to call me Duma."

The Scribe stopped at the door with a thin smile, and turned back to face the other man.

"Given the gravity of the circumstances, my Lord, I thought we might observe the protocol and procedure that ensures the smooth running of our offices, and perhaps, if his Lordship is in agreement, he would be so kind as to address me by the title I have earned."

The Sword said nothing.

"For my part, my Lord, I would prefer, with your permission, to address you by the title you were... given."

He turned to go through the door, then stopped once more, "I find it best, given the gravity of the circumstances, to remember who I am talking to."

The door closed after him with a decisive thud, and the Sword was alone.

oOo

Shortly afterwards, the Scribe sat, silent and still, gazing out of the tall windows of his teaching room, listening to the scritch-scritch of pen against paper. The room was set high in the tower, and on a morning as clear and bright as this, you could see across the city below, and on, past the walls to the hills and valleys that surrounded them. Peaceful, the Scribe thought to himself as he looked out, no sign from here of the squawking and screeching chaos that was everyday life in Bantha, nor of the whispered shadow, the mutterings and murmurs of war and worry that were quickly spreading through the streets and alleyways. From here, people went about their business as quietly as the blades of grass on the hills beyond, flowing through the city like sand in an hourglass, as the seconds slipped irretrievably by.

"Er, your Eminence?"

The Scribe paused for a moment, breathing slow and calm, before turning to face the twelve young men and women who made up his class today.
"Yes, Mister Parfort? What is it?"
"Well, your Eminence, I, er... well, your Eminence, I.. I believe we've all finished, sir."
The Scribe nodded slowly. Although teaching younger members of the Order was one of the many duties required by his position, it was one he took great pleasure in, when time permitted. It was, for him, an escape of sorts, a relief from the duties and demands he faced much of the time, the whining and insisting and requiring of an endless line of petitioners, dull-witted laymen, bureaucrats and councillors alike. Yet while he taught, while he passed on the learning and wisdom of his Order, he was free, for a little while, to revel in understanding and to share his pleasure with the few hopeful students before him, some

of whom he hoped might value knowledge as much as he.

"Very well, Parfort," said the Scribe, rising slowly to his feet, towering over the students at their little desks, "Very well. If you have all finished your transcriptions, then it is time... for a little demonstration."
The young Scriveners looked excitedly at one another, eyes wide in anticipation.
"Now, I apologise for re-treading old ground, but it is important to remember the fundamentals..." the Scribe's keen eyes flitted from face to face, "Hmm... Mister... yes, Mister Glydon."
The Scribe's gaze came to rest on a doughy, red-cheeked young man with wispy blonde hair that seemed desperate to escape from his head.
"Remind us, if you would Mister Glydon, upon what is our Order founded?"
"Um.. er, t-truth. Truth, your Eminence." replied Glydon, nervously, "Truth and knowledge."
"Very good, Mister Glydon, very good. And given that truth is at the very centre of our Order, can you tell us, if you please Mister Glydon, and if indeed you can, how do you tell the truth?"
Although no-one moved, Glydon felt the other students grow somehow further away.
"Sir?"

The Scribe smiled. Many years ago, he recalled, he had been asked more or less the same question, and had given more or less the same response.
"It's a simple enough question, Mister Glydon. How do you tell the truth? How do you find it? And how will you know it when you do?"
A slick sweat started to form on Glydon's brow, and the redness in his cheeks threatened to reach inflammatory

levels. He almost steamed with relief when the Scribe gestured to the rest of the room.

"Anyone else care to offer an answer?"

Most of the students intently examined their desks, but Parfort, sat at the front of the room, tentatively raised his hand.

"Is it... what's real, your Eminence?" he said, slowly, "I mean, is it what we know, what's proven?"

The Scribe laughed, "Well, thank you for trying, Mister Parfort, but I'm afraid it's a little more complicated than that. In fact, I must apologise, class, since I don't really expect anyone to be able to provide a simple answer, but I wanted you to think carefully about it, and I hope you will continue to do so."

"As we all know, a Keeper may gather much knowledge in the line of duty – whether it is a knowledge of combat, an understanding of magicks for those like the Seekers, who defend our interests or search for truth in hostile lands; or whether a knowledge and mastery of numbers for the Reckoners who keep track of the ebb and flow of goods and gold, who see the hidden patterns of our lives. But whatever we may learn, however much we may think we know, there is always more. The truth is... fluid, it flows and unfolds from one moment to the next, and it is our job to make sure it is not lost. To that end, we are blessed with this," the Scribe held up a small bottle of thick black liquid, "the Keeper's Ink. The lifeblood of our Order. Each day my pen must bear its weight and set down the truth – for the Ink will allow nothing else."

"Although the secrets of its origin are lost with the Ancients, one means of manufacture, one lodestone remains. Found and studied by a Scribe long before me, we were fortunate enough to discover how to unlock just a little of its potential, to allow us just a taste of the power the Ancients must have known. Since then, many have tried to uncover its full workings, reveal its mysteries, and many have failed, but with this one stone we are at least able to create a little Ink each day, enough to maintain the entries in the Great Tome."

The Scribe surveyed the room and sensed, despite his students best efforts to appear wide-eyed and willing, a waning of interest. By this stage, most young Scriveners knew the basic histories of the Order by rote. He had promised them a demonstration, not a lecture, and he did not wish to disappoint.

"Very well," he said, abruptly, "Enough history for now, if you'll excuse the pun."

The students looked blankly at one another.

"Hm. Anyway, I said it was time for a demonstration, and that is what I intend. Mister Parfort, since you were brave enough to offer an answer before, perhaps you would be good enough to clear your pen and join me here. The rest of you, gather round."

Hurriedly, Parfort discharged the little ink remaining in his pen, and rushed forward to join the Scribe behind the large desk at the front of the room, while the others jostled for view and position on the other side of the table. Under the Scribe's careful supervision, Parfort gingerly opened the little bottle sat solemnly on the dark wood, and drew a small charge of the swirling ink into his own pen. Then, much to the confusion of his classmates, he held the pen up, turning it about, a puzzled look upon his face.

"It's... it's *heavy*..." he said softly.

"Yes." replied the Scribe gently, "Yes it is."
The Scribe's blue eyes sank into the blackness of the tiny bottle, "Perhaps the truth has a weight all of its own."

For a moment the Scribe seemed entirely lost to this thought, then he turned quite suddenly to the already nervous Parfort, almost causing him to drop his freshly weighted pen.
"So, Mister Parfort!" began the Scribe, "Let us start with something simple. Might I suggest you merely write the words 'My name is Glydon' for us, in your best hand if you please."
Parfort looked uncertainly at the Scribe, who gestured encouragingly to the parchment on the desk before them. The young Scrivener took a breath, and began to write.

He gave a little sigh of wonder as he made the first strokes, as the thick, velvety ink flowed flawlessly, evenly onto the page. Encouraged by its ease, by the apparent agility of his pen, his words became more fluid, his strokes and style more extravagant, sweeping, swinging breathlessly across the page, and then...

The nib scratched dryly, awkwardly on the rough parchment, and several of the students winced, the sound scraping at their teeth like a knife on slate. Parfort dropped the pen with a yelp. He looked anxiously to the Scribe.
"It… it *stings*! Like it was burning my hand!"

"Very good, Mister Parfort, don't worry. The Ink will not allow us to set down what we know to be untrue, and that is the price of trying," said the Scribe steadily, "Now allow me to make a further suggestion. For the next few minutes, for the purposes of this demonstration, let us all agree that you will, temporarily, be known by the name Glydon, and we shall all think of you and address you as such."

The Scribe looked from face to face as each student nodded their confused assent.

"Good. Now, Mister *Glydon*, if you please, continue your writing."

"But-" started Parfort.

"If you please, Mister Glydon." said the Scribe firmly.

Parfort put pen to paper once again, and much to his surprise, finished the sentence with florid ease. He looked, open-mouthed, to the Scribe. The Scribe smiled, and glanced around as Parfort's classmates mirrored his expression.

"Now, can anyone here claim that what 'Glydon' here," he gestured to Parfort, "has written is untrue?"

One by one the students shook their heads, no, they could not contest it.

"So you see, the truth is not absolute. It is fluid, subject to context and intention, it may transform from one moment to the next, and you, my young friends, must be ready to follow it, for in that one moment it is solid and certain. Perhaps one day we will better understand, but for now we must be satisfied with this, and use the Ink as best we can."

The Scribe turned to Parfort.

"And now, 'Mister Glydon', thank you for your help, if you would be kind enough to hand me your pen, since we cannot have the Ink-"

Parfort's pen flickered on the page.

The Scribe frowned, and held out his hand.

"Mister Parfort, if you please," he began, sternly.

Parfort's pen twitched again against the parchment, although his eyes never left the Scribe's.

"Mister Parfort!"

Another flicker, then the Scribe snatched the pen from Parfort's fingers.

All eyes fell upon the fresh words resting on the parchment. The Scribe frowned.
"Mister Parfort... what is... why did you write this?" he asked, his voice a whisper.
All the colour had drained from poor Parfort's face.
"I don't know sir, I didn't! I mean, I did, I guess I did, but I-"
"Enough." grunted the Scribe. His eyes remained firmly on the page. "Enough. The lesson is over. Out. Time to go, all of you, time to go."
He looked up, suddenly, sharply, as the students hurriedly gathered their things and headed for the door.
"And no mention of this! Not till we may better understand its meaning. You hear me? – not a word!"
The students nodded meekly, and bustled out of the chamber.

Alone, the Scribe stared down at the spidery writing in the middle of the parchment. Three words, simple and small, stared back.

'Sunrise is coming'

With a grim look upon his face, the Scribe took a fresh sheet, charged his pen with the heavy Ink, and began to write.

Chapter Eight

Through rough, twisting briar, bare leafless trees, across scrub and hard earth, they walked until Joseera's feet throbbed. Wherever possible, they went across country, avoiding the roads and paths if they could, making the going that much harder. To make matters worse, Joseera found her huge companion resisted all her efforts to strike up a conversation, and each time she dropped stubbornly to the ground, insisting that she could walk no more, Fulza simply lifted her gently to her feet, saying "Little further."

After what seemed like an eternity of silently plodding, one heavy step after another, Joseera slumped onto the cold earth once more.
"Enough!" she shouted at Fulza's broad back, the squat shape of Jubal trotting alongside him.
Fulza paused, and half turned, looking over his shoulder at her with a weary expression.
"Stop!" cried Joseera, "I give up! I can't carry on any more! I can't!" she glared angrily at him as she sat, panting on the ground.
Fulza took a couple of steps back towards the girl and studied her for a moment, rubbing his jaw with one rough hand. Then he looked upwards, eyes casting about the sky, before finally he nodded at her.
"Yes. Enough." he said.
"But I – wait, what?" gasped Joseera, "We can stop? We're stopping? We're stopping here?"
"Yes." came the rumbling reply, "Stopping. Rest. But not here. There." he gestured to a flat piece of earth at the foot of three broad old trees, their tangled roots and branches and thick trunks sheltering it almost entirely on one side, forming a little hollow that Joseera thought looked as

comfortable right now as any bed she could imagine.

"We can stop, oh, we can stop, heh..." Suddenly Joseera found herself a little dizzy, and planted both hands wide on the ground before her, taking deep, ragged breaths that began to tip into relieved laughter. "We can stop!"

Somewhere deep inside Joseera felt something suddenly crumble, a little inrush of sensation filling up an empty space. As if shedding a disguise, her laughter transformed into a rolling wave of tears that took Joseera quite by surprise, robbing her of strength and breath, leaving her a mess of gasping sobs.

She climbed unsteadily to her feet and staggered past Fulza, who stood, stiffly, seeming uncertain where to look. She crossed the few yards to the dry and sheltered patch Fulza had suggested, then collapsed against one of the great trees, knees drawn up to her face, tears flowing freely now.

Fulza stood for a moment, then cleared his throat noisily. He took a step towards Joseera, then paused again, adjusting his belt and harness.

"Uh... girl." he said gruffly.

Joseera did not respond. He turned again and found Jubal watching him with a look he suspected was amusement, if the boar's face was capable of such a thing. Fulza raised a questioning eyebrow and the boar gave a dismissive snort, trotting over to Joseera and settling beside her, where the girl sniffed and smiled through her tears at the boar, before resting her head on Jubal's side. Fulza sighed and nodded to himself.

"Fine," he said to the boar, "Stay here. Keep her safe."

He took a handful of powder from a little pouch at his belt and scattered it loosely around the pair, then disappeared into the trees.

oOo

Every city is shaped by the people who live there, reflecting their hopes, dreams and aspirations, as well as their fears, their follies and frustrations. Every city then, however beautiful, has its share of dark places, and Bantha was no exception. It was in one of these dark places that Mr Glower and Miss Glass now stood.

There was a soft creak as the door opened for a moment, causing the room's solitary lamp to flicker madly, and a dark-haired man in military dress hurriedly slipped inside. He looked at the two figures before him with distrust, and bowed curtly.

"Commander Gensu, welcome, welcome!" beamed Glower, broadly, while Miss Glass returned his look with an icy stare that made him keen to look elsewhere.

"The village of Lerncos burns," he said, "And my men left it just as you instructed. We are holding the villagers in the cells beneath the Keep, but as yet we have no more information on where to find the girl."

There was a grunt of displeasure from Glass. Mr Glower was still grinning obsequiously at him, while Miss Glass' eyes bored into his skull. Gensu continued, nervously.

"I think... I think we may have been unfortunate. They claim she simply ran away, I have spoken to several of them personally, and I am inclined to believe them. She has not been seen in any of the nearby settlements. Perhaps we should..." he cleared his throat, awkwardly, "...perhaps we should look elsewhere. Perhaps it is not her."

A soft laugh came from Glass, and Mr Glower gave a sympathetic nod. "I see, Commander." he said, "But I'm afraid, even if we had not exhausted all other possibilities, there is one thing that convinces us. We cannot find her, Commander, we cannot *see* her, in spite of everything at our disposal. Each new artefact recovered affords us new power, but still she evades us. And do you know what that means, Commander?"

"W-what?" managed Gensu.

"It means, Commander, that *she has help.*" whispered Glower, with a sickening smile. "Everything else is prepared, Commander, everything! But this child holds the key, the power to turn the tide! And we would not want that power, Commander, in the hands of our enemies... now would we?"

"No." said Gensu, faintly.

Glass and Glower exchanged a look, and gave a sharp nod. "There can be no further delay. We are ready to move." said Glower.

Miss Glass stepped forward and leaned in close to Gensu, looking up at him with dark eyes, her face a scant inch from his. "Commander," she whispered, softly, and he felt her cold breath on his cheek. She came closer still. "Commander... you know what to do."

oOo

Barely half an hour later Fulza had returned, carrying a few lean rabbits in one hand, a small cloth bag stuffed with leaves and mushrooms in the other. He found Joseera in an exhausted sleep, curled against the warm bulk of the dozing Jubal. The great boar opened one eye at Fulza's approach, then with a twitch of his tail, closed it again. Fulza looked at the two of them for a moment, then set down his catch and began to make camp.

When Joseera opened her eyes, she felt a little better. There was a neat fire burning nearby, several leaf wrapped parcels on wooden skewers laid across it. Pressed against the warmth of Jubal, she didn't move, but watched quietly as Fulza, unaware that she had woken, went about his work. She watched as he methodically sprinkled more of the fine powder in a rough circle around their camp. She felt a moment of dread and almost spoke out when he hefted his great axe, but relaxed and watched with wonder as he sat and set the great axe at his side, using its edge to trim and shape the branches he had gathered. She marvelled at the delicacy and deftness of those huge, rough hands as he wove and twisted the strips of wood together with practised ease.

It wasn't until he lifted his creation and came to lean it against the trees beside Joseera that he noticed she was awake. He laid the woven branches against the trunk, twisting and pushing them into place until they formed a crude wall, extending the natural shelter of the trees, creating a little lean-to around Joseera and Jubal. Joseera was surprised how quickly it seemed to gather in the heat of the fire, how much warmer she already felt.

As Fulza drew the skewered parcels from the fire, Jubal stirred and shifted, prompting Joseera to sit up. Fulza reached over and tossed the cloth bag to the boar, who buried his snout in it, grunting and gobbling appreciatively. Then Fulza tentatively offered one of the steaming skewers to Joseera.

"Eat." he nodded, "Keep strength. Eat."

Joseera needed no further encouragement. She reached out and gladly took the wooden skewer, pulling at the hot leaves. As the sweet smell of the roasted rabbit within reached her nostrils, she felt a sudden tug at the pit of her stomach and realised just how very hungry she was. For the next few minutes the only sounds were from the crackle of the fire and the urgent crunching and munching as Joseera and Jubal competed to eat with more enthusiasm. The two finished at almost the same time, then both looked up, the remnants of their meals upon their faces, expectantly at Fulza, who, somewhat more reserved, was still chewing steadily. Fulza stopped, mid-mouthful, when he saw the pair. His laughter came so suddenly it startled Joseera for an instant, a warm, booming roll that Joseera felt in her bones. She laughed too, nervously, then turned to look at Jubal, and, realising the joke, wiped self-consciously at her mouth and face with the sleeves of her shirt, till she was certain all the grease and scraps were gone.

Fulza smiled, showing rows of wicked teeth, and continued a rumbling chuckle as he ate.

"Thought one pig was enough."

Joseera smiled too, and gave an awkward giggle.

"I'm sorry. I didn't realise how hungry I was." she said.

"No need. Hungry. Understand." came the warm reply. He motioned to the remaining skewers at the fireside and Joseera gratefully took another, eating a little more carefully now her initial hunger had been met. As she did so, feeling a little more herself again, she took the opportunity to study the figure before her more carefully, the first chance she'd really had since he surprised her on the path, which now seemed so long ago.

In the face of such kindness as he had shown her, she felt almost ashamed to think of the terror that had gripped her with that first sighting. Now, sat calmly by the fireside, he seemed to Joseera far less monstrous, despite his fearsome countenance. Her eyes traced the bulk of his broad shoulders, massive arms, seeming so at odds with the measured way he ate. She noticed the faint, pale traces of old scars that crossed his leathery skin here and there, a faded map of past injuries and conflicts long forgotten. She studied his face, hard and weathered, sharp points flashing in the wide mouth as he chewed, and his eyes, dark and deep-set. They were soft though, and their harsh surround made them seem all the more so, warm and thoughtful, and perhaps a little sad. Odd, Joseera thought, that the eyes of the men who had attacked her had seemed far less human.

Fulza glanced up from his meal to catch her staring, and Joseera, embarrassed, looked hurriedly away, a sudden interest in the remains of her food demanding her attention. Fulza said nothing though, and gradually Joseera overcame her embarrassment and met his eye again.
"Feel better now, eh? Little rest, little food."
Joseera smiled. "Yes, thank you. I – I'm sorry about before, it's just – everything's happened at once, and I don't really -" she stopped herself as felt her eyes well up again, and breathed hard to keep the tears from returning.

Once she had regained a little composure, Joseera tried to turn her thoughts to other things.
"What was that you were sprinkling on the ground before?" she asked.

Fulza pulled the little pouch from his belt, and took a pinch of the coarse powder, dropping a little into Joseera's hand for closer inspection.

"Salt." he said, rubbing at the few grains that remained on his fingers, "Iron. Few herbs, seeds."

Joseera peered at the speckled mixture in her palm.

"Keep safe." Fulza continued, "Keep hidden."

All sadness forgotten for the moment, eclipsed by her inherent curiosity, Joseera's brow knitted in puzzlement.

"Hidden?" she said, frowning, "Hidden from who? And how can this hide us?"

"Hidden from... long looking." tried Fulza, then grunted and shook his head, muttering quick, rasping words that Joseera didn't understand. "Keep hidden from... far off eyes. Far off, searching..."

"Far off eyes?" said Joseera with a confused look, "Far off- like... a telescope?"

Fulza grunted and covered his eyes with his hand.

"No, okay, not a telescope..." Joseera continued, slowly, "So... far off, but not..."

Fulza's face twisted in thought. "Far... search... like trick... power..."

"Like... oh! Far – like magicks! Like magicks!" shouted Joseera.

Fulza looked up, and clapped his great hands together. "Yes! Good! Magicks, yes!" he barked, then gestured to the little pouch, "Keep safe from far off eyes, magicks, yes!"

Joseera jumped at the outburst, then smiled at her success, but this was quickly replaced by another questioning frown.

"Okay, good, but – who can see us with magicks? Why do we need to hide? Who are we hiding from?"

Fulza shrugged, "For now, everyone." he said, simply, "We go to my home. Safe there, trust there. Till then, keep hidden, keep safe."

At the mention of home, Joseera began to look a little tearful again, though she fought to hide it. Fulza leant forward.

"For now, must keep safe, keep strong. No help to them dead." he said, in what he hoped was a comforting tone.

Joseera smiled, took a deep breath, and nodded. "Yes, you're right, thank you." she said, "I have to keep it together. I was the one who left, I don't want to let them down again."

She cleared her throat, wiped her eyes, and tried to neaten her tangled hair a little, pushing it away from her face. Then she sat, straight, hands planted in her lap, and smiled again.

"I'm okay now, I promise. Now tell me, where do we have to go?"

Fulza sat back, surprised by such resolve in one so small. Perhaps, he thought to himself for the first time since finding the seemingly helpless girl, perhaps this is not so very foolish after all. Then he tried, as best he could, to explain things in her tongue.

For almost the next hour the two strange companions talked, while Jubal snored and snorted at their side. Fulza tried, with a little frustration at first, exasperated by the search for words that wouldn't come, to satisfy Joseera's curiosity and answer her questions as well as he could. As her confidence grew though, and her skill in understanding his meaning increased, so too it seemed did her desire to know more, and Fulza found himself the target of an unending barrage of investigations. She asked about his village and his people, why he had travelled so far from home to find her, and he told her of the growing attacks and hostilities from men of the Empire, the calls for unity from many of the tribal leaders, for his people to join together and end the threat of the Empire once and for all. He explained that his tribe, few though they were, had not yet agreed to this, that there were doubts among his people, although they were under great pressure from the other tribes. He had been sent, in secret, to find Joseera, in the hope that she could help them somehow, that she might be their last chance to avoid joining the other tribes in a war against the Empire.

For his part, Fulza asked Joseera about herself and her home, and whether she knew the men who had sought to capture her, or why they were looking for her. When she explained that she did not, she thought he seemed oddly disappointed, a feeling that grew as she insisted, despite his protestations and interruptions, that no, she was not trained in magicks or the sword, no, her parents were not dignitaries or scholars, and no, she was not unusual in any particular way save that she had been in trouble with the village council more often than might be thought proper for a simple tailor's daughter.

"But I still don't understand," she said, for at least the seventh time, as Fulza handed her a rough blanket and tended to the fire, "Why me? How did you know to look for me?"
Fulza sighed. "Told you, girl. Old story. Vision."
The confused expression on Joseera's face didn't alter. Fulza gave a little shake of his head.
"Enough now. Sleep. Rest. Keep strength." he said, firmly, "We get to my village, Keshet explain. Speak better than me. Now rest."

As she drew the prickly blanket over her and settled against the still snoring shape that was Jubal beside her, she realised with faint surprise just how exhausted she was. Even so, thoughts and images whirled around her head, blurred and blended by the onset of sleep. Old story, vision, she thought. She hadn't dared tell him that she understood better than he thought. She hadn't dared tell him about her dreams.

Chapter Nine

Gaven sat by the meagre fire he had built, staring into the bright flames, tired and dejected. The fire crackled and spat, a hot yellow flicker sending out plumes of black smoke. What little wood he had been able to find had been supplemented with dry grass and the wiry leaves and branches of the tough bushes that dotted the bleak landscape, and the fire protested its poor meal with every sputter and spark.

Around him, a handful of men wandered to and fro, some also building fires, making rough camp, others tending to the wounded. There was little noise, few words were exchanged, most going about their business with a quiet sense of woe.

The leader of these men, a serious, heavy-set fellow who had been introduced to Gaven as Bear, wandered over to him now and sat, quietly.
"I'm sorry we can't offer you more hospitality, Captain," said Bear, with a faint smile, "Not what you must be used to as a soldier of Bantha herself. And not what we had hoped for either."
Gaven returned his smile. "It's more than I could fairly expect, Bear, thank you."
"Perhaps you should travel back to our town with us, Captain. You could catch your breath more easily there, hot food, hot water. And Bellheath could use your help preparing for whatever fresh evil these Savages throw at us next."
Gaven shook his head slowly, looking back to the fire. "I'm sorry, Bear, I can't I have to get word of all this back to Bantha somehow, I have to warn them. And from the

look of things, there's no time to waste." He turned to face the other man, "To that end, I need you to tell me everything you can about this... giant. We have to be prepared!"

Bear shrugged, with a bitter laugh, "I'm afraid, Captain, you know near enough as much as I. We thought we were prepared. We couldn't even slow the thing down, much less stop it..."

"But there must be more! Where did it come from? How did you come to lie in wait for it here?"

With a sigh, Bear explained that the giant had been spotted the previous morning, heading towards the neighbouring village of Bellbrook. Already made fearful and few by the Savages who had come raiding in the area, the people had watched in terror as the giant grew closer, stopping nearby at nightfall. The handful of remaining men brave and strong enough, had ridden out to meet it, but to no avail. Then, at dawn, the giant had moved off, without warning, crushing those who stood against it, and passing by the village, trampling fields as it went. The desperate people of Bellbrook had sent word to their neighbours in the town of Bellheath for aid, and so a force was mustered. When the giant stopped once again in the night, they had been able to overtake it, and prepare their ambush in a suitable place, in the hope of stopping the thing before it harmed anyone else.

"But you saw how effective that was, Captain," said Bear, ashen-faced, "We barely gave it pause. Now we must return home and hope that the Savages do not strike again before we have chance to recover."

"You say the giant stopped at night, Bear, what do you mean? Does it need rest? Why does it stop?"

"I don't know, Captain," replied Bear, "All I can tell you

is that it stopped, like a great statue, frozen it its stride."

Gaven rubbed at his weary eyes. "Then I must go, Bear, as soon as possible. If I... if it moves slowly enough, if it must also stop at night, then I may be able to draw ahead of it, warn those in its path, and tell those in Bantha what I've seen."

Bear looked at him with disbelief. "With respect, Captain, you can't be serious! You're half dead on your feet, you can't expect to-"

He was interrupted by a shout nearby, as someone pushed his way toward them.

"Gaven? Gaven! Oh, Ancients be praised!"

Before either Bear or Gaven could react, the man had wrapped his arms fiercely around Gaven, almost bowling him over in the process.

"Ah, Gaven, it's you lad! Ancients be praised!"

Gaven felt rough hands clasp the sides of his head, as his face was pulled up for inspection.

"Ah, Gaven, thank the Ancients you made it lad! Uh, I mean, Captain. Ahem. Sir."

Suddenly aware of the incredulous look on Gaven's face, the visitor seemed to catch control of himself.

"Thurro?" said Gaven, gladly, "Sergeant Thurro!"

A laugh of relief burst from both men, and Gaven put his arm firmly about Thurro's shoulders.

"Well, Sergeant, believe me, I'm very glad to see you too," he grinned, "But carry on like that and people are going to talk."

The Sergeant gave an embarrassed smile. "Yes... sorry, lad. Just glad to see you, sir."

Gaven nodded. "Don't worry, Sergeant. I won't tell anyone you care."

Now it was the Sergeant's turn to grin. "Heh, thanks. But seriously, where did you get to lad? I was worried p'raps the Savages had caught up with you after I ran into this lot makin' preparations, an' they said they seen no-one else."

"This man is one of yours I take it, Captain?" asked Bear.

Gaven turned to him, one arm still about Thurro's shoulders. "He is, Bear, he is."

"Well," said Bear, flatly, "I'm glad a little good news has come out of this."

"Bear, I'm sorry if-" started Gaven, but Bear held up his hands.

"Don't apologise, Captain. Take pleasure in it while you can. I fear there won't be much good news in the days to come," Bear stood, wearily, "And now, Captain, Sergeant, my men and I must make our way back to Bellheath. As I said, we'd be glad to have you with us if you'll come."

Thurro looked round at Gaven. "Well, sir? What now?"

oOo

"Well I, for one, am glad she ran away," came the rumbling voice of Elder Jarry, "Much rather that than whatever it is these fellows want with her." he said, gesturing to the heavy door.

He sat at a plain wooden table with Juna and Parvel Mayweather, in a dull and featureless room, lit only by what little daylight struggled though the two tiny windows set high in one of the dusty walls. In one corner, the round form of Tutty Cooksharp, hunched over the motionless body of Elder Vithru, as he gently tended to the old man's wounds.

"And you may be certain of one thing," Elder Jarry continued, "They haven't found her yet. Why else would they keep us all here, keep asking all these questions?"

Joseera's mother shook her head, rubbed at her tear-wearied eyes. "I know she's still okay. I know she is. I just feel it. I... I just wish they'd tell us why they're looking for her, why they came?"

Parvel put an arm around his wife's shoulders, pulling her in close to him.

"I wish we had some idea what in the Ancients name is going on!" he said, angrily, "I mean, those men were all wearing Empire livery. And did you see what they were taking from the carts before they herded us all in? Most of it was covered, wrapped up, but I'd swear I saw some Savage weapons. Whatever's happening here, Jarry, it's very bad indeed. And somehow, Ancients help the girl, my daughter is mixed up in it all. You may do as you like, *I* have to get out of here, I *have* to find her!"

Jarry sighed, hands at his temples. "I understand, Parvel, I do! But we have to be cautious, think it all through! Now it would help if we could begin to understand what they want from her... Are you certain there is nothing you can think of, nothing that might interest them?"

Parvel stood, and paced tersely away from the table. "Ancients sake, Jarry! You're as bad as them! There's nothing more to tell!"

Jarry took a deep breath. "What about," he said, softly, "her... origins?"

Juna stared hard at the Elder, both hands planted on the table before her. "What?" she said, "What's that supposed to mean?"

"Oh, come Juna," said Jarry, quietly, "There aren't many in the village who knew, but I remember well enough."

Parvel, teeth clenched, colour gone from his face, stepped forward to comfort his wife. "That's not fair, Jarry," he said, "We've done our best. We cared for her as if she was our own. And besides... what would anyone else know about it? It doesn't make any difference, we have to get out of here!"

The Elder scratched at an unseen mark on the rough tabletop. "Very well, Parvel, very well, I'm sorry. But surely it has crossed your mind... that it may have something to do with all of this. We must consider all the possibilities..."

oOo

A short while later, Gaven and Thurro rode across the rough land, into the dimming light. Though Gaven had told him there was no need, Bear had insisted on providing two horses, and a few simple supplies, adding that there was no-one to ride them anyway, and if it would help in the stand against the Savages, it was scant cost.

As they rode, swiftly, and in silence, Gaven wondered at what he had seen, what it meant. Men, working with, aiding the Savages, it seemed. And now this giant, terrible and terrifying, striding boldly into their land, knocking sword and shield aside like dry twigs in its path. What lay behind it? What force might they yet face? As they rode, Gaven prayed to the Ancients that the Three would know what to do. He prayed they would believe him.

It was well into the night before they stopped by a copse of squat trees to catch their breath and take what refreshment they could. As they ate, hungrily, cloaks wrapped about them against the chill, Gaven asked Thurro if he knew what had become of the rest of their unit.
"I've seen no-one else, Captain," replied Thurro, "After we got split up, I went on alone, must've been just a little ways north of you the whole while, till I stumbled on Bear and his boys."
Gaven sighed. "Well, let's hope the others had more luck than us, eh? Perhaps Grays or someone made it safely.

Perhaps they're waiting for us back home already."

They sat in silence for a moment, before Thurro spoke again.

"What's goin' on though, sir, eh? I mean, I seen some strange things, sure enough, but nothing like that giant. An' that fella back there, orderin' Savages about? There's dark things happenin'. That's for sure."

"I don't know about that, Sergeant," said Gaven, "but we have to get back to the Three. The Heart and the Book will understand more than you or I do, and the Sword... well, Lord Duma will come up with something, Sergeant. You know he will."

"Of course, of course," Thurro nodded, "They'll know what to do. Of course. They'll know what to do."

They sat a little longer, finishing their dry rations without further discussion. Then the Sergeant rose, announcing the need to answer the call of nature, and disappeared between the nearby trees, frosty grass crunching underfoot as he went. Gaven stood, and not wishing to waste any more time than necessary, set about readying the horses for their departure. He had both animals fully prepared, and had taken time to conceal any signs of their brief stop, before he began to wonder what was taking Thurro so long.

Hand on the hilt of his sword, Gaven took a few cautious steps toward the trees Thurro had wondered into, eyes straining into the darkness for a clue as to his whereabouts.

"Sergeant?" he ventured, as loudly as he dared, "Thurro! This isn't a good time fo-"

He stopped, short, as he felt something cold and very sharp press firmly against his throat, a strong hand gripping the back of his neck. Thoughts flashed through his mind, his hand tensed at his sword, but before he could make any further reaction, a cool, flat voice spoke calmly in his ear.

"Don't."

The blade turned slowly, forcing Gaven's head back.

"Release your sword, put your arms at your side. Anything else, and I'll slice your head clean off."

Gaven breathed out, slowly, and did as he was asked.

"You're a long way from home." said the voice, plainly.

Gaven tried to find some trace of an accent, some hint as to the speakers origin or intention that might help him find the right reply, but his unseen assailant was careful, taking pains not to give anything away. The voice was flat and plain as glass, betraying nothing.

"What is it you want, all the way out here?" asked the voice.

Gaven fluttered through all the possible excuses and reasons he might give, searching desperately for something that the voice might want to hear, something that might ease the steel against his throat.

The hand on his neck tightened, and the voice spoke again, "An answer, if you please."

Gaven briefly revisited all that had happened since he had set out from Bantha. He took a deep, slow breath, wondering how much worse things could get. And then he told the truth.

"I... I'm from Bantha. The Imperial Guard. My men and I volunteered to come out here, gather information, try to find out what the Savages are planning, why they move against us."

"I thought that was the work of the Keepers." replied the voice, coldly, "You're no Keeper."

"No, no," agreed Gaven, quickly, "No Keeper. My men

and I were sent... in addition. In secret. My Lord believed the situation urgent enough... he wished to..."

An odd possibility occurred to Gaven then, and he considered for a moment that it could very well be one of the Order's mysterious Seekers stood behind him. He chose his words as carefully as he could.

"He wished to be sure that nothing would escape his notice, given the importance of the matter. He wanted to be sure that, one way or another, someone would have the chance to discover what we needed to know."

The voice did not respond, and the blade did not move against his neck. Gaven went on.

"But we were discovered! Somehow they found us out, knew where we were..."

"Enough." said the voice, calmly, "I will-"

It was interrupted by another voice, somewhat coarser and more friendly, from a little further away.

"Oh, for Ancients sake, Fathom, he's tellin' the truth, what more d'you want?" it said, "We're not just 'ere for you to 'ave fun y'know."

"Yes, but he-" tried the first, finally showing some emotion as it did.

"Yes but nothin'," came the reply, "He's tellin' the truth, an' you knew that as well as I did as soon as he started talkin'. Now let the lad go, Fathom, before he takes it personal."

As the blade moved away from his throat and the hand loosened its grip about his neck, Gaven breathed a sigh of relief, and wished, not for the first time, but certainly most fervently, that he had stayed at home.

Chapter Ten

Gasping for breath, Parfort knocked urgently on the Scribe's door. He had hurried here from the Archives as soon as he had received the message, and had left considerable chaos in his wake, as well as several disapproving looks from more senior Keepers. He half-stood, half-stooped at the Scribe's chambers now, sweat pouring from his face as he puffed and panted in recovery, robes in disarray and message clutched in one damp fist. He looked hopefully at the door for a few seconds, before considering the importance of his delivery, and banging loudly on the thick wood again.

After a moment or two, the door opened a little and the tall figure of the Scribe peered down through the narrow gap.
"Mister Parfort?" said the Scribe, with a little irritation, "What in the Ancients name is it? There are no lessons today, Mister Parfort, and certainly not at this time of the morning!"

Parfort attempted to communicate through his struggle for breath. "Your – Eminen – ce!" he heaved, "I – 'm sorry! Got a – got – message! -S'mportant, y'Eminence! S'bad- Bad news!"
He held the crumpled paper before him triumphantly, as if it made sense of his address.

The Scribe raised a weary eyebrow. "Mister Parfort, I am assuming you have a message of some description for me, and I shall also assume, judging by your wild countenance, that you have read it."

A panicked expression crossed Parfort's face and he looked down at the paper with an accusatory glare. "Um, well, your Eminence, yes... it wasn't sealed... they just handed it to me! And so, I mean... I saw it, I saw it was important! So I ran right here your Eminence!"

"Don't worry Mister Parfort. I wasn't suggesting you had done anything wrong. It was simply an observation. Now..." the Scribe held out his hand, "Let's have a look, shall we?"

Parfort handed the crumpled message over to the Scribe, who gently smoothed the paper against one hand, then held it up before him. He read the message, then looked over the paper at Parfort's worried face. The Scribe looked down and read the words again, before folding the message up and placing it safely within his robes.

"Well, Mister Parfort." he said, thoughtfully, "You've done well."
The Scribe scratched at the neat bristle of his beard, blue eyes staring intently at the boy, making Parfort feel even more uncomfortable.
"Now I have another important job for you. Follow me."

The Scribe ushered Parfort through the door into his chambers, and the boy stood awkwardly on the rich woollen rug in the middle of the large receiving room.

"You're a good lad, Mister Parfort. You work hard, and you listen well. I see potential in you."
Parfort's chest swelled with pride.
"Did you enjoy my class the other day?" the Scribe continued.
The boy's eyes flickered nervously as he thought about

what had taken place at the end of the lesson, and the Scribe noticed his discomfort.
"Don't worry about that little incident, Mister Parfort. It may interest you to know that something very similar happened to me, once. The Ink takes to some people more than others, my boy. Now since you've been so diligent, and since you show such promise... how would you like to try your hand again? The information you've brought me must be set down in the Great Tome..."
Parfort's face lit up. "What, you mean - by me, your Eminence?! Really? But, I mean, is that-?"
The Scribe smiled. "It is at my discretion, Mister Parfort, and I believe you have earned it."

He led the boy over to a low oak table by the room's long, leaded window, where the thick volume of the Great Tome lay open, an ornate pen alongside it, and a bottle of the swirling Keeper's Ink. Carefully, under the Scribe's instruction, Parfort charged the pen and stood, hand hovering over the fine parchment.
"What... what should I write, your Eminence?"
"For now, keep your words simple. Set down the facts of your message as plainly as you may."
Parfort thought quietly for a moment, then began to write.

The Scribe held his breath. The boy's words flowed easily though, and within a few seconds the first sentence lay darkly on the page.

'The golden giants are weapons of the Savages, and they march against the men of the Empire.'

The Scribe let out a sudden burst of laughter, making Parfort jump.
"What is it, your Eminence?! What's wrong?"

"Nothing, my boy, nothing at all!" chimed the Scribe, "Excellent work! Carry on, carry on!"

As Parfort bent over the parchment again, continuing in his careful, deliberate hand, the Scribe looked down at him with a growing smile.

"Very good, my boy, very good. No-one can argue with the truth."

oOo

Even as the councillors began to take their places in the council chamber, the Book noticed the uncomfortable look on the Sword's face.
"What is it, Duma? You look like you've eaten something awful," whispered the Book, leaning over to him.
"I don't like this, Sofya," replied the Sword, "Whatever this is about, it can't be good. Have you seen Loulouthi?"
The Book shook her head. "Not today. She may be here later, although I think she has…"

She didn't have time to explain any further before the wide doors at the far end of the chamber opened and the Scribe entered, followed closely by Mr. Glower and Miss Glass, and several of his personal guard. He carried the Great Tome with him and strode swiftly to his place at the Order's bench. When the hubbub of intrigued whispers and murmurs died down a little, the Scribe held up a hand in apology before speaking to the assembly.
"Councillors, ladies, gentlemen, *honoured* Triumvir… I apologise for keeping you waiting. Please believe me when I say I would not have done so without good reason, and when you hear what I have to tell you, I feel certain you will understand."

The Book turned to the Sword with a frown.
"Sounds like you were right, Duma." she muttered.

"I sure no-one would disagree," continued the Scribe, "were I to describe the ascent of our honoured Triumvir as swift... sudden, even. War has a way of unearthing... unexpected heroes, bringing to the fore those who might have been overlooked in more conventional times. When Lady Sofya, Lady Loulouthi and Lord Duma arrived, we were in turmoil. Emperor Dray was gone, and the newcomers appeared, heroes of the conflict. But perhaps their inexperience in office works against them, makes them hesitant."

There was a shout from somewhere within the merchant councillors ranks, "Get to the point, Keeper!"
It was taken up by another from the tradesmen's benches, "Yes, we know you don't like havin' commoners in charge," this was met with a laugh from the rest of the laymen, "but do we really 'ave to 'ave a meetin' about it?"

Miss Glass shot a freezing look over at the tradesmen's side of the chamber and the laughter died down remarkably quickly. The Scribe, however, seemed unruffled, almost welcoming the comments.
"Yes, my friend, you speak truly, and I commend you for it! There is nothing to be gained from hiding the truth now! I make no secret of the fact that I supported Emperor Dray, that I believed we should continue our campaign against the Savages! Many of you will know that my own family were lost to Savage blades!"

"But now, by the laws of our land, this Triumvir was fairly and justly chosen. I am bound by those same laws to serve the Empire and our leaders, and by the Ancients, I have done so, not just because it is the duty of my office, but because I believe it is my duty as a man of this Empire! And while I may not agree with every decision the Triumvir have made, I defy you, *any of you*," the Scribe swept a pointed finger across the silent room, "to suggest that I have done anything less than everything I could in service of our Empire! That I have shown anything less than the diligence and dedication required of me by my profession and position!"

The Sword leaned over to whisper to the Book.
"Where is he going with this?"

"Now, my friends, we find ourselves *again* beset by a familiar enemy, *again* defending our lands and our people. This time, however, it is against a threat of unprecedented scale. Our leaders have asked us to wait, to exercise caution. But now the Savage tribes come together against us, and their forces mass to invade the Fold."

This drew gasps from several parts of the room, and prompted a low muttering from others. The Scribe raised his hand again, for silence.

"Yes, my friends. They move even now. But this is not the worst of it. Many of you have heard the whispers, the rumours of giant creatures, great armoured things at our borders. I stand before you now to assure you - these things are real, they are the weapons of our enemy, and they march against us. And for those who doubt the certainty of my findings or question what I say, I have set it down in terms that will prove it."

The Scribe lifted the heavy volume of the Great Tome,

opened it and, turning it around so others could read what was written within, dropped it down onto the table before him with an ominous boom. Those close enough could clearly see the confirmation laid out on the page in the dark Keeper's Ink, and all knew what it meant. The Ink would only set down what was true.

"I may be bound by law to serve our leaders, but I am bound to serve the Empire first. Although our honoured Triumvir may have the interests of the Empire at heart, I believe we can wait no longer. So I ask you, councillors and guardians of our people, to invoke the right due to you, the right to vote, the right to demand action. I ask you, those who have served in office long enough to have made the hardest decisions, to remember the toughest times, I ask you to muster our forces, meet these Savages in battle before it is too late, and show them once and for all that they cannot better us! You must act now, in defence of your home, and send our armies out to crush our enemy for good!"

Even before the Scribe had finished speaking, the Book and the Sword could see the outcome. A cheer had begun half way through his speech and by the end many of the councillors were on their feet, shouting approval, or stomping on the wooden floors.

oOo

A short time later, the Book and the Sword walked together through the private gardens of the Keep. The gardens were sheltered and well-tended, and although the day was cold the sun shone brightly, crisp and clear above. It was a place of unusual pleasure for both of them, a place to walk among the trees and plants, to stand beneath the sky, without fear of being accosted or required by any number of supplicants or petitioners, without the constant reminder of their office.

Today, however, neither took much joy in the exercise. They wandered in deep contemplation, almost unaware, it seemed, of their agreeable surroundings, until they reached a tired old bench, knocked together from rough-hewn wood, resting beneath a tree that might well have been its junior.

They sat together quietly for a few moments, before the Book broke the silence with a deep, melodramatic sigh, blowing out noisily through her lips. The Sword raised an eyebrow, turning his head to give her a questioning look. She smiled back at him.

"I think," she said, absently, leaning back to gaze up at the clouds above, "that this is all about to get very serious indeed, Duma."

The Sword, studying the earth at his feet, nodded solemnly. "Yes. I think you may be right there, Sofya. I hoped... I hoped there'd be something, some reason to call us back from the edge of this lunacy... but it seems not. So... we're to enter open war once again."
He leant forward, one hand absently twisting at the thin chain around his neck. " I didn't think we would be the ones to bring our people back into a war." he said, despondently.

"Duma, look -" started the Book, but the Sword stood suddenly, angrily.

"It doesn't make any sense!" he shouted, throwing out his

arms, "You know that as well as I Sofya, it makes no sense! After everything that happened? Why do they attack? How can we go to war knowing-"

"Oh, for Ancients sake, Duma, is this helpful?" snapped the Book, with startling volume, "I've said it to Loulouthi, and I say the same to you – whether we are leaders or loners, it makes no difference, so long as we give the best of ourselves. We haven't brought about this war, but it is upon us nonetheless! So act, Duma! We must do what we can, what we believe to be the right course of action, and beyond that," she smacked his arm fiercely with the back of her hand, "nothing else matters!"

The Sword looked slowly down at his arm, then up to Sofya's indignant face, and back again. "You know," he said, calm and deliberate, "I've killed men for less than that, witch."

The Book peered at him over the gold rims of her spectacles. "Rubbish," she said "You never killed a soul without trying to talk them out of the whole affair first. If half this city knew how soft you were..."

The Sword laughed, and gave a warm smile. "Thank you, Sofya."

"Pah, your secret's safe with me, I suppose..." she replied.

"You know what I mean." said the Sword, "You always were the voice of reason. And you're right. We'll do what we must. The council has made their decision, so be it."

He returned to the bench and for a moment they sat in silence again.

"Where is Loulouthi anyway?" asked the Sword, "Even if she didn't hear of the council meeting in time, she must have received my message by now."

"She had an open audience this morning," said the Book, giving him a knowing look, "They are always rather... hard on her. Poor Loulouthi... I'm sure she'll be here shortly, perhaps she is a little delayed."

The Sword said nothing, but simply nodded. Most people knew the effect the Heart's presence and abilities could have on others, but few knew the effect it had on the Heart herself.

oOo

At that moment, Loulouthi sat in her private chambers in the Keep, head resting on her arms on the small table before her. There were a few simple personal effects on the table; a brush, several small bottles and containers, and an old wood-framed mirror. The light of the fresh morning and an accompanying gentle breeze found their way in through the open window behind the table, and the cool air prompted Loulouthi to raise her head.

She looked at her face in the mirror. Tender, puffy eyes, wet tracks of the tears running down her cheeks. She stared sadly at her reflection for a few moments, waiting for her breath to come more calmly, then, with a determined sniff she set about soothing her eyes and cleaning her face, arranging her dark hair in some more acceptable fashion.

Although each of the Three held audiences with their

people, it was often the case that they tried to deal with their particular area of expertise. So it was that Duma, the Sword, usually found himself the final judge in military matters and hearings, disputes over weapons and armours, or conflicts that could not be peacefully resolved. Sofya, the Book, tended to be sought out for more scholarly disagreements, litigious or augurial issues, and questions of science and magicks. This left Loulouthi, for the most part, with affairs of the heart. In most cases, this was undoubtedly the right decision, as she was able to understand her complainants in ways that were beyond most people, share their feelings and fears, and so resolve the issue as fairly as she could. But sometimes, sometimes there were those who overwhelmed her, whose strength and depth of feeling tested the limits of her control.

So it had been that morning. A woman had come to see her, having recently lost her husband to grave illness. Her husband's brother owned the house, and intended that the woman should be evicted. Loulouthi had expected the terrible waves of grief and loss she had felt from the woman, but when she looked into the brother, she was surprised and appalled at the long festering jealousy she found buried within, how the man coveted and hated the woman for choosing his brother over him, and the sickly spitefulness that had now installed itself in his heart.

Loulouthi had always been more sensitive than most, more in touch with the feelings of others, but these days there was no escape from these feelings. She lived them, felt them, suffered them in that moment as powerfully as their owners. There were places in the city she did not like to go, despite her self control, her skill at blocking out unwanted feelings. There were places where the dark thoughts simply crept in, through sheer noise and volume, yet at least they could be avoided, or repelled. In cases like this morning, she had no choice but to open herself to whatever might lie inside these people. And then there was nowhere to hide.

Of course, she had not shown her distress in public. She had become expert, by now, in concealing her discomfort from others behind a placid mask, hiding her emotions in a serene and fixed expression. The irony was not lost on her. But despite this, she knew that Sofya and Duma would see through, that she could not conceal these feelings from them. They would try their best, as they always did, to comfort her, even though these feelings were not her own, they would subside, and there was nothing to be done.

This morning, Loulouthi didn't want to face her friends this way, especially when there were such important matters to be discussed. Instead she had walked, an image of tranquillity, back to her chambers in the Keep, had calmly closed and bolted the doors, quietly seated herself at her dressing table before letting the façade fall. Then she had crumbled, overtaken with grief, shaken and shocked by what cruelty the heart could know.

She looked again at herself in the mirror now. Her eyes were still a little red, perhaps, but there was nothing more she could do about that now. Otherwise, she thought, she looked reasonably presentable. She gave herself a little smile and looked out of the window at the day. It seemed so peaceful. For a moment more she sat and closed her eyes, feeling the sun on her face, and enjoying what little peace she could. Then with a deep breath she rose, and set off to meet her friends.

oOo

Loulouthi had found the others out by the old bench and had greeted them with a smile, brushing off their kind enquiries about her morning audience as casually as she could. She could feel the concern radiating from both Sofya and Duma, but they knew her well enough not to push any further on the subject.

Now the talk had turned to matters at hand, the Savages and other worrying reports. The Book and the Heart sat on the bench, as the Sword stood before them, several papers in his hand.

"So as you can see," he continued, gesturing with the bundle of paper, "There's no doubt from the Order. The Keepers have confirmed their information, all intelligence we have points to this. The Savages intend to stage one mighty attack, a huge force is already being assembled - to take Vas Aloron. They must realise that victory there will be hard fought despite their numbers, but if they succeed, then we're lost. There's no way we can hold them back if they have control there – they'll be able to head freely into The Fold, and attack Bantha at their leisure."

The Book and the Heart looked at each other. "Very well, Duma, I think we are all agreed that this is certain." said Loulouthi, "But what do we do? What choices do we have?"

The Sword gave a grim look. "There isn't any choice Loulouthi. We must defend Vas Aloron or everything is lost. We must move out against them."

The Book scratched her chin slowly. "I agree." she said.

"We have no alternative. But do we know what we face Duma? What about these creatures, these... giants everyone is whispering about? The rumours are running wild in the streets, but I have been able to find out very little for certain – what do we know about them?"

The Sword shrugged, "I don't know Sofya. I was hoping you may be able to uncover more than I have. The Scribe says they are a weapon of the Savages, some terrible instrument they have kept hidden. But if they hope to use them against us, our best chance is at Vas Aloron. At least we can bring up catapults, onagers, mount a strong defence." the Sword paused for a moment, and shook his head, " It hardly matters though. We've been spread out by all the fighting so far. Whatever it is we face at Vas Aloron, we must commit everything we have left to it if we hope to hold the line."

The Heart and the Book rose, and the three friends stood together, in the peace of the garden.

"It's decided then." said the Heart, softly. "We return to war."

Chapter Eleven

They came within sight of the village early in the afternoon. Fulza had woken Joseera a little before dawn and they had been moving ever since, with only a few short breaks to catch their breath. Joseera couldn't remember ever having been so exhausted in her life, but nevertheless, when she began to see the first signs of the village ahead, her pace quickened, curiosity and excitement pushing tiredness aside for now, giving her legs new strength.

In the distance she could see dozens of low, squat buildings, smooth and cornerless. Not one was more than two or three storeys high, and each was an earthy colour, terracotta reds and natural greens. Most were roofed with reeds and straw, expertly woven together, but one or two of the larger buildings had rough brown tiles laid in a shallow cone on top.

As they grew closer still, however, Joseera's feeling of excitement gave way to a growing unease. Nervousness washed over her in a cold, queasy wave, and her skin prickled on her neck as she saw movement in the shadows of the buildings, at the edges of her vision. She felt the weight of many eyes upon her.

As they turned past the first small building and entered the village proper, she saw them. Leaning against walls, peering out through glassless windows, all staring silently at her. And ahead, in the centre of the wide path that led through the village, five solemn figures stood, variously dressed in official and momentous robes, awaiting them.

Joseera had become accustomed to the look of Fulza, had, in the strange way people are capable of under the right circumstances, become used to being around him. But now for the first time she saw others like him, and all was made strange again. She was transfixed. She saw males, some Fulza's size, many considerably larger, all might and muscle, following her lazily with unabashed stares. She saw females of his race, and felt very small and fragile by comparison. Although they did not share the physical bulk of their male counterparts, the females struck an imposing figure nonetheless. Not one stood less than six feet in height, and each was long and graceful, taut muscles rippling under pale skin. If the males possessed the solid strength of a great hammer, then the females, seeming every bit as powerful, as coolly confident, would be best compared to a fine bow, poised and flexible. Savages, she thought to herself, they call them Savages. Wild. Fierce. Unrestrained. Free.

Together, they walked slowly down the dusty path, Fulza in the centre, with Joseera on his right side and Jubal on the other. As they progressed, more and more figures appeared, watching, and Joseera's discomfort grew. She pushed in, closer to Fulza, until she was almost pressed against his side as they walked, while he looked on, straight ahead, implacable as ever.

Then something hit him. From the left side of the path, someone in the crowd of bodies had thrown a small stone, which bounced off Fulza's shoulder and dropped to the path just in front of Jubal. Fulza stopped dead. When she looked up, Joseera could see his heavy jaw clench, tendons flexing and tightening.

At one edge of the group waiting for them ahead, stood a

hunched figure, a very old male from the looks of things, Joseera thought. He was bedecked with feathers and rows of beads and stones like some wild priest, and leant on a heavy, solid stick topped with a solid looking golden ball decorated with deep carvings. His thick dry skin hung about him like a heavy robe, yet he peered at them now with eyes that seemed impossibly bright for one so old. He glanced at the groups gathering on either side of the path, then fixed his sparkling eyes back on Fulza, and faintly, almost imperceptibly, shook his head.

Joseera only noticed this because she was following Fulza's eyes, trying to work out what he was staring at. And even when she did, she still wasn't sure what it meant. Fulza seemed to understand though, and with a derisive grunt, he dropped his head, took a deep, heavy breath, and continued slowly onwards.

He had taken barely two steps before another makeshift missile, a little larger than the last, whistled past them, just inches from Fulza's face. There was a shout, from somewhere within the crowd, in that rasping, burring language.
"*Kol Va'ket!*"
It was met with laughter and cheers from many of the others.

Jubal gave a fiery snort, and pawed the ground angrily, sensing his companion's mood. The boar turned awkwardly about as they progressed slowly along the path, but stayed at Fulza's side, casting his snout defensively back and forth. Joseera pressed closer still to Fulza's side, and looked nervously up at him. For a moment, he caught her eye, and gave what she took to be a reassuring look.

Another rock struck Fulza's back, the next struck Jubal's flank, drawing an indignant squeal. Yet another flew harmlessly above them, and still they walked, calmly, slowly along. Then a small, sharp stone stuck Joseera in the cheek, drawing blood, causing her to stumble and cry out, to cheers and shouts from several of the crowd. Fulza caught her under the arm, held her up and drew her around in front of him. Eyes flashing fiercely, he glared at the crowd on either side, shoulders hunched forward over her, and gave what Joseera could only describe as a roar. The terrifying, bestial noise thundered in her ears, and as she twisted to look up at his face, all teeth and fury, she doubted for a moment whether she knew anything about him at all.

Another stone was hurled at them, more openly this time, by a young male on their left. Before it could strike them, however, Fulza, one hand clutching Joseera to him, had snatched the stone from the air with the other, then whipped his arm out again, sending the stone hurtling back towards its owner. It struck him solidly between the eyes, causing him to stagger backwards and lose his footing, much to the amusement of some members of the crowd. Face darkened with anger and embarrassment, the young male leapt to his feet and started violently toward Fulza, only prevented by several of his companions, who struggled to hold him back.
"*Bash nar, Kol Va'ket!*" he yelled, as he fought to be free of those that restrained him, "*Bash nar voosa hir!*"

Fulza gave a contemptuous look, and spat at the ground before him.
"*Chik sahn hir.*" Fulza growled at him. Then he turned and looked about him, addressing them all.

"*Chik sahn kora hir!*" he roared defiantly.

There was silence for a moment, and the tiny part of Joseera not paralysed with terror wondered whether the matter had been settled. She put one trembling hand out to Jubal for comfort, and the great boar pressed against it, as Fulza turned about above them, waiting for some response. Then, as if by some unseen consent, a few of the crowd, both male and female, though mostly younger, began to step forth, standing a few paces in front of the rest. Some removed odd pieces of jewellery or clothing, handing them back to companions and friends in the throng, before turning their attention back to the little group stood alone in the middle of the path.

Joseera looked nervously around, then glanced over to the official looking Savages. The aged male rolled his eyes, and shook his head in a more obvious manner, before leaning in to mutter something urgently to the others. Before she could begin to wonder what was being said, Joseera's attention was drawn back by more movement from the crowd.

A little way in front of them on the right, someone was pushing their way through the fray. An older male emerged and shouldered his way to the front. He nodded at Fulza, and Joseera looked up to see Fulza nod back. Then the stranger walked slowly into the middle of the path. He clapped his hand firmly on Fulza's shoulder when he reached them, gave Jubal a familiar pat, and caught Joseera's eye with a look she could not fathom. Then he turned and stood at their side.

Elsewhere in the crowd, a handful of others began to step forth, five, now six, several males, two females, each with a respectful nod to Fulza before they quietly approached and stood beside him. In the end, they were eight in all, gathered in a tight circle, facing outward, surrounding Joseera and Jubal as she clung to the boar for comfort.

At the sides of the path those who stood proud of the rest began calling and goading again, barking their threats along with encouragement and support to each other. Gradually they began to advance, closing in on Fulza's little group. Holding tightly to Jubal, Joseera waited, frozen, for that spark, that little glance or movement that would cause the tension to ignite.

It never came. There was a sudden authoritative cry from large, important looking male at the centre of the group at the head of the path. It seemed their hurried discussion had been resolved.
"*Hok!*" came the voice, like an angry parent, "*Hok tura!*"
Fulza's group did not move, their aggressors paused uncertainly.
"*Mas va Kol Va'k-*" started one of the troublemakers, but the other, brimming with outraged ferocity, bellowed back, "*Mam virr su! Hok tura!*"

This seemed to be enough to cow their young opponents, and they began, petulantly, to retreat back into the crowd, retrieving belongings here and there, with muttered protest as they went. The chief, as he seemed to Joseera, now turned his attention to Fulza and his companions. He pointed one thick finger at them.
"*Muhna kirrik su va tone. Bas kar, su gan tesna kirrik. Chah, su bas Guvat.*"
This drew a general cheer of approval from the crowd, as Fulza nodded a resigned agreement. Joseera was certain she caught the old priest-Savage giving Fulza a

disapproving look. The next thing she knew, the crowd was quickly dispersing, seemingly in high spirits, and she, Jubal and Fulza were being hurried into a large, low building at the centre of the village.

"What was all that about?" she managed to ask, as they were led inside.

"Hhn." replied Fulza, with a grunt, "Welcome home."

oOo

Joseera was shown, reluctantly, to a small private chamber just inside the building. At first she had flatly refused to be separated from her companions, had hung on to Jubal's neck, until Fulza had assured her that it was quite safe. A tall female had ushered her into the little room, then slid a wooden panel across the doorway, leaving Joseera alone.

Inside, Joseera looked around. There was a plain, but sturdy looking bed against one wall, covered with blankets that were unexpectedly soft to the touch. There was a simple table, and a rough clay jug atop it, beside a small cup. When Joseera found the jug full of cool, fresh water, she poured some for herself and then sat on the bed for the next few minutes, draining the little cup again and again. Finally, her sudden thirst satisfied for now, she put the cup down gratefully, and a thought struck her quite suddenly.

It was all the right size.

There wasn't a single thing in the room, the little chair, the bed, the table, anything that would have been of any use to Fulza or his kind. All of these things would be like toys, miniatures to them, but they were perfect for Joseera. She considered for a moment whether they might belong to children of the village, but she didn't believe it. These things, all of these things, were meant for her people.

Before she could consider it further, there was a gentle rap on the wooden door panel. For a moment, Joseera's mouth flapped noiselessly as she wondered what she should say, then she told herself not to be so foolish and gave a nervous "Hello?"
The panel slid back and the aged old priest from outside stood before her. With a rattle of beads and stones, he stepped inside, swinging his great staff under the doorway and setting down a low stool he carried, before seating himself on it. He smiled, mischievously at Joseera. She lifted herself cautiously off the bed.
"Hello." she said, as clearly as she could, "I am Joseera. I came with Fulza, a long, long way, and I am here-"
The old Savage burst suddenly into laughter.

"I know who you are, Joseera Mayweather." he said, in a rich, low voice. "And, I know why you come. Which, I think, is more than you know!" he grinned.
Joseera blushed a little. "Oh," she said, "you understand me. Of course, Fulza said there were others who spoke better than him."
The Savage smiled. "For now, yes. Fulza was learning when he left. But in almost all things, Fulza learns quickly..." his eyes dropped for a moment, "Almost all."
He looked up, smiling again, "My name is Keshet, and I am '*Mudryi*' of these people - your kind call us Savages, but in our own tongue we are '*Chidri*'. As '*Mudryi*', you think of me as... one of your holy men, perhaps."
Joseera nodded. "You're one of their leaders then?"
Keshet half-shrugged. "I have some... influence. Especially in more... spiritual matters. And we must

discuss-"

"Wait.." said Joseera abruptly, biting her lip, "I have a question first. Where is Fulza now? What was that all about outside? Is he in trouble? Is it because of me?"

Keshet raised his eyebrows and looked taken aback for a moment, as if trying to remember the last time someone had spoken to him this way, then he gathered his thoughts and nodded.

"Hm, yes, questions... And I guess rest can wait. Come. Come with me."

Keshet led Joseera out of the little room and deeper into the building, down wide, high hallways, rounded and cornerless like burrowed tunnels. At one point Joseera noticed they climbed a shallow slope, and she thought to herself that they must be on a higher floor, but beyond this she knew she had entirely lost her bearings. Finally they turned down a short corridor that ended in a pair of large, stout doors, constructed of thick logs and broad metal studs. Keshet, after a moments struggle, pushed open the doors, and much to Joseera's surprise, noise and sunlight flooded in.

The doors opened onto a wide balcony, already populated by several other important looking Savages, including the chief who had intervened earlier. It overlooked a large, dusty clearing surrounded by a low wooden fence, beyond which there were rows of benches, rapidly being filled as what Joseera thought must be the whole village bustled and jostled for a seat. Then her heart jumped in her chest. She saw Fulza, alone at the far end of the clearing, gradually making his way to the centre. Just behind him, on the other side of the fence, she recognised one or two of those who had stood beside him on the path before, but it seemed they were not permitted to accompany him here.

As he walked calmly to the middle, there were growing cheers and calls from the crowd, and Joseera spotted five of the younger Savages who had faced off against them before, also making their way into the centre of the clearing. On the balcony, the chief raised one of his massive hands high, and gradually the raucous noise petered into silence.

"*Fulza, gan kora mas. Su kora, Fulza mas.*" he called out to the assembled mass. There was an expectant silence as he paused, motionless. "*Chah... kora... bas Guvat!*" his hand clenched into a giant fist and the crowd below exploded with cheers and roars, stomping and banging on benches, until the chief raised his open hand for silence once again. Joseera turned anxiously to Keshet.

"What is this? What's happening? What are they all doing here?" she asked, eyes wide with worry.

Keshet leant on his heavy staff, sunlight shimmering on the golden pommel, in stark contrast to the dark look in his eyes. "This is '*Guvat*', Joseera." he said, gravely, "This is where we settle troubles. This... for honour."

Keshet explained that many of the younger members of the village felt they should have already joined up with the rest of their people from the other tribes, that waging war against the Empire together was the right course of action. Some of the more senior Savages agreed with them, and it had been a struggle to convince them to listen to the traditional teachings of their village, to allow a little more time for the old stories to hold true. When Fulza had returned, they were unconvinced that his trip was anything more than stalling for time, and a number of challenges had been issued, in no uncertain terms. Unfortunately, since Fulza had responded to these challenges as he had, he was now honour bound to satisfy them and meet his challengers on the field. Diplomacy, Keshet stressed, was one of those few things Fulza did not seem to take to quickly. Now he had no choice but to face all those whose challenge he had directly met, in this case the four young males and one female who were facing him in the centre of the arena.

Joseera was horrified. "But it isn't fair! He's all on his own! What do they do – how do they know who wins...?" Keshet gave her a confused look. "They win when it is clear someone has won. If the enemy cannot fight, then... win."

"But they'll... why can't someone help him, please..." she turned to the towering figure of the chief where he stood surveying the scene below, and pulled fiercely at his arm. "You have to stop this, it isn't fair! Stop them, please!"

The chief looked down at Joseera with an incredulous expression, then stared up at Keshet, raising his brows with expectant restraint. Keshet hurriedly ushered Joseera away from him.

"*Mam va, mam va!*" he said, apologetically, as he dragged her back. Then he turned to her with a strained expression. "*Bash na gar*, Joseera, do you want to end up down there yourself?!"

He drew a tight breath, then gave her a slightly more sympathetic look. "There is nothing to be done, Joseera. This is how it must be..."

They watched as the chief opened his arms, with Keshet quietly explaining his actions to Joseera as they went. All eyes were looking up at the balcony, waiting for the sign to begin. After what seemed like an age, the chief balled his huge fists and punched the air above, and in the same instant there was a thunderous cry from the crowd below. Then all fell respectfully silent, as the competition began. Joseera watched, paralysed with fear both for her friend and for herself, as Fulza's opponents began to circle him, spreading out to try and surround him. What if the worst happened to him? What would they do with her? Even if they let her go or she managed to escape, she didn't have anywhere to go back to, and no way to get there. She wished Jubal were with her, at least one friendly presence in all of this strangeness.

On the arena floor, the combatants had yet to meet. Fulza stood, motionless, eyes flicking back and forth as he tried to keep track of his adversaries. They were busy positioning themselves at the moment, in no hurry to get things started, enjoying their advantage by whispering and taunting as they manoeuvred around him. Directly in front of him stood the female, a tall, slender specimen with long limbs, staring at Fulza with dark, green eyes. On her right was a squat, bulky male, shorter than Fulza but broader too, solidly built as a boulder. To the right of him, circling round behind Fulza's left side, was an odd character with a curiously snake-like movement, slim and wiry for a male, with unusual bone white hair scraped back in a tight tail atop his head. On the green-eyed female's left, the two remaining males moved to Fulza's right side, one tall and arrogant, chest puffed out like a huge cockerel as he went, the other a little shorter, with wild, black hair and a cruel, jagged scar running from his back over his right shoulder onto his chest.

The female raised her hand and gave a little signal to the others, though from her position on the balcony, Joseera couldn't see clearly enough to guess what it might mean. Nevertheless, her companions clearly understood, for as the female scraped her foot up and forward at Fulza, driving dirt and dust up in a showering cloud at his face, the boulder-like male lunged forth, right fist swinging in a great arc towards Fulza's head. Fulza was more than prepared for this clumsy assault, however, and simply ducked down, avoiding the worst of the dust, and then, staying low, swung his body round to the left, under the Boulder's fist, before coming up behind the Boulder's arm, knocking him off balance and sending him staggering towards the female. She simply laughed, her green eyes glittering, as she caught her broad companion and pushed him aside. Then all five laughed together.

They were testing him, thought Joseera, fingers clutching tight, white-knuckled, to the edge of the balcony as she looked helplessly on. They were toying with him, getting the measure of him before they truly struck. She glanced round at the others on the balcony, all watching almost as closely as Joseera herself, faces unreadable. She looked at Keshet, and he caught her eye for just a moment, giving her a sympathetic little nod, before casting his eyes back to the action.

The white-haired, snake-like Savage had placed himself directly behind Fulza now, shifting about with a strange little shuffle as Fulza moved, to maintain his position. The wild, scarred one was just beside him, and together the two of them charged at Fulza, hands outstretched in the hope of catching him by the arms. Fulza heard the movement though, and lunged forward on one leg, before pushing back with a curious dipping motion, elbows stabbing out behind him like blades. Both Snake and Scar were too committed to their action now to slow down in time, and Joseera saw Fulza's leg lock with the impact as they collided, his elbows planting deep in the pit of Snake and Scar's stomachs. Even as they stumbled backward to recover though, and before Fulza could make anything of his brief advantage, the female came at him, long legs scything the air, lightning fast, with a jutting heel aimed at Fulza's jaw. He pulled his head back, sharply, just in time, and narrowly avoided the kick, but another followed, and another, sending Fulza dancing backwards to escape them. The arrogant, cockerel male saw his chance, and with a brief wave to the crowd he ran, and dived powerfully forward at Fulza, hoping to catch him by the hips while off-balance, and so bring him to the ground. In fact, Fulza gratefully caught the Cockerel's arm, and turned, using the force of the dive to propel him as the female's next arcing kick whistled inches before his face. As he went, he pulled the Cockerel round with him, then let go, sending him crashing into the female, with just enough time to see her green eyes widen with surprise before her companion flattened her.

Fulza calmly dusted himself off, and looked slowly around, taking in each of his opponents with a measured glance. Then he stood, calm and still as before, waiting for their next move.
They weren't happy. This was clear to Joseera, even from a distance and without understanding the harsh words they were shouting at one another. They yelled and gestured at each other again, before circling Fulza once more, and gradually closing in.

Joseera wasn't sure who threw the first punch, she thought perhaps the Cockerel, but for the next few minutes the arena floor was a flurry of motion. The five surrounded Fulza, fists and feet plunging in toward him again and again, but somehow, Fulza endured. For a moment Joseera forgot her fear as she watched him move, flowing, rushing, rolling within the ring, with a grace she found astonishing for a creature of such size. She watched, rapt, as he twisted and shifted beneath each blow, absorbing, softening or redirecting its force, and turning his opponents number into an advantage. As the Boulder came to strike him, he would turn slightly into it, catching the elbow as it travelled past and leading into Scar's face. When the Snake lunged, darting in with grasping, clawing hands, Fulza pulled him further, ruining his balance before casting him off into the female's path. In this way, although some blows stuck home, Fulza weathered them, and ensured for each one that landed, his opponents paid just as dearly with the next. Joseera had just begun to wonder how long Fulza could sustain this, how long before he tired and slipped, when she saw a sudden flash from below.

While the others continued to wear down Fulza's defences, the Cockerel had circled round behind him again, and was raising both hands high above his head. Cupped, hidden within those huge hands, just for a moment Joseera saw a flash of sunlight against the cold edge of a crude, hidden blade. Everything seemed to slow down as the other four timed their movements to leave Fulza leaning back, away from them, and the Cockerel's hands began to travel sharply downwards, edge hidden in such a way that even if Fulza stopped the blow, the blade would surely slice through. Joseera screamed, threw her arms out, grabbing hold of Keshet's stick in an effort to pull herself up, over the balcony edge. Then, time stopped altogether.

There was a curious sensation, not unlike a sneeze, Joseera thought absently, followed by a light so bright it blocked out everything else. Joseera felt a strange sense of calm, although she found herself in an unfamiliar place, surrounded by shining figures. As she looked lazily from one strange face to the next, she saw glittering golden eyes, looking down at her kindly. One of the figures reached out, placing a warm hand on Joseera's cheek, and a blinding smile began to spread across its face.

"Joseera."

Before Joseera could do any more, she was back on the balcony.

With a wrench she jerked her eyes open, just in time to see Fulza turn sideways as he moved back. The Cockerel was distracted, eyes turned up to the balcony, and Fulza seized the opportunity, planting his hand on the back of the Cockerel's before completing his turn and driving the ugly blade joltingly into the Cockerel's own gut. Then he danced away, hands held high above him, open in submission. Before the other four could come any closer, someone in the crowd saw the thick blood pooling beneath the Cockerel's writhing form. The cry went up. The bout was halted.

Joseera stared down at the scene in utter confusion. On her left, the chief held up his arms once again, and called for silence. The crowd looked bewildered and dismayed, cheated of their sport and disgusted by the betrayal, but nevertheless they fell silent at their leader's behest. Fulza's four remaining opponents looked sheepish and ashamed, the female kneeling at the Cockerel's side, the others trying desperately to sink into the arena floor and disappear.

The chief turned to Keshet, calm face unable to disguise the anger in his eyes.
"Vek sh'ra Mudryi. Cohma sera vet?"
Keshet looked uncertainly from the chief to Fulza, Joseera

and back, but Joseera didn't notice. She was staring down at her friend, her companion, at Fulza, who knelt now on the earth, and stared straight back.

"*Osotik.*" He said loudly, clearly, in the silence, without taking his eyes away from Joseera's for even a moment.
"*Keshet, gan Joseera osotik.*"
Their eyes were locked together, and although the attention of the entire village was once again upon them, they did not seem to notice or care.

Keshet was casting uncertainly about, but Fulza called clearly again.
"*Keshet, gan Joseera osotik.*"
Keshet looked over at the chief, and saw a mixture of confusion and dismay on the huge Savage's face, clearly appalled at the suggestion this girl, this alien, child of another race should lay her hands upon a sacred relic. Then he stared fiercely, intently at Fulza for a moment, and made his decision. He placed a firm hand on Joseera's shoulder, and gave her a little shake, to wake her from her trance. As she turned to look at him, dazed and open-mouthed, he pressed the great wooden stick he bore into her hands, and let go.

Joseera stood there for a moment, bewildered, wondering how on earth she had come to be here. In her hands, tiny by comparison, the solid stick was more like a long staff. Her eyes drifted slowly upwards along its length, until they reached the grand golden ornament at the top, shimmering brightly, with its curious lines and patterns seeming all the darker in the bright sun. As the light danced on its surface, it almost seemed to move.

Despite the already quiet atmosphere around the arena, the

silence seemed to deepen, as if the world held its breath. The golden sphere brightened. Gently, slowly, the light turned and spread, flower-like, layer upon layer, before rising into the air, spinning faster and faster. When it seemed it could go no quicker, a bolt of blistering light, warm and wonderful, leapt between the golden sphere and the sky, and then was gone. The golden pommel sat serenely at the top of the staff. Although the sun still fell upon it, it seemed to Joseera that the light now came from within somehow.

She looked down at her surroundings almost in a state of shock, open-mouthed and foggy-eyed. As her head cleared, she saw all around her, on the balcony, in the benches, even those four remaining in the arena had taken up Fulza's position. Wherever she looked, the Savages knelt before her. Slowly, from somewhere within the crowd, a chant started, softly at first, but quickly gathering momentum until it was a thundering chorus of voices.

"*Ilos ih'vir! Ilos ih'vir! Ilos ih'vir!*"

Trembling, Joseera bent down to Keshet, and shouted over the incredible noise, "What is it? What are they saying?" Keshet looked up at her slowly, nervously, with wide, wet eyes, and struggled, thinking for a moment before answering, "They say 'light ...' no, wait not light..." he paused, staring at her with an strange expression that Joseera did not understand.

"Sun... They say 'Sunrise'."

Chapter Twelve

The Sword narrowed his eyes against the bright sun of the afternoon and stared out at the sea of faces looking up at him. The wide drill ground that stood behind the Keep was filled with people in uniform, every space occupied as, shoulder to shoulder, Bantha's soldiers and officers waited for their leaders to speak. He hated this part.

He glanced over at Loulouthi and Sofya, stood just to his right, and wondered exactly when everything had become so complicated. When it had just been the three of them, things were so simple, they had worried about each hour as it came, and action and consequence were like dawn and dusk of the same day. Now… now almost everything they said or did had some unseen effect, some unconsidered impact that would be felt in months or years to come. He tried to remember the last time he had lived in the moment, felt the adrenaline tug suddenly on his senses, holding back time like a rider hauling on the reins of his horse, and allowing him to take in every detail, every vivid colour, of every split second.

oOo

Many years before and many miles away, in a thick copse of trees, at the foot of a dusty hill spotted with lifeless scrub, two women peered out into the distance.

"How many?" whispered the first, a pretty young woman with dark curls.
"I see seven." replied her red haired companion, peering over her spectacles.
"Draw and split?"

"They look stupid enough to me."

The young woman glanced over to the next tree, where a lean, grey-eyed man was crouching low in the shade, and raised her hand in signal. He nodded his agreement and moved back, disappearing into the shadows.

She looked down at herself. She had only been wearing a light robe to sleep in, and she loosened it now, revealing a little more of the soft swell of her breasts, and ensuring it fell in such a way that her long legs were briefly visible as she moved, the curve of her thigh parting the rough fabric for a moment with each step. She shook her dark hair loose across her shoulders, and, crossing her hands lightly behind her back, gave her friend a wicked smile before stepping out into the fresh daylight.

The soldiers halted as she stepped out beyond the trees, gathering in a rough wedge behind their sergeant. She glanced quickly from face to face, and then gave the men a warm smile. Much to her pleasure, a young lad at the front, wide eyes and a short crop of thick black hair, returned the expression.

"It's alright," she said, boldly, "I'm here alone, as you can see. You have to take me back, I understand. There's nothing I can do to stop you."

At the back of the group, two of the men visibly relaxed, and began to move forward with threatening intent. The sergeant screwed up his face, all jutting chin and sharp nose, adorned with a permanent scowl, and stopped them in their tracks with a black look.
"Don't be so damn stupid," he snarled at the pair, then turned to face the woman, "You're not alone. Your type

stick together like a pack of dogs. So where are they?"

She stared hard at the man, till he almost flinched under her gaze, then smiled again, cooler now. "You're right," she said, "I'm not alone." She let her eyes flash up to the top of the ridge behind them, just for the briefest of moments, almost as if she had not wanted the men to notice.

The sergeant turned immediately, as did three of the men at the back of the group, raising their weapons nervously. The others looked uncertainly around them. The sergeant half-turned back again, attention flicking back and forth now though, between the woman and the ridge behind him.

She let out a relaxed laugh, and again gave a warm smile to the soldiers who met her eye, two of whom responded with a timorous laugh of their own.
"You must know our reputation," she said, cheerfully, ignoring the confused looks this drew, "After all, they wouldn't dare send anyone after us unprepared, or without fair warning. So you will know that we three have taken down entire squads of Savages alone. Why else would I stand here so calmly before you now, unarmed and unprotected?"

The men turned to one another with questioning looks, and a nod spread between them infectiously. The sergeant had become decidedly twitchy. "That's enough! That's enough from you… you just shut your mouth!" he shouted, still glancing apprehensively up at the ridge behind.

"Know this before you act. " she called, sharply, and they

hesitated, huddled together, eyes in all directions. "We were like you. Soldiers, following orders. But we were asked to do something we could not. We wish you no harm. We are not the enemy, but if you raise your weapons against us, we *will* strike you down."

One of the three soldiers before her looked back to the sergeant for assurance. He was met with a spitting snarl. "What are you waiting for?! Take her! Just do as yer told and kill her!"

The three soldiers nearest to the woman began to advance, but even as they did there was a sudden noise from beyond the ridge, a blasting horn sounding out of sight. The soldiers turned and scattered, some crying out, "Savages! The Savages are here!"
"Go! Grab her now and let's move!" shouted the sergeant.
One of the men lunged forward, making a grab for the woman, but she brought her arms up sharply and plunged the two short but lethally sharp blades she had been hiding in the palms of her hands into the soft, unprotected flesh at his armpits. With a scream, he dropped to the floor, almost dragging her down with him, as the other two closed in from either side. She took two quick steps back, into the shade of the trees, and as the men drew together in front of her, a huge gout of flame shot forth from her red haired friend's hiding place, catching the pair fully in the chest and face. They stumbled away, hollering and flapping at their burning hair and clothing. The three remaining soldiers, driven forward by their furious sergeant, moved in, but even as they came she caught the eye of the young, dark-haired lad who faltered and backed away, lowering his sword.

"What do you think you're doing boy?" screamed the

sergeant, "You'll do as you're damn well ordered!"
Before he could do anything further about the deserting lad however, the grey-eyed man launched forth from their left, springing into the centre, between the sergeant and his last two men. They wheeled and brought their swords to bear on him, as the two women gathered themselves and moved away.

The grey-eyed man turned swiftly, bringing his blade about in a powerful arc, knocking their swords aside. As the men swung back, he continued his spin, hooking out with his leg and bringing the sergeant crashing down heavily onto his back. He dove forward, sailing over the flailing sergeant, before turning back and driving his blade through the man's chest. Even as he did, he jerked his head back as the soldiers swords came for him again, a little too slowly though, as one of the blades sliced a bloody path across his cheek. Without pause, he leapt forward before the men could bring their weapons round again, running one of the men clean through.

The grey-eyed man pulled his sword clear and turned towards the final soldier. The two women emerged slowly from the shade of the trees behind him. The soldier made two vicious, desperate swings, but the grey-eyed man parried the first without effort, and simply stepped aside the second. The third attempt was a rash, wild horizontal slash, but the grey-eyed man spun forward, into the blow, catching the soldier's arm beneath his own, before twisting into him, knocking the soldier off his feet and taking his weapon in the process. The soldier struggled, shaking, to his feet. The points of two swords hung in the air, just inches from his neck, and beyond them stood the grey-eyed man, and his friends. The soldier glanced into the distance, where the young wide-eyed lad had stopped, panic-stricken, not knowing where best to run. The grey-eyed man looked over his shoulder with a grin at the women behind him, then turned back to face the terrified soldier, and raised a questioning eyebrow.

The soldier needed no further encouragement. Gratefully, he turned tail and ran, staggering and stumbling towards his young friend. On hearing a second horn blast from beyond the ridge, the pair hurried off, away from the sound of Savages, and eventually out of sight.

The grey-eyed man wiped absent-mindedly at his bloody cheek with the sleeve of his tunic. He and the young woman both looked expectantly at their red-haired friend, who smiled slyly and brought forth an odd looking little clay instrument. She breathed deeply, and blew on it, and as she did, the great horn sounded once again, from somewhere over the high ridge.

The young woman laughed. "You might have told us about that one, Sofya." she said.
"Aye, witch." grinned the grey-eyed man, "I almost looked for the Savages myself!"

"Now tell me," laughed the red haired woman, with an elaborate little bow. "Just what would be the fun in that, eh?"

oOo

The Sword heard a sharp noise to his left.
"Duma? Duma!" the Book hissed through her teeth, with less subtlety than she imagined. She gestured out at the mass of people staring up at them, all hope and anticipation. "Forgive me for interrupting, but I think they

might have been expecting words of some kind!"
Loulouthi said nothing, simply raising her eyebrows conspicuously.

In the drill ground before them, the sun flashed and sparkled on the finely polished buckles and helmets, like a glittering sea. It all seemed so far removed from the reality of war, brutality made acceptable by pomp and ceremony. The promise of honour and glory, when in truth there would be little of either.

The Sword gave his friends a little nod, an uncomfortable smile, then turned his attention to the men and women before him. He looked at the expectant faces, finely-kept uniforms, at the proud posture and bearing, eyes shining with respect and anticipation. How different, he thought, their beginnings from mine.

oOo

The three figures made their way hastily across a bleak and rocky landscape, as if trying to escape the searching light of the moon hanging fat and low in the clear night. Crouched low, hoods and cloaks pulled tightly around them, they followed, one after the other, across the slope of the escarpment, occasionally letting out a muttered curse as the loose scree shifted treacherously beneath them.

"Ancients' sake!" exclaimed Sofya, as she lost her footing for what seemed like the hundredth time, hands scraping through the rough debris as she struggled up and onward, "How much further Loulouthi?! They can't be following us now, surely!"

The first figure stopped briefly, turning back to glance at her companion, "Not much further Sofya, I promise, but we must get out of sight! Even if they *have* stopped, we can't risk being seen at dawn!"

At the back of the group, Duma pressed forward to steady his friend. "We won't have to worry about that running around in the dark like this," he said with a dark smile, "We'll be pounced on by some great Savage long before morning."

"Thank you Duma, a great comfort as always..." replied Sofya.

At the front, Loulouthi stopped sharply as she reached the crest of the slope, and held up a hand in warning to the others behind her. Her companions, silent now, fought their way up as quietly as they could to join her, and the three friends peered down together in wonder at what they saw on the other side of the ridge.

Beneath them, the rocks sloped sharply downwards again, curving slightly to form the sides of what seemed like a vast fissure. At the bottom of the slope, against the flat rock wall, sat a dark, alien building, broad and brooding, with jutting peaks and spires thrusting upward like great stalagmites, while numberless arches and crevices played home to deep, impenetrable shadows. As the others caught their breath and strained their eyes futilely, trying to better determine what lay before them, Loulouthi sat open-mouthed, one hand still absently raised in warning.

"Ancients be damned..." said Duma, shaking his head. "Where have we found ourselves now?"

Sofya was still squinting and scrutinizing the mysterious sight, digging around in her bag as she did so. She pulled out a small bundle of green velvet, and unwrapped it to produce a smooth glass lens, rounded with a gold band. Holding it up before her, she rubbed at the glass and muttered something quietly to herself, and as if in response, the glass gave out a faint glow. She gazed through it, first with one eye, then the other, before wrapping it neatly again and returning it to her bag, curiosity apparently satisfied.

"Let's go down there." she said, abruptly, "We can get out of sight and shelter here for the night at least."

Loulouthi turned as if surprised to find her friends beside her, before self consciously lowering her hand. "Are you serious?" she hissed, eyes wide, "What *is* that place? We haven't come all this way just to leap into the fire!"

Duma nodded. "I have to say Sofya, it doesn't look that inviting." he said, eyes still fixed below.

"I can't see any signs of movement down there, or any trace of activity," Sofya replied, "So we might as well make the best of it. One way or another, we have to get out of sight, or come morning *someone* will be looking to spill our blood, whether Savage or soldier." With that, she thrust her feet out before her, and began half shuffling, half sliding down the slope.

Duma and Loulouthi looked uncertainly at each other for a moment. "She did use the glass this time at least." said Duma with a grin. Then he gave a little shrug, and launched himself, sliding down after their friend.

Loulouthi stayed for a moment longer, staring down at the strange building below. "There's something there..." she said, softly, "Something... I feel it."
She glanced behind her, back into the distance they had travelled, and in the moon's indifferent glow she fancied for a moment that she could see a troop of men, far off, light flashing on their armours. She looked back to her friends, awkwardly slithering through the dust and drift stone, and with a quiet prayer, set off after them.

oOo

"Soldiers of Bantha! Men and women of the Empire! Some of you here today, may have faced our enemy before. Some of you may be... eagerly awaiting your first taste of action. But whatever glory you dream of, whatever you might wish for, be certain of this. The men and women who stand beside you now are your brothers and sisters, and from this moment on, you will know no finer, and could wish for no better! Whether it is your duty to follow orders or to give them, you will defend your brothers, you will protect your sisters, and together we will do what is asked of us!

"Now some of you may have heard rumours, stories, about our enemy. About the forces they muster and the powers they wield. Those of you who have faced the Savages before may be wondering what else you might face. Well, I will not lie to you. We may face an army of the Savage races such as we have never seen. But it seems that they are coming, whether we ride out to meet them or not, they are coming.

"So we will face them where *we* choose, fight them where it suits *us*. The pass at Vas Aloron will choke their advance, force them to face us head on, on a narrow front. As long as you have strength in your arm to cut down the enemy that stands before you, their numbers will not save them. This is our chance, our opportunity! If they take Vas Aloron, they will press freely on into the farms and towns of the Fold, and Bantha will be next. So we will stand now, and defend our home!

"It was said once, that one man alone could never hope to best a Savage in single combat. They were too big, too tall, too strong! Yet there are men and women here among us who have *proved* that this is not the case. We learned to turn their strengths *against* them. Remember this, my friends. We have beaten them before. Whatever their numbers, whatever new tricks they may have learned, if the Savages think to test us... we will beat them once again!"

The Sword drew the blade at his side from its scabbard, and held it high above his head. "For Bantha! For the Empire!"
His cry was emphatically taken up by the people on the drill ground, roaring voices and hands punching the air. Finally they quietened again, as the Heart gestured for silence. As she began to speak, the Sword looked on, taking in the scene. His gaze drifted from Loulouthi's face to Sofya's, and out to the hundreds of faces staring attentively up at them, depending on them, trusting them. He looked at his friends and wondered – how has it come to this?

oOo

Hidden in the shadows of one of the dead building's twisted pillars, Loulouthi and Duma stirred on thin bedrolls, around the remnants of a small fire, while Sofya stood watch, eyes fixed on the slopes above. For the remainder of the night they had rested like this, grabbing sleep while they could, and guarding their companions when their turn came. Now though, the night had almost slipped away behind the horizon, and the first true shafts of dawn were brightening the skies.

From somewhere behind them in the darkness came a scraping sound of stone upon stone, followed by a knocking, and the *pad pad* of slow footsteps.

Sofya licked her lips nervously and turned to the others, wild red hair poking here and there from beneath her hood. "Someone's here." she said, simply.

In an instant the other two were on their feet. Duma, sword in hand, its point poised in the air before him. Loulouthi readied herself, stood close beside Sofya, peering into the shade.

Slowly a strange figure emerged from the shadows.

"It's- Is it? A Savage?" breathed Sofya.
Duma stood, frozen in place, uncertain. "Doesn't look like any Savage I've ever seen..." he said.
"It is..." said Loulouthi softly, "...but something... something must have happened..."

The creature before them shared the height and rough shape of a Savage, but it lacked their weight, their build entirely. Looking impossibly old, thin hair framed its head like wisps of memory, and it clung with gaunt fingers to a gold tipped wooden staff, as if it was the only thing keeping it upright. Eyes of milky white and blue cast about before it, and then the creature smiled, all dry gums and powdered teeth.

"Ah." it said, in a voice like shifting sand. "At last."
It beckoned the three friends with a long, skeletal arm. "Come." it said, simply, "Come."

Duma moved cautiously closer. "Are you... are you one of them? Are you a Savage? How do you come to speak our language?"
"Am I savage?" said the creature, with a rasping chuckle, "No, not savage. Calm, kindly, no harm, no harm. Your language?"
 The creature lowered its wrinkled head with a racking laugh that made them wince to hear. "Very good! Very funny! *Your* langauge! Come, come."

Then it turned and began to shuffle steadily back into the shadows.

Duma turned to share his baffled look with his companions, and Sofya met his eye with an expression of equal disbelief. Loulouthi though, after staring blankly into the shadows for a moment, set off decidedly into the darkness, striding after the old creature as if there was no sense in anything else.

"Loulouthi!" hissed Sofya, urgently, "What are you doing?"
Loulouthi stopped for a moment, and half turned, with a curious frown. "Why are we here Sofya?" And with that, she disappeared ahead.

Sofya turned to Duma in amazement.
"After all the times she told me to check-" she exclaimed.

Duma raised his eyebrows pointedly.
"But she hasn't- I mean, I never-"
Duma gave a little nod, and with a shrug and a smile, set off after Loulouthi, sword in hand.
"Well really." said Sofya, indignantly to the air. Then she lifted her bag and followed on, into the dark.

They followed the withered creature deep into the stone belly of the great building. They went silently, although they shared several worried and wondrous looks, following their shuffling guide cautiously, always keeping a little distance behind despite his slow pace. Eventually, they rounded yet another featureless corner, but this time, instead of a plain stone corridor, they found themselves in a high, round hall. The chamber was tiered and stretched to the very top of the building it seemed, as a bright shaft of sunlight shone straight down from a hole up above, falling on a large stone plinth in the hall's centre. The plinth stood on a small, low platform, two shallow steps on each side.

Their guide turned calmly and laughed, a painful, crackling rattle. He held out his spidery arms and smiled.
"Welcome to the Temple of the Dead."

After a few seconds, Sofya's curiosity got the better of her, and she stepped forwards, peering up at the high ceiling, and the light streaming down from above.
"How long have we been walking?" she cried in wonder.
Duma and Loulouthi looked at her blankly.
"The sun can't be overhead already! It was barely dawn when we came inside – so how can this light be pouring in like this?"

The withered Savage gave another dry laugh and shuffled

toward Sofya. "A mystery, indeed" he said, smiling. "Now, please, follow, follow."

With Sofya staring incredulously at the light above, Loulouthi gazing around at the hall itself, and Duma turning this way and that with an uncomfortable expression, sword still in hand, the strange little group slowly made their way to low platform in the middle of the hall, where the warm light fell on the broad plinth. In its centre was a rounded hollow filled with clear water, and at the bottom lay what looked like a gnarled and twisted root, save for the fact that its surface was golden, smooth and sheer, and it seemed to shift and flow before the eyes.

Their guide shuffled up onto the platform, stopped next to the plinth. He set down the gold tipped staff, and turned slowly to face his guests.
"Now," he said, after a moment, "Ready."

In one fluid movement the creature plunged a hand into the shimmering water and pulled out the glistening root, before turning in a shower of droplets and flinging it towards them. Before they had chance to react, the strange root had expanded and grown, thin limbs and tendrils grasping, reaching for them all. As it twisted about them, wrapped itself tightly around their arms, their bodies, their legs, all three found themselves paralysed, held motionless in place.

The creature disappeared from view for a few moments, and when he returned he bore a bundle of cloth, cradled in one thin arm. He approached them, slowly, and gestured up at the shaft of light coming in above.
"This day... long past, a fading memory," he sighed.

"None left now who remember the dawn. And so... nightmares see their chance, wake and whisper promises to lonely souls..."

He turned to face the three friends, still held firmly despite their efforts to escape.

"But once more, three step forward..."

There was a long moment of silence. Cloudy eyes studied the three carefully.

"Have been waiting, waiting here, long time. Even so, she was... surprising."

The creature drew nearer, and lowered the bundle he held at his chest until they could see what it contained. From within the soft folds, round, blue eyes peered innocently out, and when they fell upon the three friends, the child smiled, and laughed.

The creature laughed with her.

"She is a good judge, I think."

It looked tenderly down at the child, then a more solemn expression returned to the withered face.

"Her family are dead, victims of endless fighting between your people and mine. She lay alone, unnoticed in the wake of the attack."

The child cooed, and frowned.

"But something was at work... I found her. Brought her here. Because she *must* survive. She belongs to old, old line, and yet... is first of her kind."

The creature gestured to the glimmering root that held them.

"In... *your* language," he said, with a smile, "call this 'The Knot'."

The pale eyes moved from one face to the next.

"It will bind you. Join you. Each of you is gifted, strong in your way... now will share that strength, each from the other. You will take this child, take her back among your people, hide her, keep her safe. Protect her until time comes."

The creature leaned close, face drawn with a desperate look.

"Our people fight, yours and mine, a ceaseless, pointless squabble. But it must *stop*. Something... something is coming, and we may be too weak to face it. Ancient things stir, and we will be caught up, ignorant and unaware, destroyed for our evils or consumed by them."

The aged head fell, gazing fondly at the child.

"Yet there is a chance. Perhaps she... will have the strength, will grant us hope. Perhaps, the light will remember..."

As the creature spoke, the daylight streaming in from above seemed to the three friends to grow brighter and brighter, beyond the bounds of reason, until the dazzling white glare eclipsed their senses, leaving nothing else.

oOo

Slowly, methodically, the soldiers trooped out of the drill ground. The Book and the Heart had said just a few brief words, and then the Sword had given the order to move out.

"We should be going with them." he said, as he watched the last squads disappear through the gate.

"We will follow in two days time Duma, as we planned." replied the Heart, leaning gently on his shoulder, "And we'll catch up with them before they reach Vas Aloron anyway. But first everything must be in place, so things run smoothly in our absence. What will be the point of any good we may do out there if everything at home falls apart?"

"I know Loulouthi, I know." The Sword put an arm around his friend. "Sometimes I just feel a little *too* much like an official."

"Don't worry Duma, neither of us think of you that way," said the Book, giving a little wink over her spectacles as she pushed past them, "An official... mascot perhaps, but even then..."

The Book swept on, calling back to them, "Now come on, we can't stand around here feeling sorry for ourselves all day, there's a lot to be done!"

With a conspiratorial smile at their friend's expense, the Heart and the Sword hurried after her, and side by side, the three friends continued in to the Keep together.

Chapter Thirteen

After what seemed like an hour or more of cloying, bewildering darkness, a hand reached out and pulled the rough hessian cloth from Gaven's head. Blinking and squinting as his eyes readjusted, Gaven turned about, taking in as much of his surroundings as he could.

He was bound firmly to a chair, he found, in the centre of a small, simply furnished wooden room. There was a plain table, upon which sat bread and fruits, one door to his right and a small window to his left, too high for him to see anything more useful than a grey sky from his seated position. On the floor beneath his feet was a thick, woollen rug, and before him, seated opposite, was a burly, heavy-set man in long robes and leathers.

The man smiled awkwardly at Gaven, revealing his remaining battered teeth, and twisted the hessian this way and that in his rough hands. The right hand, Gaven noticed, bore thick, uneven scars all around, as if it had been badly burned some while before.
"Ah... right then. Feelin' alright?"
Gaven said nothing.
The man cleared his throat noisily.
"Hm. Well. Can't blame you for bein' a little upset, I s'pose. Sorry about all this," he waved the cloth in his hands, "we just 'ave to be careful, see. 'Specially now."
Gaven nodded. "Yes, of course. It pays to be careful when you're ambushing strangers unprovoked in the middle of the night, I'm sure." he said, sourly. "Who are you?"

The man sat back, and a frown replaced the anxious smile on his thick face.

"Now, there's no cause to be rude, lad. We could just as well have put an end to you back there, with good reason an' all. So don't be thinkin' we aren't doin' you a kindness just by your bein' 'ere."
With a sniff, the man continued.
"My name's Rin Bata. You've already sorta met Fathom 'ere..."
A thin, rake like man, with fair skin and a delicate, mournful expression, stepped into view, dressed just the same as his larger companion.
"And this," the man gestured to someone behind Gaven to come forward, "this ugly one is Valien."
A striking, dark-skinned man with a broad, confident smile walked out to join the others, again dressed in what Gaven now assumed was some kind of uniform.
"There's a couple more, Finn and Caro, the brothers, but they're out takin' care of a couple o' things right now." said Rin.
"Now. P'raps you'd be good enough t' tell us yer name."

Gaven sighed, and looked wearily from one unfamiliar face to the next. "Gaven. My name is Gaven." he said, flatly.

Rin turned in his chair and gave a nod to the long, thin figure he had introduced as Fathom. In response, Fathom drew a practical looking knife, and started towards Gaven. "We're taking a risk here." he said, and Gaven instantly recognised the cold, controlled voice that had accompanied the blade against his throat a few hours earlier. "And it's not one I'm in favour of."
Fathom knelt, next to Gaven, and held the knife up before him. "So let me be clear. The instant I suspect your behaviour is anything less than innocent... I'll have this knife in you. And I'll be glad about it too."

Fathom held Gaven's stare for a moment, until it became clear that Gaven was in no mood to be intimidated, then with a self conscious little cough, he reached down and cut Gaven's bonds, before stepping back to stand at Rin's side.

"You'll 'ave to excuse Fathom." said Rin, smiling, "He takes his business rather serious, see. He's a cautious one, an' no mistake!" He turned to Fathom with a grin, and was met with a haughty sniff.

Gaven sat, rubbing his wrists where the dry rope had pressed the skin.
"Certainly." he replied. "Ancients forbid he should be frivolous with the prisoners."
Rin looked hurt.
"Now look, I think we might've got off on the wrong foot 'ere. We don't mean no 'arm if you're what you say you are, we just 'ave to be careful is all."
He turned to the dark-skinned man.
"Valien, bring the other one through will you?"

Valien nodded, and with another wide smile at Gaven as he went, disappeared through the room's small door. After a moment he returned, and behind him, unharmed and exasperated, much to Gaven's relief and amusement, followed Sergeant Thurro. The Sergeant bore a black expression which instantly brightened on sight of his Captain, and he rushed over to greet Gaven gladly, all troubles momentarily forgotten.

Rin smiled at the pair. "There now, see? No 'arm done to either of you."
Gaven and Thurro both turned to face the man with an almost identically incredulous look.

"Now 'opefully, we can put that behind us..." Rin continued optimistically, "'Cause the truth is, we might just need your help."

oOo

The rest of Joseera's day had found her in a daze, as one surreal moment followed the last. For the remainder of the evening, one or other of the towering Savages would approach, interrupting whatever else she might be doing, and with Keshet's help asking Joseera to bless them, or their child, or their family, or in many cases simply to lay a hand on them as they knelt before her. Joseera had felt awkward and embarrassed at first, and uncertain of quite what to say, although she was pretty sure that Keshet was embellishing her mutterings and mumblings somewhat in translation. By the end of the evening, however, she had accepted her lot for the time being, and reflected to herself that it was, at least, an improvement on the treatment she had received on her arrival to the the village. So, she blessed and bowed with a smile and as much grace as she could muster, even though she wasn't quite sure what in the world was going on, and Keshet no longer seemed to be doing much explaining.

In fact, the old Savage had become suddenly more nervous around her, and had spoken only a few words to her directly since leaving the arena balcony, save to translate what the next grateful Savage wanted her to bless. When Fulza eventually appeared, Joseera was surprised herself at just how glad she was to see him, and greeted him like an old friend, running over and flinging her arms around him happily.

"You're okay! Oh, thank the Ancients, you're okay!" she

looked at the dark bruises that patterned his skin, "You are okay, aren't you? What's going on? Do you know? What happened back there?"
Fulza laughed and looked down at Joseera with a smile.
"Ah yes. Questions! Of course!" he growled, "Yes. Am well, girl. Sorry too. Was... foolish."
He frowned and looked away for a moment.
"Angry. Promised to keep you safe. No help to you dead. Should listen to own words." he said, smiling again.

Fulza looked over to Keshet, stood nearby with a pained expression, clearly dismayed by what he considered to be an inappropriate display of affection. Gently, Fulza removed Joseera's arms from about his waist, and knelt beside her. For a moment Joseera was afraid he was about to ask for a blessing himself.
"Now girl. Time for answers." he said softly.
Then he rose and walked over to Keshet. The two of them exchanged a few quiet words, and from the way Keshet's eyes kept flicking over at her anxiously, Joseera guessed they must be talking about her.

Finally Fulza turned back to her.
"Come. Somewhere peaceful. Talk."

oOo

"Are you sure about this?" said Rin, gravely.
He was seated at the small table now, next to Fathom and Valien, with Gaven and Thurro opposite as they shared the bread and fruit before them hungrily.
"I'm afraid so, Rin," Gaven continued, "The only people who knew we were out there were in Bantha. Right before our mystery man and his Savage friends uncovered our position, he received a message of some kind, and

urgently delivered too. They certainly didn't seem to be looking for us before that. Now you can't tell me there's not a connection there."

Rin nodded, a worried expression on his face. "No, no, you're right. It can't be coincidence, that's sure."
Valien leant forward. "What I don't understand is the appearance of this... 'golden giant'! I mean, we hear things, out here, we listen closely, but we thought until now that these whispers were... exaggeration, the wild talk of terrified people! From what you tell us, Captain, this threat cannot *be* exaggerated. Do you think there is a connection there too? Do you think these people are providing the Savages with this kind of... power?"

Gaven sighed and shrugged. "I honestly don't know." he replied, "All I can be sure of is what I've seen, and I know I have to get word of it back to Bantha as soon as I can."
Thurro crammed the last of the apple he'd been eating into his mouth. "No disrespect or anythin'" he started, noisily, "you seem like decent enough fellas now you're done with all the sneakin' up on blokes caught short in the night. But how come you're so in the dark anyways? I thought findin' things out was part of what Keepers did?"

"As we keep telling you, Sergeant," replied Fathom, coolly, "we're not Keepers. Not any more. We still keep our eyes open, of course. But out here it's hard to be certain, and we have to be careful to remain hidden."
Sergeant Thurro looked unconvinced. "Hm. You might not be on the payroll no more, but old habits die hard, I'd of thought."

Rin breathed out heavily, shaking his head. "If all of this is true, Captain, if the Savages really do have such powerful support and inside intelligence, then you're right. Bantha must hear all of this as soon as possible. Sergeant Thurro?"

Thurro had been eyeing Fathom suspiciously, but now his attention turned to Rin. "Eh?" he replied.
"You're from Norfenn, right?"
Thurro smiled, nodding. "Aye, right enough. Thought I recognised your accent."
Rin smiled back. "Sergeant, Bantha's less than a days good ride from here. Would you be willin' to head back alone, carry the word?"

Gaven and Thurro exchanged a confused look.
"Well… of course," started Thurro, "but why… I mean-"
"Why would he go alone? I'll ride with him!" interrupted Gaven.

Rin frowned, rubbing thoughtfully at the curious scars on his hand. For the first time Gaven noticed that Fathom and Valien bore similar scars.

"Captain. D'you think you'd recognise this mystery man of yours if you saw him again?"
"Well, yes. I mean, yes, definitely. I won't forget that face. He looked right at me."
Rin nodded.
"From your description, Captain, I've a notion just who your traitor might be. But you're the only one who can say for sure. So if you're willin', Captain… I need you to come with us."

oOo

Fulza, Keshet and Joseera sat in a large, square garden in

the centre of the large main building of the village. It was like a little oasis, a tranquil space with many plants and trees, little pools and streams of water. One small door, small by Savage standards at least, led back inside. Around the middle of the garden there were several carved wooden benches on which they now sat, and at their feet, at the heart of it all, a small sun was etched into the stone floor.

The air was warm and quiet, and for the first time in days, Joseera felt relaxed. She pushed off her boots, and leant back, eyes closed, letting the soft sunlight bathe her face.
"Oh, it's beautiful here," she sighed, "whose garden is this?"

Keshet laughed uncomfortably. "Is... yours, Joseera Mayweather, I suppose." he said.
Joseera sat forward and looked at him, wrinkling her nose. "What?" she asked, "What do you mean, mine? I've never even been here before!"

Now it was Fulza who laughed. Keshet looked sharply at him, but Fulza simply turned away, admiring the plants and smiling to himself.

Keshet sniffed and rubbed slowly at his temples. "You forgive me, please, Joseera Mayweather. Although I supported Fulza, sent him out... I... I was not sure what we might find. I hoped, of course, something to support our faith, something we might use to spare our people from conflict. But to find someone as truly... special as you..."
He gave a sideways glance at Fulza, who shrugged lazily.

"Happened just as stories said. No surprise." He looked over at Joseera and gave what she thought was a wink.

"Saw you. Found you. Knew you, girl."
They continued to stare at one another until Keshet interrupted.

"I should explain, Joseera. I will try, best I can."
The old Savage breathed deeply, and looked up at the sky, as if seeking inspiration.
"A long time ago, Joseera, before we can truly know, our stories tell us that the peoples of the world lived together, yours and mine. They were guided by great and wise leaders, known to us as... *Ilo'Seri*."

Joseera's eyebrows raised, and she looked over at Fulza, but he did not return her gaze.

Keshet continued, "For many, many years, there was peace and prosperity, and this was made possible by the Ilo'Seri. They drew upon the power that surrounds us, from the earth, from the sky, what they called Seri-gae. It is said they could see into the hearts of others, that they could bring light and life, that even the sun itself was theirs to command. They ruled with wisdom and honesty."

Joseera leant forward now, intrigued, elbows on knees, face resting in her hands.

"But some of the people grew jealous and greedy. They wanted to take the great power of Seri-gae for themselves, and they worked in secret to do so. The peace was ended, and many great battles were fought. The world was burnt and scarred, the Ilo'Seri disappeared, dead or gone, and the people struggled to survive amongst the ashes.
"A handful of my people, those who had served the Ilo'Seri until the very last, kept safe a few remnants and effects, swore to honour the Ilo'Seri's memory and

remember them in stories passed from one to another.

"So it is we tell these stories, Joseera. The line of the Ilo'Seri was gone, forgotten and lost. But the stories say that in the darkest times, one of our people will venture out into the world, and the last of the Ilo'Seri will be known to him."

Keshet sat quiet for a few moments, looking expectantly at Joseera, who mirrored his expression as if she wasn't certain he had finished. Then, all of a sudden, she seemed to realise what he was suggesting.
"What?! Me?! But... I'm... I mean, I'm just... I'm not-"
"Yes, you Joseera. How else do you explain all that has happened?"

Joseera looked as though she had been slapped. Her mouth moved wordlessly, and she looked helplessly back and forth at Fulza and Keshet. Fulza leant forward, studied her intently.
"Think, girl. In woods, first time we meet. Was first time you see me?"
"What do you mean?" whispered Joseera.
"Saw you girl. Heard your name. In my sleep. In my dreams. Knew you."
Joseera stared at Fulza with a far-off look in her eyes.
"All this time." she murmured softly, "I… I've seen you. Those dreams... It was you."

oOo

Outside the small, sheltered cabin, Sergeant Thurro looked down at Gaven from his saddle. His horse had been fed and watered, and now it stamped the ground idly, eager to move. Thurro gave an unconvincing smile.
"Well Captain, best be on my way. With the bearings and

directions they've given me, should be an easy ride. An' hopefully we'll see you back home in Bantha in a few days, eh?"

Gaven nodded and smiled warmly up at his friend.
"I'll be back as soon as I can, Sergeant, believe me. In the meantime, you get the word to Lord Duma and the others. Maybe put in a request for some leave for me too." he grinned.
Gaven held his hand up, offered it to Thurro, and the older man grasped it fiercely.
"Be safe, Gaven. And be careful. This lot seem alright, but... just watch your back, eh? Come back to Bantha in one piece."
Gaven nodded solemnly.
"You too, Lem. You too."

For a moment the two friends simply stood silent, hands clasped together. Then with a nod, Thurro gave his horse the little encouragement it had been patiently waiting for, and set off for the city. Gaven stood and watched him go for a little while, enjoying the peace, the whisper of the leaves in the wind. For a moment he might have believed all was well with the world.
"Be safe, Lem Thurro." he murmured softly. Then he pulled up the dark hood on his fine green cloak, and turned back towards the little cabin.

oOo

Joseera sat, staring intently into space, in silence. Occasionally she would shake her head just slightly, or raise her eyebrows just a little, and that was enough, despite Keshet's protestations, to convince Fulza there was still work in progress somewhere behind the girl's wide eyes, work that should not be disturbed. So, the two Savages sat, awkwardly, silently also, and waited.

Eventually Joseera seemed to come round, to register the huge figures seated in front of her again, but the distant look did not entirely disappear.
"Am I... who am I?" she said slowly. "I... I don't recognise this person. I don't recognise any of this. Am I... still me? Or... do I have to be someone different now?"

"Well of course Joseera, you must be aware of great responsibility that-" started Keshet, but Fulza's heavy hand grasped his shoulder, accompanied by an equally weighty look, and stopped him in his tracks.
"Same girl." said Fulza, gently, carefully. "Still ask lot of questions. Still little annoying. Same girl."

Joseera gave a desperate little laugh, and smiled shakily at Fulza.
"Tell me something then. One more question. Those men, those soldiers who came to my village. It was because of this, wasn't it? Because of me?"

Again Keshet started, "Joseera, you mustn't-".
But again he was interrupted by Fulza, who said simply, "Yes."
Now it was Keshet's turn to give a look of displeasure.

"I see." replied Joseera plainly. Tears welled in her eyes, but she held her head up, and continued, "What do I do?"

This time Keshet looked to Fulza first, irritably, before replying. "There is a place Joseera. Very old, very special... from the time of the Ilo'Seri themselves. If their secrets lie anywhere, it will be there. It is... difficult journey though. The quickest way is... dangerous to say the least. Aurren'ai Vale... we must prepare you for worst possible..."

Fulza watched Joseera closely as the old Savage spoke, and saw her quicken, jerking breaths clutching at her chest. He rose, suddenly, and raised a hand to silence Keshet, drawing a look of frustrated indignation from his senior before Keshet looked at Joseera, and realised his mistake. With an exasperated sigh, Keshet nodded at Fulza, before standing and straightening his robes.

"Perhaps you need little... time Joseera" he said, awkwardly. "I will leave you alone. Discuss these things little later."
Then the old Savage turned and headed slowly back inside.

Once he had gone, Fulza stepped close to Joseera, and knelt calmly before her. She was biting her lip almost hard enough to draw blood, fists clenched, white, at her sides.
"What do I do?" she mouthed.

Fulza smiled. "First, girl, breathe." he said, softly.
Joseera laughed unsteadily, then nodded, drawing a few deep, ragged breaths, before wiping at her eyes and rubbing her face.

"You trust me, girl?"
"Yes." sniffed Joseera.
"Sometimes, girl, they say I do not think of... future."
He gestured at the bruises on his face with a smile.
"But I say, sometimes best. Forget all else, remember now. So. Want to help me, help family?"
Joseera nodded slowly.

"Want to stop fighting? Want to help all?"
Again, Joseera silently agreed.
The great Savage stood before her. "Then forget rest. We go, together, tonight."
He held out one huge hand, and Joseera took it. The she gasped, loudly, startling Fulza.
"What girl? What is it?"
Joseera looked up at him earnestly. "What about Jubal?"
Fulza threw his head back in a relieved laugh. "Yes! Jubal too! Three of us, together we go."

Joseera smiled. "Thank you, Fulza. Whatever in the Ancients name is going on, thank you. You're... a good friend. Now, tell me, where is it we have to go?"
Fulza looked down at the slight, brave girl in front of him with a frown.

"In your tongue, is called... the Temple of the Dead."

oOo

A short while later, in a secluded part of the village, a small building, little more than a hut, a large, rough pair of hands fumbled with a small glass ball, awkwardly twisting the metal bands that encircled it. A soft light began to bloom in the heart of the sphere, and the rough hands lifted it to a mouth of pointed teeth. The coarse lips struggled with the unfamiliar words.

"The ..girl. Was here. Gone now. He takes her ..to the Temple, certain. But ..was here. Joseera Mayweather was here."

Chapter Fourteen

The first thing that anyone entering the Aurren'ai Vale would notice was the stillness and the silence. One could identify, almost to within a few paces, the point at which the Vale's geography and flora ceased to allow sounds, echoes, breezes from the world outside to enter. It was as if everything outside had simply ceased to be, and many travellers coming to the Vale for the first time would waste a good spell simply pacing back and forth, in and out of the Vale, a look of wonder and confusion on their faces. Then again, a good many travellers turned back altogether at this point and refused to ever set foot in the Vale again.

Fulza, Jubal and Joseera had broken camp early and been moving all morning. They had slipped out of the village late in the evening and despite all Keshet's arguments he had eventually let them go, agreeing that perhaps this was the safest and quickest way. Before they left though, he had presented Joseera with his staff, golden pommel still and solid again as if she had dreamt its opening. She had been uncertain how to receive such a clearly momentous gift, but had tried her best to express her gratitude, even if the significance was lost on her. Now though, she was feeling more grateful than ever, leaning heavily on the thick staff as she reached the top of yet another steep hill and began the descent into the thick woodland beyond.

As Joseera crossed the boundary she gasped, looked around her, eyes wide, and took a few steps back to experience the odd sensation of entering the Vale again. She was just about to turn back for a second time when Fulza caught up with her, and with a slight frown and one large, firm hand pushed her onwards.

"No stopping," he offered, by way of explanation.

"B-but the noise, the *sound*... it's like... well, there isn't..."

"Hmh. Yes. No noise. No sound. No lick of wind. Tricks of the Vale. The trees. The plants. No matter. No stops," he replied, continuing ahead on the path.

Joseera glanced nervously around her once more, then, staying close to Jubal she hurried on after her stoic companion.

The trees and plants of the Aurren'ai Vale grew thickly and the path quickly turned to a track, then to nothing as the forest seemed to crowd around them. For almost an hour they walked at a steady pace in silence. Fulza took the lead, with Joseera trailing a few paces behind, Jubal always at her side, almost as though the great boar could sense her disquiet and wished to provide a little comfort as they moved. Finally they broke through the tree line and came out into a small, grassy clearing. Fulza threw down his pack and began to make camp.

Joseera was glad to feel the sun on her face again, and was about to make comment to that effect, but Fulza stopped her in her tracks.

"No talking," he said gruffly.

"No talking, no chatter. Stay close, make fire, no rest till then," said a rough voice into her ear from just behind her. Joseera started and turned suddenly, then again as she found no-one behind her.

A small twig hit her in the side of the head.

"Make fire!" growled Fulza, although his voice sounded

distant, as if far beyond the trees.

He gestured emphatically at the ground, so Joseera gathered her wits and set about it. Fulza walked a few paces off and for a moment she considered asking him if he planned to help with the hard work, but then she saw him digging around in the various pouches at his belt, a concentrated look on his face, and thought better of it.

Joseera gathered a few pieces of dry wood that lay scattered about the ground nearby and as her brother had taught her as a child, she dug out a small pit in the earth, surrounding it with as many stones as she could find. She broke the wood into suitable lengths and arranged them in a little pyramid, piling the smaller bits and pieces underneath to serve as kindling. As she worked, she watched Fulza curiously. He had collected a mixture of the powders he carried into one great hand and now walked slowly and deliberately around their little camp site, sprinkling a handful of the mixture onto the ground with each step, and muttering quietly to himself.

He appeared not to notice her progress at all and once she had finished her work, she sat silently watching him. While she waited, quietly, her mind drifted back to her final conversation with Keshet, before they had left the village. She turned the words in head, wondering at the strangeness of it all.

The old Savage had not been best pleased when Fulza told him they were leaving alone, that night. Eventually though, Fulza had managed to convince him that it was the safest way, that the three of them could travel unnoticed, and far faster than a large group. Even so, Keshet had insisted on speaking to Joseera alone before she left.

"Firstly, Joseera," he had said, with an almost fatherly affection, "You must promise to listen to Fulza when you reach Aurren'ai Vale. I have taught him all I can to keep you safe, but you should know a little of the place too, Joseera. Stories say that many people used to live there. That it was a lush and fertile place. But when traitors rose against Ilo'seri, Aurren'ai was the first place they struck, as it was seat of Ilo'seri rule. Stories say that those who lived there were unprepared, that many hundreds, maybe thousands, fell victim to usurpers. But even as they stole Ilo'seri's power, twisted Seri-gae to their own ends with terrible devices they had built, the land was corrupted, flooded with the spiteful energies released, and with blood of those who fell. Since that time, stories say Aurren'ai Vale fell silent, and now it plays tricks of its own on those who stray into forest."

Then Keshet had leaned close and Joseera had noticed how tired he seemed. His sunken eyes were heavy with worry.

"Joseera, since you arrived in village, I have spoken with our leaders. They have received word that your people plan to march a great army into heart of our lands, take them from us once and for all, that they gather at place you call Vas Aloron. Almost every one of Savage tribes travels there, to unite, to stop this force before it reaches our homes. There is even a group from this village travelling there now. But it does not make sense, Joseera. Fighting had slowed between our people. Uneasy, perhaps, few problems here and there, but for the most part, we have left each other to our business. Then, few months ago, attacks begin with no warning, from western mountains all the way to eastern sea. Attacks by trained men, skilled fighters, brutal and merciless. Word comes that your people have simply been preparing, waiting, and that soon they will wipe us from the land. So my people fight back. And no-one seems to care why. Yet hundreds will die at Vas Aloron, Joseera, on either side. And if all this is allowed to continue, many more will die. If war is truly allowed to begin again, then it will not matter why or how it started. It will not matter until someone has won. You must travel through the home of Ilo'Seri, Joseera, you must find secrets within the Temple of the Dead. We have little time, and no other hope."

"You certainly seem to be putting a lot of faith in me, Keshet." she had said to the old Savage, "But what if I'm not one of these 'Ilo'Seri'? I don't feel special. What if I don't know what to do?"

Keshet had reached out to her then, and placed his worn hands on her shoulders.
"When attacks started, Fulza's dreams became clearer. For first time, he described your face, could hear your name. This cannot be coincidence, Joseera Mayweather. His belief sent him out into hostile lands, to find you, on the strength of a dream and stories of an old fool such as me. Even I doubted. Ilo'Seri in our stories are not... like you. But he believes in you, Joseera. You must start to believe in yourself."

She had been sat, lost in her thoughts for a full half hour before Fulza finally walked over to join her.

He sat, heavily, on the ground beside her, and began to poke critically at her construction, rearranging the odd stick here and there when he found fault with it. Then Fulza took a small, leather bound parcel from his belt, and opened it to reveal a well used flint and striking stone. With practised ease, he sent showers of tiny sparks into the little bundle of fibres, and once they began to burn, he eased them into the pile of wood, then, blowing and poking here and there, coaxed the fire to life.

When he was satisfied, he turned to Joseera with a weary smile.
"Am sorry, girl. Have to be sure we are safe. This..." he gestured outward at the forest around them, "...dangerous place."

Joseera turned and looked out at the dense trees and vegetation. It had grown steadily darker since they had stopped, and now, in the dusky light, Joseera felt suddenly enclosed by the thick forest. As she turned and looked about, she thought she saw figures, pressed against the tree trunks at the corners of her vision, leaning, peering in at them, though when she turned again to see them she found nothing but plain wood. The more intently she stared, the more she began to see shapes in the bark of the trees themselves, twisted faces, hands, pressing outward from within. She shook her head, and told herself not to be so foolish, that the dim light was playing tricks on her eyes. She pressed closer to the warm bulk of Jubal, ever dependable, who lay snoozing, gently snoring at her side. For a moment, she thought back to the Furrindoun Woods near her village, so long ago now it seemed, and how frightened she had been when her attackers had closed in. It was different now, of course, Fulza was here, and she knew he would protect her, that she would be safe with him.

Joseera turned back to look at Fulza and was unnerved to find him doing just the same, casting about anxiously with his eyes, her nervous expression mirrored on his face. She swallowed, mouth suddenly dry. She couldn't remember seeing him like this, no matter what they had faced before.

"Fulza? What is it? Are you okay?"

His eyes snapped towards her, sharply, almost as though she had said something wrong, but then his face softened, and he nodded.
"Yes. Yes, okay."
He smiled again, and Joseera wondered to herself, surprised that this broad, rough face, the rows of pointed teeth, could make her feel at ease, could give a smile she was as glad as any in the world to see.

"Am sorry, girl, if I scare you. This place... I have never set foot within. Is sacred place. And cursed one."

Joseera watched him closely, waiting quietly for him to go on. He took up a stray stick that lay on the ground beside him, and began to poke absent mindedly at the fire.

"Have given what protection I can," he said, gesturing at the pouches hanging from his belt, "Even at edges of Vale, trees steal voice, play tricks. But... feel... something, out there. Something unfamiliar. And from look of you, girl, you feel it too."

Joseera gave a sudden shudder, as a chill ran up her spine, and she glanced nervously about.

"Know this, girl. I will protect you with all strength I have. Know Jubal will do same."

At the mention of its name, the great boar gave a lazy

snort, and flicked one ear, bringing a smile to both Joseera and Fulza's face for a moment. Joseera gave the beast a friendly scratch. Then her eyebrows furrowed in an expression Fulza had grown to recognise, and he braced himself for the inevitable question that followed.

"You know, Keshet said he had his doubts, before he met me. That the Ilo'Seri in your stories weren't like me. What did he mean by that? Do you think I did something wrong, acted the wrong way?"

Fulza drew a slow, deep breath and studied her for a moment. When he eventually spoke, his voice was soft and thoughtful.
"No, girl. Done nothing wrong. In our stories, Ilo'Seri not like you. Not like your people. In our stories, Ilo'Seri look like mine."

They both sat quietly then. Fulza gently harried the fire, as if searching for answers in the embers. Joseera stared into the glow, and tried to forget the growing dark beyond.

oOo

Sergeant Lem Thurro had ridden as far and as fast as he dared before it was too dark to go on, and had broken camp at first light, continuing his journey just as swiftly. It was partly a sense of duty and urgency that drove him to ride as hard as he did, but also the sense that as long as he pushed, as long as he focused on nothing but the task at hand, then his mind would not wander and he would not think about his fear, for his friends, for his home, for himself. So he rode, legs burning, arms aching, as his horse sweat and thundered beneath him. When he saw the shapes of Bantha, the familiar jumble of odd spires and peaks growing in the distance, both man and horse felt the inspiring surge of a journey almost ended, and somehow found a last burst of speed.

A short while later, Thurro handed the reins of his horse over to one of the stable lads outside the city gates.
"Now take good care of him, lad," he said, as he handed over a few more coins than strictly necessary, "He's worked bloody hard, so see he gets a good rub down and a good feed, 'stead of that muck you usually give 'em, eh? And as for the rest... well, you know what to do."

The boy looked wide-eyed at the generous payment piled in his hand and nodded with solemn enthusiasm.
"Yessir! I'll take proper good care of 'im, sir! 'Ave 'im all rested and ready by the time you gets back sir! An' don't worry 'bout the rest sir! I'll take care of it sir, no problem! Thank you, sir!"

As the boy continued to call his gratitude, Thurro trudged on, up the broad slope that led the last short distance to the city gates, waving his hand over his head in acknowledgement of the boy's thanks without turning back. 'Sometime soon,' he thought to himself as he forced his aching legs to keep plodding forward, 'I'll find someone to give me a nice rub down an' all. An' hopefully someone a mite prettier than my young friend back there.'

Finally Sergeant Thurro stood looking up at the vast wooden doors that were the city's east gate. A wave of relief took him by surprise, almost bringing tears to his eyes, and requiring several deep breaths and noisy clearings of throat before he managed to regain his composure. He was home.

Once he had gathered himself, Thurro walked over to the smaller guard gate to the side of the main gates, a narrow, heavy construction of studded wood and thick iron bands, with a tiny hatch at around face height. Thurro gave three firm knocks and had to wait only a moment before the little hatch snapped open and an unfamiliar, frowning face peered out.
"Yes?" it asked, abruptly.
Thurro was taken aback. "Oh, er... hello... er, who are you? Where's Tinley?"
The face looked unimpressed. "'E's not 'ere. But I'm not the one knockin' on the bleedin' 'atch, am I? So more to the point, who in the Ancients name are you?"
"Ah... er, right. It's just it's usually.. well, anyhow..." Thurro cleared his throat and adjusted his uniform. "Sergeant Lem Thurro, Imperial Guard. Returnin' with urgent reports for the Three."

Thurro stood and waited patiently while the face cast a suspicious eye over his battered uniform, the stripes and insignia on his arms. Finally, with one last look of general disapproval for good measure, the face gave a curt nod.
"All right then. S'pose you better come through."
The hatch snapped shut and after the clatter of bolts and locks subsided, the door swung open a way, just enough for Sergeant Thurro to squeeze inside.

The disapproving face, it transpired, belonged to the equally disapproving body of Frankin Cuttle, an ageing Guardsman from the Keepers Tower, transferred to the gate from his usual quiet post in the Tower archives, and clearly none too pleased about it. Thurro was at least faintly reassured to see that the man's frown was apparently a perpetual expression of general disapproval with the world at large, and not something directed at

Thurro alone. He asked Cuttle what had happened to Tinley, the young soldier he had expected to find on the door.

"Hah. Off to Vas Aloron wi' the rest of 'em I should think. Practic'lly every feller capable of swingin' a sword 'as gone off. Imperial Guard, City Militia, army, whole lot of 'em. Left all the rest of the work to the likes of us." he sniffed. "Anyhow. You wait 'ere. I 'ave to go and find someone to take responsibility for lettin' you in t' the city..." Cuttle gestured to a simple chair in the corner of the tiny, square gate room, and then banged wearily on the door leading deeper into the city walls. "...since they don't seem to think I know what's what, and all that, 'spite the fact that I been serving since 'fore they was crawlin'..."

As Cuttle continued to mutter his long list of grievances, another hatch snapped open and shut, the door clicked open to let Cuttle through, then Thurro was alone.

It was only a few moments before the door opened again and Thurro was joined by two more unfamiliar men in uniform. The younger of the two, an earnest looking blonde fellow, stood smartly to attention against the wall inside, and eyed Thurro with zealous intensity. His companion, an older man with jet black hair and a probing eye, stood before Thurro, hands clasped behind his back.

"So... Sergeant...uh..." began the dark haired man.
"Ah – Thurro, sir. Sergeant Lem Thurro. Imperial Guard, 1st Keep Battalion, sir."
"Ye-es. Sergeant Thurro." continued the other, "Well, Sergeant, I am Commander Gensu. I'm afraid I must apologise for the confusion at the moment, Sergeant. Unfortunately most forces have been mobilised to Vas Aloron. Presently, that leaves me as the senior officer here."

"Oh, I see. Very good, sir." said Thurro, uncomfortably.
"Now, Sergeant, I understand you have an urgent message for Lord Duma, correct? So, if you'd like to explain it to me, I'll make sure it reaches him as quickly as possible. In the meantime, we'll see that you get some hot food and a good ale, Sergeant, you look exhausted, man!"

Thurro opened his mouth as if to speak, then closed it again. His eyes jumped between Gensu's steady gaze and the pips of office on the Commander's arm. He cleared his throat unhappily.
"Uh-hm... If you don't mind, sir, I think... uh... I think I'm s'posed to deliver this message myself. Sir."

Commander Gensu said nothing for what seemed to Thurro like a very long time indeed. Instead he just stared plainly at the Sergeant, lips pursed, before nodding silently. Then abruptly, he gave a broad smile.
"Well, Sergeant, I suppose it's nice to see a commitment to your duty! Seeing it through to the bitter end. Understandable, of course. Very well, Sergeant, very well."
Thurro gave a sigh of relief.
"Thank you, sir. No disrespect meant, sir, of course. It's just, I was given very particular instructions, sir, you know how it is."
"Of course, Sergeant, of course." laughed Gensu. "But I'm afraid you'll have to excuse me, in that case. I am, as you can imagine, in great demand at present! Lieutenant Ripfer here will see that you get what's needed."

The Commander turned and nodded at the blonde haired man waiting stiffly by the wall, who saluted sharply in response. Then, with one last smile in Thurro's direction, he was gone.

The blonde man stepped smartly forward and held out a hand to Thurro.

"Lieutenant Kai Ripfer, Sergeant, at your service. Now, would you like to clean up first, or would you rather get straight down to business?"

Thurro shook Ripfer's hand gladly. He had never enjoyed dealing with officers, and was relieved that the Commander had been so agreeable.

"Nice to meet you, Lieutenant. I'd be happy if we could just get everything sorted out first."

Ripfer responded with a bright grin.

"Very good, Sergeant." he said. He pulled open the narrow door leading on into the city, and gestured for Thurro to head through.

"After you, Sergeant. After you."

Chapter Fifteen

Joseera awoke slowly, not because of any disturbance, but because she was so cold. It took her a few seconds to remember exactly where she was, and it was still too dark to see very much. She reached one hand down to pull up the rough blanket she had been covered by, and with the other stretched out for Jubal's warm bulk. She found neither.

Blinking, still not entirely awake, Joseera lifted her head to look around. There was no sign of the fire that had still been gently burning when she fell asleep. There was no sign of the clearing where they had made camp. And there was no sign of Fulza. Instead, she found herself surrounded by dark leaves and vegetation on all sides.

Joseera came to her senses very suddenly then, but she surprised herself by staying quite calm. Breathing slowly, as deeply as she could, she checked carefully around her. She still had all of her own possessions it seemed, and the rough blanket lay on the earth by her feet, as though she had simply kicked it off herself while sleeping. At her side she found the staff Keshet had given her, pommel curiously bright in the forest darkness. It gave her a little soft light to see by, and she stared briefly at it in wonder, almost forgetting her situation. Then, steadily, she got to her feet and began to consider her options.

As she peered into the thick wood surrounding her, she could discern no particular path, could not make out a clear way to head if she moved off. So instead, she stayed put, leaning on the staff she was becoming quickly fond of, and thought. Somehow the smooth, heavy wood beneath her fingers helped her think, helped her focus. The gentle glimmer from the etched golden ball atop the staff, soft and warm, somehow made her feel safer, kept her calm. She thought back to the beginning of her journey and how often tears and panic had gripped her then. It seemed almost like a dream now, as she stood there alone. If only I could have seen myself, she thought. Perhaps it would have given me strength to know how much braver I'd become.

Then, abruptly, she screamed out loud.

From the corner of her eye she had seen movement, a figure right there in the trees beside her. She half turned, half stumbled away from them, raising her staff defensively before her, heart suddenly galloping in her chest. She stood, tense, breath rushing in her throat.

Nothing.

Trees, wood and darkness. But as she stood, frozen, she noticed that... yes, there was a shape, misshapen wood, vaguely person-like. She laughed, nervously at herself. Oh yes, how much braver she'd become...

The twisted trunk of the tree before her lent itself, in the dull light, to a ripe imagination. Two bulging knots in its bark offered themselves as a head and perhaps a protruding shoulder, the larger of the two even having a convenient hole to serve as a mouth, mid shout. A drooping branch, splayed shoots at its end, served as an arm, gently reaching as the branch shifted and swayed. Joseera gave a sigh of relief. At least Fulza wasn't here to see how silly she'd been, like a child at bedtime, jumping at shadows. The dark, she thought to herself. Unfamiliar surroundings. Her eyes playing tricks on her.

She had just begun to gather herself, to steady her breathing and rally her nerves, when it happened again. Someone, something, a presence right there beside her. She turned, her reaction more measured this time, and as she half expected, she found nothing before her, no-one waiting, lurking there in the darkness. Just a tree, quiet and still, branches spread wide, roots like long legs, buried in the cool earth.

When she felt it the third time, Joseera did not turn fully, instead looking sharply over her shoulder at the empty space, the trees stood patiently beyond. Still the feeling persisted, and she felt the hot rush of sudden shock being steadily replaced by the icy grip of a real and growing fear. Her hands tightened, knuckles white against the dark wood of her staff as she fought for control of her feelings.

"*Joseera.*"

A voice, a word on the wind, like the rustle of leaves, so faint that even in the same moment she wasn't certain she had heard anything at all. The adrenaline, perhaps, the fear. Her ears playing tricks on her.

"*Joseera.*"

It came again and her fears became firm. One voice at first, from elsewhere this time, then joined by another, and another, and another, still another, until it seemed that every whispering breeze, every branch, every leaf in the deathly silence of the forest was screaming her name in the stillness as the motionless trees pressed inward.

She stood there alone in the quiet and the darkness, clinging to her staff to keep her upright. Eyes tight shut, teeth clenched, face contorted as the noise in her head continued to grow.

Her eyes playing tricks on her. Her ears playing tricks on her. What was it Fulza had said? The Vale plays tricks of its own.

oOo

Lem Thurro had not, in his opinion, led a particularly remarkable life. Those who knew him, however, might well have disagreed, and with good reason. He had come to Bantha as a young man, little more that a boy in truth, from the Norfen town of Buckweald. His family were butchers, but Lem, like so many young men, had rebelled against a simple life in the family business, and drawn by the promise of adventure and excitement, had come to the city to find his own way. Upon his arrival, the city had quickly brought him back down to earth. Life was difficult and expensive for a young lad with no friends and no prospects, and Lem had spent the better part of a year learning a healthy respect for hard work and small kindnesses. When the campaign against the Savage tribes in the north had started, Lem's ideas of adventure once again got the better of him. Since then his service had seen him through two more wars, taken him across the Empire from the mountains to the Eastern Sea, over the waters to the wilds of the Silund and back. There were few who could say they had seen so much or travelled so far.

None of this mattered to Lieutenant Ripfer. Commander Gensu seemed to think that he enjoyed his work too much, but Ripfer really didn't see the problem. He *did* enjoy his work. While others fussed and puffed and pondered in bureaucracy around him, Ripfer liked to think of himself as a man of action. He got things done. And as a matter of fact he had just such a thing to do now.

"After you, Sergeant, after you." he said, holding the door open for the old fool and waving him through.

The instant that Thurro stepped into the doorway and presented his broad back to the Lieutenant, Ripfer made his move. His left hand slipped over Thurro's left shoulder and under his chin, lifting his head and taking a firm grip on his throat. At the same time the Lieutenant's right hand went to the long, narrow dagger at his belt, and brought it fluidly forth, driving it hilt deep into Thurro's back just below the shoulder blade in one continuous motion. The point travelled through Thurro's chest at an angle, piercing his lungs and heart before the very tip poked from his breast.

Thurro shook and convulsed as his body fought for breath that would not come, clutching helplessly at the searing pain in his chest. He felt himself falling gently backwards, then felt hands upon his shoulders lowering him to the floor. Above him, upside down, he saw the blonde haired man smiling down at him. He tried to speak, but found his mouth and nose filled with hot tarry blood, and choked instead.

The blonde haired man laughed. "I'm sorry, Sergeant, I didn't quite catch that!"
He crouched down, his fair hair and cold smile swimming in Thurro's vision, dancing in black and purple clouds.
"I'm afraid we've got plans for Bantha, Sergeant. And we don't need the likes of you running around spreading all

sorts of rumours and gossip, see? Still, I don't think that will be a problem now, Sergeant, will it? Seems to me you've forgotten what it was you wanted to say."

Lem Thurro wasn't really listening anymore. He thought of a girl he had known, a long time ago, and a laugh that made him smile without knowing why. He thought of his friends and hoped they were safe, and that they would forgive him for letting them down. And then, Lem Thurro was gone.

Outside the gates, the stable lad looked through the small bag the old Sergeant had given him. The coin was all for him, the Sergeant had said, more than the lad saw in a month, if he took good care of the Sergeant's horse. Oh, and one other task, simple enough. There was a note, tucked into the saddlebag. He wasn't to read it, the Sergeant had said, although truth be told the lad didn't know how, just to see that it got to Lord Duma's stable hand. He'd know what to do with it, the Sergeant had said. With a shrug, and a comforting jingle in his pocket, the lad set off.

oOo

Fulza spun furiously in the darkness. He could just make out the shape of the trees and branches surrounding him, but nothing more, and every instinct he possessed was telling him nothing was right here. Most importantly of all, there was no sign of Joseera. He roared and bellowed her name into the black, turning about, not daring to move lest it should be in the wrong direction, away from her. Then, suddenly, in the distance through the trees, he thought he saw her. It was brief, just a flash of soft blue, the cloak that she wore, but he plunged into the darkness anyway, in case she should wander any further. Strength flaring in desperation, he crashed powerfully through the trees, shattering branches and splintering bark in his fury, but for every spindly limb that he knocked aside, a dozen more took its place, smothering, twisting and pulling at him. He turned to free his wrist where it had become caught up, and saw another faint flash of blue somewhere off to his left. He struggled to turn, but the branches pushed back, trapping and wrapping his arms, holding him firmer and faster the harder he fought.

Eventually in a cocoon of vine and thick wood, he found himself unable to move at all. You promised, he thought to himself. You promised to protect her. He roared out her name until the trees shook.

oOo

There had been silence in the dusty cell for some time. Juna and Parvel Mayweather sat quietly on one side of the wide table, arms wrapped around one another, while Elder Jarry sat alone on the other, one hand rubbing insistently at his temples.

"Look, Parvel, Juna…"
"That's enough, Jarry. There's nothing more to say." said Parvel, flatly.

There was a noise from the corner of the room, as the huge frame of Tutty Cooksharp rose and stood. The big man turned to face the others, his soft face wet with tears.
"He's dead." he said, to no-one in particular, "They killed him."
Parvel quickly skirted the table and knelt beside the form of Elder Vithru. He checked at his wrist, his neck, his

mouth. There was no sign of life.

"Tutty's right," said Parvel, turning back to face the others, "He's gone. I guess... I guess he was just a little too frail to recover from such a beating."

Juna's hands covered her mouth as fresh tears welled in her eyes. Jarry stood, slowly, shaking his head. "I'm sorry, Tutty, I'm so sorry. He was as good as a father to you, I know..."

Tutty looked down at Vithru's body, then at Jarry. "They killed him." he said again. His eyes travelled over to the thick wooden door of the room, and his huge hands curled into fat, heavy fists.

"It's time to go now." he said.

oOo

Joseera knelt, staff planted before her, eyes closed, forehead pressed against the cool wood. She trembled slightly and gave an occasional whimper through her juddering breath. Save this, the air was deathly quiet and solemnly still.

Bright coloured explosions, flashes of pain danced before Joseera's eyes as the voices grew impossibly louder, whirling and spinning about her as she felt the dry branches flail and grasp at her skin.

"*ComewithusbewithusstaywithusJoseeracomewithusbewithusstaywithus...*"

The sound was a screaming roar in her head, ever increasing even as she thought it could be no louder, grow no greater, somehow the noise expanded, doubled and redoubled itself endlessly.

"ComewithusbewithuspleaseJoseerastaywithusJoseeraplease..."

Her skin burned, and she pulled herself tighter in as the limbs of the trees whipped and pulled at her, clawing and begging, desperate to draw her in. In agony, head pounding and eyes streaming, Joseera tipped back her head and peered up, along the length of the staff at the sky above, praying for something, anything, to relieve her, to swoop down and save her before she tipped into madness.

"Comewithusstaywithusbewithuscomewithusbewithus..."

She saw something odd.

The round, golden pommel at the top of the staff was still glowing, glimmering soft and warm in the darkness. Joseera looked at the gentle light and felt suddenly calm. The terrible noise, the rushing trees were still there, but somehow... distant, pushed into the background.

"Comewithusbewithusstaywithus..."

She fixed her eyes on the glow, but there was still something... something strange about the light that she couldn't quite put her finger on. Then it hit her. The light wasn't coming from the staff.

"Comewithusbewithuspleasestaywithus..."

As she stared and wondered, something else caught her attention. With the sound and the chaos around her dampened, she could hear another voice, something else calling her name, although this one wasn't like the others. This voice was rough and ragged, hoarse. This was a voice that she knew.

"*Comewithusstaywithusbewithus...*"

Calmly, Joseera stood up.

"*Comewithusstaywithusbewithusplease...*"

She listened to the thunderous noise, and looked down about her at the thin branches and leaves brushing her skin.

"*Comewithusbewithusstay...*"

She looked up into the night sky, and felt the warmth of the sun on her face.

"*Comewithuspleasestay...*"

"No." she said.

Joseera took a deep breath of relief and looked around the camp site in the bright morning light. The sky was a clear, vibrant blue, and the sun's rays danced on the top of her staff, warm glow reflected in the gold.

A few feet away, Fulza stood, heavy arms windmilling dangerously through the air, eyes wide with panic as he roared, "Joseera! Joseera! Jos-"
He stopped, abruptly, frozen in place when he saw her. Joseera couldn't help laughing out loud at the sight as he stood, arms outstretched, with a bewildered expression.

Fulza frowned, then self-consciously lowered his arms, before stepping towards her.

"Girl. You're okay."
Joseera smiled. "We're all okay." she said, happily, and looked down to Jubal. The great boar stirred in confusion and cast an accusatory look at the pair, as if to demand an explanation for such an interruption so early in the morning. When none was forthcoming, Jubal stood to stretch and yawn, shaking off the memory of a most peculiar dream.

Fulza placed one huge hand gently on Joseera's shoulder. "Girl. We must go. Not safe he-"
"Not yet, Fulza," interrupted Joseera, "you and Jubal wait here. I won't be long."
She turned and walked back towards the tree line.
"Girl!" started Fulza.
"I won't be long! I just have a couple of things to take care of!" she called back, "Get the camp packed up, we can leave as soon as I get back!"
The she disappeared into the trees.

For a long moment Fulza did nothing but stand and stare after Joseera. He was brought round by Jubal rolling one of the packs over, nudging it against Fulza's leg. Fulza looked down at the boar, then back off into the woods. With a shrug, he started packing.

She had been gone for little more than a quarter hour, when he was disturbed by a commotion, some way off in the forest. As he looked up in concern at the sudden swish and rustle, Fulza was amazed to see a graceful flock of delicate birds rising from the canopy. They lifted, swiftly, into the sky, gossamer wings shining gold and white in the bright sun.

Fulza stood, enchanted. He watched them wheel and soar

higher and higher, until he could no longer see them at all. When Joseera returned a little while later, smiling as she emerged from the thick trees, she found him still standing there, staring up into the sky.

Chapter Sixteen

In a quiet field some way to the north, the morning found all was well and peaceful. A handful of green and blue wild birds, called Tooroos after the song they made, sat in the wide old tree at the corner of the field and welcomed the new day. It was warm now, but a soft dew remained on the long, untended grass giving it a frosted look. A gentle breeze drifted playfully through the flowers and long stalks. Had anyone sat there at that time, in the fresh morning, they might have been forgiven for believing all was well with the world.

If there had been anyone sat there at that time, the first odd thing they would have noticed was the birdsong ceasing. The Tooroos all fell quiet, sitting quite still on their perches in the broad tree. The field began to sparkle. A hundred thousand dewdrops danced and shuddered where they sat, or else fell to the earth, glittering and twinkling as they went. The leaves whispered a rhythm on the branches, in time with the vibration in the earth. And if there had been anyone sat there at that time, and even if they had not noticed any one of these odd things, they would certainly have heard the growing sound, coming slowly closer.

Thung. Thung. Thung.

The colossal figure approached steadily, each step covering a dozen metres or more. Its pace was measured, the giant showed no signs of hurry. The bright morning light flashed and shone on the great golden body, picking out the odd markings carved there, and scattering bright flashes across the grass.

When the giant reached the boundary of the field, the youngest and most foolish of the little green and blue birds could not resist taking to the air for a closer look, and despite the frantic chirping of his companions, wheeled in tight circles around the giant. Emboldened by his excitement, he flew closer and closer still, finally alighting on the giant's crested shoulder.

The giant stopped. Slowly, the great head turned to face the little bird. The morning held its breath. The little Tooroo could not have flown away even if it had tried, transfixed as it was by the two dark eye holes in the giant's metal face, deep and mesmerising. Somewhere, deep, deep within that utter blackness, there was a tiny glow of golden light.

For a minute or more they remained that way, bird and behemoth. The grass dared not sway, the leaves dared not rustle. Then, without warning, the giant strode on, impassive face turning into the distance once again. The little Tooroo leapt into the air, and flew hurriedly back to the safety of the old tree, where for today at least he would sing a very different song. Before long, the golden giant was a distant shape, flashing gold in the sunlight as it went. But the distant footsteps could still be heard as it moved.

Thung. Thung. Thung.

On the shores of the Kursfell lake far to the east, the waters surged onto the land, as if desperate to escape the confines of the lake itself. A roiling wave tumbled ahead of the glittering figure at the centre of the lake, as it strode implacably through the water, submerged to the chest but travelling just as steadily as though it were on dry land.

In the vast forest of the Timark to the the southwest, several woodsmen would tell the terrified people of their villages, after a few ales, how they had seen a giant, clad in golden armour, striding through the forest in the distance, head and shoulders clear of the treetops.

On the steep slopes of the Long Hills, a lone golden figure walked tirelessly upwards through the sharp rocks and shale, its great footsteps the only sound in the cool air. Once it had passed, the air was still again, and the hills were silent.

oOo

There was no such peace north of the Fold. The wide, grassy plains to the south of the Vas Aloron pass were filled with the armies of the Empire. They sat at the mouth of the narrow corridor, rugged slopes of the Long Hills rising sharply on either side. Everywhere, the air was filled with bustle and chatter, hundreds of men wandering to and fro, tents of all shapes and sizes surrounded and filled with drinking, talking, sharpening and planning. With no time to marshal troops together, to create cohesive units, it was a somewhat messy affair, scattered bands and groups of men all having answered the call to arms. By far the most organised and numerous were the soldiers of Bantha, and by the authority of the Three, their General, a leathery old man by the name of Tarrett, had taken overall command of the Imperial forces. Powerfully built, even now, with bright blue eyes made all the more striking by his pale white hair and moustache, Tarrett was doing his best to give the men some sense of unity, to provide at least a little focus, but he was faced with a difficult task. A great number of the men were not professional soldiers, but rather carpenters, shopkeepers and the like, those who bore arms only when the need arose. Despite anything the General could say or do, these men knew little about controlling their fear, and it was fear that gripped them now.

Some way in the distance on the other side of the pass, beyond the steep sides their enemy gathered. Too far off to see clearly, but close enough to make out hundreds upon hundreds of huge Savages. While the trained men set their jaws and readied their weapons, they could not entirely escape the whispers and murmurs of the others, passing on stories of a single Savage tearing people in half bare handed, their terrible wolves and beasts clawing their way through dozens of armed men. When the cold wind blew through the pass, the whispers would fall silent for a moment, and the roars and jeering howls of the enemy were carried to them on the wind, which was worse.

General Tarrett was just in the process of dividing up squads of trained soldiers to head each group of militia, in the hope that this would provide some discipline and guidance to each unit, when the cry went up.

Two lone Savages, unaccompanied by even their beasts, were making their way through the pass towards them, weapons held out in front, handles towards their enemy, in the Savage sign of truce. The men went silent after the initial babble died down, all watching the progress of the two broad figures.

Hurriedly, General Tarrett mounted his horse and called three of his commanders and a handful of guardsmen over to join him. Once they had regained their composure, they rode slowly out into the pass, away from the ranks of their men, and waited anxiously for the Savages to reach them, to hear what message they might bear.

The Savages approached slowly, cautiously. The men could not read the expressions on their animal faces, but they moved calmly and their weapons remained steadfastly out before them. One of the guardsmen, smooth-faced and certain, gave a snort of disapproval.

"Hn. Don't know what in the Ancients name these things could have to say that I'd be interested in hearing. We should start with this pair, then cut down the bloody rest of 'em an' all."

General Tarrett gave the man a withering look, learned from years of command. The guardsman tried to hold on to his arrogant air, but couldn't quite manage it and shrunk a little in his saddle.

"What's your name, soldier?" asked Tarrett.

"Uh... hn. It's Hant, sir." replied the guardsman, slowly.

"I see. And did I ask for your opinion, Mr. Hant?" Tarrett continued.

"Well... no, sir, but I-"

"Did I give you leave to speak, Mr. Hant?"

"No, sir."

"No sir. And yet here you are, sharing your unwanted opinions nonetheless. So let me ask you a question, Mr. Hant. If we were to attack, right now, throw everything we've got at these creatures, what do you think would happen?"

Hant faltered. "I... Well, sir.. I-"

"Some of these men, Mr. Hant, have never used a sword to cut down anything more than a few weeds. So if there is a chance, Mr. Hant, a hope of an alternative to sending them to be torn apart, then I for one will be very interested in hearing what these creatures have to say."

Hant sat silent, cowed, on his horse, while the General turned away to stare back out at the approaching figures.

"I fought these creatures the last time," he said softly, "and one thing we can be sure of. Even if we manage to beat them here, even if we succeed in holding the pass... they won't go down without a fight."

The General turned to look at the men waiting alongside him. "Make no mistake. If we cross swords with these Savages today, the price will be heavy, and we'll pay it in blood."

oOo

Jen Cullen was deeply unhappy. A feeling, he reflected miserably, that had started more or less straight after he had first run into Glass and Glower, and persisted more or less continuously up to the present moment.

True, his life had not been perfect before, but he had carved a place for himself, had been respected, feared even, and he had been in control. Now he found he was afraid to do so much as speak without being instructed to. And as for poor Pash... Cullen had always thought him a little too talkative, but that would never be an issue again after what they had done to him.

The real problem was things seemed to be getting worse. Being sent running all over the place, digging out their strange treasures, mysterious objects with an unpleasant air, that had been bad enough. But at least they had been able to do things their own way. The man he and Pash had been sent to serve now was a humourless devil, and he treated Cullen and Pash like slaves, animals, responding swiftly and harshly should they ever question their master. He was known as Aleph, Seeker Prime, the very finest the

Order of Keepers had to offer. Cullen, who had met many unpleasant individuals in his life and line of work, was terrified by him.

The Seeker Prime dressed plainly, in functional but fine leather and light mail, with a heavy black cloak and broad hood. He and his fellow Seekers were armed to the teeth, but as far as Cullen could tell this was just a precaution, as not one of the five of them had drawn a weapon of any kind on their journey so far, despite the fact that they had taken out any Empire patrols they had come across. When they ran into a scouting force of a dozen men, Cullen had hoped for a moment that he might escape, but the Seekers had responded calmly when challenged for identification, then attacked without warning, striking out with deadly force, turning any weapon unsheathed against its owner. As they had neared their destination they had encountered three Savages, and Cullen had thought all their troubles might come to a brutal end together, but the Seekers slaughtered them coolly and precisely, without comment, which frightened Cullen more than he had thought possible.

And now, here he found himself, scrabbling through the darkness behind Pash, one failing torch to light their way as they stumbled along the cold corridors. Given the choice upon seeing the strange building, half-buried in the sand and dust, with its crazed points and spires protruding like the spines of some great creature, Cullen would have turned back and kept running until he was safely home in Bantha. As it was, the Seeker Prime was at his back, so here he found himself, he and Pash, sent in to scout the way, or more likely to spring the traps.

They had been crawling in almost complete darkness for

what seemed like an hour or more, when Cullen, who had grown tired of trying to see where he was going some while ago and had long given up looking, ran into the back of Pash. He was about to make an irritated complaint, but as he raised his head to speak he caught sight of what had stopped Pash in his tracks, and stayed silent instead.

Before them the narrow stone corridor opened out into a vast, vaulted chamber. High in the curved ceiling above, they could see an opening, letting in faint traces of daylight. At the centre of the chamber, in the dim wash of pale light, they could make out a skeletal figure hunched on the steps at the foot of a simple stone plinth, head bowed.

Pash looked questioningly at Cullen, but before they could decide on a course of action, the withered figure lifted its head and looked towards them.
"Ahhh... at lassst... come innn... come in."
Its voice was a dry, dead sound, all shifting ash and paper, and it seemed to lack the strength to even stand. Cullen wondered how long it had been trapped in here. He took a few cautious steps towards the creature.

The creature's skin hung from it like old cloth, and its clouded eyes swam lazily, but it seemed to know where Cullen was well enough. It gave him what he thought must be a smile of some kind, before beckoning to him with one wasted hand.
"Yesss... come..." it gasped, "Time heeeere... at last... Ancientssss come..."

Cullen took another step, and was glad to feel Pash stood beside him.

"What d'you mean, 'Ancients'? We're no Ancients. What is this place? Who are you?"
The creature laughed, like a gentle desert wind.
"No Ancients, no... but... touched by them... This day is done... No need.. to ssstay in darkness now... Come.. come innnn to the light..."

Cullen and Pash shared a glance, then looked back at the helpless, crumpled thing on the steps. They walked slowly forwards until they stood next to the creature in the fading light from above. The creature raised its head gently to meet them, and gave another arid smile.

Pash grabbed Cullen's arm suddenly, making him jump, and turned to look at him, eyes wide with amazement.
"Jen... Jen! Ancients be praised, Jen, it's a miracle!" he gestured madly at his mouth, "I can speak, Jen! A bloody miracle! I can-"
He was cut short with an almost comically blank expression on his face by a crossbow bolt, which pierced his head at the temple and buried itself deep in his skull. For a moment he stood, blinking and gasping, then he toppled lifelessly backwards.

Cullen barely had time to register his surprise before watching Pash fall, horrified. He turned towards the narrow entrance to the great chamber to see Aleph, Seeker Prime, striding purposefully forth, crossbow rising again. He managed a desperate "No!", before the second bolt stuck him solidly in the chest.

It was like walking into a wall. He heaved for breath but found there was no air to be had. His face creased in frustration for a moment, then Jen Cullen fell to the floor, dead.

Aleph continued forward, reloading the crossbow with calm assurance, the rest of the Seekers close behind.
"Your services are no longer required, Mr. Cullen." he said, with a thin smile.

The creature at the steps, if it was afraid, did not show it. Instead it sighed and raised its head towards the Seeker Prime.
"Of coursssse... Shadows, always clossse... None left who remember now... None but me..."
Aleph looked critically at the wasted creature.
"How utterly pathetic." he said.

With what seemed a supreme effort of will, the creature hauled itself to its feet, and shuffled painfully towards Aleph.
"And you... my friend..." it said, insistent, "Good or bad, this day isss done... There isss one more thing... you mussst do..."
Aleph cocked his head curiously.
"I think you may be right there." he said. He fired his crossbow again.

At such close range, Aleph's aim was infallible, and the bolt hit home, striking the creature squarely in the breast with a dry crack. And with a dusty puff it flew cleanly out the other side, clattering on the stone steps of the plinth.

Aleph raised his eyebrows appreciatively. It was rare that the Seekers encountered something they had not anticipated. Unfazed, Aleph stepped forward.
"Very well." he said, and even as the creature reached out to him, smiling weakly, Aleph took a firm grip on its arm. He did not, however, have the chance to exact his violent

technique. As his hand closed firmly on the creature's skin, he saw a flutter of pain cross its papery face, and then it smiled more broadly than ever. Without a sound, the dry lips mouthed a single word.
'Sunrise.'
Then the creature crumbled, leaving nothing more than a pile of dust and ash before him.

Aleph frowned.
"Now that *was* unusual." he said, thoughtfully. He looked to the other Seekers, and gestured to the bodies of Pash and Cullen, and to the pile of ash. "Check them. We don't need any more witchery."

As the others did as he commanded, Aleph stepped up to the plinth and examined the twisted golden object that lay submerged in clear water in the shallow recess on top. He smiled. Then he pulled a speaking globe from his belt and twisted the metal bands to the appropriate position.
"Yes, Master, it's here, just as you said it would be."
Aleph paused for a moment, light from the globe flickering.
"Yes, Master, I have everything I need. The Three will not be a problem."

oOo

General Tarrett and his men waited in anxious silence as the two Savages drew ever closer through the pass. When they were almost close enough to hail, the General saw a flicker of movement in the rock above them on the hillside, and his instincts flared, a desperate sense that something was amiss. Even as his arm rose in alarm, as the words of warning were still forming in his mouth, he saw a handful of men in dark cloaks and leathers break cover, high on the side of the pass, and loose a volley of arrows at the two Savages below. The Savages were dead before they hit the ground.

Arm fixed in the air, voice frozen in his throat, General Tarrett heard, with terrifying clarity, the roar of fury go up.

oOo

Relentless, with singular purpose, the giant strode tirelessly onwards. In the rugged flats of the Switch, the day was peaceful, save the faint, rhythmic sound.

Thung. Thung. Thung.

Chapter Seventeen

They had broken clear of the thick woods of the Vale some time around noon. Now in the warmth of late afternoon, the sun sat fat and lazy in the sky as Joseera, Jubal and Fulza trudged steadily on. The vegetation had thinned as they progressed and now they marched through dry dirt and rock, yellow-brown monotony of the landscape broken only by the occasional pioneering weed or scrub. They walked silently, in the kind of dogged trance a prolonged journey inspires.

It was Jubal who broke the peace. The great boar stopped moving so suddenly that Joseera, following close behind and paying little attention, busy considering what had happened in the Vale, almost tumbled right over him. Jubal ignored her though, instead snorting and sniffing urgently ahead. Fulza drew up behind them and found Joseera squinting into the distance and shaking her head.

"I don't know what it is." she said with a shrug. "Something is bothering Jubal, but I can't see anything."
Fulza smiled. "Maybe see more than him. Pigs not known for good eyes. But smell... smell something long before see it."

He leant forward and put a hand gently on the boar's back, and in response Jubal turned to look at Fulza, before scraping at the ground and flicking his snout repeatedly into the distance.
Fulza looked grim. "Someone coming." he said. "Riders. Horses."

Sure enough, a few minutes later they saw several hooded

figures appear from the jutting rocks ahead. From where she now lay, pressed flat in the powdery dirt, Joseera watched the horses pick their way through the rocks, weaving steadily closer. There were six riders in all, and although it was difficult to discern any further details, Joseera could see bumps and bulges that suggested the riders were well armed. She turned her head to Fulza, who lay low beside her.

"They're coming this way." she whispered.

Even as she spoke the riders halted, as the one in the lead signalled something to his companions. Quickly they moved their horses back the way they'd come a little, before one of the group dismounted and moved off to the side, disappearing amongst the rocks.

"Not good." grunted Fulza. "Perhaps smell us too."
A deep frown creased his heavy forehead, and the sharp teeth were bared.
"What should we do?" asked Joseera tentatively, "Do we show ourselves?"
"No girl." came the answer, "Know their dress. Men of Empire. Killers."
Joseera looked confused. "Of the Empire? But... then maybe I can talk to them, or..."
Joseera's head was suddenly filled with pictures of the soldiers burning her village, beating her friends. They had been men of the Empire too.
"...or maybe not." she finished softly. "But how can you tell? That's not a normal uniform, I've never seen it before."
"Hm. I have." snarled Fulza. "Stay here."

He gave a nod and a little gesture of one hand to Jubal, and the boar hunkered deeper into the dry earth in response. Then, taking one last glance at the riders, Fulza slid himself out of their hiding place and moved silently away. Joseera gave a nervous sigh.

"Do you think anything will ever go smoothly, Jubal?" she asked.

If Jubal had an answer, he didn't share it.

As she watched, Joseera saw Fulza emerge behind a group of low rocks ahead, stealthily approaching the riders with animal grace. Once again she found herself surprised by the natural ease and flow of his movements despite his solid bulk. Then, to her horror, she noticed one of the riders who had slipped away moving soundlessly towards Fulza, around the next outcrop of rock. She could not tell if either was aware of the other, but if both continued on their present course, they could not help but meet. Biting her lip to keep from calling out, she looked over to check the rest of the riders. Just at that moment, one of them turned in her direction and looked up, briefly, into the sky, sunlight illuminating the face beneath the dark green of his hood.

Joseera gasped. Then she stood upright with her mouth hanging wide open.

Instantly the sharp points of several blades and arrows were trained in her direction.

"Joseera, no!" cried Fulza, startling the rider nearest him, who swiftly turned and levelled his weapon fearlessly at Fulza. In reply, Fulza launched forwards, hands reaching for his great axe as he went.

Joseera did not notice any of this. Every ounce of her incredulous attention was fixed on the rider whose face she had seen.

Fortunately the rider had more wits about him. When he saw Joseera appear from her hiding place, he threw back his hood, eyes wide, and when his companions raised their weapons he flung out his arms, shouting, "Wait! WAIT!"

Even Fulza and his would-be adversary froze in their place, eyeing each other suspiciously.

As Joseera watched, open-mouthed, the rider climbed slowly down from his horse, peering intently at her. His companions exchanged uncertain glances. He took a few careful steps towards her.

"Joseera?"

"Gaven?"

oOo

Although they were not entirely ready for their enemy's charge, and much of their arsenal was still unprepared, the armies of the Empire responded swiftly. This was thanks in the main to the more experienced, professional soldiers who moved quickly, with practised efficiency. So it was that the first line consisted mostly of trained men, many of whom had met the enemy in battle before. They were mounted, which gave them an advantage of speed that the enemy could not match, and swept forward together, a rumbling wave of steel and dust. A shade more than three hundred abreast, stretching from one side of the pass to the other. They rode in the hope that a strong cavalry could halt the Savages charge and break through their lines, striking out with hoof and blade and fist at any who drew near. They were preceded by arcing banks of arrows, loosed even as the horses thundered forth, thinning the enemy's front line and slowing their advance.

For their part the Savages had few trained warriors, most of whom were tasked with leading one group or another in the charge. But although they lacked training, there was not one among their number who was not a born fighter. Most shrugged off the arrows that lodged in their thick skin, not piercing the hide deeply enough to inflict any real damage. Those who were unfortunate enough to be more seriously struck, shafts protruding from heads, necks and chests, were borne onward by the sheer weight and strength of those at their back, or else they fell, and were overrun by the surge of bodies that followed.

The two sides flooded the pass, roaring inevitably towards each other. When they met, a long peal of thunder filled the air, as one after another flesh and weapon clashed.

Everything had happened too quickly for General Tarrett and his escort to return to the point of command. In a way, Tarrett was glad. Although he had some small talent for leadership and strategy that, coupled with his long service, had raised him to the lofty office of General, he was at heart a soldier. In a matter such as this, he would have much rather stood shoulder to shoulder with his men and face to face with his enemy than stay and pull strings from far behind the lines. Besides, what did strategy matter now? This had all come upon them too soon, before their hasty preparation could be completed. The field catapults and ballista had not been in position, or ready for firing, and the organisation of the men was unfinished. The Three had not yet arrived to lead them. No, the time for strategy was past, thought Tarrett. All that would matter now was how long and how hard they could fight.

The General and his men had joined up and ridden forward with the flood of mounted men, and now found

themselves five or six from the front, hacking and chopping at any Savages who managed to press through the wall of hooves and blades ahead. Tarrett turned and glanced worriedly along the line. Some distance away to his left, he could see a dozen or so of the cavalry, less experienced men, had broken through the Savage's line altogether, and were pressing further into their ranks. Tarrett had fought the Savages before. It was not the same as fighting men. They would not turn and run, would not rout. Even as he watched, one man after another was dragged from his horse into the churning fray below, and torn, literally, limb from limb.
He yelled an order over to Hant.
"Hant! Hant! Get over there and tell those men to hold the bloody line, for Ancients sake! Never mind the glorious charge, we move together and keep the line strong! Go!"

Tarrett turned his attention to the bloodied Savage clawing at him from his right. He swung his broadsword in vicious arcs, hacking at the creature. On his third swing, the sword lodged deep in the Savage's skull, splitting its face and halting its assault instantly. Tarrett tugged at the sword as the Savage crumpled, almost pulled from his saddle, but at the last moment the blade came free.

Ahead, two men at the front had fallen, along with their mounts, and those around them were struggling to shore up the gap created. Although there were plenty of riders to take their place, the Savages had taken up the carcasses of the horses, and were using them as both shield and ram, protecting from the strikes of the soldiers, whilst at the same time pressing them back.
"Stand fast! Cut through!" shouted Tarrett, before urging his horse forward against the press, and beginning himself to make heaving slashes in the belly of the dead horse

before him. The men surrounding him quickly followed his example, and within a few moments they had reduced the bodies to chunks of meat. Spurred on by this success, the men pushed up, and the line once again stood strong. They were a fearsome sight, covered in the blood and bile that filled the air, teeth bared, steeds wheeling and stamping at any who came too close.

Yes, thought Tarrett, as he roared and swung with the rest of the men, the time for strategy is gone. All that will matter now is how long and how hard we can fight.

oOo

As they stood, fiercely hugging one another in the afternoon sun, the pair seemed entirely unaware of the tension that surrounded them. Joseera pulled her head back a little to look up into the other's face and placed her hands on his cheeks in wonder.

"Oh, Gaven, Gaven, Ancients be praised, it really is you! But what are you doing here?
"I might ask you the same thing, Joseera," replied Gaven with a smile. He cast a worried frown at Fulza. "Especially with the company you're keeping..."

For a moment Joseera looked surprised, but then she reminded herself of what she had thought the first time she had come across her Savage companion. Taking Gaven by the hand, she led him to Fulza. The other riders held their places, weapons still at the ready, but Fulza took a long look at Joseera, then lowered his.
"Hope you know what you're doing, girl." he said, softly.
Joseera smiled. "Gaven, this is my friend, Fulza. And that great thing over there," she pointed at Jubal, whose pink

snout was now poking out over the top of the rocks that had concealed him, "is Jubal. Fulza, I'd like you to meet my brother, Gaven."

For almost the next hour, once Gaven had introduced Rin, Fathom, and the others, they listened intently to Joseera as she recounted the events that had led her to them, often with a look of amazement on her own face as she recollected the terrible and remarkable journey from her home to the present. She was careful to leave out, however, the strange light she had experienced in Fulza's village, and Keshet's explanation of the Ilo'Seri. Joseera still wasn't entirely sure what to make of it all herself, but she felt pretty sure she knew how her big brother would react. She wondered if Fulza might give her away, but the big Savage seemed to understand, and said nothing. When she'd finally finished, Gaven sat shaking his head in disbelief.
"My own little sister, safely come all this way... I can't believe it! Little Joseera..."

It was Fulza who took charge of the situation.
"Now. You tell us." he said. "I see men dressed like you. Fine leathers. Sharp blades. Bad news for my people. Done bad things. So now you tell us, what you do here?"
Gaven's face flushed with colour, and he stepped angrily towards Fulza.
"We've done bad things? Us?! Your monsters have attacked people from all-"
Joseera stepped nervously between her brother and her friend, but much to her relief Rin took a firm hold of Gaven's arm before he could continue.
"Hold on, think, lad!" urged Rin. "Can't you see it now? He's no more guilty than you are!"
Gaven paused and licked his lips uncertainly, eyes still

fixed on the Savage, while Fulza frowned, peering at Rin.

Rin shook his head and continued. "It's just as we thought, lad. Someone has been talkin' to the Savages, givin' them information. But what if that someone wasn't really workin' *with* the Savages after all? What if they had their own plan all along, while we was all busy fightin' each other? Think about it, lad..."

Gaven seemed to relax a little, and gave a slight nod. He directed a question at Fulza.

"Why did your people begin attacking our lands? Why do you move out against us?"

Fulza paused for a moment before answering.

"Attacks start, no reason. No warning. Men come, kill our young, raid our villages. Soon after, received word. Men plan to take lands. Destroy us for good. So, leaders decide, tribes must unite. Fight together, once and for all."

As Fulza spoke, Gaven continued to gently nod, while at the same time the colour drained from his face.

"My men and I were sent out to investigate all the sudden and unprovoked attacks by Savages. We were warned that they had united, that they planned to destroy the Empire, take our lands for themselves. We were told to prepare for war."

He took a step forward, and offered a hand to Fulza.

"It seems I owe you an apology, Savage. And..." he looked over at Joseera's worried face, "...my deepest thanks. I still don't quite understand why or how, but you've kept my little sister safe all this time."

Fulza didn't reply, but he stepped forward and took Gaven's hand.

Rin spoke up again. " Now I think we can probably shed a

little light on things for you too. You said you'd seen men dressed like us before? Well, we're not what you think. We're wearing Empire colours, specifically those of the Order of Keepers, it's true, but we don't work for 'em. Not anymore. We deserted, ran away when we were asked to do some... disagreeable things. Since then, we been on our own, tryin' our best to figure out what in the Ancients name is goin' on."

Fulza's eyes narrowed, and Joseera looked confused.
"The Order of Keepers?" she said, amazed. "But... everybody has heard of the Scribe and the Keepers! Are you all Keepers? Gaven?! Are you a Keeper?"
Her outburst brought a sigh from one of the other riders, a long, slender fellow with a cynical expression.
"Oh, for Ancients sake." he said. "Were you listening at all? We *were* Keepers. Were, as in, in the past. We're not Keepers any longer. Not since this..."
He pulled off his right glove and held up his hand, exposing the twisted scars and mottled skin that covered it.
"...the Scribe and his friends Glass and Glower had us testing the Ink, testing the truth... They were using it to look for something, and they didn't seem to care at what cost."

Gaven put his arm about Joseera's shoulders.
"Please excuse Fathom, Joseera. He takes a little getting used to." Gaven raised his eyebrows in Fathom's direction, and was met with a haughty sniff. He went on. "None of us are Keepers, Joseera. In fact, we think they may be the ones behind all of this."
Joseera was baffled. "What? But they... they're part of the Empire, they've always been... Why would they?"
Gaven shrugged. "We're not quite sure yet Joseera. That's

what we're doing here, that's what we're trying to find out. I was sent from Bantha to gather information, find out where and why the Savages were attacking, but I discovered something unexpected. There were men working with them, alongside them, helping them, feeding them information and who knows what else. I was on my way back to Bantha to tell the Three when I ran into... some other problems. Then I met Rin and his friends."
Rin nodded politely.
"At first I thought they were Keepers, but when they told me what the Order had done to them, was doing to others... Rin thinks the Keepers may be the ones working with the Savages, and since I'd seen one of these traitors in the flesh, he asked me to help him find out."
Rin raised a hand. "Although from the sounds of what you're tellin' us, seems like the Keepers have got plans of their own."
Gaven nodded. "But I'm afraid that's not all. When I escaped from..." he looked awkwardly at Fulza, who seemed not to notice, "...the enemy, I... I saw something I still can't quite explain. A... a giant, a great golden giant striding across the land. I was lucky to escape with my life, as when I arrived, it walked through two hundred armed and trained men who lay in wait for it as if they were nothing. So now, Savage, I ask you – is this some weapon of your people? Some secret device? What power moves against us?!"

Fulza was silent for a long moment. Then he frowned.
"Girl. We must go. Get to the Temple." he said, simply. He began to gather his things.
Joseera turned to him in surprise.
"Wait, Fulza, what? We just found Gaven, we can't just leave! What is it, what's wrong?"
Fulza stopped, with a sigh, and turned back to Gaven.

"I can promise you, Gaven, brother of Joseera, this giant is no weapon of my people.

"Then who-" started Gaven, but Fulza raised one huge hand.

"Do you know stories, legends of my people?" asked Fulza.

Gaven glanced at Rin, who simply shrugged, then he shook his head. "No, no I-"

"In stories of my people - I do not remember exact words, cannot speak your tongue well – in stories of my people, the giants will wake when the end is near."

oOo

With a gasp of exertion, Tarrett swung his broadsword out before him, slicing almost clean through the neck of the Savage that bore down on him. With his right foot, he kicked out, pushing the body away. He wiped blood and sweat from his eyes, and took stock of the situation. It wasn't good. For his own part, he had lost his horse, taken down by some great cat sinking teeth into its neck. His armour had been badly dented by the fist of a hulking Savage, cutting into his left shoulder and preventing him from raising that arm much higher than his chest. He still had strength and had not yet received a wound serious enough to slow him, but he was tiring, he knew, and he could say the same for the men who fought beside him.

The Savages, however, were relentless. They fought heedless of pain or injury and with an animal fury. The only thing that had allowed them to hold out for so long, thought Tarrett, was that the Savages lacked order and tactics, frequently allowing themselves to be separated from their lines and cut down by the clamour of swords which then surrounded them. But despite this, Tarrett knew, the Savages were winning.

As he looked down the line to his left and right, he could see only pockets of cavalry remained, bunched together in patches to make the most of their dwindling advantage. Elsewhere, the real soldiers had all fallen and the line was an undisciplined rabble of civilians and militiamen, flailing and scattering hopelessly. Every Savage is as fearsome as the last, thought Tarrett, while we are running out of true fighters.

As he stared out at the field, lost for a moment in melancholy, a broad shouldered male Savage battered aside the man in front of him and before Tarrett could react, landed a juddering blow to Tarrett's chest. He stumbled backwards, breastplate cracked. Instinctively, he raised his sword before him, but felt the sharp pain flare in his shoulder. He tried to keep the sword high with his right hand alone, but exhaustion bit at his muscles and the blade fell. The wide Savage leapt forth, heavy forearms crashing down onto Tarrett, dropping him painfully to his knees. Helpless, General Tarrett glared defiantly up into the grinning face of his monstrous assailant and readied himself for the killing blow. The Savage gripped his throat, raising the other hammer fist high above its head. Then it froze.

The grin dropped from its face, and was replaced by a look of confusion as a foot of steel burst forth from its chest and slid out under its chin. Briefly, Tarrett met the now peaceful eyes, then the huge body was heaved aside, replaced by the gasping figure of Hant, one hand outstretched to Tarrett.
"Come on, sir! Not time to rest just yet! Up you get!" shouted Hant, as he hauled the bewildered General to his

feet. "We have to retreat a little, sir, regroup! Something strange is going on! The attack seems to be slowing up, sir, and some of them are falling back!"
Hant slung one arm around the General's shoulders and half dragged him back through the lines, calling out orders as he went.
"Fall back! Fall back to a single line at the rocks!"
After a few moments, General Tarrett gathered his wits and began to help Hant reorganise the men.

oOo

The people of Bantha and the skeleton force of soldiers who remained, most too old or too young to go off to Vas Aloron, were completely unprepared for the attack on the city. Despite their protests and terrified screams, most of the citizens could do nothing as Gensu's men took control of the streets. The few pockets of resistance here and there were quickly and unceremoniously crushed.

Commander Gensu was pleased. He had been uncertain at first when he was instructed to take the city, but in fact things had gone very smoothly. It had been even easier than expected. All that remained was Bantha's great Keep, where he knew the Three were waiting even now. He had been promised, however, assured that the Three would be taken care of before he and his men went in. He didn't know how, or by whom, but he didn't much care, so long as it was done. Commander Gensu drew a deep breath, and gave the order to breach the door.

Within the Keep, the Three were making hasty plans. The Sword stood, hand planted on the wooden table, a crumpled note pressed beneath it.
"We have to act quickly." he said, grimly, "This is from

Sergeant Thurro, one of Gaven's men, although there's no sign of the Sergeant himself. One of the stable guards said it was passed to him by a horse-hand."

The Book puffed her cheeks and frowned. "Don't tell me," she said, "it warns of an imminent attack on the city."

The Sword gave a dry laugh. "Not quite." he replied. "Firstly, it confirms what we feared of the giant. Gaven has seen it with his own eyes, south-west of Bellheath. He doesn't seem certain how it is connected with the Savages, but the thing apparently breezed though two hundred men without slowing. It was heading along the river, towards us."

The Heart shook her head. "What does that matter right now, Duma?" she asked. "We have to deal with the problem at hand."

The Sword nodded. "I'm getting to that."

"Oh dear." said the Book.

"Yes. It may not matter whether this giant is controlled by the Savages or not. The second thing Thurro tells us is that there are men of the Empire working alongside the Savages, providing aid and resources. I imagine it's the very same men who attack Bantha now."

The Book scratched thoughtfully at her chin. "Then... Vas Aloron?"

"Perhaps simply a way to distract us, tie up our men and empty the city." agreed the Sword.

"How much of the city do they hold, Duma?" the Heart asked. "Can we reach the Keeper's Tower? The Scribe and his men?"

The Sword sighed. "I don't think so, Loulouthi. Gaven and his company believe... they believe that the Order is behind this."

"But... they're the ones... it was their intelligence, that led our forces to Vas Aloron!" gasped the Heart. "And the

Scribe?"

"I don't know, Loulouthi, I don't know." the Sword replied.

The Book sniffed. "Well, no use worrying about that right now." she said. "Whoever is behind this has made a grave mistake, eh? If they think they can simply take the city by force while we three stand by, then they have deeply underestimated us, and they will be sorely disappointed."

The little woman turned to face the other two, her eyes burning. "Duma, how many men do we have left in the Keep?"

"Fifty or so, I'd say." he replied, "Most will be down in the barracks if they've any sense, readying arms"

"Good. Can you go down and rally them?"

The Sword smiled, and nodded.

"I'll go up to the Council rooms and gather the few men we have there." said the Heart, resolute. "I should be able to get an idea of the size of force we face from there too."

The Book adjusted her glasses. "Very well." she said. "If I can get to my study, I can get a message to Vas Aloron. We'll meet at the inner gate as soon as we can. And then we'll show these fools whose city this is."

oOo

At that very moment, many miles away, Aleph, Seeker Prime, stood looking calmly down at the twisted golden shape before him.

"Now," he said softly to himself, "let's see."

Before him he held out a small, dark object, pitch-black and shimmering. Quietly, he began to speak some well practised words. He seemed faintly surprised when a cold, blue light began to grow about the dark shape, but he did not allow himself to be distracted, calmly continuing to speak the words he had memorised for this very moment.

The cold light seemed to take on an almost liquid nature, flowing and dripping down onto the twisted golden thing beneath. Eventually the golden shape was barely visible, encompassed in a shell of cold and shimmering blue.

Aleph silently placed the dark object back into its pouch, and drew forth his speaking globe. He twisted the metal bands into position, and spoke two words.
"It's done."

oOo

In the Keep, the men looked on in fear as the Sword, who had been in the middle of addressing them, was suddenly silent, dropping onto one knee. He clutched helplessly at the air as a strange, blue haze appeared around him, until it surrounded him entirely, and he was still.

The Book staggered forward, clutching at the edge of the bench in her study. It took her only a moment to realise what was happening, and she threw out her hands in desperation. Within a few seconds, the strange light held her, motionless, in place.

In the Council chamber, the guards called out in concern to the Heart, but she did not answer. She stood, a shimmering, cold light around her, hands pressed to the glass of the great window that looked out over the front of the Keep. With horror in her eyes she watched, unable to move or turn away, as Gensu's men finally broke through the gate below.

Chapter Eighteen

It did not take much discussion to establish that Gaven and the others would join Joseera, Fulza and Jubal in travelling to the Temple of the Dead. Fulza was not open to negotiation as far as the destination was concerned, and Gaven refused to be parted from Joseera now that he had found her. Rin quickly concluded that if the Temple was of some significance in the events unfolding, they might well find the answers they needed there at any rate.

They had not been moving for long, coming upon a long, low dip where the trail sank between two great sheets of stone on either side, when Jubal once again stopped short and began sniffing suspiciously at the air. In an instant, Fathom was down from his horse, and with a nod to Rin, disappeared into the rocks and shadows nearby. Joseera twisted round in the saddle where she sat, in front of her brother. "Where is he going?" she asked, quietly.
Rin answered in a low voice, "Fathom may be a little short on charm, but he's a fine scout – could of trained for a Seeker one day I'd reckon. An' if he slips off now, it might just give us the edge over whoever's out there see, if they don't know he's about."

Just as Rin finished speaking, several figures began to appear over the crest of the path ahead. Fulza turned and flattened himself against one of the large stones at the side of the path. "Will stay out of sight. Maybe let you pass quietly." he looked darkly at Rin, "Maybe friends of yours."

Rin shook his head slowly as more of the men came into view. "No. No friends of ours I think." he murmured,

"They may not be flyin' a flag, but that's the Tower Guard uniform they're wearin'. They're with the Order."
Gaven turned anxiously to look at him. "Will they know who you are Rin? Do you think you might be able to pull rank?"
Rin pursed his lips thoughtfully. "I don't know." he said. "Just let me do the talkin'."

In full sight now, there were around twenty men approaching at a march in rank and file, preceded by two others on horseback. The green and grey of their uniforms stood out in odd contrast against the sandy yellows and browns of their surroundings, and their polished swords and buckles glittered conspicuously in the red evening sun. When they caught sight of the little group on the path before them, one of the mounted men, most glittering and conspicuous of all, held up a gloved hand and the company behind him came to an abrupt halt. He nudged his horse a few paces further towards Joseera and her friends and peered at them suspiciously.

"Good evening, Master Keeper," he began, addressing Rin, although the tone of his voice did not quite match the respectful words he uttered, "Do you require some assistance, perhaps?" The man's gaze lingered on Joseera and she felt Gaven's arm tighten around her waist.
Rin replied, "No, thank you Captain. We have been a little unfortunate, but our business is well in hand. Now, please don't let us keep you, we have to be movin' on."
Rin began to walk his horse onward, but the Captain raised his hand once more.

"If you'll indulge me for just a moment longer, Master Keeper. I do apologise, but these are... uncertain times, as you will of course understand. Might I be so bold as to inquire exactly *what* your business is out here?"

Joseera felt Gaven's breathing quicken behind her, but Rin remained calm.

"Not that it's any right of yours to question a Keeper, Captain," he said, tersely, "but I suppose, given the circumstances... We're takin' our young friend here -" he motioned to Joseera, "- over to the Seeker Prime, *without* delay."

At the mention of the Prime, the Captain seemed suddenly less sure of himself. "Ah, well..." he began, awkwardly, "...I'm sorry, Master Keeper. I don't wish to cause delay in the affairs of the Seeker Prime. Nevertheless, I'm afraid I'm under very strict orders here, Master Keeper, if I could just see your-"

He was interrupted by the second mounted soldier, who had drawn level and now made a few hushed comments to the Captain in a low voice, too quiet for Joseera to make out. While he spoke though, the Captain did not look at the man, instead fixing his eyes first on Rin, and then very firmly on Joseera. After a few moments the Captain smiled and made a quiet reply to his companion, who nodded sharply, then briskly returned to the waiting soldiers.

With a sniff, the Captain addressed Rin again. "I think it best, Master Keeper, if you hand the prisoner over to us. We'll take care of things from here."
As he spoke, Joscera noticed with growing anxiety the rest of his company spreading out across the path, adjusting belts and harnesses, loosening swords in their scabbards.

Rin replied through clenched teeth. "That's not going to

happen, Captain. And the Seeker Prime is going to hear of your insolence."

"Is he indeed, Master Keeper?!" snorted the Captain, "Or should I perhaps say, *former* Keeper. On the contrary, I think he might congratulate me for bringing justice to those who disgrace the Order! And if that girl is who I think she is, he might just give me a bloody medal."

He gave a flick of his hand to the men behind him, several of whom began to advance menacingly.

"Now don't make this difficult, Rin Bata," he called, "You may be able to cause us some trouble, but your little band is no match for twenty armed men. There's no way you can take us all on!"

"You're right Captain." replied Rin cooly, prompting a smug smile from the other man, "But you see, I'm hopin' I won't have to. *Fathom!*"

As the Captain's smile faded, the advancing men looked confusedly about, one or two drawing swords and glancing out at the rocks around them. As they did so, a fizzing, brown object, no larger than a man's fist, landed in the dirt before them with a soft *thup*. The men looked down at the lumpen ball of clay, at the tiny, sparkling fuse that protruded from it, and a couple even managed to open their mouths to shout the beginnings of a warning to the others, but before the sounds were fully formed, the little ball exploded in a flash of sparks and dust.

Through the haze and chaos, Joseera thought she saw a thin figure launch itself into the fray from the rocks above, then as several of the soldiers burst forth from the roiling cloud of smoke towards her, she heard the Captain's voice yelling out, furiously, "Take the girl! At all costs, whatever it takes, the girl!"

Joseera twisted round to see her brother, only to find Gaven looking at her with a distant and unfamiliar expression. "What is it, Joseera? What have you done?" he whispered, with a frown. "What do they want with you?"

Before she could answer, they were interrupted by a cry from Rin. He had leapt down from his horse and was facing four of the soldiers, charging towards him. Swiftly, he drew his weapon, and holding it flat across his body before him, rushed forth, catching three of the soldiers and hurling them off their feet. The fourth man however, managed to slip by, and ignored Rin altogether, instead running furiously at Joseera and Gaven, sword waving.

"Look sharp, Gaven!" called Rin, desperately, but even as Gaven stepped in front of Joseera and began to draw his sword, the soldier was stopped brutally in his tracks. Fulza stepped out from his place amongst the rocks and with a massive backward swing of his arm, sent the soldier hurtling back through the air over Rin's head, only to disappear into the smoky cloud of cries and clangs beyond. Fulza moved towards Joseera, but Gaven remained determinedly in place between them, hand on sword, a mixture of fear and uncertainty on his face.

As the three remaining soldiers before Rin struggled to their feet, he turned to look back at Joseera, Gaven and Fulza.
"If anybody has any bright ideas," he shouted, "now would be a good time! We won't be able to hold 'em for long!"

oOo

General Tarrett was confused. A short while earlier he had been certain that the battle was lost, that Vas Aloron would fall, that the Savages would take the pass and push into the Fold with ease. But for some reason the Savages assault had slowed and instead of the relentless drive that had almost overwhelmed the Empire's forces, Tarrett now saw some Savages moving back, or holding rather than continuing to press forward. He was grateful, of course - it had granted them just a sliver of breathing room, space enough to reorganise, bolster their front line and defences, bringing them back from the brink of defeat. But he was also confused. General Tarrett was a career soldier and had seen enough conflict to understand the ebb and flow of battle. What he was seeing now made no sense, and that worried him.

"I don't understand it, Hant!" he shouted over the din, as a field medic did his best to dress the General's wounds. "They had us! They'd broken the line, and even where they hadn't, we had nothing but a rabble at the front! What in the Ancients name are they up to?"
"I don't know, sir, but whatever it is, we'd better thank 'em for it!" replied Hant, "Even if they've got something up their sleeve, at least we've had a chance to get things sorted! They'll have a harder time pushing through now, that's for sure!"
Hant had managed to drag the General clear and out of harms way for the moment. From their position on a slight slope at the side of the pass, some way behind most of the fighting, they could see that the field weaponry was almost prepared, catapults and ballista stood waiting the command to fire. Meanwhile, ranks of men formed up and moved forward as one.
Tarrett turned to the medic fussing at his side. "I'm fine,

I'm fine, for Ancients sake, man. That'll do well enough for now, go and find someone in real need!" he turned back to Hant, "Well, we'd better be ready. There's something not right here, Hant, that's for certain!"

Hant shrugged. "They've missed their chance, sir. Now that we've got everything in place, we'll hammer them back if they try and push again!"

As if to prove him right, one of the catapults was finally made ready and let loose a great chunk of stone. The missile sailed over the Empire lines and came down some way into the Savage forces, crushing those at its destination, then rolling onward to scatter or flatten those beyond.

Hant laughed. "See what I mean, sir? It's our turn now!"
Tarrett shook his head uncertainly. "I hope so, Hant. I don't like it, it doesn't make sense, but I hope so."

Thung.

oOo

"What in the Ancients name was that?" shouted Gaven, as he unceremoniously kicked away another soldier who had come too close. He stood side by side with Rin now, while Fulza and Joseera remained behind him. After Fulza had dispatched the last guardsman, Gaven felt fairly sure that Joseera was as safe as she could be, so long as she stayed next to the hulking Savage. Ahead of them, Fathom and the others had spread out across the path, and although the smoke from their entrance was clearing, they were still managing to keep most of the soldiers at bay, darting around them, spinning and tripping them this way and that, using their number against them. Somewhere in amongst the chaos, several of the soldiers swore they had seen a great boar charging back and forth, and several others would confirm it when they came to.

"Did you hear it?" Gaven continued, loudly.
"What are you talkin' about lad? Hear what? I can barely hear a flamin' thing over their racket!"
Rin was right. The din of shouts and cries of frustration from the soldiers as they swung at their assailants and found nothing but smoke and thin air was deafening, but Gaven was undeterred.
"No, not that, there was something else! Off over the ridge there, something... something like – like metal! Like a... gong, or a great bell!"
Rin knocked aside an oncoming sword and then struck the owner solidly in the face with the pommel of his own weapon, sending the man crumpled and unconscious to the ground, before screwing his face up at Gaven. "Are you going soft in the head lad? A gong, for Ancients sake? What is a -"

Thung.

"There!" shouted Gaven, "There, tell me you heard that!"
Rin frowned, and nodded. "Aye lad, I heard that. I don't know what it was, but I heard it. Are... are you alright, lad?"
Gaven had gone suddenly pale and his face bore a solemn expression.
"I know what it is, Rin. I've heard it before. The giant I told you about? That was it. That was the sound."

They turned and looked about them in the direction the noise seemed to have come from and sure enough, they saw it. Only the great head was visible at the moment over the high rocks, gleaming brightly in the red evening sun, still some way off, but drawing closer. Clearly the soldiers saw it too, as a cry went up from the Captain again, "The girl! Quickly, before it's upon us, the girl, the girl!", and his men redoubled their efforts. Hurriedly, desperately, Gaven ran back to where Joseera and Fulza stood, both of them staring open-mouthed at the golden figure appearing in the distance. At another time, Gaven might have laughed at the similarity of their expressions, but now he grabbed hold of his sister by the shoulders and drew her close to him.

"What is it, Joseera? What aren't you telling me? I'm your *brother*, Joseera, for Ancients sake!"
Joseera looked at him with tears in her eyes, but her gaze was steady and her voice didn't tremble. "I know, Gaven, I'm sorry." she said, softly, "It was all too much to explain right away, and there's no time now. But you *are* my brother and so you have to trust me. I don't know why and I don't know how, but somehow... I'm *important* in all this. I have to get to the Temple. Fulza believes it, and now so do I."

Thung.

Gaven looked hard at her for a long moment. Then he shook his head. "I can't believe I'm doing this." he said, with a sigh. "You were always important to me, my sister. But... you're not the little girl I left at home, Joseera, that much is certain. Very well. I hope you know what you're doing."
His hands dropped from her shoulders and he stepped back, taking in his sister's determined expression and the huge Savage behind her. "Go then. We'll hold them here as long as we can."

Joseera leapt forward and caught her brother in a tight hug, surprising him, and then he flung his arms firmly around her in response. Meanwhile Fulza let out a sharp whistle, bringing Jubal charging out of the melee, trailing bits of battered armour and torn uniforms behind. Fulza knelt and spoke a few soft words to the great boar, then stood silently. The two faced each other for a few quiet seconds, Savage and beast, then Jubal turned and charged back into the fray. Fulza turned to find both Gaven and Joseera looking at him.

"Can't come with us. Can't climb the rocks." He gestured to Gaven, "Will stay with you until we meet again."
Joseera gasped. "But Jubal-"

Thung.

Fulza held up a broad hand. "No time to argue, girl." he knelt again and waved her over, helping her climb onto his back and fix her arms about his neck. Then he stood, with Joseera clinging to him, and approached the rocks at the path's edge.

There were several awkward thumps from nearby, and Rin's voice called out urgently. "Gaven? Gaven! If you don't mind, lad, I could do with – *ugh! Get out of it!* - I could do with a hand!"

"Be careful, Joseera. I'll see you soon." said Gaven.
Joseera fought the lump in her throat and simply nodded, for fear that anything else would give her away. Gaven gave a faint smile and headed back towards Rin and the others. Joseera held on tightly as Fulza launched himself up among the rocks and began to climb. Then she heard

Gaven's voice call out again.
"And Savage! Savage?!"
Fulza paused on the rocks and turned to look back.
"Look after my sister Savage! Or you'll have me to answer to!"
Fulza said nothing, but met Gaven's eye and gave a slow nod.

"Gaven!!" came Rin's voice again, "Gaven! I'm not a miracle worker, lad, get over here!"

Fulza turned his attention back to the rocks, pulling himself upwards with powerful arms, and in just a few moments Joseera's brother and the others had disappeared from her view.

oOo

On the battlefield, there was chaos. Some of the men had begun to turn and run the moment the great figure had appeared from behind the mountainside. Others bravely held their position, trying their best to maintain control and rally those around them. Some did nothing, neither running nor fighting, standing fast in simple, blind panic.

From their position at the valley's side, Hant and General Tarrett watched, jaws slack, numb, as the golden giant strode inexorably towards them.
"It's true..." murmured Hant, as much to himself as to the General, "Everything they said... it's true. Unstoppable weapons... machines..."
Tarrett did not respond. Instead he began to march unsteadily down the slope, as fast as his injuries would allow.
The terrified Hant called after him. "General? General!

Where are you going? General!"

General Tarrett did not look round. But he shouted back to Hant as he went. "Let's get things in order! This is it, Hant, this is it! We need to pull ourselves together and *bring that thing down!*"

For a moment, Hant didn't move, uncertainty freezing him on the spot. But then a soldier's training kicked in and he ran hurriedly after the General.

They fought their way through the tide of fleeing men, sweeping those who still had control of their senses along with them. Under Tarrett's orders the nearest catapults were hastily turned and reloaded, furiously wound to fire as far and as fiercely as they might, and on the General's command, they loosed their missiles one after the other. As they sailed, no-one dared breathe.

The first and second of the projectiles missed their target entirely, hurriedly aimed as they were, coming down instead somewhere within the Savage ranks. The third, however, was directly on, smashing into the giant's chest in a shower of dust and shrapnel. A sudden cheer went up among the men, screaming and hollering their approval with red faces and wild eyes, but it died just as quickly.

Even as men jostled and pushed around him, General Tarrett looked on in disbelief. The giant still came steadily, patiently onward, but worse that that, there was not a mark or a scratch upon it. All the noise and madness around the General seemed to disappear into the background, and he simply stared at the giant through glazed eyes, listening to the ringing footsteps.

Thung. Thung. Thung.

"General? General? General!"
Hant's voice brought Tarrett out of his reverie. Dazed, he turned to find Hant shaking him by the arm.
"General! I- I think you need to hear this, sir!" Hant motioned to a young soldier stood beside him. "Tell the General what you just told me!"
"W-well, sir, y'see," the boy stammered anxiously, "It's not theirs, sir! I've come from the front line, sir, and it's doing for them too, sir, it's not theirs!"
Tarrett frowned. "What in the Ancients name are you saying, lad? You're not making any sense!"
The boy looked uncomfortably at Hant, who nodded for him to go on. "It's not theirs, sir, that thing, that giant. It's doing for them too, stamping all over any of 'em that's in its way. They're running away from it, sir, *they're running away!*"

It took a moment or two to sink in. Then Tarrett hauled himself up onto the side of one of the catapults, climbing as high as he could, and strained his eyes into the Savage ranks. It was true. There were Savages running in all directions, panic and disorder seemed everywhere. And those unfortunate ones who could not escape the crush, who could not move away in time, were caught beneath the giant's great feet, ground into the earth.

Tarrett climbed shakily down from his perch, and took hold of Hant.
"Get the order out. Draw the men back, all of them, and as fast as you can. They should not engage the Savages, or seek to hinder them in any way. Get everyone out. And send a rider to Bantha, right now. Strict orders - not to stop until they reach the city. Understand?"
Hant shook his head, nervously. "Very good, sir. But what

is it? What's going on?"

Tarrett took a deep breath and stared out at the golden figure again. "Ancients help us, Mr. Hant, I don't know. But we'd better find out."

Thung.

Chapter Nineteen

Joseera lost track of exactly how long she had been clinging on to Fulza. After he had scaled the jagged rocks, they had skirted some way north from the edge overlooking the path, to avoid being spotted by anyone below and wasting the opportunity Gaven and the others had bought them. Then, since Fulza was able to move so quickly over the rough terrain, it had seemed sensible for Joseera to remain on Fulza's back, so there she stayed, hanging on as tightly as she could while Fulza rushed onward, bounding across the stone and scrub underfoot. They did not speak as they travelled, but Joseera could sense that something had changed in Fulza. He moved with a simple urgency and determination, not slowing at all until the light began to falter and they came to the crest of a steep slope above what Joseera knew must be the Temple of the Dead.

The vast building, if it could be called that, for it seemed more like some strange rock formation, looked uncared for and abandoned. Here and there parts of the structure were crumbling or had collapsed altogether, and much of it was overgrown with wild plants and vegetation. At its base, however, Joseera could see several dark archways that remained clear, leading into the Temple, although she could make out nothing beyond.

Gently, Fulza lowered her to the ground, then crouched at the edge of the slope, peering down at the Temple with a frown.
Joseera was concerned at his silence. "Fulza, are you-" she began, but much to her frustration, Fulza raised a hand to quiet her, not even turning to look at her.

She sat back on her heels in irritation. "Fine then. If you're not even going to tell me-"
Fulza shot her a serious glance. "Quiet, girl." he growled. "Something not right here. This place. Not as Keshet said."
Joseera forgot her complaints for the moment, and leant forward again, putting her head next to his.
"What is it?" she whispered, "This can't be the wrong place?"
Fulza shook his head uncertainly. "No. Not wrong place. Temple of the Dead, is certain. But looks... empty, wrong."
Joseera's brow furrowed for a moment as she too stared down at the sprawling structure in the dimming evening light. She shrugged. "But it *is* the Temple. We've come this far. What difference does it make now?" she said. "We have to at least go and investigate, Fulza. After all," she stood, staff planted at her side, and looked at him with wide, clear eyes, "what else are we going to do?"
Then she began to carefully pick her way down the slope.

Fulza smiled to himself. The girl had a point. He climbed to his feet and started off down the slope after her.

oOo

Although his face betrayed no signs of his struggle, the Sword's eyes flickered and fluttered with effort. He strained against the invisible bonds which held him, all of his strength, every ounce of his will focused on freeing him from the strange blue light that kept him frozen in place. It was no use. No matter what he did or tried to do, the Sword could not escape.

At first he had been bewildered, confused, as if afflicted

by some mysterious ailment, when his limbs began to stiffen and seize. But as he looked around the barracks room at the reactions of his men, as he heard their cries of fear and wonder, and saw for himself the shimmering blue glow creep along his arms, he quickly realised there was some more sinister force at work. When the light gripped him completely, he found with slight surprise that he could still direct his eyes well enough, still see and hear those around him. With frustration, he watched his men begin to panic.

When the doors burst open there was nothing he could do but watch in horror, unable even to close his eyes against the sight, as a horde of Gensu's troops poured in. The Sword's men were caught unprepared, equipment half ready, unarmed and dishevelled, and most fell beneath the Tower Guard's blades in a matter of seconds. Those few who had their wits about them, who managed to grab a weapon or shield, were dispatched swiftly afterwards, overwhelmed by superior numbers and arsenal. In just a few short minutes, the Sword found himself surrounded by the lifeless bodies of his men and jeering Tower Guards, hurling insults and picking at the spoils of their victory.

More soldiers continued to flood into the Keep and the Sword watched helplessly as they were dispatched to secure other parts of the building. He wondered and hoped that Sofya and Loulouthi might still be free, able to act, and tried to suppress the feeling in his heart that they were as helpless as he. Then, as he watched, the crowing figure of Commander Gensu appeared in the doorway. When Gensu's eyes lighted on the Sword, a broad smile spread across the Commander's face.

"Well, well, Lord Duma!" laughed Gensu, across the room. He motioned two nearby soldiers over to him, and gestured to the Sword. "Check him."

The two men looked uncomfortably at one another, then slowly inched their way cautiously towards the Sword. When they eventually reached his side they shared another nervous glance and an unspoken argument of jerking heads and nods took place, before one of the men poked awkwardly at the Sword's arm, then stepped hurriedly away. When the Sword neither moved or responded, the two became bolder, and satisfied themselves of his condition with a growing series of pushes and shoves.

"That's enough!" called Gensu, dismissing the pair. Then with a nod, he carefully approached the Sword himself, bending on one knee to look into his face.

"The great Lord Duma..." said Gensu, smiling softly. "Can you hear me? Ah yes – I see in your eyes that you *can* hear me. Well, Lord Duma, no doubt this is a surprise, eh? I have always suspected your talents to have been somewhat exaggerated, but even so... the mighty Sword brought to his knees like *this*, eh? Humiliating, to say the least."

Without warning, Gensu's hand shot out and struck the Sword sharp and hard across the face. Although he could not respond, the Sword felt the sting of the blow nonetheless.

Gensu's face grew cold. "Your time is done, *Lord*. This weakness, this pitiful diplomacy is over, it's time for those with vision and ambition to take charge, those who have *earned* the right! When our Master takes control we will enter a new age of knowledge and power, and the Empire will *grow* again!"

Commander Gensu stood, staring down at the Sword with

contempt. "For my part, I think I will enjoy your position. Finally our enemies will learn to fear the Imperial armies again. There will have to be many changes, of course, but perhaps there are one or two things I may keep around..."
He leant forward, pressing his face close to the Sword's. "...the Lady Loulouthi, for example... I might be able to think of some... use for her." Gensu gave a sickly smile. "In fact, I've probably wasted quite enough time with you. Perhaps I'll go and pay her a visit right now. We can get to know one another."
Gensu straightened up again, and with a snort launched a wad of spittle at the Sword's face, before giving a mocking bow.
"Goodbye, Lord Duma." he said, and marched swiftly away, leaving the Sword knelt in the middle of the barracks as soldiers hurried by, a warm, wet strand creeping down his forehead.

Although his face betrayed no signs of his struggle, the Sword's eyes flickered with effort.

oOo

At Vas Aloron, there was an uneasy, hushed air. Men worked quietly and with focus, swiftly going about their business with solemn determination. Many were packing up kit and horses to depart, a steady stream of figures trailing back into the Fold with bowed heads and still tongues. Those who remained did their jobs with sober concentration, and there was little chatter.

General Tarrett was exhausted. The medics had encouraged him to rest, but he had flatly refused, knowing that there was still far too much to be done in the light of the evening's events. He was still reeling, in truth, from so many surprising and unexpected turns, but he was trying hard to maintain some sense of order and control, as much for himself as for his men. Tarrett had given the order for everyone except the professional soldiers to make their way back to their homes as quickly as possible. He saw no sense in keeping tired and terrified men needlessly. With a deep sigh he looked out at those still working in the pass and wished he could send them all home.

After the initial panic at the golden giant's arrival, a number of curious things had occurred. In spite of the frenzy of confusion and fear, a great number of the men had quickly rallied when they saw the catapults launching against the giant, and took it upon themselves to organise an attack in any way that they could. They had launched spears, swords and arrows against the thing, and failing that, a hail of rocks and stones beat upon its golden hide. In admiration and amazement, General Tarrett had watched as several of the men began to heave great slabs and boulders into the giant's path. Yet more astonishing was the reaction of the Savages. Since the moment of the giant's appearance the struggle between Savage and soldier had lessened, and as the huge figure strode further into the pass, the fighting had ceased altogether, as man and Savage realised the giant bore no allegiance to either. When they saw the efforts of their prior opponents, however, the Savages too had begun to quickly rally, and then they had begun to help. Dumbfounded, Tarrett had seen a team of strong Savages swiftly bring up a dozen or more thick ropes, then stretched out to their full length. Taking the ends of the ropes in his broad hands, one of their number had run, brave and wild, across the giant's path as closely as he dared. At the other side, many more Savages joined him, taking the ropes and pulling them taut. In the moments before the giant's foot drew against the lines, the General had seen several men running *towards* the thing, catching hold of the ropes and hauling alongside the Savages, giving whatever help they could.

The Savage runner had done well, and the line had crossed too close and too quickly for the giant to notice, if it was aware of such things. One great golden foot had caught firmly against the ropes and a furious cry went up from the men and Savages at each end as they fought to hold fast. Breath stopped in his chest, sound choked in his throat, Tarrett had watched for what felt like an eternity as the golden figure stalled, suspended in its place. Then, unbidden, a cry had rushed out of him like water from a dam, and his fist leapt into the air. *The giant faltered.* Unable to free its great foot in time, the colossus had pitched forward and finally fell, landing on its hands and knees with a thunderous force, sending man and Savage alike sailing into the air amidst a shower of dust and earth.

Within seconds, the giant had been surrounded with figures hammering and beating it, climbing and pulling at it, stabbing and thrusting. Briefly, it seemed almost dazed, and the great head had turned this way and that, seeming only now to notice its tiny assailants. Then, as if their assault was no more than rainfall drumming at its hide, the giant had begun to right itself. It straightened, then drew one huge leg up, lifting itself onto one knee. And there, as the sun's last glow disappeared behind the mountains in the west, it stayed.

And there it remained, even as General Tarrett looked at it now, lifeless, motionless and impervious to harm, shining coldly in the moonlight of the cloudless night. Several of the men had suggested that perhaps it had been damaged somehow, perhaps the fall had stopped it for good. Tarrett had his doubts. Nonetheless, once it had become clear that there would be no further activity from the giant, at least for the time being, he had begun to send men home. Not long afterwards an officer had approached with a message from the Savages, and with the help of those who understood a little of the Savage tongue, they had managed to open communications. Thankfully, both sides had conceded that there should be no more hostility tonight. Now groups of men and Savages worked alongside each other, some roping the giant to the earth lest it should shift again, other still trying in vain to scar or scratch its skin.

Tarrett watched impassively, only half seeing. Despite his exhaustion, his mind was racing. For the first time since the battle had begun, Tarrett had time to think back to the beginning of the fray, to the mysterious figures who had fired without order on the Savage envoys. His conversation with the Savages had confirmed some suspicions and raised some terrible questions, especially regarding their motives for conflict. Tarrett was, he now realised, fairly certain who those mysterious individuals were. He had seen men dressed in that way on a few rare occasions, when his duty had called him to the Keeper's Tower. Men of the Order. Seekers. He shivered and pulled his cloak tighter about him. If he was right, nowhere was safe.

oOo

Parfort scuttled anxiously along the corridor, struggling with the heavy weight of the Great Tome, desperately trying not to fall behind. Ahead, the Scribe, flanked as ever by Mister Glower and Miss Glass, whisked impatiently on, calling back to Parfort only to hurry him along. In the past, the young Scrivener had never had any problems keeping up with the old man, but in recent days the Scribe had seemed possessed by some vernal energy, and now Parfort found it hard to keep pace. As they swept through the hallways of Bantha's Keep, he tried his best to avert his eyes from the destruction around him, splintered doors and shattered windows, and from the grisly bodies of the Keep's guard and staff. He slowed as he stepped around the body of a maid, a girl surely younger than him, face pale, eyes staring into nothingness.

If he was honest with himself, Parfort thought, he didn't really understand what was happening. He knew that he had sworn into the Order, that he owed his life and loyalty to the Keepers and the Scribe. He had listened very carefully to all the speeches and lectures about the good of the Empire, progress and knowledge. He had dutifully copied the texts about the Order's purpose and responsibility. But now he felt far out of his depth. He didn't understand. Parfort felt sure that the people of the Keep were not the ones they should be fighting or harming. Not the ones they should be killing.

"Come along, lad, keep up." came the Scribe's dry voice again, startling Parfort out of his distraction. They climbed yet another flight of wide steps, and finally stopped at a broad set of doors in a pointed archway.
"Hm. The great council chamber." rasped the Scribe.
Mister Glower gave a sickly smile, "But today there will be no debate, Your Eminence."
The Scribe turned and looked down at Parfort with a pricking glare. "Wait here, my boy, unless I call for you. We won't be long."
Parfort swallowed uncomfortably and gave a frantic little nod. He barely recognised the old man any more.

Gratefully he stood to one side as the Scribe disappeared into the council chamber followed by the creepy Glass and Glower, and the heavy doors swung shut behind.

Left in the silence of the corridor, Parfort tried not to think too deeply on what he had seen as they made their way through the Keep. His eyes darted nervously about, struggling to avoid the motionless figures lying just in sight on the cold floor at the far end of the hallway. Their stillness seemed almost accusatory. His eyes fell on the cover of the huge book clutched to his chest, and although he knew it was not permitted, he opened the pages to the most recent entry.

The thick parchment unmistakably bore the absolute black of the Keeper's Ink. The words he read, in flawless copperplate hand, did little to make him feel any better.

Inside the council chamber, as expected, the Heart stood frozen at the far end of the room. The Scribe did not expect, however, to find Commander Gensu with her, one hand tightly on her hip, the other buried in her robes as he pressed close at her side, whispering hotly in her ear. When the doors closed with a gentle *thud,* the Commander turned suddenly, then stepped tightly away from the Heart with a flustered expression.

"Ah... uh, your Eminence, hn. I didn't, ah... I didn't realise you were with us already. Um."
"Clearly." replied the Scribe, coolly.
"I'm... Well, I-I'm afraid I, uh-"
The Scribe interrupted him by simply holding up his right hand, giving a thin smile. Then with his left hand, he took up a battered little book that hung about his neck on a thin

leather cord, and flicked through pages thickly covered with scrawl and scribblings. He turned to look back at Mister Glower and Miss Glass.

"Perhaps we should find out what the good Commander is *really* afraid of..."

With a pen that seemed to simply appear in his other hand, he began to write.

While Glower grinned approvingly and watched over the Scribe's shoulder, Miss Glass held Gensu in a frosty stare that almost pierced the skin. She took a few delicate steps toward the man.

"Yes, Your Eminence. Write his secrets... and I'll show them to him." she whispered.

Gensu dropped suddenly and painfully to his knees.
"No, no, wait! No, Your Eminence please, I meant no disrespect, please!"

The Scribe paused, and looked up from his little book.
"Is the Keep secure, Commander?"
"Uh, yes, yes, quite secure, your Eminence! We hold all areas and have men throughout, your Eminence!" blurted Gensu, desperately.
The Scribe nodded. "Very well, Commander. I am sorry to interrupt your... negotiations, but I'm afraid I need to speak to the Lady Loulouthi alone for a few moments. I suggest you see to Lady Sofya and Lord Duma."
Gensu nodded frantic agreement from his position on the floor. "Yes, your Eminence, very good. I'll see to it right away!"
"Very well, Commander. Go."
Gensu scrambled to his feet, and, cutting a wide berth around Miss Glass, made his way out of the room in an awkward dance of deference and haste.

Once the Commander had gone, the Scribe gave a loud sigh.

"It seems you are not to have your fun with the Commander today, my friends," he said.

Mister Glower laughed. "As long as it is your wish, Your Eminence, we will not be disappointed."

Miss Glass raised her eyebrows. "I'm sure the Commander's time will come, Your Eminence," she said.

The Scribe gave a little chuckle, and nodded. "Quite right, I'm sure, Miss Glass. Although I imagine the Commander hopes it will not be at your hand!"

Glower gave another fawning laugh.

"Now, my friends, please watch the door, while I have a little... conversation with Her Ladyship here."

Miss Glass and Mister Glower both gave a slight bow, before returning to the door at the far end of the room. The Scribe turned his attention to the Heart.

"Now, Lady Loulouthi. I'm afraid I must apologise for the behaviour of my men. Not the sort of thing you're used to, I'm sure.

There was no reply from the Heart, stood quite still in a soft blue light.

The Scribe tutted. "I think it impolite not to face one another if we are to have a reasonable discussion, wouldn't you agree?"

He raised his left hand, and with a grimace, made a twisting gesture. As he did, the Heart spun round quite suddenly where she stood. He took a few steps forward and drew his hand slowly towards him. The Heart slid forth across the floor, feet dragging indelicately in the thick pile of the rug beneath her. When she came to rest before one of the chamber's plush chairs, the Scribe stepped closer and pushed her unceremoniously down into the seat.

"Now, we can finally talk, face to face."

The Scribe pushed back the heavy hood of his robe and released the chain about his neck, letting the whole thing fall to the floor. The Heart's eyes betrayed her disgust and surprise.

The Scribe was covered in streaks and patches of dried blood, on his skin and in his clothes. His left eye was dark and bloodshot, all white replaced by an infected red. At the centre, a crimson iris glared out angrily. Around the eye rough shards of dark stone and metal had been forced into the skin, leaving it twisted and puckered where they jutted from the surface. There were other, similar wounds in sight elsewhere on his body, the back of his right hand, his left forearm, his chest, each with those dark foreign lumps driven in, nestled into ugly scabs. Where his pale skin was still visible, dark veins seemed close to the surface, like a network of poison beneath.

When he looked into her eyes, the Scribe gave a sickly smile. "Ah, Lady Loulouthi, always so concerned for the feelings of others. I can assure you, there is no need to worry about me. I can *see* more clearly than ever."

He walked slowly behind her chair, and turned it a little, pushing it forward until she sat at the wide table in the middle of the chamber. Then he drew up another chair and sat close beside her.

"Do you know why this city is here, my Lady? Why it began?" he asked. "Few do. The Ancients, our predecessors, our forebears settled here, and deep beneath our feet they built something beyond our feeble imaginings. And although we may have forgotten their wisdom, lost all such knowledge… there are remnants, whispers, for those who know where to look. Somewhere beneath this Keep, Lady Loulouthi, somewhere deep, deep below there is a neglected little door. And behind that door I believe I might find one such remnant, one such whisper. An artefact. Old. Ancient, even."

He leant closer still and reached out towards her neck. Then, in one sharp movement, he snatched the thin chain of office she wore, tearing it roughly from her. The Heart could feel his thick breath against her cheek and feel the flecks of spittle as he spoke.

"Now I have very little time, Lady Loulouthi, and there is one more thing I must be certain of. I need to know everything about the girl, Joseera Mayweather. I need to know what happened all those years ago, out there in the Temple. And, my Lady, I need to know *now*."

The Heart fixed him with a defiant glare.

With a narrow smile, the Scribe placed a fresh sheet of parchment on the table before the Heart and took her right hand with his own, the dark little lumps protruding from the raw wounds below his knuckles.

The Heart stared. The stone, she thought, in horror, the Scribe's Ink...

Squeezing her fingers he pressed a pen into her grip, and holding her hand with his, began to write.

"I think you'll tell me, my Lady." he whispered. "I think you will."

oOo

They had made it to the base of the Temple without incident, and now Fulza and Joseera stood side by side at one of the low archways, tentatively peering into the darkness beyond. Although the moon was high and bright in a clear sky, the light did not extend into the Temple at all and neither could make out anything but sheer blackness within.

Joseera turned and looked up impatiently at Fulza. "Well? What do we do now?" she asked.

Fulza continued to peer into the darkness, answering absently, "What you mean, girl?"

Joseera shrugged. "I mean – what do we do? There's no-one here, right?"

Fulza looked down at her uncertainly. "No. No-one here."

"But you thought that there would be? Something or someone in our way at least?"

The big Savage chewed at his lip. "Yes... Something. Someone." he nodded.

"Maybe waiting inside then?"

"Maybe waiting, yes."

"So it's not safe to go in?"

"Probably not, girl."

"But we have to go in?"

"Hm. Have to go in"

The two stood and looked at each other in silence. There was no breeze.

"Go in front, girl. Stay very close."

They crept tentatively forward, Joseera leading, Fulza protectively arched over her, one hand resting firmly on her shoulder as they went. Much to their surprise, as they edged further into the darkness, Joseera's staff began once again to gently shine, providing a slight but welcome bloom to light their way. Steadily they travelled deeper and deeper into the Temple's belly. The path twisted this way and that, cutting off the little patch of moonlight left outside and leaving them alone in the staff's meagre glow, with nothing but blackness beyond.

They walked in silence, steady and slow, until Joseera found she had lost all sense of how long they had been moving. In the absence of sight or sound, her breath sounded loud and laboured, and for a horrible moment she was convinced that Fulza had vanished from behind her, that she would find herself alone. She stopped suddenly and turned, only to find him looking gravely down at her. Much to his surprise, she flung her arms about his neck and hugged him warmly. For a moment, he froze, taken aback, but then put a hand upon her back and pressed her closely to him.

"Still here, girl." he said, gently. "Now, go on. Must go on."

She drew back to meet his eyes. "Together." she said.

"Together." he agreed.

Eventually the narrow passage gave way to a huge, high chamber, and it could not have come soon enough for Joseera. She felt as thought they had been creeping through the darkness for hours, but even so, she was amazed to see a faint shaft of daylight drifting in from a hole in the roof high above. The vast space seemed otherwise deserted, and largely featureless, save a simple platform in the centre where the dusty light fell. She stepped forward in astonishment, peering up into the haze.

"Fulza, look! Is it possible? How can it have taken all night?" she exclaimed. "Fulza! Fulza?"

Joseera turned, and with a gasp, her hand went to her mouth. Fulza stood in the narrow entrance to the room, fixed in place by four sharp blades pressing at the sides of his neck and under his arms. Four men, two on each side, held the long hafts of their weapons firmly and calmly, ready to run Fulza through should he make an unwelcome move.

In the shadows beside them, a dark figure leant forward on the rock where he sat.

"Hello Joseera." said Aleph. "I've been waiting for you."

Chapter Twenty

Much to her pleasure, the Book was causing Lieutenant Ripfer considerable irritation. As soon as she had known what was happening, in the precious seconds before the light had immobilised her completely, she had thrown up whatever defences she could muster, in the hope that she would at least make life difficult for whoever was responsible. So far, she was not disappointed.

The young Lieutenant had entered her study with an arrogant air, gloating and swaggering as if he himself had been the one to subdue her. When he had attempted to approach her, however, his manner had quickly changed. The simple protective charm she had established caught him entirely by surprise, throwing him off his feet and knocking the air from his lungs, drawing a host of muffled sniggers from the three soldiers accompanying him. Although the soft light entrapping her prevented her from smiling, the Book's eyes sparkled with amusement nonetheless, and this was not lost on Lieutenant Ripfer. He had leapt to his feet with a petulant scowl, and commanded his men to try in his place. They had rushed forward in the hope that an aggressive approach might be the key, and had met with the same fate as their Lieutenant. From her shimmering prison, the Book had watched the bullish figures sprawled on the floor, and given silent thanks that she had at least been caught out in her own study, where her practise was at its strongest. Ripfer glared at her with impotent fury, and the Book had met his gaze with relish, hoping he could still read the gladness on her face.

They had thrown things and thrust things, leapt and

crawled, to no avail. Perhaps half an hour or more had passed, yet despite their increasingly inventive efforts, Ripfer and his men were no closer to a solution, she knew. Sadly, thought the Book, neither was she. When satisfied that she was safe for the time being, she had turned her mind to the light ensnaring her, in the hope that even if she could not devise a means of escape, she might at least better understand her predicament. So far, she had been without success. The light did not appear to conform to any arts or magicks she could think of, and seemed unwavering in its hold. It did not help that she was subject to constant distraction, as these fools insisted on continuing their masochistic efforts to lay hands on her.

Her attention was brought entirely back to the room when the study door opened. The soldiers had been full of noise, shouting encouragement and advice to one another as they made their attempts, but now they fell silent. Wrapped in the long robes of his office, hood drawn low, the Scribe walked purposefully into the study, closely followed by the curious figures of Mister Glower and Miss Glass. He stopped, and surveyed the chaotic scene before him. The men were suddenly cowed.

The Scribe sighed, and muttered quietly over his shoulder to Glass and Glower. "It seems I must take care of every *detail*, does it not?"
Miss Glass simply nodded, but Mister Glower gave a sycophantic giggle, agreeing, "Indeed it does, your Eminence, indeed it does!"
The Scribe's eyes lighted on Ripfer, who squirmed miserably. "Lieutenant. You are in command here, I assume?"
Ripfer gave a painfully keen salute. "Yes, your Eminence. That is correct, your Eminence."

The Scribe nodded. "Then perhaps you would be so kind as to explain exactly *what* is causing your delay? My instructions were quite clear, and *time* is very much of the *essence* here, Lieutenant!"

Ripfer's face flushed a hot pink. "Uh, yes, your Eminence. My apologies for... keeping you waiting. We have been trying, your Eminence, but... the witch has-"

"When you say 'witch', Lieutenant," interrupted the Scribe, sourly, "am I to understand you mean 'the Lady Sofya'? Because if that is the case, *Lieutenant*... it is somewhat disrespectful, wouldn't you say, Miss Glass?"

Miss Glass eyed Ripfer with contempt. "I would, your Eminence. Given his sluggish performance, I would suggest the Lieutenant remembers the proper order of things, and his place in them."

The rest of the men in the room considered their boots as intently as they could, blood drained from their faces. Ripfer's voice was tight when he continued, and sweat glistened on his brow. "Yes, of course, forgive me, your Eminence. I meant... we have been trying, your Eminence, but the... Lady Sofya has... some protection in place. Some use of her... *gifts*, your Eminence. It's proved impossible to draw near her."

The Scribe gave a loud and abrupt burst of laughter, swiftly joined by Mister Glower, and the three soldiers visibly flinched.

"Does she, indeed!" he cried. "Ah, dear Lady Sofya, ever the trickster! Shrewd and devious to the last, eh?"

The Scribe reached out with his left hand, and pointing to an empty glass flask sitting on a nearby bench, gave a flick of his fingers in the Book's direction. The flask leapt from its place and flew across the room, but before it could strike the Book something knocked it aside, leaving it to shatter on the stone floor.

The Book's eyes flickered nervously. That, she thought, was unexpected. That was a worrying development.

The Scribe sighed. "Very impressive, Lady Sofya, especially given the circumstances under which you were working. Unfortunately, my Lady, I have no more time for games, however entertaining they may be."

The Scribe began to move forward, and as he came closer the Book saw for the first time what was clutched in his right hand. Two familiar shapes of shimmering gold dangled from the delicate chains he held, two shapes very similar to the symbol of office she wore about her own neck. Suddenly, the Book was afraid.

As the Scribe neared, his left hand pressed at the strange lump upon his chest, hidden beneath his robes. The Book felt a momentary nausea as the Scribe breezed through her barrier without pause or exertion, then her eyes widened in horror as the tall figure drew close enough for her to see clearly beneath the hood, to see his face. This face, disfigured and distorted as it was, brutally augmented, was not the Scribe she knew. The dark shards buried in his skin glittered, reflecting the soft blue light around her.

The Scribe bent forward, leant in close, and pulled gently on the little length of chain that was visible outside the Book's clothes, bringing her emblem of office out from its hiding place.
"You were always my favourite, Lady Sofya." he whispered. "A woman with a little *vision*, at least. But, I'm afraid now I must leave you. I have most *pressing* matters to attend to, and now I finally have everything I need."
With a sudden jerk, he yanked the chain painfully from her neck.

The Scribe paced impatiently back towards the door, waving dismissively at Lieutenant Ripfer as he went. "Thank you, Lieutenant. Lady Sofya shouldn't cause you any further difficulty. Remain here for the time being. Mister Glower, Miss Glass, we are ready, I think!"
With that, the Scribe and his lackeys were gone.

The soldiers in the study breathed an audible sigh of relief. Ripfer gave the Book a noxious smile.
"Well," said the Lieutenant loudly, "now that everything's taken care of, if we must stay here we may as well enjoy our success! Let's see if there's anything decent to drink, shall we?"
The suggestion was met with grateful approval from the other three men, who began to examine the various shelves and cupboards that littered the study for anything that looked faintly alcoholic.

Ripfer himself made his way over to the Book, and began to look in the cupboards beside her.
"Thought you'd got the better of us, didn't you?" he puffed, mawkishly, "Thought you'd got it all figured out!"
He had discovered two bottles of wine in the cupboard, one red, one white. He looked critically at each for a moment, then pulled the cork from the red with his teeth and took a deep swig. His face screwed up in an expression of distaste, and he passed the bottle off to one of the other men.
"Ugh! I'd have expected a little more from the shelves of the grand Lady Sofya!" he spat, "Still, better than nothing, I suppose! To your health, witch!"
Ripfer pulled the cork from the other bottle and raised it at the Book, before drinking deeply from that one too. He scowled again and passed the bottle on.

"Yuch! No better!" he cried, "Perhaps it gets better the more you drink though, eh?"

From her frozen position, the Book observed the carousing men pass the bottles between them with an almost scholarly interest. She watched as Ripfer held his stomach for a moment and gave a queasy belch. If she could have raised an eyebrow, she would have.

oOo

Joseera called out to Fulza in concern.
"Fulza? Are you okay? Are they hurting you?"
The Savage could not move his head or look at her, thanks to the sharp spear points pressing firmly into his neck below his jaw, but he answered her as steadily as he could, through clenched teeth.
"Am okay, girl. Be calm."

Aleph laughed delightedly, then jumped down from the rock where he sat, out of the deep shadows, to where Joseera could see him a little more clearly. He was a tall man of about her brother's age, and athletically built. He wore stout leathers and light mail, with a long cloak and hood, very plain in appearance, all dark browns and black. Although the rest of his men had their hoods drawn up, Aleph's was down about his neck, and revealed his thick, dark hair and tanned, smiling face, green eyes sparkling at her. He sauntered forward, one hand hooked into his belt, the other playing with a little stone, pitch black and shiny.

Joseera frowned at this attractive figure and his easy stance. She gripped her staff tightly before her.
"Who are you? What do you want?" she growled.
"Oh really, Joseera, so hard, so direct?" he spread his arms

in mock disappointment, "I'd have hoped for a little more... frailty from a sweet little thing such as you." He smiled warmly at her, and Joseera found herself fighting the urge to smile back.

"Still," he continued, with a wry glance at Fulza, "perhaps it's the company you keep."

Joseera shook her head, tried to clear the downy thickness from her thoughts. As she looked at Aleph, she felt strangely tired. Perhaps he could help her, find her somewhere to rest.

"Now then, Joseera," Aleph went on, green eyes caressing her, quickening her breath, "I think you should let me take care of you... I'll take care of everything from now on... You'll have nothing more to worry about... nothing at all." He stepped close and drew his hand from his belt to gently stroke Joseera's cheek. His touch was warm, and she closed her eyes softly.

In her mind's eye Joseera saw her home. She saw her bed, and her house, her mother and father. She saw a peaceful day, beneath a clear sky. Then with a flash she saw the flames as her village burned, saw the terrified faces of those that she loved. She saw her brother's face, and heard his voice urging her onward. She saw Fulza, dear, dependable Fulza, always beside her.

Joseera's eyes snapped open, suddenly fierce. She jerked away from Aleph's hand with a shout, and instinctively lashed out with her staff, catching him on the arm and knocking the little stone he had been toying with from his grasp.
"No! Get away from me! Stay away!" she screamed at him, staff thrust out defensively.

Aleph scowled at her angrily. He had not changed, physically, as far as Joseera could tell, but he looked colder somehow. His eyes seemed to sit deeper in his face, and now she noticed the cruel sharpness of his features.

"Very well then, Joseera." he snapped. "I suppose it was a little optimistic. Have it your way."
With lighting speed he lashed out and ripped the staff from Joseera's grasp, throwing it off into the shadows. With dismay, Joseera watched it skitter into the darkness. Aleph turned back and struck her a ferocious blow across the cheek with the back of his hand, sending her sprawling into the dirt, eyes streaming, head spinning. Dimly she heard Fulza protest and then cry out as his captors reasserted their control.

Aleph strode over to where Joseera lay, and taking a firm grip on her neck with one hand, lifted her roughly to her feet. Then he flung her backwards, and she landed heavily on the steps at the foot of the plinth in the centre of the room, her head bouncing painfully on a hard corner, splitting the skin. Joseera felt a wet heat spreading through her hair and across her face. She pressed at it with her hand, and looked numbly at the slick blood on her palm when she drew it away.

Aleph approached her again, and she lifted her arms in an effort to protect herself.
"Oh, don't worry, Joseera." he laughed, dryly, "I need you alive, child. Now. I must apologise for my rudeness. You asked me who I am and what I want, and I have yet to answer you."
He sat, relaxed on the steps beside her, leaning on one elbow as he spoke.

"My name is Aleph, and I am the Seeker Prime, finest servant of the Order of Keepers. That is who I am. You are Joseera Mayweather, descendent of the Ilo'Seri, and that, Joseera, is what I want."

Joseera frowned at him through the haze, and he smiled.

"Surprised, Joseera? You shouldn't be. The Order has access to knowledge and understanding far beyond the means of most. We knew what you were before you did yourself, child. And now...His Eminence has need of you, the Order stands on the brink of true greatness, and whether you know it or not, child, you are the key to unlock it all! The knowledge and power of the Ancients lies at our fingertips. His Eminence has sought out their relics, the remnants of their arts… and now it seems the greatest power of all lay right beneath our feet. And you will help us harness it, Joseera! The secrets you carry will make us unstoppable!"

He laughed, softly, and gave a wry shake of his head.

"Of course, we did not expect you to be so... troublesome. I've been searching for you for some time. When I gave the order to burn your village, I felt certain that would flush you out, but no... You have caused me some frustration, Joseera, and more than a little embarrassment. Still... I suppose you are not entirely to blame for that. Your... large friend here was there to help you along the way, wasn't he?"

Aleph stood and walked slowly over to where the others were holding Fulza.

"What do you say, Savage?" asked Aleph, "Are you to blame for all this trouble?"

"Leave her alone." managed Fulza. "I will-"

"Hah! You will what, Savage?" spat Aleph. "You imagine you can threaten me?"

Aleph pressed one hand to his lips thoughtfully.

"You know, Savage, I find it remarkable that you have formed such a bond with this child. A base creature like yourself, protecting one of us. Perhaps she sees you as... a pet. In fact, there *are* age-old histories that say we once lived side by side, your people and mine. Difficult to believe, I know. But I suppose at some stage we must have surpassed you, risen above the vulgar animal and become your superiors. Intellectually. Culturally. Physically."
This prompted an angry grunt from Fulza. "Hn. Let me go. We will see."

Aleph smiled. He turned and walked a few paces away, so that he stood in the centre of the ground between Fulza and Joseera.
"My thoughts exactly, Savage." he said, "My thoughts exactly. Since you have caused me quite so much irritation, I feel you owe me a little amusement in return. So, I propose a deal to you, Savage. My men will release you. The way out, and your freedom lie behind you, and we will do nothing to hinder you should you wish to run away with tail between your legs. Alternatively-"
Aleph opened his arms wide in invitation.
"-you may face me in combat. My men will do nothing to interfere. If you can best me, Savage, in this if nothing else, you and Joseera will be free to go."

Joseera struggled to lift her head on the steps where she lay. She called out to Fulza, although doing so made her head pound madly and her ears buzz with noise. "Fulza! Don't listen! Don't let him-"
"Joseera! Be calm, girl." Fulza called back. "After all, what choice?"

Aleph clapped his hands. "Very good, Savage! Very good!"

He removed his cloak and sword belt, tossing them both to one side, before signalling to his men. Two of them roughly removed Fulza's axe from his back, and stripped the knives and tools from his harness. They also removed the thick belt from his waist, eyeing the many pockets and pouches suspiciously. Then they took up their spears again, and all four backed away slowly, leaving Fulza alone in the doorway.

Aleph gestured behind Fulza.
"The door is there, Savage. If you doubt your strength."

Joseera dragged herself painfully up onto one arm so she could see what was happening. She blinked and rubbed at her face with her other hand to clear the blood and tears from her eyes.

For a moment the two figures simply stood, facing each other across the empty ground, as if trying to divine the others weakness or perceive their strategy. Then, without warning or indication, Aleph's right hand flicked out, and launched a tiny dart, concealed in the palm of his hand, straight at Fulza. It lodged loosely in Fulza's chest, and hung there pitifully. For a moment Joseera feared he would collapse, or choke in the hold of some terrible poison, but instead he simply looked disdainfully down at the tiny dart, before plucking it from his breast with a derisive snort. Then the great Savage gave a terrible roar, and launched himself forward with the speed that had surprised Joseera so many times before. Arms thrusting out, muscles surging, he flew murderously towards Aleph.

But somehow, Aleph was faster.

In astonishment, Joseera watched as Aleph swept and

flowed around Fulza like smoke, impossible to catch, and punished each missed attempt with a stinging strike of his own. He used the Savage's greater size and bulk against him, always staying unnervingly close, inside Fulza's reach, whilst dipping and spinning around the Savage's heavy limbs.

At first Joseera thought they may fight each other to a stand still, as Fulza simply seemed to shrug off Aleph's blows, but then she realised he was beginning to slow. Fulza turned as if confused, mouth hanging open strangely, eyes squinting and blinking. Aleph, meanwhile, appeared to know exactly where to hit the Savage, focusing his assault on vulnerable targets, the throat, the knees, beneath the arms.

Eventually, dazed and desperate, Fulza threw a lethally powerful punch straight at Aleph's chest, but the Seeker turned to his right, avoiding the blow by a whisker. In a flash, Aleph wrapped his right arm around Fulza's wrist, and smashed at the Savage's elbow with his left, pulling Fulza off balance, and sending him crashing to the earth. The Seeker saw his opportunity. Aleph continued to turn, bringing his heel and then his fists smashing into Fulza's temple again and again with a sickening crack.

Tears ran freely down Joseera's face, streaking the blood. She tried to call out, but her throat was tight and dry, and she could not find her voice. As she watched, Fulza, insensible now but impossibly dogged, tried to raise his head from the ground, eyes rolling crazily, jaw slack. Each time he rose, Aleph would send his head solidly into the earth with a sharp, heavy blow, a wet smack echoing round the stone walls of the Temple. Again and again the great Savage rose, again and again the Seeker punished him for it, until Fulza's face was a slick mess of blood, and Joseera could stand it no longer.

She tried to push herself up onto her feet, but her vision swam and she found her legs weak. Her feet slipped from under her and she fell on her back at the foot of the plinth. Consciousness almost escaped her as she lay there, but the edge of the soft sunlight filtering down from above fell just on her face, and something in the light gave her strength.

"Joseera."

Joseera frowned, and looked drunkenly up into the glow. Far, far above, as she gazed up through the hole in the high, curved ceiling, she could see a delicate bird. It sailed peacefully in a cloudless sky, warm sun dancing on golden wings.

"Not far Joseera."

From the corner of her eye she could see Aleph, now finished with Fulza, striding purposefully over to where she lay. Gently, as if helping someone else up, Joseera lifted herself, leaning against the plinth, up into the light.

When he saw her rising again, Aleph quickened his pace. She was tougher than he had expected, it seemed, and his patience with her irksome ways had all but run dry.

"So close."

The voices ringing in her head were clear now, and Joseera felt a growing strength as she lifted herself higher. Her hands gripped the edge of the plinth and she pulled as hard as she could, heaving herself up to lean on the side. Panting, she looked down into the shallow bowl carved into the top, at the cool, still water within. The warm sunlight fell on her back and shoulders, soothing her. Before her she could see a faint golden shape, twisted like a root, constrained and suffocated by a thick blue shroud. She smiled.

"*Now.*"

Aleph bounded up the steps to the plinth arms outstretched, reaching for Joseera. Even as he grasped for her, Joseera extended one finger down into the water.

The effect was instantaneous. The dusty strand of sunlight falling through the roof was replaced by a blistering brightness, suddenly a thousand bright shadows and points of light circled quickly outward from the beam, and the many nooks and alcoves in the walls were lit up from within. Everything was bathed in warmth. Aleph cried out in fury and pain as the blinding light burst across his vision, raising his arms in a hopeless effort to deflect the glare.

On the earth where he lay, the unconscious Fulza cried out as the glow touched him, and then quieted, and lay still.

In the shallow bowl, the blue shroud darkened under the blazing light, tightened, and shattered, fading to nothing in the brilliant glow. The twisted Knot of gold beneath bathed in the warmth and gleamed.

In the centre of it all, Joseera gave an exhausted laugh. Then Aleph, cursing, eyes streaming, found her in the brightness, and struck a brutal blow to the back of her head. For Joseera, the light turned to black.

Chapter Twenty-One

Mister Glower, Miss Glass and the Scribe stood before a dusty and neglected door. Made of heavy darkwood, and bound with thick iron beams and braces, it sat, unmoving and intractable, in the deep stone wall far beneath the Keep. Countless ravelled cobwebs crossed its surface, and in the centre of its bulk lay a blackened, round plate, three odd holes evenly placed around it.

The Scribe's face lit up in near childish excitement as he watched the whimpering Parfort slot the three gold emblems into their assigned places. He was close now, he knew, on the edge of greatness, knowledge that had been lost and hidden for centuries was almost within his grasp. Knowledge that would bring with it inevitable power.

For the fourth time at least, Parfort's hands slipped, and one of the keys fell, tinkling, to the worn stone floor. The Scribe gave an irritated scoff.
"Fire and flood, Mister Parfort, pull yourself together! We do not have time to waste with incompetence!"
The young Scrivener tried to suppress the welling tears and panic.
"Y-yes, your Eminence! I'm sorry, your Eminence, they're just – it's an awkward fit, your Eminence, and-"
"I'm not interested in excuses, Mister Parfort!" barked the Scribe, "I told Mister Glower and Miss Glass here, that you showed promise! Do *not* give me cause to regret my recommendation!"
"Yes, s-sorry, your Eminence! I'm sorry!"

On their journey down into the deep tunnels and chambers beneath the Keep, Parfort's misery had grown exponentially. As they had progressed, the Scribe had become more impatient, and the little party had moved more and more urgently. Parfort had found himself almost running at times to keep up, looking on in horror as each unfortunate individual to cross their path, whether servant or soldier, was dealt with more swiftly and more brutally than the last.

"Nothing must stand in the way of progress, knowledge, the next step, my boy!" the Scribe had cried.

Parfort wasn't sure that anything could.

Eventually the boy's shaking hands overcame their task, and Parfort stood at the door with fingers splayed, pressing each of the keys into their place at the same time. The Scribe's frustration seemed tempered by the boy's success.

"Finally, Mister Parfort, very good. Now... press and turn the whole plate as one, down on the left..."

As he spoke, Glass and Glower took a few cautious steps back, and motioned for the Scribe to do the same, which he quickly did. It was infuriating to watch the lad stutter and fumble at every hurdle, but the Scribe had come too far, was too close to his goal to risk any problems now. He would not fall prey to some trick or drudge's trap. Not now.

He narrowed his eyes as the boy slowly twisted the plate round as far as it would travel, finishing its journey with a decisive *clunk*. The Scribe held his breath, and waited. For a moment there was no sound save that of the boy's heavy breath. Then, a sudden *click*, prompting a terrified yelp from Parfort, who jumped, flinching away as the solid door swung open.

The Scribe's eyebrows lifted in mild surprise. As simple as that then, he thought. Almost disappointing.

He swept forward, Glass and Glower close behind, past the outstretched Parfort, who lay shivering in relief.
"Come along, Mister Parfort!" he called behind him. "We still have a great deal to do!"
The young Scrivener dragged himself miserably to his feet, retrieved his torch from the old iron holder on the wall, and slipped through the narrow doorway.

They travelled silently on along a thin, cold passageway, damp walls glistening in the firelight, until eventually they came to an arch that marked the end of the glum corridor. As they continued into the dim and musty chamber beyond, Mister Glower drew a dull, black rod from his robes, short and narrow like a pen. He held it high in one hand, and to Parfort's surprise, it began to glow. Dimly at first, like a firefly or nightflower, a strange, blueish purple light, gradually brightening until it burned like a flame. There was no heat though, rather the light felt cold, spreading, malignant, through the darkness, as if feeding on the shadows. Parfort shuddered.

To distract from the sickly light, he held up his own torch and directed his attention outwards, gazing around him at the chamber they traversed. His mouth rounded in silent marvel at what he found. All about them, as far into the gloom as Parfort could make out, they were surrounded by row upon row of shelves and tables, stacked high with parchments and papers. Huge books, gargantuan tomes with curious bindings were strewn around, and a thick layer of collected dust sat placid and peaceful atop it all. Parfort faltered in his step. All his life he had been fascinated by such things, drawn to the mysteries that lay hidden in the words, enchanted by the tales and stories found within. His time in the Order had taught and conditioned him to value and respect what could be found set down by pen and ink.

The boy called out to his master in wonder.
"Your Eminence... your Eminence, look! So much... so many of them! What is it all, your Eminence, where did it come from?"
The Scribe paused, and cast a sour look over his shoulder.
"We don't have *time* for *games*, Mister Parfort. This does not concern us."
Then he walked on.

Parfort's brow creased in confusion and amazement.
"B-but, your Eminence, i-it's-"
"No *time*, Mister Parfort!" said the Scribe again. "Now wait here, boy. Keep your wits about you. If there is any disturbance from beyond, you will let us know immediately. Understood?"
Parfort swallowed nervously, then gave an uncertain nod. The Scribe grunted his approval.
"Hnh. Very good. Now, Miss Glass, Mister Glower? Shall we proceed?"
"Certainly, Your Eminence." replied Glower.
Parfort watched as the three figures moved slowly away from him, eerily lit by the flickering violet rod. They continued across to the far wall of the wide chamber, and disappeared through a narrow doorway.

For a few moments Parfort stood, shivering, in the tiny island of warmth cast by his wavering torch. Beyond the little pool of light, the darkness stretched into the distance, and it reflected the boy's mood perfectly. Parfort felt lost.

oOo

When Fulza opened his eyes, he was surprised to find bright sunlight filling his vision, and the dark blur of a figure at his side. He blinked, clearing the fog, and the blur gradually sharpened, until much to his surprise he recognised the solemn face of Gaven Mayweather, Joseera's brother, by his side.

Fulza breathed deeply. The last thing he remembered was being in the damp darkness of the Temple, fighting a losing battle against the arrogant Seeker, and the taste of earth on his lips. Now he could feel the sun's warmth on his face, the air was fresh and clear. And there was Gaven, the girl's ignorant brother, eyes dark, frowning down at him. Fulza wondered if he was dead.

He tried to lift his head, to sit, and swiftly decided he couldn't be dead. If he were, there was no way his body could ache as it did. He winced, and Gaven quickly put a firm hand on his shoulder, pushing him back to rest.
"Where is she, Savage?" he said, "Where is my sister?"
Fulza frowned. The more he came to his senses, the worse he seemed to feel. His head throbbed.
"Bash na gar…Where... where am I?" he managed. "What happened?"
Gaven frowned again.

As he lay there, Fulza cast his eyes about, taking in the transformation that had taken place within the Temple. Above him, through the hole in the high roof, the sun's broad beams poured in, bathing Fulza and the ground around him. The light danced and sparkled in the clear water that lay in a little pool atop the plinth, and played on the twisted gold therein, casting myriad reflections out around it. Fulza watched the shimmering patterns on the Temple walls, a thousand points flickering on the rough surface.

His astonishment got the better of him for a moment, and he tried to rise further, but a sharp pain lanced through his head and he fell back with a grimace.
"Joseera…"
"Yes, Savage, Joseera. Where is she?" responded Gaven, urgently, but it was no use.
The sharp pain thickened and spread through Fulza's skull, and his eyes fell closed once more. The warm sunlight played across his skin, and the great Savage slept.

oOo

As the dawn came at Vas Aloron, men and Savages alike were preparing to leave. The exhausted Tarrett had presided over several slow but fruitful negotiations with the Savages, and had been better pleased with the result than he could have hoped. Shortly afterwards he had retired to the few remaining tents to collapse into a complete and dreamless sleep. When Hant arrived barely two hours later to shake him rudely awake, it took the General some moments to remember where he was. He rubbed clumsily at his eyes, then fixed Hant with an accusatory glare.

"What? What is it, man? What do you want?"
"I'm sorry, sir. Sorry to wake you. But it's moving."

The words had the same effect as a pail of cold water, and Tarrett was suddenly alert. The events of the previous day rushed back into his mind with a jolt. With a nod, he stood, pushed back the tent door with aching arms, and stepped outside. He was met by a cold gust of wind, making him shiver involuntarily. Blinking, his tired eyes took in the scene, grateful for the grey morning.

The great golden giant was in the same place as it had been all night, kneeling as if in prayer, covered all about with a wild criss-cross of ropes, variously staked into the ground or secured to nearby rocks and trees. But even at first glance, Tarrett could see that the huge figure *had* shifted slightly, the vast head had moved.

He turned to Hant. "What happened? What caused it?"
Hant shook his head. "I.. I don't really know, sir. There was nothing much going on, to be honest most were leaving the thing well alone by then. But it just... just moved."

Even as they looked on uncertainly, the thick clouds that rolled across the sky broke for a moment, and the bright sun, still all but hidden by the mountains, cast a few sparkling rays across the valley. Again, the giant moved. Only briefly, a shifting of weight and the sound of straining ropes, but both men knew what they had seen. They were not the only ones either, as concerned shouts of warning went up from all directions.

Tarrett frowned. The wind was strong, and the light was growing inevitably. He had to wait only a few moments before another flash escaped and the giant shifted again. As realisation dawned with the day, Tarrett looked at Hant with round and watery eyes.
"It's the sun, Hant. By the bloody Ancients, *it's the sun*."
Hant's eyes narrowed for a moment, then widened again as he nodded in agreement.
"Ancients be praised, General, I think you're right."

Before they could do anything about their discovery, almost as if in response, the round edge of the sun finally began to emerge from behind the mountains. Shining directly now, the light pierced the grumbling clouds and began to sweep down the hillsides opposite and across the pass. The moment it struck the crest of the great head, the giant moved in earnest.

Just for a second, it seemed as though the crazed network of ropes and chains might actually hold the thing in place, but then with a deep, creaking wail, the restraints gave way. Stakes and anchors leapt up on flailing lines, while trees and rocks were ripped, altogether from the earth. The giant did not strain or pause, straightening as though all their work was nothing, and then, it began to walk.

Cries and yells rang out as men and Savages rushed clear of the giant's path, and others resumed their attacks with rocks and arrows. None of this, however, seemed to matter to the giant. It ignored the havoc around it quite completely, choosing instead to march solemnly onward, into the Fold, great strides eating up the ground.

"Where is it going?" murmured Hant quietly, as the giant moved into the distance.
Tarrett looked grimly at him. "Ready the men." he said firmly. "We leave immediately."

oOo

It was some time before Fulza awoke again. When he did, however, he was glad to discover that his head no longer hurt, and his limbs felt strong and rested. For a few minutes he didn't move, enjoying the feeling. It seemed a long while since he had felt truly relaxed.

When he sat up, he found Gaven nearby, busy readying a pack for travel. He didn't seem to notice Fulza move, and instead of calling out, Fulza quietly watched him working. The man had little in common with his sister. Where her hair was fine, red-golden, his was thick and dark. While Joseera's features were small and delicate, her brother's were broad and strong. As Fulza watched though, he saw that although Gaven bore little physical resemblance to his sister, there were other things that made their relation clear. Something about the way the man moved, with confidence, certainty, reminded Fulza of Joseera. Something of the determined expression on his face, jaw set, brow creased. A dauntless sense of courage.

Gaven turned to pull one of the worn straps tight, and caught Fulza observing him.
"You're awake." he said simply, continuing his task, "You've been out for a while."
Fulza grunted. "Hnh. How? What happened?"
Gaven laughed dryly. "I was hoping you could tell me, Savage." he said. "Rin and the others went after the guardsmen. That creature of yours led me here, and when I arrived I found you lying here alone, looking as though you'd taken on the whole Silund nation, and lost. No sign of my sister, or anyone else."
Fulza nodded, slowly, and looked down at the simple dressings applied to his wounds. "And you… help me?"
"Don't thank me, Savage." replied Gaven with a sniff, "I just did what I could. If you died, then the chances of me finding Joseera would be pretty slim, I'd say. I didn't know your kind heal like that though. So fast."
"So fast?" asked Fulza, frowning, "What you mean?"
Gaven shrugged. "I did next to nothing, put on field

dressings as best I could. Before I could think of anything else, the worst of it started to knit unaided."

Fulza tentatively pulled back the rough cloth covering his shoulder, and found no sign or mark of injury beneath. Hurriedly then, he sat, and pulled away the rest of the loose bandaging, and found similar results beneath. He stood, and found himself feeling as fit and as strong as he ever had.

Gaven sat eyeing him, cautiously. "What is it, Savage? Something wrong?"

"Nothing wrong." Fulza replied. "This... you did not do this?"

Gaven slowly shook his head. "No, Savage. Like I said, I thought perhaps it was the way with your kind. Another thing that makes you so bloody hard to fight."

"No." said Fulza. Then he found his eyes drawn to the bright stream of sunlight falling into the chamber from the the high roof, and to the glinting golden shape that lay in the small raised pool beneath. He walked slowly over to the plinth, silently noting the blood dried on the steps at its base, and lifted the twisted thing gently from its resting place. "This is not way with my kind. Maybe yours..."

Taking a little of the cloth that had bound him, Fulza carefully wrapped the golden shape in it.

Gaven raised his eyebrows, and shouldered his pack. "Either way, Savage, you stand healthy again, great, good, fine news. Now if you're finished recovering, perhaps you can finally tell me where we're going?"

Having placed the little bundle carefully in his pack, Fulza remembered something else. The attacker had knocked Joseera's staff from her hands... He wandered to the edges of the large chamber, peering into the corners until he found it, laying in the dust. He turned back to the dark haired man, who stood with one hand holding the strap of his pack tight across his chest, an impatient expression on

his face. Fulza found himself thinking of Joseera again.
"Where we're going?" he replied, in confusion.
"Yes, Savage." Gaven said, flatly. *"Where did they take my sister?"*

By the time they neared the outside of the Temple, Fulza had told Gaven all that he could recall about their encounter with Aleph, describing as best he could the Seeker's raving description of the plans for Joseera, and that he had said he needed her alive. He was surprised when it seemed that Gaven was familiar with Aleph, but not that this familiarity did little for Gaven's mood.

"Aleph. Seeker Prime, the Scribe's attack dog." Gaven had growled. "A thug who hides his brutality behind duty and learning. Curse his hide, I'll slit him from top to bottom if he hurts her."

Fulza had been about to ask more, but he was interrupted by a familiar and delighted squealing from beyond the Temple arch. As he cleared the doorway into the daylight, a great boar charged happily towards him, sliding to a stop at his feet in a cloud of dust.
"Jubal!" exclaimed Fulza, and knelt to greet the boar, gladly welcoming the rasp of its rough tongue on his face.
"Once it had brought me here and led me inside, it insisted on waiting out here, standing guard I suppose." Gaven nodded, grudgingly, "I will say this for the thing; it is certainly loyal, and it fights like a bloody demon."
Fulza turned with a smile as he continued to rub warmly at the boar's back and flanks. "Thank you. Jubal and I have known each other since both little more than pups. Is a good friend."
"Well, you should thank him then. The beast brought me here at least, it would've taken me twice as long to find

this place without it."

Gaven walked out onto the dry, baked dirt beyond the Temple's shadow.

"Now. We should get moving, Savage. It's a long way back to Bantha from here, that's sure. There'll be no time for rest or stop."

Fulza nodded his agreement. "I'm ready, Gaven Mayweather. We will find your sister."

Gaven's jaw tightened. "Let's go." he said, simply.

They set off at a steady pace, heading south east along a dusty trail. As they went, the path sank between high ridges of dry sandstone, turning the world around them into sheets of terracotta pinks and reds. The sun was a pale shape behind a mask of clouds, and a strong wind blew down into the valley, whipping the dry dust and sand into their faces, leaving them squinting at the way ahead.

They had been moving for less than an hour when they felt an odd vibration in the earth beneath their feet, and shortly afterwards began to hear a familiar but unwelcome sound ringing in the air.

Thung. Thung. Thung.

Gaven and Fulza turned to look at each other in silence, both knowing what the noise meant. As they looked behind they saw the shining shape of the giant growing, marching steadily forward, already clear of the ridge that sheltered the Temple far behind them.

They began to run along the narrow valley floor, the ringing footsteps growing ever louder as they went, resounding on the valley walls. When they turned again, the giant was almost on top of them, no more than a dozen great paces away, towering and terrible, glittering gold. The ground shook with each thunderous step, and the air shuddered with the sound. The giant was heading straight for them.

Fulza looked around at the dry red slopes on either side. He glanced, wild-eyed, back at the great figure.
"Climb! Climb! Get out of valley!" he shouted.

They tried in vain to scale the dusty slopes, never making it more than a few feet before the brittle red sandstone gave way beneath them, sending them sliding back to the bottom in a swirling haze.

Thung. Thung. Thung.

Then time ran out, and the giant was upon them. Desperately Gaven, Fulza and Jubal threw themselves across the dirt to avoid the impact of the first great foot, and pressed themselves low as the second swung ominously over them, dull rush of air humming by as it went.

"It's Bantha!" screamed Gaven from the dirt, over the thunderous noise of the giant's passing. "It must be heading for Bantha! Why else?! What else could it be?!"
Fulza raised his head from the dust and cast a frantic glance up at the giant.
"Stop! Wait!" he cried, in desperation.

Thung.

The second great foot swung down and landed ahead of them, shaking the ground and sending a rolling blast of dust and stone sweeping outward. Then the other, began to

rise again, and travel forward. Gasping helplessly, stinging dirt whipping his face and eyes, Fulza planted Joseera's staff in the dirt before him, using it to heave himself up, and cried out again.
"STOP!"

The giant's foot returned to the earth a few dozen feet away from them, and the giant paused in its stride. For a moment, no-one moved or dared breathe at all, and everything was still. Then the great golden head slowly turned and looked down, until its gaze rested inescapably on the tiny figures in the dry earth below.

Chapter Twenty-Two

Many miles away, Commander Gensu chose exactly the wrong moment to return to the Keep's barracks.

He had left the council chamber in a bitter cloud, bemoaning the lack of appreciation for his efforts and inflicting his sullen wrath on any soldier foolish enough to stray too close. He consoled himself with the thought that when the dust had finally settled, he would have everything he wanted. Of course, technically he'd answer to the Scribe, but the old man seemed to have less and less interest in normal things, obsessing instead over dusty relics and forgotten history, sometimes disappearing for days to pore over another piece of primitive scribbling. The day to day running of things, thought Gensu, the people, the city, the things that mattered, would be left to him. Whatever he desired, money, women, fine clothes and wine, would all be in his grasp. Who knows, he mused, a smile creeping back onto his face, perhaps in time he would even be able to get rid of the old man.

By the time he descended the steps leading to the barracks, Gensu's daydreaming had vastly improved his mood, and he turned the corner into the long, high room with a broad grin and a spring in his step, relishing the opportunity to deal more sternly with Lord Duma, since the Scribe had all he required of him for now. The entrance from the Keep opened onto a wide, raised platform that was used to deliver address to the men, and offered a view across the large chamber. Gensu stood and surveyed the scene, the crowd of soldiers filling the space, laughing and cheering as they pulled down flags and heraldry. He nodded in appreciation of their achievement.

His achievement. His victory. Bantha would belong to him.

When his eyes finally settled on the Sword, his good mood instantly dissolved. The strange, blue light surrounding the man, binding and subduing him, was fading. As Gensu watched, the Sword's head lifted, and a small, gentle smile crossed his face.
"Oh... no." whispered Gensu, simply.

It was a strange sensation. At first the Sword did not move or react as he felt the forces that restrained him being weakened, for fear it was another trick, or the product of his desperate imagination. When he was certain though, when he felt the freedom of movement returning, he gave silent thanks to whoever or whatever was behind it.

The Sword rose slowly to his feet, and heard the panicked orders fall from the lips of their commander, "Destroy him! Quickly! Quickly you fools, cut him down, *cut him down!*"

He smiled again. The order came too late.

He shuddered, enjoying the flood of instinct, of balance, of strength flowing back into him. He swung his right foot back behind the other, drawing his blade, surveying the room and taking two of the Scribe's men down even as he turned. There was a chaos of clatters and clangs, as dozens of soldiers jostled and shoved, hurrying to ready their weapons, encircling him, surrounding him.

They were many, he thought. Many, but not enough. Not today.

"If you wish to leave," the Sword called out, as loudly as he could, "go now and never return! If you stay and stand against me, be warned, I will give no quarter! You will find no mercy here!"

The words hung in the air, and hesitant glances shot around the room. From his vantage point Gensu could see a few of the men on the opposite side of the room, near the outer door, quietly lowering their weapons and slipping away. Crimson-faced, he screamed out furiously at the men again.

"What are you waiting for?! He's just one man! You have your orders, now *cut him down!*"

This, it seemed, was enough to tip the balance, and the room erupted in shouts and noise as the men surged forward, engulfing the Sword completely.

For a few tense seconds, Gensu could not see the Sword at all, just a great clamour of limbs and weapons, waving and flailing, pressing inward. Unblinking, breathless, he watched and waited, jaw clenched, knuckles white.

At the heart of the melee, the Sword dodged and crouched low, and as he drew his blade clear of the first assailant, pulled the man's body down on top of him, protecting him from the blows he could not deflect. He slashed out at the knees and calves of those nearest, and as they screamed and stumbled backward, slowing those behind, the Sword pushed upwards as fiercely as he could, driving the body he bore into the air and scattering those around him.

Commander Gensu looked on in horror from the edge of the room as the Sword reappeared in an explosion of men, then turned and wheeled about, his blade flickering through the air, shimmering, singing as it arced and fell. No matter which way the soldiers struck or where the blow came from, the Sword's weapon was always there to stop it, or twist it into another, before returning with a vengeful riposte.

Gensu had, of course, heard the stories and tales folk told of the Sword and his gift with the blade. As a military man, he thought he'd known better than most which bore some grain of truth and which were the wild fairytales of children and drunks. His opinion was rapidly reversing. To say the Sword had a gift was a foolish description at best. A gift suggested prowess, some natural ability, but this... Gensu stood, frozen for a moment, considering whether to rally his men and co-ordinate their efforts or to pull back those he could and retreat, when, from the midst of the storm, the Sword's eyes lighted on him across the room for the briefest of moments. Commander Gensu forgot his concerns, turned, and ran.

oOo

As she stomped down the corridor, occasionally swigging from the bottle of fine Timark red in her hand, dispatching any soldier who challenged her in as imaginative as way as she could muster, the Book had to admit, she was enjoying herself.

Just a few minutes earlier, the irritating young Lieutenant had been standing in front of her, drunkenly expounding on 'order' and 'progress', when without warning, the strange light surrounding the Book had suddenly faded. For a moment they had shared a look of surprise, before the Book seized her opportunity and gave the astonished Lieutenant a hefty and entirely unladylike boot in the stomach. This sent Ripfer stumbling backwards where he collided heavily with the other soldiers.

The Book had barely had time to enjoy the pained expression on his face before the explosive mixture he and his men had consumed did the rest. The results were decidedly messy.

After she had cleaned off the worst it, the Book had calmly wandered over to the small fireplace on the other side of the room, and reached into the small polished wood cabinet that stood nearby.
"Could've told you if you'd given me the chance, eh?" she had sniffed, "This is where I keep the good stuff."

She had uncorked the bottle without ceremony, and taken a deep draft, before adjusting her glasses with a loud sigh.
"Right then." she said to the empty room. "Let's sort this mess out."
She had crossed the room again, picking up various bits and pieces as she went, odd looking things wrapped in thick twine, little jars full of curious liquid, charms and trinkets on thin leather straps, depositing them about her person here and there, in pockets, on wrists, in the folds of her robe. When she reached the door she gave one last absent-minded look back, as if to ensure there was nothing she had forgotten. Then, with a nod, she marched determinedly out of the door, taking the bottle with her.

oOo

The Heart was hurrying along the familiar stairways and corridors, travelling quickly down towards the base of the Keep. She was trying to think clearly, sensibly, but her rage was making it difficult to think straight at all. Of course she was angry with the Scribe, with the Keepers, with their men for this unthinkable betrayal, their barbarous actions, but she was also angry with herself. How could she have been so blind to this? So ignorant? She stormed onward in a red haze.

Although she was largely unaware of it, she met little resistance as she forged on, the soldiers in her path driven off in horror and fear by the tangible wave of fury she exuded.

It was only when she saw a man burst through a wooden door ahead of her, driven by a gout of white flame, that the Heart caught hold of herself and stopped for a moment.

"Sofya?" she called. "Sofya, is that you?"

She sighed thankfully, choked with relief, as the familiar figure, crowned with a flare of wild red hair, stepped through the ruined door, bottle in hand. The Book took another quick gulp, then peered at the Heart, wrinkling her nose as she took in her friend's frenzied eyes and violent demeanour.

"Ancients, Loulouthi, are you alright? You look quite a state!"
The Heart nodded shakily. "I think so, Sofya, I'll be fine. It's not important right now. The Scribe, have you seen him? Has he taken your chain?"
"I'm afraid so, Loulouthi. Duma's too." said the Book. "How much does he know?"
The Heart looked suddenly lost. "I'm sorry, Sofya. I couldn't help it..."
The Book placed a hand on her friend's shoulder.
"What has he done to himself, Sofya? How could this happen?"

"I don't know, Loulouthi." shrugged the Book. "But I don't imagine our being set free is part of his plan. So whatever it is, we have to act quickly."
The Heart nodded again, more firmly this time, and the two set off together for the lower floors.

They had descended another two floors without incident and were making their way along the wide public corridor, when a figure barrelled around the corner ahead. The man's dark hair was slick with sweat and plastered his face, and his attention seemed to be focused entirely behind him. Consequently he had travelled a good distance down the corridor towards the Book and the Heart before he noticed them. When he finally looked up in their direction, a cold lump formed in the Heart's chest as she recognised the face of Commander Gensu.

Clearly he recognised both of them too, as his face contorted hatefully, and he drew to a halt. He eyed the women contemptuously, before drawing his long sword free of its scabbard, and stepping slowly toward them.
"Well. The witch *and* the whore." he snarled. "It seems *everyone* has been granted leave to wander off as they please! Unfortunately for you, I'm going to have to cut short your little excursion."
He levelled the fine steel of his blade at them, and advanced down the corridor.

The Book snorted derisively. "Pff. Really, we don't have time for this."
She strode ahead of the Heart, spreading her hands at her waist. The Commander did not turn or move away though, and the Heart felt a sudden knot of misgiving wrench at her gut. This man, however repulsive, was not fool enough to be unaware of the Book's unusual skills. Her

mouth opened to shout a warning to her friend, but she was too late. The Book's hands thrust out forcefully before her, sending a sudden blast of air rushing at the man. There was an odd sound, like a sharp intake of breath, and the Book was cast from her feet, flung against the hard stone of the walls, where she fell to the floor and lay still.

Gensu laughed.
"Heh. Arrogant witch. Like all her kind. They think their art raises them above the rest of us." He turned his eyes hungrily to the Heart. "Did she think I would be foolish enough to step into this Keep without some protection from the likes of her?"
The Heart was shaking now, as he continued his progress along the corridor towards her, almost lazily, enjoying her discomfort. Some part of her wanted just to turn and run away.
"What have you done to her?" she said.
Gensu smiled, and with one thumb, pulled at a leather cord about his neck, drawing a small, pitch-black carving of metal and stone from beneath his tunic.
"His Eminence tells me this little thing is older than Bantha, beyond the senses of the witch's arts, and your particular... talents. Though truly, I could not care less where it came from. I'm just glad to see it works."
He was close now, and he lowered his blade to his side, in order to step nearer to the Heart, near enough that she could smell the familiar heat of his breath. She breathed as steadily as she could, and fought the urge to retch. Gensu raised his other hand, and stroked her cheek slowly.
"Now. We were interrupted before. And I, my Lady," his fingers stiffened, and he gripped her face cruelly, "I was not finished with you."

Tears welled in the Heart's eyes, and Gensu chuckled. He pushed her back, against the wall of the corridor, and pressed himself close against her.

"Tears already, my Lady? You had best save a few, I think…"

The Heart clenched her teeth, and blinked to clear her vision as best she could.

"You know well enough the dangers of Duma's blade…" she whispered, voice cracking. Gensu gave a disdainful laugh.

"And you were prepared for Sofya's arts…" the Heart continued. "But do you know who is most dangerous of all?"

Gensu's body forced her hard against the wall, and his hand tightened about her throat. His other hand dropped the blade to the floor, and began to pull at the fabric of her dress, drawing it roughly up about her waist. He leaned so near his lips were almost against hers. "Tell me." he hissed.

The Heart's face was a pale picture of revulsion, her mouth curled in loathing. Dark shadows spread beneath her eyes, and her eyes burned furiously.

"I am." she said.

Her hands leapt upwards and clapped about Gensu's face, and for a moment he bore a look of fury at the attack, fit to kill her for her insolence. Then he met her gaze. The Heart's eyes seemed almost to pull in the light around them.

"Now, Commander. I'm going to make *you* feel something."

With a deep breath, steeling herself, the Heart gathered the myriad feelings that had assailed her over the past few hours. The terror and agony of hundreds of innocents assaulted and killed in the Keep, the grief and anguish of those left alive, the sickening pleasure and exhilaration of those who had gloried in their conquest. One by one, as she had felt them, she gathered these feelings up, building and swelling within her, almost overwhelming her. Pain. Fear. Torment. Despair. One by one she collected them all. She reached out with her mind until she found Commander Gensu. She thought back to his visit in the council chamber.

"Goodbye, Commander." she said, softly. Helpless, Gensu began to sob.

A few minutes later, she knelt, shaking, at Sofya's side, as the Book peered concernedly up at her.
"Loulouthi? Ancients save us, are you alright?" asked the Book, rubbing painfully at her head where it had struck the stone. "I can't believe I was so foolish, to be caught out by so silly a trick, eh? Although I must be honest, I couldn't see he had some protective art or other! But you, Loulouthi, look at you! What happened?"
The Heart smiled weakly at her friend. "It doesn't matter, Sofya, its done, he's gone. He won't be troubling us again."
The Book studied her for a moment. "Loulouthi... He came to you didn't he? While we were trapped like that, he came... I - Loulouthi, I'm sorry."
The Heart shook her head. "Sofya, there was nothing you could do. Nothing any of us could do."
The Book pulled herself up, and put her arms warmly about the Heart.
"Oh, Loulouthi." she said. "Well. He got what he deserved. I'm glad you're alright."
"You too, Sofya." replied the Heart, helping her friend up.
"And now we are both on our feet again, we have more

pressing matters to attend to.

"Hm." said the Book. "So. Let's find Gideon Prow."

The pair headed off down the corridor together, leaving it empty save for the shivering figure lying on the cold stone floor. Whatever remained of Commander Gensu lay on its back, softly whimpering, eyes open but unseeing, cast adrift and lost.

Chapter Twenty-Three

It was a long time before anyone moved, or said anything at all.

The wind blew tiny sandstorms along the valley floor, as Fulza simply lay in the dusty red earth, propped up on Joseera's staff, a near comical look of incredulity on his face, suddenly struck dumb. Gaven was much the same, and even Jubal seemed frozen in stunned silence.

For the giant's part, it neither shifted nor made a sound, but Fulza could not tell whether this was because it was waiting, or thinking, or simply stopped altogether.

Eventually, Gaven found his voice, although his eyes remained fixed on the towering figure standing before them, as if his gaze alone were keeping it there.
"It... it stopped, Savage. It stopped. It just... it stopped, right there."
When he replied, Fulza's eyes too remained firmly on the giant.
"Yes... see that."
Gaven gave a strange, nervous little laugh.
"What did you do, Savage? How did you stop it?"
"Good question." replied Fulza, slowly, "Don't know..."

A curious frown spread across Fulza's face, and he thought hard of Joseera and what had taken place in the Temple. He looked up, thoughtfully, at the giant.
"What did you do, girl?" he murmured softly to himself, "Why did it stop?"

"*You request it.*"

Like a thought not his own, the answer sounded in his head, and Fulza leapt to his feet as if stuck by lightning, and stood tense, with wild, round eyes. The reply caught Gaven so off-guard that he let out a startled shout, and thrust backwards in the dust, while Jubal snorted in sympathy.

The sound was a strange one, made up of noises that had nothing to do with the world of words and speech, but that somehow formed themselves into a voice when put together. It was like talking with a rockfall, rumbling down a mountainside, or a peal of thunder, rolling across the sky. There was a metallic quality too, and the sharper sounds seemed to ring and echo in their heads, hanging in their minds.

Fulza steadied himself. He stared up at the golden figure and breathed deeply. There was no sign that the giant had spoken. No sign of life at all. Fulza squinted, and rubbed at his eyes in an effort to clear the dry dust from them. As far as he could tell, the giant hadn't moved. In fact, it looked so still, so fixed and solid that for a moment he questioned whether he had really heard anything at all.

"Gaven Mayweather...?" he said, in a flat tone.
"Savage?" came the hissed reply.
"Gaven Mayweather, did you hear that?"
"Yes, Savage. I heard that." replied Gaven, emphatically.

Fulza peered up into the dark eye holes in the giant's golden face. In the blackness, there was a faint light.
"You can speak." he said to the giant.

"*Yes.*"

oOo

The Sword hurried down into the lower levels of the Keep, removing any of Gensu's remaining men he came across, and doing his best to direct the few terrified staff and servants who had escaped the initial attack to safety.

As he descended past the stables there was a hammering on one of the thick doors that led from the lower Keep out to the horse pens. A voice called out to him from behind the door.

"Lord Duma! Lord Duma! What's happening? Is the Keep secure?"

The Sword paced over to the door and peered through the narrow wooden bars at the top.
"Who is that? Corporal... Win... Winnow, is it?"
The man's relief was palpable through the bars.
"Yes, my Lord, that's right. Corporal Jan Winnow. And I'm very glad to see you, my Lord, if you'll forgive my saying so."
The Sword nodded. "Same here, Corporal. But what are you doing down here?"
"I'm with the Horse Guard, my Lord, my men and I came down when the trouble started in case there was need for us to ride out. But while we were preparing the horses, a load of the staff started turning up, shouting about the Keep being breached and there being soldiers causing havoc inside, butchering anyone they could lay hands to. Well, me and my men, there's only eight of us here, my Lord, but we gathered up as many of the staff and civilians as we could, and then we barricaded ourselves in here, figured it was the safest place. I hope you don't think

we've done wrong, my Lord, we just thought it best to protect those we could until we knew what in the Ancient's name was going on."

"How many are you in total, Corporal?" asked the Sword. Winnow shrugged. "I'm not quite sure, my Lord, I'd guess... about sixty or so? We managed to get most of those from the lower floors down here in time."

The Sword grinned, and thumped the door in delight, causing Winnow to jump.

"Well done man, well done! Now can you open the door, Corporal? I have a job for you."

As the Corporal and his men began to clear the door, the Sword informed him of the situation.

"The rest of the Keep has been taken, as far as I can tell, Corporal." he said, "Thanks to you, things aren't quite as bad as I feared. You've saved many lives. But I don't know where Lady Sofya and Lady Loulouthi are, or whether they're safe. I have to assume that they were... incapacitated, just as I was, but I can't be certain that they are also free now. I need to find them as quickly as possible, Corporal, and I'm going to need your help."

"I'll do whatever I can, my Lord, of course," replied Winnow, helping his men drag aside the last of the benches they had piled against the door. "But perhaps you should come take a look out first, my Lord, before you say things aren't so bad as you thought, if you'll forgive my saying."

The Sword frowned, and Winnow hauled open the heavy stable door, and beckoned him inside.

"Out that way, my Lord, you can see right over to the square." said Winnow, pointing at one of the small windows set in the stable's thick stone walls.

The Sword gave the Corporal a questioning look, and crossed the room to look out of the little window. What he saw drew the colour from his face. There were hundreds of soldiers busying themselves outside the Keep and in the square beyond, most in Banthan uniform, but all wearing the rich red of the Keepers as a sash, or about their arm. The Scribe had an army. The Sword cursed himself for his foolishness.

"Ancients take them! This is Gensu's doing! He... he arranged the detachments, who was sent to Vas Aloron, who stayed behind. He and Prow *planned* this, made sure all those loyal to us would be out of the way!"

He slammed his fist angrily against the wall.

"Damn them both! I should... I should have made the arrangements myself, I should have thought..."

Corporal Winnow stepped nervously forward. "You couldn't have known, my Lord. You couldn't have expected such treachery. None of us did."

The Sword turned away from the window, a thunderous look on his face.

"I will gut these traitors if it's the last thing I do." he growled. "Corporal, keep these people safe. I'll return as soon as I can."

oOo

The city of Bantha was old, and although there were many of its residents who proudly claimed that their families had lived in the city since the very beginning, there were none who knew for certain when that beginning might have been. On the surface, Bantha's long life was evident in the mishmash of styles and designs in the buildings, the wild sprawl of its twisting streets and alleys. But that would take you back no more than a few hundred years at the most. In order to go further into Bantha's history, you would have to dig a little deeper. Buildings with doorways and passages in cellars that had long been sealed up, forgotten places buried in the foundations, layer upon layer of the city's life hidden down below.

Bantha's great Keep was no exception to this. It had stood on the same spot in some form or other for as long as record had been kept, and likely for some while before that. Over the ages it had grown and spread, as one ruler after another had altered and expanded in prosperity, or rebuilt and adjusted after attack. Down beneath the wide corridors and bright chambers now in day to day use, lay a labyrinth of abandoned spaces.

The Book and the Heart did not have far to travel before they found evidence of the Scribe's passage. On their way, the Book had grabbed a torch from its holder, and it was only the torch that gave them light now. No-one had cause to see to the lamps down here, since these parts of the Keep were never used. For the most part, they were kept locked, dark and unsafe as they were, and the Three had seldom found the need to venture in. The Book looked critically at the old door that led on into the bowels of the building, now swinging lazily on its rusted hinges, lock torn from the rotten wood.

"Hnh. I suppose we should have done something about this door long ago. A determined child could have broken through here." she said.

"I don't imagine it would have made any difference, Sofya," replied the Heart, "the Scribe is certainly more than a determined child."

The Book sighed. "Yes, of course, Loulouthi. What does it matter now? I just keep wondering how we could have let this happen? How could we be so unprepared?"

The Heart smiled. "I think it was you who told me, Sofya, not so very long ago, to deal with the situation in hand rather than worrying about how you got here."

The Book turned, raising her eyebrows at her friend.
"Well," she said, after a moment. "I'm sure I put it better than that."
"Oh, I'm sure!" laughed the Heart, "I'm sure."

They continued on, descending several levels further, down winding stairwells, into the depths of the Keep. They passed the heavy door to the archives, finding the emblems, the three keys left behind, still sitting in the circular lock, and had walked only a little further into the darkness beyond the door, when they came upon a somewhat greater obstacle. Ahead, the narrow passageway had entirely collapsed. The walls and ceiling had tumbled inward, and now their way was blocked by a solid wall of stone and earth, the floor before it strewn with rubble and dirt. They approached as closely as they dared, studying the roof above them with uncertainty.

"What in the Ancient's name?!" exclaimed the Book, as she examined the wreckage. "This is his doing. It must be!"
The Heart, stood a little further back than her inquisitive friend, shook her head slowly.
"I don't understand, Sofya. It doesn't make sense."
The Book spun round, wild hair echoing the torch in her hand, a furious expression on her face.
"This is his doing! Him! He doesn't want us following him, so he's brought down the cursed ceiling!"
"No, Sofya, that's not what I mean." said the Heart, "Is there another way round? Some other way that leads through there?"
"What?" spluttered the Book, "Honestly, Loulouthi, you know as well as I do that this is the only way to..."
She stopped, and her anger subsided as realisation swept across her face.

"Oh. How silly of me. I didn't even stop to think, let my temper run away with me. But you're quite right, Loulouthi. It doesn't make sense. Why would anyone seal up their only way out?"

oOo

For some reason he couldn't quite explain, Fulza felt much calmer now as he stood before the giant, and Jubal, sensing this, had crept up beside him. Gaven didn't seem to share his sentiment, as he had carefully gotten to his feet and stood warily some distance behind, weapon drawn as if he might be able to defend himself should the giant take exception to the circumstances.

Fulza glanced back at him. "Don't think sword will save you, Gaven Mayweather, if it comes to that." he said.

"Maybe so, Savage." replied Gaven, "But if it's all the same to you, I'd rather have it in hand than not, if it comes to that."

Fulza shrugged, and stepped forward again, looking up at the unmoving face.

"You hear me?" he called.

"*Yes.*"

Fulza swallowed hard. He wasn't entirely sure what he was doing.

"Said… stopped because I request it. Why? Why listen to me?"

The answer didn't come straight away, and again Fulza wondered whether the giant was thinking, or had heard at all.

"*A spark. A long forgotten flame. Would hear what you have to say.*"

Fulza shook his head in confusion. "Flame?... What flame? What do you mean?"

"*Remnant. Memory of a time long gone. Had thought no such thing remained. None but my brothers and I.*"

Fulza steadied his breath. Although he heard what he presumed was the voice of the giant, it did not seem overly friendly, and he was not inclined to test its temperament.
"What are you? What is it you want?" he called.

"*At our creation, we were named Sun Kings, and we slept.*"

The giant's eyes began to burn darker, more fiercely then, and Fulza shifted nervously.

"*Now men betray the earth again. Greed. Hunger. Have learnt nothing. Our sleep is disturbed. The Ilo'seri gone. We will fulfill our purpose.*"

Fulza tensed in frustration. "What does this mean?!" he shouted, "Where are you going?"

"*The city of the Ancients will crumble and fall. The device will be destroyed.*"

Gaven lurched forward and shouted out, suddenly. "The city... Bantha? Are you talking about Bantha?" shouted Gaven, lurching suddenly forward, but the giant appeared not to hear him, or even if it did, not to respond.
Fulza called out again. "You say Ilo'Seri gone? Have not gone! We... seek one now, gone to the city!"

At this, the giant's burning eyes softened a little.

"Ilo'Seri..."

Gaven tried to seize the opportunity. "Yes, Sun King! She... she lives, she has gone to the ancient city! We follow her now to help her!"
The giant stood, motionless, while Gaven continued.
"We must... we must find her, and help her! We will help her to... to save the city, to save them all!"
He quickly realised that he had said something wrong, as the Sun King's eyes darkened and flashed.
When the unearthly voice came, it was sharp and cold.

"No. Circle must be broken. The Ilo'seri failed. We have watched and waited. Seen a hundred thousand pointless lives. Betrayal. Greed. Hunger. They have learnt nothing. We will bring an end, and the sun will still rise."

Fulza was beyond fear. The Sun King's answers angered him now, as he thought of Joseera, alone and needing him, needing them all. Teeth bared, he roared back at the giant. "No! Cannot be only way! Will not believe it! What use is that? Joseera lives! We have not found each other and fought here for nothing! She has not suffered for nothing! I will not allow it!"
As his temper flared, Gaven noticed with alarm that Joseera's staff began to grow brighter and brighter in Fulza's hand, until he found he could not look at it directly. He shielded his hands with his eyes, then peered through them in disbelief as the light seemed to spread to Fulza himself. The Savage shone, as if something had been ignited inside him, and the light danced on the Sun King's golden skin.
Fulza railed on, relentless and unaware, "You say Ilo'Seri

failed, but have not failed! She still lives!"
The giant paused, but the light in its eyes never waned. Finally, an answer came.

"*Perhaps... Perhaps there is a way. Perhaps this Ilo'seri... perhaps... she may remember.*"

With that, the giant bent down on one colossal knee, and lowered its left hand, palm up, to the ground before Fulza. He stood, looking at the great fingers, the metal joints. Then he looked up into the giant's face, and stepped up onto its outstretched hand. Jubal hopped quietly up alongside him.

"Savage! What are you doing? This is madness!" hissed Gaven, desperately.
Fulza turned, looking steadily back at him.
"For your sister, Gaven Mayweather. We have to go. We have to go to the city."
Gaven stared hotly back at him for a moment. Finally he shrugged and shook his head, before climbing up to join Fulza and Jubal.
"Very well." said Gaven to the giant above. "Take us to Bantha."

oOo

The Sword stood anxiously on the great stone stairwell that spiralled up the rear of the Keep's main building. He had considered and dismissed several possibilities already, and was beginning to run out of ideas. On his way across from the stable block he had encountered several of Gensu's men, some of whom had foolishly elected to stand and fight rather than run in terror at first sight of the furious Sword, and he had dispatched them in short order, not even breaking his stride as they ran at him and fell in quick succession beneath the curt swing of his blade. When he had reached the main building though, he found it strangely deserted. He had already investigated the Council chamber several floors above, finding nothing, and had thought to continue upwards to the Book's study, when he had come across several soldiers lying in the quiet halls who bore the mark of Sofya's indelicate touch.

He paused, uncertainly, trying to imagine where his friends might have headed, assuming of course, that they had gone of their own free will at all. Finally he concluded that even if he did not find Sofya in her study, he might at least uncover some indication of her whereabouts, and set off again, bounding swiftly up the steps.

When he reached the study high in the broad tower, he found the door wide open, and the room apparently deserted. From the doorway he peered in at the chaos of papers, flasks and odd looking instruments, and reflected that it would be difficult to tell whether the room had been disturbed or not, given that everything looked very much as it usually did. When he ventured in and discovered the remains of Ripfer and his men, however, he drew his conclusions quickly. They had found the Book up here, that much was certain, and from the looks of things Duma was willing to stake his life that the little woman had left of her own volition too.

The Sword stepped over a sloping pile of books to investigate further, when he happened to glance out of the study's wide windows. He stopped short, then turned, all else forgotten, and walked slowly over to stare silently out, unblinking, mouth widening noiselessly.

He stood for a moment just looking, one hand pressed against the cool glass as he took in what he saw.
"Oh no." he whispered softly. "Not now."

Chapter Twenty-Four

When the giant stood, taking Fulza, Jubal and Gaven with it, borne in one vast golden hand, all exclaimed aloud in a mix of fear and exhilaration. The giant raised them up until they could clamber safely across to its shoulder, though Jubal skittered and slipped on the shining metal, needing Fulza to haul the boar to safety. Once installed however, they rested quite securely, nestled in the curved ridge that rounded the giant's shoulder. The view was truly remarkable.

Fulza looked back at the Temple, in the distance behind them. The tall points and spires leapt madly into the air, wrapped with vines clinging and climbing. Columns and dark arches stood silent around the Temple base, and for a brief moment, as the drifting clouds dampened the sun's glare, Fulza thought he could see a faint column of light disappearing into the heavens from the Temple roof.

Before he had time to think further on it however, the giant set off, and with a breathtaking rush of air they surged forwards, the giant's great legs carrying them swiftly over the land below.

For a while, they rode in silence, heads poked out over the ridge, admiring the sights sweeping past below. Eventually though, the cold wind grew too much for them, and they slid back below the edge, pulling their cloaks tight about them, while Jubal curled up as small as possible for a creature of such bulk. Crouched low and looking up at the golden face above, Gaven decided, despite Fulza's insistence that he should not disturb their bearer, that he had other questions.

"You said you would help your brothers?" he called, loudly, "Does that mean there are more like you?"

"*We are three in all.*"

"So where do you come from? How did you get here?"

"*We few were left behind. We found ourselves alone. So we listened and we waited. We slept beneath the earth until the need arose.*"

Gaven rubbed at his eyes in frustration. The giant's replies were more like riddles than answers. He took a deep breath, and puffed noisily out.
"But why? What is your purpose? Why were you left?"

"*If all else failed, we would not.*"

Gaven was about to continue his interrogation, but stopped short when he turned and noticed Fulza watching him with a barely hidden smile on his face.
"What is it, Savage...? Something wrong?"
Fulza shrugged. "Nothing wrong, nothing wrong. Are certainly Joseera's brother, that is all."
Gaven gave a questioning look. "What is that supposed to mean, Savage? Of course I'm her brother, I don't see what-"
He stopped short, mouth wide open, mid-sentence.
Fulza frowned. "I'm sorry, Gaven Mayweather, I didn't mean to-"
"No, Savage, look!"
"What?"
"Look, there, Savage! Look!"

Fulza turned, eyes narrowing to see a high wall of snow-capped peaks looming ahead, and stretching off, unbroken, on either side, as far as he could see.

"It's the western range of the Long Hills." shouted Gaven, "They shield the lands of the Fold beyond... I can't believe it, I can't believe we're here already! Such a distance, and we've covered it as if it were nothing!"

Fulza peered out at the looming mountains growing in the distance. "We are close then. Close to the city."

"Well, yes, but... this is no use!" Gaven exclaimed, "The Long Hills were not rashly named, the range stretches from the banks of the Pulchren right up to the northern Fold! We're too far south, it will take hours to reach the nearest pass!"

The Sun King's voice rang in their heads, unbidden.

"Our path lies ahead."

oOo

The Sword stared silently out from the study high in the Keep. The windows were wide and long, crossing three sides of the room, and afforded him an excellent view. The city stretched out in all directions below, and beyond the walls to the north and west lay the familiar green of the Fold. To the east, the broken greys and browns of the Pulchren's rocky shores, and the river flowing tirelessly by.

"Why now? Why right at this moment?" he said, then laughed softly at himself, "Foolish, Duma. This can be no coincidence. There is a connection here, undoubtedly."

No matter which way he turned, the Sword could not

escape the sight of the golden figures advancing in the distance. Two giant shapes clad in shining gold, marching in a steady rhythm. The nearest came from the north-east, toward Vas Aloron, and was close enough now to just make out the flutes and folds of its armour, glittering in the sun. The other approached from the north-west, and was still some way from the city, but it came just as steadily, and showed no signs of slowing.

The Sword worked to quell the doubts that grew within him, jaw tightening with his resolve as he denied any sense of hopelessness. He breathed deeply, and tried to focus on what could be done, instead of what could not.

The giants came with a constant pace, it seemed, and the Sword judged by this that the nearest would not reach them until nightfall. That was time enough to prepare. If these things marched with the enemy, he would see to it at least that their passage was not easy.

He stood watching for a moment longer, feeling colder than the day could merit, and shuddered, feeling for a moment as though the eyes of those golden figures fell on him.

"Ancients take you," he growled at them. Then, with a frown, he turned and set off back down into the Keep, to seek out the Book and the Heart.

oOo

As a small child, Parfort had been unlike most of his friends. While they played games of soldier and Savage, fighting battles with sticks and imagining glory,

Parfort had found the reality of these past conflicts more interesting. Much of his time was spent buried in some book or other, to the delight of his teachers and the frustration of his friends. He was offered a place with the Order of Keepers relatively young, and his parents, a proud but poor couple, had gladly accepted. Though it meant they would see very little of their son, the Order brought a certain status, and guaranteed that their child would be well educated and taken care of. By his sixteenth birthday Parfort had attained the rank of Scrivener, highest available to a novice, and amongst those to be tutored by the Scribe himself. While his childhood friends idolised the great athletes and warriors of the Empire, Parfort looked to the Scribe as his paragon of learning and understanding.

He did not know what had happened to that man. Peering off into the blackness at the faint purple glow from the door of the next chamber, Parfort reflected glumly on his situation. He had sworn to obey the rules and teachings of the Order, and therefore the Scribe, but now found himself questioning both. Since the age of eight, the Order had been his family, his world. Where could he turn if not to them?

He kicked despondently at the stones beneath his feet, sending the fat wreathes of dust that gathered there spinning off into the dark, invisible currents of air twirling them silently across the floor. The slight breeze also disturbed the thick layer sat on the pile of hefty books closest to him, and dust long undisturbed tumbled noiselessly over the edge to its quiet fate below, revealing the dark words sprawling across the faded leather cover. *'An Historie of the Cities: Bantha the Destroyer'.* Parfort's eyes wandered curiously over the title. He glanced nervously off, at the glow from the door the Scribe had taken, accompanied by the ghoulish Glass and Glower, and saw no change. Then, not for the first time in his life, Parfort sought escape between the pages of a book.

'During Ilo'Seri rule, four cities grew and flourished, and the old power, called 'Seri-gae', the strength of earth, was plentiful. The Ilo'Seri grew fewer as the people spread, but still they guided and taught, making sure the balance remained, that the Seri-gae was respected and used with great care.

But some among the people became greedy and mistrustful. They thought the Ilo'Seri kept the Seri-gae for themselves, and so they plotted to steal it from them. They read the old stories of the birthing of the world, when all creatures were said to be equal, and took their name from them, calling themselves 'Children of the Ancients'.

These few, Children of the Ancients, worked in secret, building terrible machines unlike any before them, tearing Seri-gae from the earth and casting out dark fire. They leapt upon the four cities and ripped them piece from piece, drawing even the power from the Ilo'Seri and turning it against them.

The city of the south was razed almost to dust, and the Children of the Ancients took it for their own. They rebuilt it in twisted form around a great device that would draw Seri-gae from the heart of the world itself, and used captured Ilo'Seri to further its creation.

Their evils twisted the Children of the Ancients so that none would know them. Even as it granted them power, their misuse of Seri-gae warped and distorted them, extending their short lives and consuming their bodies, leaving them grasping and wraith-like, ever hungry for more. Still they walked among others though, using their new gifts to conceal their true form.

The last Ilo'Seri dreamt a desperate plan. A brave few allowed themselves to be captured by the Children of the Ancients in the hope that they might subvert the great device, and bring about its failure.

Uncertain of success, the remaining Ilo'Seri and their followers prepared for the worst, a failsafe. In the ruins of the fallen cities, three golden giants were built. Three people were chosen from among the survivors, and the Ilo'Seri drew forth their spirits, and sealed them into the great golden bodies. So they might weather the Ancients weaponry and outlast whatever disaster came to pass, the Ilo'Seri formed these golden giants to draw their strength from a source of Seri-gae beyond the Ancients grasp - the sun itself. Named Sun Kings, the giants would move against the Ancients if all else failed.

The Ancients used the captive Ilo'Seri, and began to activate the great device, ripping Seri-gae from the deep heart of the world. But the Ilo'Seri were ready, and resisted. Their efforts stopped the device, but not without cost. A huge and terrible wave of force swept out across the land, wiping out those receptive to Seri-gae, Ancient and Ilo'Seri alike, along with a great many others. The great device was sealed, it lay inert and abandoned. The Sun Kings, alone now and without purpose, stood in monument, and waited.

The Ilo'Seri and Ancients were gone from the land.

The surviving peoples gradually rebuilt their worlds. In time, some forgot their fears and returned to Bantha, began to settle and build in the ruins, echoes of the Ancients influence still showing here and there. Others spread far across the edges of the land, eschewing what they had known before, perhaps in fear of where it might lead them, choosing instead a simpler existence, and trusting only in what they made and crafted themselves.'

Parfort felt sick. His stomach shrank into a tight, painful knot, and the back of his throat gave a acid sting. With one shaking hand he reached into his robes and drew out the folded parchment he had torn from the Great Tome.

'*I, Gideon Prow, Scribe of the Order of Keepers, will wield the power of the Ancients.*
The Triumvirate, leaders of the Empire, will yield their keys.
Joseera Mayweather, child of Ilo'Seri blood, will undo the seal.
The Sun Kings, devices of the Ilo'Seri, will fall.
I, Gideon Prow, will release the power beneath the city, and neither Man nor Savage will prevent it.'

When a voice called out to him from across the room, Parfort was so surprised and terrified that he almost dropped his torch. When he turned to see the svelte and ominous figure silhouetted in the doorway, he struggled to regain his composure at all.

Miss Glass watched him for a moment with a predatory indifference.
"Been doing a little reading, boy?"
Parfort didn't answer.
"Well, didn't you hear me before? I said His Eminence

has need of you. Now, come along."

In a sickly pool of shifting violet light in the next neglected chamber, surrounded by an utter blackness on all sides, the Scribe smiled as he and Mister Glower investigated the object before them.

"Here we are, Your Eminence," said Miss Glass, as she followed Parfort in, "He was distracted by a little... research of his own."

The Scribe did not turn, attention focused wholly on the dusty shape he studied.
"Hn. Yes, yes. Very good. Thank you, Miss Glass."

The object looked to Parfort very much like a peculiar sort of sundial. It rose to a little more than waist height, widening at each end, with a sturdy column between. The top was flat, for the most part, save a hollowed out section in the middle that dipped like a bowl, and four narrow metal struts that stuck up around the edges. It was made from a dark stone, pitch-black and solid, but all around it was inlaid with odd, jutting pieces of metal that stood proud in a curious pattern.

The Scribe examined it closely, reverently, tracing its edges with his hands, but never making contact.
"Quite... quite incredible! The Font of the Ancients... and to think the city itself draws *Seri-gae* to this point!" he murmured, as he turned his head this way and that, exploring every aspect, every surface of the thing.
Mister Glower leaned in to point out several concentric rings laid around the edge. "As you see, it will be raised by this control, using the methods we have shown you, Your Eminence. Your control of the fragments is

outstanding, it should prove an easy task to you now."

"Excellent, Mister Glower. We are ready then."

"The real test begins once the Font is in place," called Miss Glass coolly, taking up place beside them, "Are you certain we have all we need?"

The Scribe smiled, humourlessly. "I have spoken to Aleph. He assures me everything is in place."

Miss Glass gave a low bow. "Then you are indeed ready, Your Eminence. It is written. Nothing will stand in your way."

Despite his anxiety and his general sense of unease, Parfort could not stay his curiosity. Calling on the tattered remnants of his courage, the young Scrivener spoke up.

"W-what is it, your Eminence? What... what is it for?"

He was half expecting another angry outburst, and was prepared for such, but the Scribe surprised him by answering with a warm enthusiasm, as if he welcomed the question.

"Ah, Mister Parfort... This... this should excite you more than any book, should thrill you more than any story. This, Mister Parfort, is the Font of the Ancients, the crowning glory of their achievements, and the key to the secrets of this city. It is a gateway, Mister Parfort, to a universe of knowledge, lost and forgotten, and an endless source of power..."

The Scribe turned to face his young charge, and pushed back his hood, let drop his cloak, to reveal his disfigurement. His good eye twinkled gleefully, and the strange light from the rod cast swirling patterns in the dark shapes protruding from the Scribe's flesh. The same swirling shapes were mirrored in the dull metal of the object behind him.

"This is progress, Mister Parfort, this is the future of our Empire, a new beginning! And it starts, Mister Parfort, with me."

As Parfort watched, horrified, the Scribe spun back to the mysterious object and with Glass and Glower's direction, began to shift the metal rings that encircled the wide rim. As he did, the light from the little rod in Glower's hand spat sharply, then was extinguished altogether, only to be replaced a second later with a brighter blaze that seemed to come from the object itself. The Scribe became a tall silhouette, surrounded by a fiery purple-white, and Parfort stumbled backwards in surprise, dropping his own torch and falling to the ground, throwing up his hands against the sudden glare.

"Your Eminence, what's happening?!"

The Scribe didn't answer.
"Yes! I see the pattern! Now, like this..." he shouted instead.
Parfort wasn't sure exactly what the Scribe meant, but after a moment he called out again.
"Perfect! Then let us rise!"

The ground where Parfort lay began to shake.

oOo

The Book and the Heart had wasted no further time in the passage deep below the Keep, once they had established there was no way through. They had tried at first to shift a few choice sections of the collapse, in the hope that they may be able to find some small opening, but to no avail. The Book had debated whether there were any arts she might employ to shift the rubble by other means, but concluded there was nothing that could be done without returning to her study first, and even then she was greatly concerned that any disturbance could affect the floors above, creating even greater damage.

Consequently, they had returned the way they came, back up into the Keep, and were surprised to see the Sword descending the great stairwell as they emerged.

"Duma! Where have you been, eh?" the Book called up to him, gladly, "Taking it easy somewhere, I assume?"
"Ah! At last! I've found you!" replied the Sword, advancing down towards them, "Good to see you both. I'm glad you're safe, very glad."
The Heart and the Book exchanged a brief look of trepidation on seeing the Sword's expression, then walked to meet him at the foot of the stone steps.

After a few minutes of explanation and discussion, all three wore the same expression.

The Heart shook her head. "There are so many questions to answer, but in the mean time, what do we do right now? Duma, how long do you think we have?"
"It's hard to say." replied the Sword, with a shrug. "If these giants keep a steady speed, then I'd say the nearest will be on us by dark."
The Heart gave a deep breath, and nodded. "Very well then. That makes things simple at least. We know how much time we have."
The Book who had been silent for a while, kneading at her temples, suddenly gave a loud snap of her fingers, and

shouted out, startling the other two. "That's it! That's it! It must be!"

"What is it, Sofya?" said the Heart.

The Book seemed not to hear, and slapped the top of the banister in frustration. "Ancients curse him! We must find that *snake*."

As used as the other two were to the Book's manic ramblings, the circumstances pressed their patience thin.

"What are you talking about, Sofya?" said the Sword, tersely, "This is no time for puzzles! You mean the Scribe?"

"Yes, yes, of course the Scribe," replied the Book, "but that's the key, Duma! He will have to make his move now, he has no time!"

The Sword grimaced, and looked to the Heart for help. She gave a little nod, and laid a hand on the Book's shoulder.

"What do you mean, Sofya? We don't follow your thoughts so swiftly."

With a frown, the Book looked from one to the other. "For all his tricks and bravado, Prow still seemed nervous, irritated at being kept waiting," she said, calmly, "He was impatient, went on about not having enough *time*. Now, whatever it is he's up to, do you think he'd be worried if he knew these giants were on their way to aid him, eh? Why worry? In fact, why risk taking the city at all until such a force arrives?"

The Heart and the Sword began to nod in understanding.

"These things are not coming to support him..." said the Sword, slowly.

"They march *against* him!" finished the Heart.

"Exactly." the Book continued, "Which means he has as little time as we do. The reason he's in such a hurry is he knows these things are on their way, eh? All we need to do, is find him first."

"I thought you said you couldn't follow where he'd gone?" said the Sword.

"It's true..." replied the Heart, "but there must be some other means of getting out. He wouldn't seal himself in with no hope of escape."

"Yes." said the Book, "and wherever he comes out, he will have to do it soon. We must be there when he does."

"The oldest plans of the Keep lie in the Keeper's Tower," the Heart said, "We will never reach them now."

The Sword scratched at his jaw. "What about the Council's repository?" he said, "Old Firman always insisted on keeping a working set of records, especially those relating to the city and its rule. Said he never trusted the Keepers to know what was really important, Ancients bless him."

The Book smiled. "It's a good place to start, Duma. How can we reach it?"

"The stables," replied the Sword, "There's a Corporal of the Horse Guard and his men there who have managed to protect many of the staff."

"Oh, thank the Ancients!" said the Heart.

"Yes, they barricaded themselves in when they realised what was happening. There are too many of the Keeper's men outside for us to risk leaving through the city, but since Winnow and his men were sealed in we can be certain none of the invaders got through there. He can take us out of the south river gate, and from there we can make our way round to the main west entrance. The Council halls are only a few hundred yards inside."

The Book nodded. "You know," she said, "in some ways, I miss this. The three of us, like this."

"What do you mean, witch? No help, no time, and almost no idea what we're doing?" asked the Sword.

"Exactly," grinned the Book, "Simpler times, eh?!"

"Now as then," said the Heart, "we stand or fall together.

Duma, lead the way."

oOo

When the day began to darken, the Sun King had reached the lower slopes of the Long Hills, and had begun to climb without any change in pace. Fulza, Jubal and Gaven were already feeling the effects however. As the evening drew on, the temperature had begun to drop anyway, and now as their altitude steadily increased, they found it was quickly becoming unpleasantly cold. There was little to be done, and for the most part they simply hunched low, arms wrapped about them in silence. occasionally casting an uncomfortable glance upwards at the snow lying on the peaks above.

As it was, their fear of the peaks proved premature. When the last wisps of daylight eventually fell behind the horizon, without warning the Sun King stopped. Much to Fulza and Gaven's dismay, they found themselves halfway up the side of the mountain, no fire or furs to keep them warm, and worse yet, trapped thirty feet in the air in a shelter of cold metal.

Gaven looked angrily upwards, kicking at the golden hide. "What are you doing? Why have you stopped? At least let us down for Ancient's sake, we'll freeze to death up here!"
Fulza began digging around in his pack.
"Look." he said, urgently. "See if anything to burn. Can start fire. Then I will find a way to climb down."
Gaven looked blank for a moment, then the words sank in, and he nodded his understanding. He knelt, and began to rifle through his pack, pulling out anything he thought might feed a flame.

Fulza stood to peer down over the golden rim at the hard earth far below, leaning on Joseera's staff to steady himself. His eyes searched for some safe passage down, and for any scant shelter this barren place might offer.

"Hold on, Joseera," he muttered, softly to himself, "Will find a way, girl."

Gaven called from behind him, "Savage?"

Fulza did not turn. "Keep looking! Must stay warm!"

"Savage… I think you may have solved that problem…"

Fulza was about to protest, but before he could form a response, he felt a gently growing warmth above his shoulder. He looked round, and found the golden head of Joseera's staff shining with a soft glow.

Silently, Fulza turned and sat, holding the staff reverently out before him. He and Gaven watched in wonder, and even Jubal was transfixed as the light grew and spread, encompassing them all.

Deep within the Sun King's eyes, a response bloomed, and the great golden body steadily began to move again.

The Sun King continued its climb, and Fulza looked out at the snow. After a while, he found he wasn't cold at all.

Chapter Twenty-Five

When the way became steeper, the Sun King grasped at the jutting rocks ahead, and pulled itself upward in addition to driving on with its great legs. The climb afforded the giant's passengers an even better view of their surroundings, and they marvelled at the fierce beauty of the peaks and slopes around them.

As he sat atop the swaying giant, watching the snow slip past, Gaven thought of his life at home, in Lerncos. He remembered how excited his sister, and the other young ones of the village would get when there had been a good snow, thick enough to have fun in. She and her friends would head out into the village square and cause mayhem, perhaps declaring war on Gaven and some of the older boys, Thom Lallow and Robb Fossley, until the air was thick with flying snow. It seemed to Gaven now almost like a dream, half remembered upon waking. He wondered what his little sister was doing now. He wondered if he would ever see her again, and if he did, whether she would forgive him for not being there when she had needed him most.

Joseera had always complained that her life in the village was dull and unexciting, the people boring and unimaginative. She had envied her brother deeply when he left for the great city, asked him a hundred questions whenever he returned, and often loudly proclaimed that she would leave too, just as soon as she could, and find excitement for herself. Gaven laughed to himself, and wondered whether his sister would feel the same now. Then he imagined what the Elders might say if they could see her now, and that made him laugh even more.

Jubal snorted in faint surprise at the sudden noise, and gave him a peculiar look.

"Something funny?" Fulza asked, with a bemused expression.

Gaven smiled. "I'm sorry, Savage," he said, "I was thinking of my sister. How keen she was for excitement even when she was little, always desperate to find some sort of adventure."

Fulza nodded. "Hah. Girl certainly knows how to find trouble I think."

"Yes." replied Gaven, "She always did."

They sat in silence for a moment, then Fulza continued, softly.

"I am sorry, Gaven Mayweather."

Gaven turned, eyebrows raised. "What for?"

"For... all of this. For your sister. For failing her."

"No, Savage, you... you did what you thought was right... And you did protect her. If it weren't for you, who would have helped her when our village was attacked, when she was alone and scared, hunted in the woods? I wasn't there for her then. You were. And I thank you for it, Savage... Fulza. I thank you."

Fulza frowned uncertainly, and Gaven turned to look solemnly at him.

"And anyway," he continued, "we will both be there for her now. All that matters is that we find her."

The golden figure, gleaming beneath the pale moon in the fields of pristine white, climbed silently and steadily onward.

oOo

Bantha's Triumvirate were operating at the peak of their

effectiveness. In many ways they were at their best under pressure, when allowed to depend on one another, rely on their individual knowledge and their common understanding. The Three marshaled the resources at their disposal with decisive proficiency, driven by the urgent awareness that their time could run out without warning.

On their arrival at the stables, they had found the nervous Corporal Winnow doing his best to keep the people in his charge calm and prevent any outbreak of panic, in spite of the clear threat outside. He was beginning to run out of ideas when the Sword returned with his companions, and was very grateful to see them, as their appearance did more to boost the morale of the terrified Keep staff than anything the Corporal had been able to come up with. Winnow was also glad to hear their plan; leave the Keep and get out of the city by the simplest and least noticeable means possible.

So it was that they all, staff, soldiers, the Corporal and the Three, hurried along the low, narrow passageway that led down to the tiny river gate. The gate was never used these days, almost forgotten, a relic of the days before the Empire, when Bantha had stood against many sieges. The river gate, which lay at the waterline, just wide enough for one little narrow boat to squeeze through, had allowed Bantha to continue to receive supplies regardless of any force outside on land.

As the passageway neared the gate, it dropped steeply, and the freezing water of the Pulchren rose up around their chests. There was little light, and the going was slow, as many of the staff, already terrified, were struggling to maintain their composure. Eventually though, the disparate group began to make their way, one by one, out into the river's edge beyond, where Winnow's men helped to haul them, shivering, up the banks to safety. The sight of the towering golden figures striding forward in the distance did nothing to ease anyone's nerves.

The Three were the last to make their way out into the dimming evening beyond the city walls. The Book splashed her way ashore, eschewing all proffered assistance from any of the waiting soldiers, and began to stomp determinedly up the banks to safety. The Sword, at the rear, paused at the doorway though, looking back along the dark passageway. As she made her way through the cold waters to the bank, the Heart glanced round to see him standing there.
"This is not defeat, Duma," she called to him, "We will find what we need and return."
He looked back at her, and gave a faint smile, then started out after her towards the shore.

Once safely on land, huddled in the growing shadow at the foot of the great wall, they began to make arrangements. The Book and the Heart set about explaining things as plainly as they could to the staff and servants, leaving the Sword to deal with the guardsmen.
The Sword drew Winnow quietly aside. "These people are cold, and exhausted, Corporal. You yourself have done more than enough, and deserve whatever respite you can find. Take them away from the gates, up to the horse stead there, you'll find blankets and a few supplies at least. Then move on, head out to one of the farmhouses, and keep them safe."
"Yes, my Lord, of course," replied the weary Winnow, "but what about you? Are you not coming with us?"
"No, Corporal," said the Sword, "we still have work to do here. We're not going to let that traitor do this to our

home."

Winnow nodded, and returned a stoic smile. "Of course. Good luck, my Lord. Ancients be with you."

The Heart was trying to maintain her patience, dealing with a group of obstinate Councillors who seemed to think their safety superseded that of the servants, when a thin, tired looking couple approached at her side, politely begging her attention.

"Excuse me, my Lady, if you have a moment, please..."

They were, like almost all of those gathered there, a bedraggled sight, a man and a woman with filthy, soaking clothes and dirt streaked across their faces, but the Heart looked more carefully than most. Their clothes were of simple cloth, but neatly stitched and well made, their manner was respectful and good natured. When she looked into the couple, the Heart felt not only the chill of exhaustion that they all shared, but another, greater cold, a deep, biting loss.

She frowned at the Councilmen still clamouring and arguing before her.

"Gentlemen, that's enough! This is not a negotiation and I will not be moved! Now unless you want me to ask the good Corporal to leave you here by the riverside to fend for yourselves, I suggest you quiet your complaints!"

Cowed, but still muttering protest, the men shuffled away, and the Heart turned her attention to the worn couple, waiting patiently beside her.

"I'm sorry about that. Now, how can I help you?"

The pair seemed unsure of how to behave, and the man gave an awkward little bow before replying.

"Uh.. thank you, my Lady, thank you. My wife and I,

we're looking... well, we were hoping to find our son, my Lady. He works in the City Guard."

The Heart frowned. "Well. There is little I can do, I'm afraid. At this moment I cannot be certain even who remained in the city, and who rode out for Vas Aloron."

The man nodded, and his wife spoke hurriedly.

"Oh, of course, of course, we understand that. We were just hoping to find out anything at all, we'd be grateful for whatever you can tell us." The man nudged her with his elbow. "My Lady." she added.

The Heart smiled. "Very well then. What is his name?"

The woman looked confused. "My Lady? We thought you might remem-"

She was silenced by a sharp look from her husband.

"Thank you, my Lady." he said. "Our son is Captain Gaven Mayweather."

The Heart tried very hard not to let the surprise show too obviously. It was hard to tell, the years had changed them, and of course, the mud and dirt made it more difficult, but she saw now, recognised the faces before her...

"Mayweather." she said, slowly. "I see."

"We're sorry to trouble you, my Lady," Parvel continued, "but-"

The Heart shook her head. "No, please, don't apologise, it is I who am at fault! It is... Parvel, Juna... It's been such a long time... You must forgive me, please, I didn't recognise you at all..."

"Please, my Lady, there's no need." replied Parvel. "Why would you know us? It's been so many years, and you have plenty to worry about I'm sure. It's just... things have been very bad for us... we hoped you may favour us with a little help. Our home, Lerncos, was attacked, burnt to the ground-"

"Lerncos... yes, I remember," said the Heart, "And I

remember hearing of the attacks in the west. One of the deepest forays by the Savages into our lands."
Parvel looked confused. "Savages? My Lady, we were attacked by men from the Tower."
The Heart's eyes widened.
"And... the girl?" she asked, softly.
"Joseera disappeared just before, my Lady," said Juna, tears gathering in her eyes, "We haven't seen her since."

As the couple expanded on their story, the Heart's look of amazement grew, then was gradually replaced by a look of dark anger. She called out to the Book and the Sword, who saw her face, and came with swift concern.

The Three bid the Mayweathers go with Corporal Winnow, as there was little else to be done for them here, but left them with the promise that they would send word if they heard anything of their children. When the couple and the rest of the group had set off with the Corporal and his men, the Three shared a worried look.
"He was looking for the girl," said the Heart, simply.
"And may have found her, by the sound of things," said the Book.
"If he found her, then we have already failed her once," said the Sword, "Let us make sure we do not fail her now."

The Three hurried along the wall, and reached the towering gates of the west entrance. They ran untroubled through the deserted barbican and into the street beyond, when the Heart glanced up, and cried out.
"Oh! Sofya, Duma, look!"

They turned in time to see the closest of the giants reach the far north-east city wall, golden head looming above the high battlements.

"Ancients preserve us. Look at that thing." said the Sword, quietly.

As they watched, the giant reached out with one great hand and took hold of the top of the wall, crushing the crenelations and sending heavy chunks of stone tumbling down onto the buildings below. Then, it stopped. As the last rays of the sun disappeared behind the mountains, the giant simply froze, perfectly still, where it stood.

For a moment, the Three stood frozen too, not daring to move lest they somehow freed the thing.
"It looks," murmured the Book, carefully, as if afraid to disturb the silence, "like we may have been given a temporary reprieve."
"We need to reach the repository, quickly. And we need to find that girl."

The other two nodded silent assent, then together they moved purposefully away.

oOo

At that moment, Joseera Mayweather was, in fact, closer than any of them may have believed.

The first thing she was aware of was a splitting pain in her head, but when she tried to lift her hands to her face, she found herself unable, her arms tightly bound behind her. She opened her eyelids slowly, wincing as a flickering light stung her eyes. Blinking, she waited for her vision to clear, and took in her surroundings.

She found herself sitting in what she took to be some kind of cell, propped up against a cold wall. The floor was damp and dirty, strewn with bits of hay and ragged cloth, and her hands felt rough stone behind and beneath. Her clothes were a little tattered, but it seemed that although her pack was nowhere to be seen, nothing had been taken from her person. Her father's sword sat awkwardly in its scabbard, pommel pressing into her side.

Gradually, painfully, she raised her head a little and extended her appraisal. She sat near one corner of the room, to her right, and two torches were set in brackets above her. Their meagre light did not stretch far enough to fill the space however, and Joseera could not be sure how large the room was, as beyond the torch glow the stone walls receded into darkness.

A few yards before her sat a plain wooden chair. Seated on it was Aleph, watching Joseera closely, and neatly dressed in dark robes, having changed from his Seekers leathers and chain into more traditional Keeper's attire.

Joseera groaned.
"Ancients sake, what now?" she rasped, finding her voice dry and unfamiliar.

Aleph smiled broadly.
"Oh, don't concern yourself with me, Joseera. Awake at last, eh? I was beginning to be concerned."

Joseera rested her head against the clammy stone. As she spoke, her fingers investigated their restraints, and found them wanting.
"Where am I?" Her voice cracked. "What do you want?"
Aleph leant forward on his chair.

"You're in Bantha, Joseera, the great city. I've been looking after you, but now its almost time for us to visit His Eminence the Scribe, and then you're going to help him change our world."

Joseera gave a dry laugh. Concealed behind her, her hands squeezed agonisingly through the worn ropes. "Why would I help you?"

Aleph gave another charming smile.

"Oh, don't worry Joseera. It's a very simple task. In fact you might say you were born for it."

Joseera smiled coldly back. "I'm sorry. I'm afraid I have other plans."

Summoning every ounce of strength she had left, picturing her brother, his family, her friend Fulza in her mind, Joseera tore her hands free from their bonds and drove herself forward against the wall. She pushed upwards with her legs and launched herself towards the Aleph, whose smile was replaced for a moment with a look of mild surprise. As she flew, Joseera pulled forth the knife from her belt and brought it before her, thrusting it out towards Aleph's chest.

Without even rising from his seat, Aleph sliced upwards with one hand, catching Joseera on the wrist and knocking her blade aside. He drew his right leg up tight against him, and planted his foot on her chest, before kicking out, sending her flying backwards to slam against the wall, knocking the breath from her body and re-opening the raw wound from the Temple on the back of her head.

Aleph sighed.

"Well, Joseera." he said, calmly, "You certainly do have spirit, I'll grant you that."

A cold feeling crept through Joseera's body. She felt gingerly at her head, while waiting for her breath to return.

Aleph stood gracefully and stepped forward, kneeling in front of Joseera. He took hold of her arm. His grip was fantastically firm, and with one hand he pulled her close to him.

"Honestly, Joseera," he said, coolly, "I'm too soft. No good will come of it."
He grinned and released her, leaning back, hands raised. "But really, where did you think you would go?! You be civil, Joseera, and I will make this all easy for you."

Joseera sank back where she lay.
"Whatever you want," she spat, tasting blood in her mouth, "I won't help you. You'll have to kill me first."
Aleph laughed. "Oh, there'll be time for that, Joseera. Don't you worry."

oOo

The Three had wasted no time. They had met little resistance, as the bulk of the Scribe's forces seemed to be concentrated around the Keep, but the handful of men who did cross their path were dealt with swiftly. They found one lone pair looting a fine carpenter's house, the craftsman and his wife lying dead outside. The two soldiers threw down their weapons when they saw the Three approaching, begging for forgiveness, that they had been misled. The Sword wore a dark scowl, but returned his blade to its scabbard, and was about to address the men, when the Book stepped forward and threw out her hands, burning the pair down in an instant.

The Sword tuned to her with a look of surprise. "Sofya, they had put aside their weapons."
The Book did not look at him, eyes fixed instead on the bodies of the carpenter and his wife. "They made their choice, eh?" she said, flatly.
The Heart said nothing.

They reached the Council buildings without further incident, and made their way swiftly inside. Casting blessings on the fastidious and obsessive nature of the Council librarian, Firman, they found what they were looking for with ease. They cleared space on the broad, old table in the middle of the repository, the Book spread the dry parchment out across it.
"This is dated the oldest," she said, weighing the corners with whichever dusty books were nearest at hand, "Look, the entire northern living quarters are missing altogether! That puts it well before even Emperor Horun's time…"

As they peered down at the crumpled document together, their brows furrowed, and their hearts sank.
"This… this is incredible…" gasped the Sword.
"There must be miles of passages beneath!" exclaimed the Heart, "How deep can it possibly go?"

The Book gave a deep sigh, and was about to speak, but stopped short as there was a thunderous noise from outside, and the solid stone of the repository floor literally shook beneath their feet.
"What in the Ancients name now?" cried the Book, "An earthquake?"

They ran quickly together, out of the wide door that faced the Keep in the distance, and even as they did the tall tower that stood in the middle of the Keep's central building collapsed and fell inwards. It tumbled, breaking up as it went, showering the lower roofs with heavy blocks of stone, crashing through in places. Elsewhere, the walls seemed to bulge and buckle madly, tiles slipped and fell loose from their fixings. All across the great building, glass shattered, bricks warped and cracked, until it seemed the whole structure swayed.

"Ancients save us... what is it?!" cried the Heart.
The Book frowned. "Something beneath," she said.

Chapter Twenty-Six

It was near dawn when the Sun King began its final descent into the Fold, Gaven, Fulza and Jubal still perched upon its shoulder. The sky was gradually beginning to brighten, although the sun was not yet visible on the horizon.

Gaven and Fulza had first spotted the city in the distance as they cleared the high ridge at the top of the Long Hills, but in the darkness it had been difficult to make out clearly, a broad shape scattered with tiny lights. Now though, they drew closer by the moment, and the growing day afforded them a better view. Gaven was gladdened by the sight of the city itself, the vast sprawl of buildings he knew so well. But his fervor was tempered by the little groups and lines of people he saw moving away from the city, and by the two motionless golden figures stood at the high walls.

"Those others," he called to the Sun King, "they are your brothers?"

"*I am the first. We are three in all.*"

"And they're waiting, they need the sun?" Gaven continued, "Before they can move, I mean?"

"*Seri-gae. The light drives us.*"

Gaven turned excitedly to Fulza.
"That means we have a chance, Fulza, we can reach them before they destroy it all."
"Yes, maybe," said Fulza, "But what do we do?"

Gaven chewed his lip thoughtfully. "I'm not sure yet. Perhaps this one can convince the others to listen. And then we go and find the Scribe."
Fulza smiled uncertainly. "Sound like your sister, Gaven Mayweather. Sounds simple"
"Well, let's hope it is, Fulza," he replied, smiling back, "let's hope it is."

A frown crossed Gaven's face, and he called out to the Sun King again.
"Why the sun?" he asked. "If whoever made you could do all this, why not something to drive you, to power you?"

"When the world dies, when all is dust... the sun will still rise."

"I see." said Gaven, softly. "Please, hurry."

oOo

Bantha's Keep was now little more than a twisted shell. Most of the roofs and upper sections had collapsed in on themselves, and only the thick outer walls of the lower Keep remained, although even these were cracked and crumbling, large chunks falling away.

The Three stood, ashen faced, in disbelief.
"How is this possible?" murmured the Sword, as much to himself as anyone else.
"At least it was empty, Duma. I have a feeling we were meant to be inside right now, eh?" replied the Book.
The Heart took a deep breath. "This is what it has all been for." she said, quietly.
The Book gave her an inquisitive look. "I'm sorry, Loulouthi?"

"You remember, Sofya. We all do." the Heart replied. "The creature said that something terrible was coming, but that the child could bring hope, there was a chance... The Scribe didn't bring the giants, but they're here because of him. Whatever it is he wants with Joseera, whatever it is he's doing, it isn't finished. We have that chance. We have to stop him. We have to try."

They began to walk together along the wide street that led back to the Keep.

As they rounded the building and turned, they quickly saw that getting back to the Keep would be an almighty struggle in itself. They had managed to escape the building almost unnoticed, had faced scarce resistance on their entry through the north-west gate, and the reason for this now became horribly apparent. The Scribe's forces were concentrated around the ruined building, hundreds of men stretching from the Keep's shattered doors, along the broad causeway, and spreading across the wide market square.

The Three stopped in their tracks.
"Well. This will complicate things..." started the Book.
"Of course, it makes sense. He doesn't need to hold the rest of the city now. He just needs to make sure he isn't disturbed..." said the Heart, "Is there another way...?"
"I think not, Loulouthi," replied the Sword, "The river gate will not have survived the collapse. There is only one way to reach him now."
"We have no choice then," breathed the Heart, "There are... so many. Do you really think we can?"
The Sword frowned. "Does it matter?" he said.
"The only thing that *matters*," remarked the Book, impatiently, "is that there is a snake in our house. These

traitors have slaughtered their own people, betrayed their trust, and they stand in our path."

"Well then." said the Heart, softly. "We must act. And we must do it now."

The Sword nodded. "Yes, Let's go." He drew his weapon from its scabbard. "Let's go and meet them."

The Book pushed up her sleeves and straightened her glasses. "Good. We'll have an end to this, one way or another, eh?"

oOo

Within the Keep, Parfort was stretched far beyond what he considered to be the limits of his sanity. He lay, trembling, on the ground, a few yards from where the Scribe stood clutching tightly to the Font, Glass and Glower close at his side. The sound from the Font was stronger now, and a faint sheen of purple-white light danced over it. This seemed almost normal though, thought Parfort, in comparison to the growing chaos that surrounded them. The normal rules of nature appeared to have been revoked, and the floor on which they stood was rising, up through the Keep, bringing great stones and wooden beams crashing down towards them, only to be turned harmlessly away by some unseen force at the last moment. The ground shook underneath them, and beyond the edges of the platform it fell away entirely as they rose, until Parfort realised they must be atop a great column, pushing its way to the surface. He curled up, covering his head with his hands, praying loudly for it to stop.

Eventually it did. When Parfort felt the thunderous shaking cease, he cautiously slid his hands away from his face and was astonished to find himself under the open sky, on a circle of stone about a dozen yards across. He sat slightly, and saw the ruins of Bantha's Keep littering the earth, jagged remnants of walls and odd half-rooms undisturbed, made lunatic by the devastation surrounding them.

The Scribe turned to face him.
"We are almost ready. Now, Mister Parfort, are you all right? It was a difficult journey. You're doing very well indeed." said the Scribe, in velvet tones. "Now, come here, my boy. I have a very special job for you..."

Despite everything he had seen and learned, years of training and discipline cannot simply be erased, and something within the young Scrivener swelled with pride. He wiped at his eyes and clambered up on shaking legs, staggering uneasily towards his master. The Scribe took his arm when he drew closer, and led him to the Font.

"Mister Parfort, you have an auspicious task indeed. One of particular significance, one that will mark the beginning of a new age!"
The Scribe beamed at Parfort, as Glass and Glower stepped up behind the boy and took a firm hold of his shoulders. Parfort smiled uncertainly back at his master.
"Th-thank you, your Eminence... I'm glad to help, your Eminence, if I can..."
The Scribe laughed. "Of course you are, Mister Parfort, of course you are. A new beginning, and you will be the one to start it all! You are about to change the shape of the future, Mister Parfort, to change the world."

While Glass and Glower remained close behind the boy, the Scribe leaned close in to him, and spoke in almost fatherly tones.
"We have something in common, you and I, something

that sets us apart from other people. An... openness, an ability to feel things others might miss. I saw it the day you took so well to my pen, to the Keeper's Ink, my boy. You have a gift, Mister Parfort, just as I do. And now I want you to help me. I want you to use that gift. Step forward, boy, place your hands on the Font. Let yourself feel the powers that lie within it, just as you did with the Ink, and open it, my boy. Open it for the Order, for the Keepers, and for me."

Glass and Glower gave Parfort a gentle but insistent push, propelling him towards the dark shape. The boy gave a nervous glance back to the Scribe, who smiled proudly, and gestured for him to go on. Parfort placed his hands on the large curved struts protruding from the Font as directed.

For a few moments, nothing happened. Parfort felt the anxiety rising in him, afraid that he had somehow failed, and was about to give up and turn back, hopelessly, to his master, when he felt something flicker beneath his fingers. Like a cold breeze, the feeling prickled across the skin of his hands, and something within the dark metal shifted, like a light reflecting from some unseen source. He opened his eyes wide and twisted to look round at the Scribe, calling out as he did.
"Your Eminence! I can feel it! I can feel a power, Your Eminen-"
There was a sickening sound, fluid being drawn through a tiny space. Parfort remained standing for a few seconds more, his eyes still bearing a look of innocent wonder, although his skin stretched drum tight over his bones. Then he dropped silently to his knees, and fell softly to the floor.

The Scribe chuckled in amazement, as the struts on the Font widened, and several knurled metal ridges extended from beneath its top.

"Well," he said, "it seems I once again owe you my gratitude, my friends. There was nothing in any of the writings about this! Were it not for your matchless research, I would not have been prepared."

Behind him, Glass and Glower shared a strange, dead look.

"Our pleasure and our duty, Your Eminence, we are glad to be of service, always." oozed Mister Glower.

"Indeed. A sacrifice, required to give life to the ceremony. It was often the way, lest such things be taken... lightly." added Miss Glass, coolly. "And now, Your Eminence, we must press on. Time is of the essence."

The Scribe approached the Font, a cruel smile on his face.

"Yes, yes, quite right, Miss Glass, of course. Aleph is on his way with the girl now."

"A great moment, Your Eminence." said Mister Glower, stepping forward to place a hand on the Scribe's shoulder. "The power of the Ancients will be yours!"

"There will be no-one to challenge you!" hissed Miss Glass, at his other shoulder, "Even the Sun Kings will kneel and serve your vision!"

The Scribe laughed, and placed his hands reverently on the curved spines of the font before him.

"Yes..." he whispered, "And you will sit at my side, my faithful friends. Our enemies will burn, and my Empire will span the world."

oOo

Aleph was grateful for the good fortune that had allowed Joseera to fall in his lap. The Scribe had been pleased when he had heard of the events in the Temple, although

Aleph had not been complete in his description of events. He had the girl, after all, which was the important thing, and Aleph was keen to curry his master's trust and favour, especially since it seemed the Scribe would soon be the unquestionable authority in these lands. Aleph was intelligent, and well-studied. He understood the implications of what the Scribe was doing better than most in the Order. A selfishly practical man at heart, he could quite plainly imagine the benefits that would come from being at the right hand of such a power.

So now, despite the fact that he considered such work far below someone of his learning and ability, he carried the struggling girl swiftly through the narrow streets. He was cautious, although the streets beyond the Tower were largely deserted, but he knew better than to let complacency make him sloppy, and wanted no mistakes, no more unexpected complications after whatever it was that had happened in the Temple before he managed to blindly grab Joseera and fight his way out.

It didn't take him long at all to cover the short distance, and before he knew it he was in sight of the forces in the square outside the Keep, without problem. He was taken aback when he first sighted the ruined building, surprised by the scale of the destruction. The Scribe had explained to him what would happen, but nevertheless, to see such a thing first hand was disturbing, even for a man such as Aleph.

He didn't allow it to slow him for more than a moment though, and quickly pressed on, passing through the ranks of men stationed outside, Tower Guard and Imperial Army, all wearing the Keeper's red. Many knew his face, and those that didn't recognised the authority of his dress, parting respectfully before him, some saluting, some even cheering as he passed.

"Ancients aid you, Seeker Prime!"

"We have the city, Seeker Prime, the Savages are next eh?!"

"The giants *do* serve the Tower, Prime? Are we victorious?"

"Where is His Eminence, Seeker? Have you seen him?"

Aleph paused, and looked around at the expectant faces. He took a deep breath.

"My friends!" he shouted to the assembled troops, "His Eminence is safe and well, and at this very moment he oversees the destruction of the Keep, symbol of our weakness, hiding away behind our walls! His giants will free the city, and lead the march to conquer the Savages, and anyone else who stands against us!"

Cheers and echoing cries went up at this.

"I take this traitor," Aleph continued, indicating the slumped form of Joseera over his shoulder, "to His Eminence now, guilty of colluding with our Savage enemies, consorting with them, and-"

Aleph stopped, mid-sentence and stared off into the distance, at the wide path leading into the square from the northern side of the city. Three lonely figures were approaching with steady determination. Three unmistakable figures.

Some of the men turned, following his gaze, and a confusion began to spread.

"Is that? It is! It's them!

"What do we do? I thought they was-"

"What are they doing here?!"

Aleph overcame his surprise at the sight, and his instincts kicked in, telling him he had only a few moments to grasp control of the situation and direct it in his favour. He called out again.

"Men of the Empire! These three have escaped His Eminence's attention! Slipped away like rats while their Keep fell! These three would have you living in fear, giving up your land to the Savage foe, stealing from their own people to give to the enemy! His gracious Eminence the Scribe has revealed the truth to us, and now they return to prevent him from freeing us! Believe that I speak for His Eminence the Scribe, believe me when I say that whoever brings him their heads will know riches beyond his dreams in the new Empire! Now take them! Take down those who have lied to you, misled you, weakened you! Kill them and let us all be free and strong!"

It worked. Aleph grinned, eyes burning brightly with the rush of adrenalin, as the roar of the men around him grew, and they began to charge murderously off towards the Three.

"Yes! Go, my brothers! Go!" he shouted again and again, as he turned in the opposite direction. Joseera shifted awkwardly on his shoulder, beginning to wake, and he grunted, adjusting her weight. He glanced up, and looked for a moment at the deep red of the slowly brightening sky. An omen, perhaps. Then he hurried away, towards the remains of the Keep, where his master awaited.

oOo

Gaven and Fulza, perched atop the Sun King, had almost reached the west gate by the time the sun began to shine across the Fold. Even as they covered the last short distance to the city wall, Gaven saw the other giants begin to move, and yelled frantically at the Sun King to hurry. They stood at the north of the city, by the main gate, and even now were effortlessly dismantling it, tearing out great chunks by hand to make way for them to stride into the city itself.

"*We will go, and speak with them.*"

"No, please, no time! Set us down here. Can get into city this way!" protested Fulza.

They looked down at the little out-buildings, lights still burning in the windows of the stead and stables next to the open city gates, long since deserted by the guards.
"Are you ready, Gaven Mayweather?" asked Fulza.
"I think so. Once we get into the city we should be able to get a better idea of what's going on." he replied.

Fulza turned back to the Sun King for a moment.
"Please, help us, when time comes. We will find her."

"*You cannot hurry the dawn.*"

Fulza grunted in frustration, but Gaven cut in insistently.
"But what good will it do?! The dawn might come, the sun might still rise... but what good is it? What use is it, any of it, if there's no-one left? No-one to see it? If we have a chance, a hope of stopping things before they go that far, we have to try, and you have to help us! What good is the sun if there's no-one to feel its warmth?!"
An unexpected sound, strange and grinding rang deep within the Sun King's golden belly.

"*Very well, sparklings. I will try.*"

Chapter Twenty-Seven

Juna and Parvel Mayweather stood in one corner of the battered stable building, the gnarled Elder Jarry and the bulky figure of Tutty Cooksharp alongside them. They were engaged in a heated discussion with the exhausted Corporal Winnow and an awkward man-at-arms.

"Look, I really must insist." the Corporal continued, as he had for the past few minutes. "You cannot remain here. We must leave now and head further out! This is your last chance!"
Juna shook her head. "No, I'm sorry, Corporal, really, but we can't go! We have to wait for our children."
"We're not leaving without them." added Tutty Cooksharp, simply.
The Corporal looked nervously up at the big man.
"Fine, it they wants to stay, let 'em stay." grunted the man-at-arms. "We give 'em fair warning. It's not our problem if they won't listen."
"Now there's a smart fellow." said Elder Jarry, "Just listen to him, Corporal, and leave us be, please!"
"Please, Corporal, we understand what we're asking. We'll take our own chances, you don't have to feel responsible for us." said Parvel.

They were interrupted by one of the young lads who had been posted on watch outside, running, full pelt, into the little stable.
"There's one coming!" he shouted, at the top of his voice. "There's one right here! It's coming this way! Get out, get out! Everybody go while you can!"

Thung. Thung. Thung.

Everyone rushed outside, and on sighting the great golden figure approaching, panic erupted. People rushed back inside, gathering up belongings, and shouting about how it was 'every man for himself', and 'what was the point of waiting'.

For a few minutes there was chaos, while arguments erupted, possessions were claimed and families gathered. All the time the giant grew closer, ringing footsteps growing in volume, adding to the madness. Having finally ushered everyone outside, Winnow was about to try and restore some order, when Parvel grabbed his shoulder fiercely, causing the man to wince in surprise.
"Hey! What do you think you're doing?"
"That's my work!" shouted Parvel, pointing off into the distance. "That's my flaming work!"
The Corporal looked at him as though he were mad.
"What are you talking about, man, you're not-"

Everyone turned and followed Parvel's finger. Sure enough, the giant was close enough now that they could see a man sat high on the giant's shoulder, in military uniform, wrapped in a dark green hood and cloak. Next to him, sat the powerful figure of a Savage, alongside a dark, hairy mass of fur.

Gasps of fright and confusion spread through the group. Was the giant being controlled? Driven? Did it serve man or Savage? Then Parvel, who had been peering at the giant with a look of disbelief, spoke again.
"That's… that's one of my cloaks." he said, dully.
As they watched, amazed, the man atop the giant seemed to spot the little group and point over at them. Some hurried back inside again, but the rest stared on as the

giant, seemingly at the man's behest, stopped, and carefully lowered its passengers onto the ground, before straightening again, and marching away from them, north along the city walls.

The travellers began to approach the stable buildings, and several of the soldiers recovered their senses, and their prejudices with them. The man-at-arms and several more readied their weapons.
"A Savage! A flaming Savage! Draw swords, boys, draw swords!"
"That's my bloody cloak!" said Parvel again. "Don't tell me it isn't, I'd recognise my own work anywhere, nobody else can blend that colour!"

As they came closer to the strange pair, the figure in the green cloak stepped forward, pushing his hood back about his shoulders.
"You there! What's happening here?" it cried. "Who's in charge?!"

Corporal Winnow, brandishing his sword before him, called back. "Don't come any further! Identify yourself!" then, to his men, "Hold your ground, hold fire!"
The man-at-arms spat and growled, "Are you mad, Winnow? Never mind that, men, shoot the bloody thing down!"
The bowmen looked in desperation at each other, but they were trained to know their enemy. They raised their bows, knocked arrows, and began to draw.

The figure in the green cloak stepped angrily forward, casting one arm out in front of the Savage, the other levelling his sword straight at the bowmen.
"Hold your fire!" he roared, "I am Captain Gaven

Mayweather of the Triumvir's Guard, and anyone who strikes this creature will die in that same instant!"

Parvel's mouth dropped wide open. His wife grabbed hold of Winnow's arm.
"Corporal." she said, astonished. "That's our son!"

oOo

Aleph picked his way through the shattered walls and half-rooms that were all that remained of the Keep, until he reached the broad platform in what had been the Great Hall, where the Scribe stood waiting, Glass and Glower ever present at his side.

"Very good, Aleph," called the Scribe, as he saw the Seeker Prime approaching, "very good. Now bring her up here."
Aleph bounded easily onto the platform, even with Joseera's weight upon his shoulders.
"Here she is, Your Eminence. A little bruised, but otherwise unharmed."
"Excellent, Aleph, thank you. Lay her down there, next to the Font."

Aleph placed his load down gently on the stone next to the strange object, alongside the motionless figure of Parfort, and Joseera slumped over onto her side with a faint groan.
"Everything else goes well, Your Eminence. The city is ours, and any… uncooperative parties are being dealt with as we speak," said Aleph, giving an extravagant bow before approaching the Scribe.
"Flawless work, as ever, Aleph. And the Sun Kings?"

Joseera's eyes crept painfully open. Her head pounded

terribly, and she breathed softly, not daring to move lest the pain grow worse. As her watery vision cleared, she was faintly surprised to see another face, that of a young man not much older than her, inches away from her own. He looked desperately pale, his lips a soft, wintry blue, but his eyes still bore a weak flicker of life.

"You're her, aren't you? You're Joseera..." he murmured, his voice a breathless whisper.

Joseera frowned. "Don't speak," she whispered back, "Save your strength, please, you look so cold!"

"He's going to use you..." the boy continued, sadly, "He's going... to make you open it... whether you want to or not..."

"Don't worry about me! Just stay quiet, and stay still."

"Lis... listen to me!" the boy sighed, brown eyes pleading with her, "You can stop him! You can! They resisted before! The Ilo'Seri, they stopped it! And you... you are... Y-you can do it. I know you c-can."

A slight shudder passed through the boy, and his eyes seemed to release Joseera, drifting off into the distance. She twisted against her restraints, and cried out, "No! Don't go! Just... just stay quiet, don't go!"

"I think she's awake, Your Eminence." said Aleph, turning his attention back to the figures laying beneath the Font.

"Very good, very good." said the Scribe. "I'm sure she wouldn't want to miss a moment. Especially as she has such an important role to play..."

The Scribe approached and knelt, pulling forth a long, slender knife, running it gently along Joseera's cheek, a strange smile on his face.

"Finally we meet, Miss Mayweather. Destiny can only be avoided for so long..."

He ran the blade slowly down her neck, and traced along

her arm until he reached her wrist. There, he stopped, and turned the sharp edge against her skin.

"But now that you're here, Miss Mayweather, we have everything we need..."

He thrust the blade neatly under Joseera's bonds, and cut them with a long stroke, before doing the same to the ropes at her ankles. As her limbs slid free, Joseera tried to sit, but her head rang and her vision swam, and she sank back with a dull groan.

Aleph watched, carefully disguising his disapproval. An ornamental knife, certainly not one that had ever tasted blood, and, it seemed, not one that ever would.

"Might I humbly suggest we leave her bound, Your Eminence, as a precaution? She has proved surprisingly resilient, quite liable to cause... difficulties, if the opportunity presents itself."

The Scribe turned his head, and gave Aleph a sideways look.

"Thank you, Aleph, your concern is noted," he said, then with a smile to the others, "but I think it's time this young lady learnt to co-operate, wouldn't you say Mister Glower, Miss Glass?"

Miss Glass didn't seem to respond at all, but Mister Glower made up for it, clapping his hands with a fawning laugh. "Quite so, Your Eminence, quite so!"

Then Miss Glass turned to Aleph with a faint, cold smile. "Thank you for your help, Seeker. We can manage now."

Something about her expression troubled Aleph, and he gave an involuntary shudder. He got the curious feeling that he was not as well-informed as he might have thought.

The Scribe did not notice the exchange, all his attention being focused on Joseera. Her eyes narrowed with a contemptuous glare, as the Scribe bent low, leaning close to Joseera's face.

"Did you hear me, Miss Mayweather? It's time to change the world."

oOo

There was an odd scene around the small stable buildings, with Fulza stood on one side and a handful of bristling soldiers on the other. In the middle of the tension, was a melee of tearful hugs and greetings.

"I can't believe it's you! Mother, Father, you're here, you're really here! Mister Cooksharp, Elder Jarry!"
Even the Elder, not normally given to displays of emotion, had tears in his eyes.
"Well, well, Gaven. I must say, it's good to see you too, lad, very good indeed!"

Juna grasped her son by the shoulders.
"What's happening here, Gaven? After Joseera disappeared, we were so worried, and then after everything that happened, we thought she'd never know where to find us, we'd never see her again! Then we come here to find you, and find all this… What are those things? Those giants?"
Gaven sighed. "I'm sorry Mother, really, I am. But there's no time to tell that story now."
He turned and gestured back towards Fulza.
"This is Joseera's friend, a good friend, Fulza. He has risked his life to keep her safe from the moment she left the village."
Fulza looked uncomfortably at the earth, knowing the question that would follow.
"Well then, Mister... Fulza. I think we owe you our thanks.

You've kept our daughter safe, and whatever anyone else might have to say about it," she looked disapprovingly at the soldiers stood behind her, "that makes you a friend to us too. But where is she? Where is Joseera?"
Fulza gave an awkward frown.
"Your daughter... your daughter was taken."
Parvel and Juna frowned back.

One of the soldiers whispered to another, a little too loudly.
"Ancients save us, it can speak normal!"
Elder Jarry fixed him with a scowl.
"Haven't you got anything better to do?"

The exhausted Corporal Winnow made one last attempt to take charge of the proceedings.
"Please, everyone, we must go now! Right this moment, please!"

Parvel and Juna looked desperately at their son.
"I have to stay." Gaven said to them. "Fulza and I, we'll find her. We can stop this."
"Then we're staying too, Gaven." said Parvel. "We don't want to lose you again."
"Me too." Tutty chimed.
"Well" said Elder Jarry, with a shrug. "We might as well stick together."

"Suit yourself, it's your funeral!" said the man-at-arms. "Come on Corporal, let's get out of here!"
Winnow waved his arms in exasperation. "I tried! I warned you!" he cried. Then he turned, and joined the group of people hurrying off into the Fold.

Gaven looked at his parents with a serious expression.

"Mother, Father. I need you to wait here. Fulza and I have to go," he gestured towards the city gates, "that way."

Juna shook her head. "No, Gaven, don't be foolish, please!"

Gaven met her mother's eyes with a steady gaze.

"There's no other way, mother. Joseera is in there. Alone."

Juna and Parvel looked at their son anxiously, then turned to each other. A silent understanding seemed to pass between them.

"Very well, Gaven." said her father. "We'll wait for you here, right in this spot. Is there anything we can do to help?"

"I don't think so, father. Say a prayer or two perhaps."

oOo

At the great northern wall of the city, there was carnage. Most of the people were long gone, those who still could escaping the city by other means, seeing the golden giants approaching that way. Some, however, had recklessly come to fetch treasured possessions or valuable belongings from their homes and places of business, while a handful of the Scribe's men had been stationed there and bravely stayed at their posts. Now the air was filled with panicked screams and yelling as the giants tore down the wall and proceeded into the city, advancing steadily, knocking and pushing aside any building or obstacle that lay in their path.

The Sun King approached them as quickly as it could, heading along the wall from the west. When it saw them press through, it pulled at the wall beside it, heaving it outward so the stone fell away from the buildings within. It stepped thought the gap, into the city, and reached out to the others with its voice as it neared them.

"Brothers, hold! Strange news! A spark of light remains!"

The foremost of the giants turned its great head slowly. Its voice rolled into the ether in response.
"*What good is a spark? They live in darkness. Wasting their own brief lives, taking others. We know our purpose. We will bring an end.*"

"*It is too late for a spark. Too late for hope.*" replied the other. "*We know our purpose. A new day will come. The sun will still rise.*"

"No, brothers." said the first. "*It is never too late for hope.*"

Chapter Twenty-Eight

The Three had almost reached the wide square before any of the men began to take notice of them. Even then, the spread of interest was slow, as one nudged another, and that one in turn alerted his superior. They seemed uncertain of who it was that approached, and although they may have had their suspicions, it was quite improbable that the Empire's rulers should be walking, unaccompanied, through the city they had lost, dressed in filthy clothes and covered in dirt.

Were it not for Aleph, the Seeker Prime, they may have crept closer still, perhaps even come upon the men with an element of surprise. But instead, when the Seeker's cry went up, suspicions were validated and doubt evaporated, and several hundred men, hungry for glory, charged.

The Three stopped and stood, together, as the crowd approached. The Heart breathed deeply, and tore away the bottom part of her already frayed gown, freeing her legs to move more easily. She drew the two short and wickedly sharp stiletto blades from her belt, and readied them in her hands.
"Well, my friends," she said, "whatever happens, I'm glad to be standing beside you."
The Sword smiled. "Glad to be standing beside you too, Loulouthi, but please, don't be so defeatist. We're going back to our Keep, that's what is going to happen."
The Book agreed. "Yes, Duma. Let us not forget what these men have done, eh? I don't know about you, but I've got a little anger to work through. Now, enough talking. Their numbers make them bold. They charge as if to overrun us… Loulouthi?"

The Heart nodded. "You're right. They have a lot to answer for..." The Heart's brow furrowed, and her eyes began to darken, "Let's rattle their confidence."
"Just when I was beginning to tire of bureaucracy," laughed the Sword, "Together then."

The Heart took a few steps forward, and faced the onrushing group. She drew her arms out wide, teeth bared, face twisted in concentration. The approaching men roared bestially, a blood lust truly upon them now, buoyed up by the shouts and cries of those around them. They waved their swords wildly above their heads and rushed to cover the last few feet between them and their prey, desperate to be the first to strike, to claim their place in history. If they had watched more carefully they might have seen the shadows in the air, like a wisp of black smoke around the Heart's hands. They might have noticed the colour drain from her face, and may have seen the darkness of her eyes. As it was, they charged closer still.

Without warning, the Heart raised her head with a sudden, jerking motion, and threw her hands down behind her. Like a cloud passing overhead, dimming the day and bringing a sudden chill, a wave of unseen energy blasted outward, sending a curl of dust spreading before it. The nearest man's face knotted in a look of horrified confusion, and though his scream was uninterrupted, it changed from one of rage and strength to that of terror and revulsion. Eyes rolling in his head, he kicked at the earth in desperation, trying to reverse his travel, throwing himself back into the men behind. One or two of the men, perhaps less foolhardy than the rest, tried to slow, but it was too late. Momentum and the weight of those behind prevented it. When the shadow touched them, a change came over each man, sweeping through the crowd like a terrible wave, bringing chaos as those still charging up behind collided with those fleeing at the front.

The Heart stumbled as she came to her senses, and fell to one knee, the effort she had expended taking its toll. Her friends were ready though, and moved alongside her, the Sword supporting her and helping her up while the Book stepped in front, a wicked smile on her face as she pushed her glasses to the top of her nose and rolled up her sleeves.

The first wave of men had come to an ungainly halt, sprawling on the ground as others piled up behind, but some began to push their way through, while others regained their senses and their composure, and shakily found their feet. The Book wasted no time. She quickly brought forth a handful of slender glass tubes from her robe, and swinging her arm out in front of her, tossed them into the crowd. Where they landed, they shattered, sending out little fragments of glass and a shower of the watery red liquid within, causing some minor annoyance to those nearby, followed by derisive shouts at the missiles ineffectiveness. But those struck by the liquid shouted louder and with greater fury than the rest, and when they were jostled or pushed by those behind, they found their temper uncontrollable. Within seconds, a dozen of the men were savagely attacking those around them, hacking furiously at anyone within their reach. Confusion grew as the rest of the men struggled to escape their blows, or fought back, even striking each other as they tried to determine friend from foe.

The Book's hands darted into her robe again, and pulled out a tightly bound leather pouch. Drawing forth her little knife, she slit the leather at the top, and, stepping across in front of her companions, cast a thick grey powder down onto the floor in a large semi-circle before them. As it touched the ground, it began to darken and smoke, and even as the last of it fell, a wall of fierce white flame leapt up, shielding the Three behind it.

The Book turned away from the blaze, back towards the Heart and the Sword.
"Well," she shouted above the noise all around, "we have slowed them down at least... Now the real work begins, eh?"
The Sword narrowed his eyes against the bright flames, peering through at the men beyond. "How long will it burn, Sofya?" he asked.
"Like this? Two, maybe three minutes at most."
As she spoke, one of the men just visible through the flickering heat had found a skin of water from somewhere, and flung it on the fire. The next second he disappeared with a yelp behind the great gout of flame that resulted.
"Well, maybe longer if they keep that up. Idiots." continued the Book, "But not much. It was all the blackroot I had, I took everything I could before leaving my study."
"Three minutes, or thirty, it doesn't matter." said the Heart, "We can't hold here anyway. We have done what we needed, stopped their charge. We haven't time to wear them down at this bottleneck. As foolish as it is, we must press forward."
The Sword gave a grim nod. "You're right, of course, Loulouthi. Are we ready then? Like we used to, hold a circle, I'll take the lead. Call out if one breaks the line behind."

The Three prepared themselves, and even as they did, a few bold men leapt over and through the lessening flames.

The Sword cut them down with cold precision, before their feet had even found the earth again, but more took their place, and as the fire shrank further still, so the soldiers courage grew.

"Here it is then!" cried the Sword, "If we are split, we meet beyond the doors of the Keep! Now, together!"

It seemed that a charge by their vastly outnumbered opponents was the last thing the Scribe's forces were anticipating, and for a moment this worked in the Three's favour, as surprise slowed the soldiers responses, allowing the Sword to cut a wicked swathe a dozen feet into their ranks before they truly grasped what was happening. All the time, the Heart remained just at his right shoulder, guarding their side and rear, while the Book moved at the left, holding off any who approached that way.

For a while there was only the sound of clashing weapons, wordless cries of pain or fury, grunts of exertion and impact. The Three slowly, slowly crept toward the Keep, inching forward until they were buried deep within the lines of their enemy, who pressed on all sides. The Sword fought like a demon, blade dancing before him as if possessed, and none entered the wide arc of space in front of him without paying dearly for their incursion. As his foes struck high, swinging their weapons overhead, the Sword countered with a block of astonishing ferocity, sending their blows bouncing back, before slashing low and wide, deadly sharp edge of his blade slicing muscle, severing hamstrings, sending another row of men collapsing to the ground to be trampled by those behind. When the next man thrust low at the crouching Sword, he deftly knocked the tip of the man's blade into the earth, before planting the flat of his foot on the weapon, tearing it from the bearer's hands. Then he rose up, swinging high and fast, splitting the man near in two.

At the Sword's back, the Heart and the Book fought with no less intensity. Those soldiers who attempted to flank the group, or approach from the rear thinking they would find a less dangerous opponent, were cruelly disappointed. Many who neared the Heart found their temper softened, or their conviction shaken as she met their eyes, found that in truth they lacked the certainty to strike down this gentle thing, or the confidence to attempt it. Some turned away altogether, forced by fear and anguish to fight against the flow of men at their back, and those who did not found their pause a fatal one, as the delicate daggers the Heart wielded again and again found gaps in armour and yielding flesh. On the Book's side, chaos reigned. Although the Book's cruel little knife danced back and forth when needed, more than half the blows that brought down her enemies were launched by them in the first place. Men staggered and fell about in confusion, some blinded by fantastic flashes of light, others deafened and senseless from a sudden thunderclap. In the middle of it all, the Book's hands flickered and flew, tracing curious shapes in the air, drawing odd objects and trinkets from her robe as needed, while her eyes flitted from one target to the next. Her brow twisted and creased with concentration, and although her teeth were clenched and her jaw tight, all the time she wore a wild little smile that alone was enough to unnerve those around her.

However, the Scribe's men were persistent, and numerous. Despite the Three's best efforts, each man they brought down was replaced instantly by another, and eventually the Three began to tire. A sudden push by several men on the Sword's left meant they closed behind him, forcing him to move quickly forward, and separate from the others. The Book and the Heart were left back to back, holding their ground, and the Sword found himself beaten even further from them by a series of brutal attacks. Unable to focus his attention on a single front, defending all sides, he found himself forced to move at the whim of his attackers as he deftly spun and wheeled, deflecting countless strikes. The Heart and the Book, meanwhile, found themselves in a stalemate, still able to fend off the onslaught of those around them, but unable to move lest they leave their back unguarded.

The Scribe's men saw their opportunity, and redoubled their assaults. Officers called furiously upon them to seize the moment, and bring on the bloody conclusion. Strength and courage bolstered, a roar rose up from the throat of every man, and they swung their weapons with new vigour.

For a moment, the Book faltered, sweat pouring from her face, and she miscast a charm, a meaningless shape hanging in the air. It was a moment too long. Although she quickly resolved it, her lapse provided an opening that was gladly filled with steel, and a reaching blade slipped through and cut her deeply at the shoulder.

The Heart heard her friend cry out in pain behind her.
"Sofya! Sofya? Are you alright?!" she called uncertainly, not daring to turn her attention elsewhere even for a second.
"Yes- ah... yes!" came the embattled reply, "Yes... but, Loulouthi... I don't... We can't hold this!"
"Concentrate, Sofya! Don't let go!" the Heart shouted back, although she knew her friend was right.

Around the Sword, things had come to an uncomfortable

balance. The men surrounding him had fully recognised their advantage, and now made the most of it. There was none among them who could best the Sword individually, they knew, but he was tiring, and they knew that also. So now, the Sword found himself in a space of his own, the soldiers around him staying just out of reach until he was forced to turn his back, at which point they lashed out from behind him. The Sword turned and turned again as the soldiers baited him relentlessly, each blow just a hair's breadth closer to its mark. He was not sure where in the crowd beyond Sofya and Loulouthi now lay, but from one side, as he twisted again to meet the next blow, he could hear terrible roars and cries, sounds seeming almost inhuman.

The next blow never came. As the Sword rounded and raised his blade to meet it, the soldier now before him turned suddenly away, halting his swing inexplicably. Nonetheless, it was a chance. The Sword cut him down, and pressed forward into the gap, but before he could bring his weapon to bear on the next man, a colossal fist appeared high above, and hammered down on the soldier's skull with crushing force. Two great arms reached out, and swept aside the surrounding men as if parting water, and the Sword's eyes widened in disbelief as a muscular Savage, bare-chested and bloody, emerged after them. The Sword stood frozen, blade steady in his hand, but the Savage made no move to attack. Then a soldier at his right yelled out, charging forward with a wild thrust. Even as the Sword turned to meet him, a heavy blade fell on the soldier from behind, pulverising his armour at the shoulder and splitting the man almost clean to the waist. As the body fell lifelessly forward, it revealed a familiar figure.

"Good to see you, my Lord! Looks like we arrived just in

time!"

"Tarrett! Tarrett, Ancients save us, man!" cried the Sword, looking about in amazement as dozens of the General's troops appeared, alongside more of the tall Savages, cutting a path through the Scribe's terrified men. "But how-? Never mind. My friends?"

"The Heart and the Book are with us, my Lord, we came upon them first! We followed the golden giant, but when we reached the city we found them still, frozen by the darkness. Then we saw the east gates lay wide open, and the ruins of the Keep. We hurried through the city as quickly as we could!" shouted the General.

The Sword nodded gratefully. "Very well then, General. The Scribe is behind this, and he remains within. We must press through to the Keep!"

"Yes, my Lord! As you command."

Although tired from their race back to the city, Tarrett's men were enraged and dismayed by what they discovered, and their fury overcame their weariness when they found themselves face to face with the traitors responsible. They alone may have been enough to rout the Scribe's forces, but as it was they were accompanied by the frightening presence of the Savages, and together they made swift progress. The Three reunited at the head of the charge, and those few of the Scribe's men who were yet foolish enough to stand and fight fell quickly. Before long, the Three stood outside the Keep's shattered doors.

Chapter Twenty-Nine

Gaven, Fulza and Jubal hurried through the winding streets of Bantha, searching for some sign or indication of which way they should travel. The few people they passed met them with odd, hostile looks, and each time Gaven called out to them in the hope of some direction, they hurried away, clearly deciding they had enough problems of their own, never mind a soldier and a Savage seeking to head *into* the city, with a large, threatening pig at their heels.

"This is hopeless, Fulza, How will we know where she is?!"
Fulza gave a grunt. "Be calm, Gaven Mayweather. You know this place. What lies at the centre? Need to see where the trouble lies. Find Joseera there, for certain."
Gaven breathed deeply, and chewed at his lip. "The city is built around a great open square. The Imperial Keep lies just to the south of it, overlooking the river, while the Keeper's Tower stands in the east."
"Very well then, Gaven Mayweather. Let us head for the centre, find our bearings from there." replied Fulza, setting off down a side street.
"Alright, Fulza." called Gaven after him, "But where are you going? You don't know the city!"
The big Savage turned for a moment. "Simple. Approached from west, came through west gate. Head east, will find the centre."
He pointed up, into the morning sky. "Over there, is east. We follow the sun."
Gaven looked round and gave a little laugh.
"Yes, of course." he said. "Of course we do."

oOo

On the platform, Joseera grimaced as the disfigured face of the Scribe grinned down at her.

"Ah, excellent." the Scribe purred. "You *are* awake after all. Good morning, young lady."
Joseera groaned. Her head pounded madly. "You." she managed. "What did you do to the boy? Why did you hurt him? He can't have done anything to you."
The Scribe smiled. "Oh, Mister Parfort was extremely useful. I just helped him realise his... potential. And now, Miss Mayweather, I'm going to help you."
"Hah. I know what you've done." Joseera replied, defiant, "You're a liar. You don't want to help anybody, you're not anything you say you are."
"On the contrary," said the Scribe, "I will lead us into a new age of understanding. There are always those who fear the unknown, young lady, who stand in the way of progress."
Joseera coughed painfully. "Whatever you want from me, I won't give it to you."
The Scribe laughed loudly. "Oh, I think you will, Miss Mayweather, I think you will." He smiled at her, thoughtfully. "Aleph was right. You're not as fragile as you seem. All the better, I suppose."
"It doesn't matter what you say. I won't do anything for you. You're wasting your time."
The Scribe sighed, and sat back. "Ah, Miss... may I call you Joseera? It is Joseera, isn't it? I hope you don't mind, I think we are beyond such formalities."
Joseera said nothing, simply scowling back at him.
"Joseera, you are going to do exactly as I ask, and I will tell you why. You cannot have failed to hear of, perhaps you have even seen, the mysterious golden creatures,

giant, lumbering things walking our lands. Well, Joseera, they are coming here, right here, to this very spot. They are coming for me, Joseera, and they are going to destroy this city and everything in it. I can stop them. With your help, I can stop them."

He stopped for a moment, and watched her, seeing the uncertainty on her face. He smiled again, but a cruel smile now, one that made Joseera afraid.

"Now perhaps you do not care about the city, Joseera, perhaps you do not care about the many thousands of people who live here, their homes, their lives. Perhaps I have misjudged you, and your conscience. But I think there may be people here that you *do* know. That you surely *do* care about. In the corners of this building, Joseera, in the cells below there are people from some little village, a tiny place, you may have heard of it. Now what was the name again…? Ah yes. *Lerncos.*"

Joseera frowned, and a chill spread through her body. "What?"

"Yes, Lerncos, that's it." the Scribe continued. "Lerncos. Brought here after the tragic attack on their village by the… Savages."

Joseera struggled angrily against her bonds. "You're lying! You're lying, they can't be-"

"Oh, but they are, Joseera!" the Scribe interrupted, grasping her face suddenly in one hand, pulling her close, "I was looking for *you*, my girl. It was all because of you. Now you have a chance to put it right. Do as I ask, and you can save them, Joseera. Your parents would be so happy to see you, they have talked endlessly about you…"

Joseera gritted her teeth, trying not to let her feelings show, but the tears welling in her eyes betrayed her.

"My parents." she whispered. "What is it? What is it that you're trying to do?"

The Scribe leaned closer, till she could smell the rank sweetness of his breath. "I am going to free myself from the limitations that the Ilo'Seri put in place. I am going to harness the power they were afraid to use. The legacy of the Ancients, the immeasurable force of Seri-gae will be at my disposal."

He smiled, and ran a sharp nail down the side of Joseera's face.

"The only things standing in my way now are the remnants of a failed race, mindless guard dogs left behind. In order to stop them, Joseera, in order to control them, I need the touch of their creators, the touch of the line of Ilo'Seri. Your touch, Joseera. Your touch."

Joseera's breath was ragged. "And you'll let them go? You'll let them all go, my family, the others, you won't hurt them?"

The Scribe grinned. "I have no need of them, Joseera. You have my word."

The preparations were quickly made. The Scribe took his place near the centre of the platform on one side of the Font, while Aleph helped him to remove his outer robe, along with other bits and pieces, accoutrements of office now unnecessary. Mister Glower and Miss Glass helped Joseera to the other side of the Font, and showed her where to place her hands, explained that this should simply be enough, that she should let the power flow naturally, and not to fight it lest it cause her harm. Nervous and uncertain, Joseera stood between them, tears rolling silently down her face. She wished there were someone here she could trust, someone to tell her what to do, the right course to take. She thought of Fulza. She thought of her brother. She thought of Elder Jarry and the others from her village. She thought of her parents.

"I understand. I'm ready." she said.

Calmly, the Scribe took hold of the knurled metal handles on his side of the Font. Joseera expected some movement or response, but everything was still, and the Font remained as cold and dead as ever.

"If you please, Miss Mayweather." chimed Mister Glower, just behind her.

Joseera breathed deeply, and stretched out her hands. She held them, shaking, in the air, inches from the cool metal.

There was an impatient sigh from Miss Glass. "Now, girl!" she said, and reaching forward, clutched Joseera's forearms in a fierce grip, thrusting her hands onto the Font.

For a moment Joseera felt an almost pleasant sensation, reminiscent of how she had felt in the Temple, looking up into the warm light overhead. But the moment passed quickly. The strange feeling grew and kept growing, its sweetness swiftly becoming sickly, overwhelming, filling her stomach and throat with an oily wave of nausea. Still it grew, and Joseera tried to pull her hands away from the font, recoiling from it all, but found the cold metal now hot and fluid, flowing around her hands and encasing them up to the wrist, sticky and unyielding. It held her firm, and she lost the strength to fight anyway, as the nausea overtook her and she retched. She would have fallen, heaving, to the floor, but the Font held her up. Still the flow of power grew, but there was nothing pleasant in it, no warmth at all. It was cold, and absolute. A piercing, ringing pain, a needle of burning ice driven up through the soles of the feet to the back of the eyes. Joseera screamed.

On the other side of the Font, the Scribe wailed strangely as the metal danced with purplish light, flowing across his hands and up about his arms and body. Aleph started forward in alarm, concerned that something was amiss, but Miss Glass stepped forward and barred his way, placing her hand flat upon his chest, with a touch like a block of ice.

Mister Glower gave his usual simpering smile. "Do not worry, Master Aleph! This is as it should be!" he shouted, over the strange noises of the two figures locked around the Font. He turned to face the Scribe. "Your Eminence? All is well?"

The Scribe slowly turned his head to look at Mister Glower, a slack smile on his face, and a crazed look, as if he had never seen the man before. He laughed, drunkenly. "Ah... Mister Glower! I-I feel it... I feel it, Mister Glower! Such power... such... an endless reach, Mister Glower! Endless!"

Glower smiled back. "The connection is made, Your Eminence, you may safely release the Font! You must stay close by until the process is complete, but you may move freely!"

Cautiously, the Scribe uncurled his fingers and gently released the metal he had been gripping so tightly. The shimmering purple remained though, dancing across his skin, and his whole body seemed to take on a pale glow, as if a pure white fire burnt within. He looked around at his companions and a manic grin split his face.

"I feel it!" he shouted again, and turning out to the ruins around him, his eyes lighted on the towering remains of the great stairwell, twisting madly off to nothingness nearby. He reached out a hand into the air before him, fingers spread wide, then slowly curled it in a fist, and as he did, the stairwell twisted and cracked as though constricted, before finally crumbling in a thunderous shower of stone.

"I feel it!" the Scribe howled out again, as behind him at the Font, Joseera screamed too.

oOo

In the Fold beyond the city's north gate, people had stopped, setting down their belongings and supplies, and turning back to watch the incredible sight unfolding at the city walls. One of the golden figures, it seemed, stood before the others, and now led their way forward, forcing its way through the cluttered streets, pushing walls and buildings aside. Not one of the people quite understood what was taking place, and most were terrified by what they saw, but none could tear themselves away, transfixed by the sight and the sounds, the rumble of stone and the ringing of golden metal.

The Sun King was struggling to quicken its brothers. They moved slowly, convinced of their inexorable destiny. It did not falter though, or slacken its pace, forging onward and opening a path for them. Again and again it called out as it went.

"Hurry brothers, hurry! There is hope! A spark remains, there is still hope!"

oOo

Outside the Keep, the arrival of Tarrett's forces and the Savages had brought the area under control. There were still small patches of fighting here and there, where the Scribe's men had barricaded themselves into nearby buildings, or fought on the retreat into the narrow streets and alleys, but for the most part the situation was in hand. The Three stood with the General outside the entrance to the Keep.

The Heart was giving their thanks again. "And please, General," she continued, "pass our sentiments on to your men. They have done a great service to us."
"The Savages too, General, let them know we are grateful." added the Book. "What is the arrangement there, anyway?"
The General shook his head uncertainly. "When the fighting is done? I'm honestly not certain, my Lady. For now I'm just glad to have them beside us instead of against us. As I understand it, when they learnt what had happened, how they had been misled, they were even angrier than we were. I wouldn't want to be the Scribe if they get their hands on him."
The Book smiled. "I see, General. Well, thank them if you would. Now, talking of the Scribe, we must be going, eh?"
"Let us come with you, my Lady."
"We need you out here, Tarrett." said the Sword, "We can't risk them taking this position back, or following us in. Besides, we don't know what to expect in there. Better we go and test the waters first."
Tarrett sighed. "If you insist, my Lord, we'll hold here, of course. But at least take a few men with you. We can spare a handful, that's sure."
"Very well, Tarrett." said the Sword, clapping the old General on the shoulder, "One squad, get them moving. And be careful out here."
The General was pleased and relieved. "You too, my Lord." He turned and yelled out in a soldiers voice to several nearby men. "You there! Ready arms, get over here! You're inside, with the Three, your lives for theirs, understood?!"
The men quickly secured their gear and hurried over. A chorus of "Yes sir!" filled the air.

The Three stepped unchallenged through the outer doors

of the Keep, which hung in splintered pieces from their hinges, with Tarrett's men close behind. Once inside, all looked around apprehensively at what remained. It resembled more the ruins of some long abandoned fort than the mighty building they knew so well. The heavy inner gates still lay open, broken apart when Gensu's men had breached them, and the Three stepped cautiously through, uncertain what to expect beyond.

They found themselves in a wasteland of rubble and wood, punctuated with the remnants of furniture, scraps of cloth. Here and there patches of sky were visible through crooked holes in the ceiling, and in places the odd wall or doorway stood alone, forlorn amid the wreckage.

The Three knew the building well though, and no amount of damage could have robbed them of their bearings.
"To the Great Hall?" said the Heart, in a low voice.
"Aye," replied the Book, "makes sense to start there at least. We'll have an idea of what is still standing too."
The Sword turned to the soldiers waiting patiently behind. "Stay quiet. We'll stick together for now, so follow close as you're able. No noise, not a sound, not even if you see the foe. Send a signal forward unless you're certain that they've already spotted us. Understood?"
The soldiers looked one to the other, then silently nodded. Together the little party began to creep slowly deeper into the Keep.

Before long they had reached the remains of the receiving rooms that had stood on the north side of the hall. The interior damage seemed worse here, and only a few jutting slabs still stood to indicate where the boundaries of each space had been. For the most part, it was a wide open space now, and in the middle of it all a low platform rose, two or three feet clear of the destruction that surrounded it.

The Three crept closer, careful and low, pressing in against whatever cover presented itself. On the top of the platform there was an odd ripple in the air, as if from a great heat. Several figures stood, all attention focused on the strange object in the platform's centre.

The Book, crouched behind a huge fallen beam, signalled to the others, concealed against the curved remnants of the old hall doorway.
"That's him!" she whispered. "The Scribe! But who is that with him?"
The Sword peered carefully around the corner of his hiding place.
"His lackeys." he whispered back. "Glass and Glower, I believe, and the Seeker Prime. I see the girl too. And it looks like a young lad on the floor there. One of his students perhaps?"
"Either way, they're preoccupied." said the Heart. "There's no way to approach them without being seen, we should move now, while they're distracted."
"You're right. There's no choice." replied the Book. "But go carefully."
"We'll flank them then," said the Sword, "for caution's sake. Sofya, you head round to their right, I'll move to the left. Loulouthi, the men will stay here with you, when you see us ready, approach them from here."

The Heart continued to watch their quarry closely as her companions made their way warily through the rubble. She need not have worried, however, as the figures atop the platform seemed quite oblivious, allowing the Book and the Sword to move without fear of notice. When she saw they were ready, she took a long breath, and stepped out from behind the broken wall.

They moved slowly at first, ready for some reaction from the Scribe or the others, but none gave any sign of responding. As they drew nearer, they saw that the girl stood with her eyes closed, and the Scribe's attention was entirely focused on the ugly stone and metal thing between them.

Closer and closer to the platform they came, the Sword and the Book from each side, and the Heart followed by the handful of Tarrett's men. Finally it was Aleph, glancing nervously around him, who spotted their approach.
"Your Eminence! Your Eminence, we have visitors!"
The Scribe turned with a scowl. When he saw who it was stood before him however, his expression twisted into an ugly smile.
The Heart shouted out in frustration.
"Curse you, Gideon, what are you doing? What have you brought upon us?"

When she heard the voices, Joseera's eyes snapped open, sore and bloodshot, ringed in red. Her head lolled madly as she tried to focus on the newcomers, keep her vision from swimming with the pain.
"Who are you?!" she howled. "What are you doing here?"
"That's enough, Miss Mayweather, leave them to me! You concentrate on the task you've been given!" snarled the Scribe, over his shoulder. Mister Glower and Miss Glass moved silently nearer Joseera, staying close at her side.

The Heart stepped forward again, as close to the edge of the low platform as she dared.

"Young lady, you've nothing to fear. We are friends... old friends, though you may not remember us. This man is making a terrible mistake, but we are here to put things right. You have a choice, you don't have to listen to him any more."

Joseera's eyes flicked back and forth at the people around her. Her brow, slick with a cool sweat, knotted in confusion.

"You... you don't understand... It's too late! You have to get away. You have to go *now*!" she called out.

"I said that's enough, Miss Mayweather!" spat the Scribe, then he turned angrily to Aleph, "Well, you truly are a protege... perhaps a little economical with the truth of events which befell you in the Temple, Aleph? Or is there another explanation for the three corpses walking and talking before us, eh?"

Aleph frowned unhappily. "Heh... Your Eminence, I-"

"Oh, spare me." The Scribe drawled, "You can explain later. For now, go and make sure we don't have any more uninvited guests!"

Aleph's face reddened, tendons rippling in frustration along his jaw. "Yes, Your Eminence. Of course."

He bowed curtly, and giving the Three a wide berth, headed back towards the entrance to the Keep.

As Aleph went, Mister Glower left Miss Glass with Joseera and crept forward, muttering something into the Scribe's ear, too quiet for the rest to hear. The Scribe giggled manically in response, and gave a mischievous nod

"Well, Gideon," said the Heart, shaking her head. "It seems we underestimated you. That is to our detriment. But it needn't be too late, Gideon, we can still fix this. Together."

"Oh, please," the Scribe replied with a contemptuous scoff, "Give me a little credit at least. It is time for a new chapter in our Empire's history, and *you* will not feature in it. You should take the girl's advice. Get out of here while you still can."

"You should teach them a *lesson*, Your Eminence. Let them see how they underestimated you... show them how *strong* you've become!" hissed Miss Glass from beside the Font, eyes burning with a curious hunger.

The Scribe pursed his lips in thought. "Yes... perhaps you're right, Miss Glass... a little test..."

The Book and the Sword lost their patience at the same moment, and stepped forward together. The Sword drew his blade and held it before him, levelled at the Scribe's throat.

"I've heard enough, Gideon." he said. "This ends now."

The Scribe simply laughed.

"I've told you before, Duma. I'd rather you addressed me according to my position. And as of today, you may call me *Master*."

"Oh yes, very good, Your Eminence!" cooed Glower, grinning and clapping his hands fervently, "Master of all! Now show them, Your Eminence, show them!"

The Sword moved steadily forward, and motioned for Tarrett's men to follow.

The Book scoffed, and began to fish in her robes for something. "Have you lost your mind, Scribe?" she said. "You'll be lucky if we leave you standing at all!"

The Scribe nodded. "I must say, you have all been far more troublesome than I anticipated. I had presumed you would be buried beneath the ruins of your Keep.

Thankfully, how you escaped, how you recovered, none of it matters now. You're too late. I am the only one who can stop those golden things outside your walls from tearing down your precious city. And whether you believe that or not, there is nothing you can do. I will unite the land under my power, and every man, every woman, *everyone* will kneel before me, and we will wipe the Savage filth from the earth."

Behind him, having returned to Glass and Joseera, Mister Glower practically drooled with excitement. "Yes, yes, now show them!"

The Sword sighed.

"This is a joke, Prow." he said, irritably, blade still thrust straight and sharp before him, moving closer to the Scribe. "Your men outside are beaten. We have escaped your traps. I won't listen to any more of your lies. You've failed, it's over!"

"Ah, Duma," replied the Scribe, "As usual, you really don't understand, do you? It's too late. I haven't-"

He was interrupted by a sudden shout, the harsh, cold voice of Miss Glass cutting through the air like a scalpel.

"Enough talk. Remember our terms! Do as you're bid, and show them, *show us all, now!*"

The Scribe flinched at her voice, face twisting in a strange mix of resentful irritation and what looked like fear. For a moment the Heart and the Book looked at each other in confusion, but the Sword's patience had run entirely dry. He swiftly covered the short remaining distance between him and the Scribe, before drawing back his blade and sending it in a fast, flat sweep at the Scribe's neck.

The Scribe turned back to see the blow sailing toward him

and lifted his arm. The Sword cried out in surprise as his weapon was knocked aside, torn from his grip and sent spinning, clattering into the wreckage of the Keep. He had no time to recover before the Scribe swung his arm back again, planting his palm solidly against the Sword's chest, sending him sailing backwards, and over the platform's edge.

The Book gasped in amazement, but reacted quickly nonetheless. She gathered her wits, a quick motion in her fingers, and sent a roiling blast of white flame searing towards the Scribe. When it reached him, however, he seemed to almost to play with it, reaching out with his other hand and twisting it about his arm, before turning it back, roaring, at the Book. She threw up her hands in alarm, calling up a desperate defence, but it was not quite enough to save her from the impact itself, and the blast launched her too away, off into the rubble.

Tarrett's men had watched the exchange wide-eyed and open-mouthed, but now they gathered their senses. Their young lieutenant waved his sword in the air, and shouted out a simple order.
"Now, lads! Take him! FORWARD!"
The Scribe sneered at them over his shoulder, and waved his hand at them in a dismissive sweep.
"No, lads... *back!*" he snapped.
As the sweep of his arm moved past each man, one after another was hurled violently off into the darkness beyond, breastplate crumpling as if under some terrible blow.

The Heart was still stood at the edge of the platform. She could feel the panic rising. She made no move to approach. Instead she fixed the Scribe with a steady, searching gaze.

"Stop this, Gideon." she said, as calmly as she could. "This isn't who you are. They wouldn't want this. Your family wouldn't wish to see you this way. Your father, Gideon… think of your father. Everything he wanted for you…"

Just for a moment the Scribe paused, and a look of doubt crossed his face.

"My father…? What could you know? Those creatures took him…"

"Yes," replied the Heart, softly, "unfairly taken in defence of his land, untimely… but think, Gideon! Would he have wanted this? Was he so cruel a man?!"

The Scribe's good eye shone, and wandered into the distance. "He was a good man… a good man."

Miss Glass grabbed a handful of Joseera's hair, and yanked her head sharply back, causing her to cry out. The Scribe looked round in surprise.

"Focus, Your Eminence!" rasped Glower, smile still plastered on his face but quite vanished from his voice, "Draw strength through her, and *focus!*"

The Scribe turned back to the Heart with a scowl.

"Gideon…" started the Heart.

"Save your games, Lady Loulouthi!" he barked back, "Don't try to play with me! Whatever you may think you know, it's... it's too late! Now, I have other things to attend to, so... goodbye, Lady Loulouthi."

He raised both hands before him, then flung them outwards at the Heart, and a howling rush of wind ripped forward, tearing at her clothes and stinging her skin. The gale lifted her and flung her carelessly into the shadowy ruins beyond, where she struck the hard stone of a shattered wall, and fell limply to the floor.

The Scribe looked pleased with himself.

"Good, good." he muttered. "A little messy perhaps, but a good test... very good..."

He turned his attention back to the Font, where Mister Glower and Miss Glass stood with Joseera. He pressed his hand against the dark thing buried in his chest.

Glower smiled sweetly at him "Yes, very good, Your Eminence, very good. You're doing *so* well." he purred.

Miss Glass fixed the Scribe with an icy stare. "Almost there. Now let's finish this."

The Scribe stared silently back for a few moments.

"Perhaps this power is enough," he whispered, almost inaudible, "perhaps *you* are no longer needed."

Mister Glower tutted loudly, looking hurt. "Tsk! We're so close, Your Eminence, so close! The Sun Kings are almost upon us, take them and we all get what we want! No need to quarrel!"

Miss Glass smiled. "Almost there. Then you will have *everything* you desire, and we can go on our way..."

The Scribe said nothing. After a few seconds he gave a dull nod. His brow furrowed in concentration, and he seemed lost in thought for a little while. Then, ever so slowly, a faint smile crept across his face.

"Yes..." he breathed softly, his head tipping back in delight. "Yes... I hear them. The Sun Kings will answer to me!"

In the wreckage, the Sword lifted his head with an awkward groan. He tried briefly to move, and felt a sharp stab of pain in his side. My ribs, he thought, most likely broken. With a sigh, he rested his head back against the stone. Above, the sky seemed peaceful, the new day was brightening. From where he lay, he could see through the ruined Keep, to the city beyond. He could see the golden figures. As he watched, they advanced steadily. He closed his eyes. We've failed, he thought.

oOo

When Gaven, Fulza and Jubal reached the edge of Bantha's great square, the buildings cleared and for the first time they had a clear view. To the north, they could see the massive shapes of the Sun Kings, steadily approaching, and just to the south, what remained of the city's Keep. When they saw the devastation and bedlam surrounding the crumbling building, they knew immediately that they were in the right place.

There was considerable disorder outside the Keep, and on seeing both men and Savages running here and there, Gaven thought for a moment that there must be fighting, and was ready to rush forward, weapon drawn, although in all honesty he could not say for certain on which side he might belong. Fortunately Fulza caught his arm before he made his decision, prompting him to pause, and watch.

Gaven quickly realised that, much to his amazement, the two sides were working together. There was a great deal of confusion, not least because each struggled to understand the other, but there could be no doubt about it, they had a common purpose. Now and then there were shouts and gestures to the north, pointing at the Sun Kings, before another flurry of activity erupted, preparations being made.
"You don't all speak our language, then?" whispered Gaven, as they neared the hustle.
"Hmn. No, Gaven Mayweather. No more than you speak ours."

Nervously, trying to avoid any unwanted attention, they

walked slowly through the crowd of bodies hurrying this way and that. Although Jubal drew a few strange looks from some of the soldiers, Fulza kept the boar close at his side, and most of the men were too busy to give the matter further thought. They had come within fifty yards of the entrance to the Keep, when a huge Savage, with two great tusks protruding from his jaw, ringed with decoration and carvings, stepped into their path. He looked squarely, and suspiciously at Fulza.

"*Kol Va'ket... bash su va hir?*" growled the big Savage, its voice a low, threatening rumble.
Fulza's muscles tightened. "*Ma'bas kirrik. Tura, shah?*"
The big Savage's eyes briefly lighted on Jubal, and then studied Gaven for a moment. "*Gar yem sin? Shah?*"
"*Chah. Gan sar.*" Fulza turned, and gestured behind, at the golden figures in the distance. Then he pointed into the Keep. "*Ilos ih'vir, kamcha. Skothi va hir. Mam va Ilo'Seri.*"
For a long moment the big Savage remained quiet, its expression quite unreadable to Gaven. Finally it gave a slow, deliberate nod.
"*Kal kera.*" it said, then turned and walked away, without looking back.

As they wove their way through the remainder of the crowd, the last short distance to the doors of the Keep, Gaven leaned in to Fulza, keeping his voice low.
"What was all that about? What did he say to you?" he asked.
Fulza gave a deep breath and looked straight ahead.
"'Good luck', Gaven Mayweather. Said 'good luck'".

Chapter Thirty

They crept through the remains of the Keep's splintered door, and looked around at the expanse of debris beyond.

Gaven puffed his cheeks, taking a deep breath.
"Are you all right, Gaven Mayweather?" asked Fulza, quietly.
"Yes, Fulza, I think so. It's just... I know this place. To see it like this... I can't believe my little sister is really involved in all this."
The Savage laughed dryly. "Think I would like to know sister you talk of. Joseera I know is bound to be." he said.
Gaven laughed back.
"Alright then, Savage. Let's see what we can do."

Cautiously, quietly, they picked their way deeper into the ruined building. They had not come far, however, just reaching the remains of one of the long corridors that led up to the receiving rooms, when they saw someone swiftly approaching.

At the other end of the crumbling walls, Aleph was extremely pleased when he recognised Fulza in the distance. He would be glad of the opportunity to vent a little frustration.
"Well, well!" he said, walking confidently towards them. "Look who we have here! A second chance, it seems, and no need for me to rush away and spoil things this time."

Fulza glared angrily at the arrogant figure. Gaven caught his arm.
"Careful, Fulza." he whispered, cautiously. "I recognise his robes. A Seeker, he is dangerous, beyond a doubt."

Fulza growled. "Met before. In Temple. Took your sister."
Gaven's expression hardened. "Ah. Did he, now?"

"Well now, it must be Captain Mayweather too. What do you say?" Aleph asked. "Would you like to come and see your little sister's big moment? Or perhaps your large friend here would like a rematch?"

Fulza stepped forward, sharp teeth bared.
"We have come for the girl." he rumbled.

"Oh," replied Aleph, mockingly. "It seems your kind just can't accept defeat, can you, Savage?"

Aleph ran swiftly towards them, bounding over the uneven ground. Fulza walked determinedly forward to meet him. But as the Seeker drew close, just as Fulza began to reach for him, Aleph launched a fine spray of reddish dust flying into Fulza's face. Fulza hands went instantly to his eyes, and he roared out in pain, while Aleph dropped flat to the ground, sliding between Fulza's legs, and rolling up onto his feet behind the great Savage.

Gaven dashed forward, pulling his sword from its scabbard as he ran, but Aleph spun to meet him. Though the Seeker seemed unprepared, both hands still high in the air, his right leg whipped around after him, sweeping up out of nowhere, hard heel catching Gaven squarely in the side of the head, entirely by surprise. Gaven staggered sideways, vision reeling, and collapsed on the rocky floor.

Fulza groped blindly behind him, keeping his arms out wide in an effort to maintain some kind of defence, while Gaven, on hands and knees, struggled to clear his head. Aleph stood between them, a look of contempt and disappointment on his face.

"Pitiful. How did you expect to help her if that's the best you have to offer? I hoped for some challenge at least. Still, no use dragging things out now."

A wicked, narrow blade slid out from the sleeve at his right hand.

The Seeker moved quietly towards Gaven, now up on one knee.

"Time's up, Captain." Aleph smiled.

"Wait," Gaven replied, blinking, leaning heavily on his sword, "wait... you forget one thing."

The Seeker looked unimpressed. "Oh?"

There was just long enough for Gaven to see the Seeker's expression of smug satisfaction vanish on hearing the rasping, angry squeal somewhere in the shadows to his right. Aleph turned, reactions quick as thought, just in time to see eight hundred pounds of tusk and muscle hurtling from the darkness.

With impressive speed, the Seeker launched himself into the air, tried to leap, to clear the boar, but it was not enough. Jubal hammered into his legs with avalanche force, sending Aleph spinning head over heels, landing on his front in the stone with a brutal impact. As he went though, the blade in Aleph's right caught Jubal's flank above the foreleg, and the boar skittered and fell as he completed his charge. The boar squealed again, a high note of pain this time, and Fulza cried out in concern, arms flailing blindly towards the noise.

Gaven was on his feet now, and swung his sword over his head, bringing it down in a blow to take the Seeker's head, but with an almighty grunt of effort, Aleph rolled, and the blow missed its mark, instead slicing the flesh at the back of the Seeker's shoulder. Then he rolled back, trapping Gaven's weapon under his left arm, and lashing out with the right, sending the cruel little hidden blade stabbing deep into the inside of Gaven's thigh. With a howl, Gaven fell, clutching at the fast blooming flower of red. Aleph picked up Gaven's sword, and climbed painfully to stand.

Cursing and spitting, blood coursing from the wound at his shoulder, and with one leg unnaturally crooked, the Seeker turned back towards Fulza, who was closer now, eyes streaming, feeling his way cautiously closer to the sounds of struggle. Aleph gripped the hilt of Gaven's weapon tightly, and raised it high above his head.

Fulza focused his attention, tried to clear his mind. He listened closely, desperately searching for the clues to guide his movements. When the Seeker tensed to make his final strike, Fulza rose suddenly, one great hand shooting out and catching Aleph tightly by the neck. The Seeker's surprise was palpable, eyes bulging wildly as much in shock as anything else. Fulza lifted him effortlessly into the air, reaching out with his other hand and snapping Aleph's weapon arm, leaving it hanging by the Seeker's side. Then the Savage drew back and closed his huge fingers into a broad fist. Aleph gave a faint whimper, which was followed by a terrible crunch as Fulza released his hold and hit the Seeker as hard as he could, sending his body bouncing limply into the broken stones.

Gaven hobbled over to where Fulza knelt, hands at his face, clearing the dry dust from his vision.

"Fulza? Are you okay? Can you see?"

The Savage grunted. "Ugh. Yes, can see. Ground fireroot. Coward's trick. Jubal?"
Gaven looked round. There was a lot of blood, and the boar was holding one front leg up lame, but did not seem too distressed.
"He's badly cut, but he'll live."

Gaven helped Fulza wipe the worst of the clumping powder from his swollen eyes, then Fulza began to search through the little pouches and bags at his belt, pulling out strips of plant and rag, dried herbs and powders. The Savage quickly bound Gaven's wound, and saw to Jubal's cut. Gaven had seen many field dressings in his time, but made a note now to find out more about the Savage's methods, impressed by their effectiveness. As soon as they were able, they continued into the Keep.

"Can we be sure that she's here, Savage?" asked Gaven, as they picked their way onward, "What if they're keeping her somewhere else? Somewhere more secure?"
Fulza looked ahead into the ruins. "No, Gaven Mayweather. Joseera is here. I feel it."

oOo

On the platform, the Scribe was becoming impatient.
"What is this? What's happening?" he demanded, "I can feel them, I can hear the Sun Kings voices in my head! Onerous, dull dronings, filling my thoughts, but I cannot grasp them! I thought the girl was supposed to make them vulnerable, make them listen!"
Mister Glower smiled as though receiving an unwanted gift. "Yes, Your Eminence, we are almost there... There are... unexpected difficulties..."
Miss Glass knelt next to Joseera, pulling the girl's head

back cruelly. Joseera's eyes rolled back in her head blindly, showing all white. She seemed quite unaware of those around her.

"The child is tenacious!" hissed Miss Glass, "This intransigent little bitch is fighting the flow, slowing things down."

"Well, *fix* it! All your promises, all your talk… now do something about it!" the Scribe snapped.

Miss Glass scowled at him. "It's *you* who needs to do something, Prow. Show some backbone! Take control, pull the power through her, force her to let go!"

"Miss Glass is correct, if indelicate, Your Eminence," interrupted Glower, "*you* must find her thoughts, shake loose her hold. Take hold of the Font again, and break the child!"

"Hah! What use are you? Must I do everything myself?!"

Miss Glass began to rise. "Watch your mouth, Prow. We have guided your hand. We could tear it off just as easily."

Mister Glower gave his companion a strained look, then addressed the Scribe again. "We are so close now, Your Eminence… just a little more, the Empire will be yours and we will be free! Take the Font, Your Eminence, the girl is exhausted, she cannot resist much longer!"

The Scribe wore an angry look, but approached the Font nonetheless, and reached out his hands to take hold of the twisted handles again.

Before his fingers closed, a voice rang out somewhere in the ruins beyond.

"Wait!"

The Scribe looked up, snarling with irritation.

"Oh, fire and flood, what now?! Aleph? Aleph! Ah, useless, all of you! Useless!"

He turned from the Font and peered into the darkness at the intruders. As he did, the furious scowl he wore twisted in amazement.

"No... it couldn't be... so foolish? After all the trouble you have caused, now here you are? Just in time to witness my ascenscion!"

Gaven ignored his words as they continued to advance towards the platform.

"Stop what you're doing, Scribe," he said, trying to sound as commanding as he could. "It isn't too late."

The Scribe laughed uproariously. "Oh really? I must stop what I'm doing, Captain? Why don't we ask someone else's opinion?"

With a cruel smile, the Scribe held out a hand towards the pale figure hunched by the font, hair lank and slick with sweat, jaw slack.

"Well, Joseera, what do you think? *Is* it too late?"

For a few seconds Gaven stared in silence. He had not recognised the wretched figure as his sister. As realisation dawned, he cried out in dismay.

"Joseera! Joseera!"

His voice seemed to call his sister back from wherever she had gone, and she gave a sobbing cry, before calling back to him in a dry, pained voice.

"Gaven?! No, Gaven, what are you doing here? Get out of here, please, Gaven, please, *go quickly*!"

"Shut up!" snapped Miss Glass, "Prow, we have no time for this!"

"This will only take a moment!" barked the Scribe, angrily. "Well, this *is* nice. A family reunion it seems."

Gaven, forgetting his injured leg altogether, hurried forward toward the platform's edge, before Fulza could reach out to stop him.

"No, no, wait! You don't need her! Take me in her place, she's my sister, my blood! Whatever it is you need, I'll do it, you'll have it! You use me, curse you! *Use me!*"

The Scribe looked out at Gaven and laughed heartily.

"Oh, how sweet. Unfortunately for you Captain Mayweather, I'm afraid you have an inflated sense of your own importance. Your blood has less in common with your sister's than you think, and certainly isn't worth anything to me..."

"Don't listen, Gaven, please, go, *get out of here!*" rasped Joseera desperately.

"Your Eminence..." chimed Glower.

A sly look crossed the Scribe's face. "But perhaps you could provide... some *amusement*."

Gaven climbed up on to the edge of the platform and faced the Scribe.

"Take me." he said solemnly. "Let my sister go, and take me."

With a sneer, the Scribe flung one hand out dismissively, sending a purple-white bolt arcing towards Gaven like lightning. It struck him squarely in the chest, and he flew back off the edge of the platform, landing heavily against Fulza, knocking the Savage from his feet. The crackling energy spread, dancing across Gaven's skin and leaping to Fulza and Jubal, sending convulsions tearing through their bodies. Joseera let out an anguished scream.

oOo

Thung. Thung. Thung.

Amidst the shards of splintered wood, torn cloth and crumbled stone, a low ringing, growing slowly louder, brought the Heart to her senses. She wasn't quite certain at first where she was or how she came to be there, but she didn't worry herself, instead staring up at the grey sky, listening to the pealing bells, wondering how long she had been here. She felt well rested, she reflected. Perhaps she had slept here. If she had, it must have been a long and peaceful sleep. But why would she sleep here, amongst the ruins of this place? Perhaps someone had brought her here while she slept, laid her down upon the stones. Or perhaps...

A dream? The Heart remembered the Scribe with a jolt, and sat stiffly upwards. A lancing pain shot through her temples, and she clutched at her head with a gasp, feeling sticky blood matting her hair. Blinking, clearing her eyes and her thoughts, she looked out across the rubble. No, she thought, not a dream.

Unsteadily, she climbed to her feet. She began to walk, stumbling the first few steps, towards the platform in the middle of the ruins. As she went, she saw several strange figures lying on the ground. A man, a beast and a brute. She saw others approaching from either side. A tall, athletic man with pale grey eyes, one arm clasped tightly to his side. A short, bookish woman with a shock of wild red hair, limping awkwardly.

Thung.

They reached the figures on the ground together, and stopped silently beside them. The Heart and the Sword watched, while the Book cast her hands in the air over them, dispersing the strange energy, loosing their muscles

and calming their minds. Fulza struggled to his knees, but Gaven remained where he lay, face contorted in pain and confusion. His hands grasped feebly at the Book's tattered robes.
"Don't leave - her... please, don't leave her..." he gasped.
Gaven's eyes rolled dully, and he fell back, pale and weak.

At the Font, the Scribe had resumed his assault on Joseera, and cackled in delight as he felt the power within him continue to grow, but his laughter was cut short by a deafening rumble of metal and stone. At the jagged edges of the outer walls, a pair of huge golden hands appeared, followed by another, and another, irresistibly tearing away the stone in great chunks, sending it crashing down to reveal the golden figures beyond. In the clouds of dust and thunder, the Sun Kings stood, vast silhouettes framed in the ruptured walls. They began to advance steadily into the ruins, stepping easily over the shattered stone and knocking aside obstructing beams and buttresses like cobwebs.

Thung.

"Your Eminence..." pleaded Glower.
The Scribe frowned.
"Yes. Enough games. Enough distractions. Time to claim my destiny!"

The Scribe renewed his grip on the Font, knuckles white, brow twisted in concentration.
"It is set down in the Ink! The Three, the Sun Kings, all will fall! The power of the Ancients will be *mine*!"
He summoned all his strength and called up a rush of dark energy from the Font, forcing it through the conduit that was Joseera by sheer will, and causing the girl to let forth

a shattering howl. Enveloped in the blaze of Seri-gae, the Scribe joined her cry, letting his own voice soar with anger and hate.

"Yes! Give in to me, girl! Let the power flow to me! Let it out, child, let it *all* out!"

Now a change came over the girl. The corners of her eyes began to darken and dim, creeping circles of black invading the pale porcelain of her face. Twisted black and purple tendrils spread themselves malignantly across the white of her bare arms, a sickness seeping under her skin, tracing her veins.

Thung.

Behind the Scribe, Glass and Glower paused, and looked uncertainly at one another.

"Ah... Your Eminence... Your Eminence?" Glower began, voice wavering between subservience and desperation.

"Prow!" Glass cut in, with a hiss, "What are you doing?! Use the lodestones, you fool! Channel the power to Glower and I!"

"Your Eminence, *listen* to her!" Glower barked, his mask of civility cracking with the strain, "You cannot hope to control the Seri-gae alone! Let us help you! As we promised! As we *agreed*!"

Thung.

Beneath the crackling force that surrounded him, a thin smile crept across the Scribe's face. He turned to peer over his shoulder at Glass and Glower with a strange expression.

"I'm afraid... I'm afraid that won't be possible. There's been a... change of plan." said the Scribe in a cool, flat tone.

"What are you talking about?!" spat Glass, angrily, "All our efforts! The power will kill you or the Sun Kings will crush you! Your greed will waste it all for *nothing*!"

She crept forward, hands cast out at her sides, claw-like, fingers curved and sharp as talons.

"We have *clawed* our way back into this world, and we will *take* what is ours!"

Mister Glower's eyes burned hatefully, and his temples pulsed and rippled with an inhuman fury.

"This power is ours! It was stolen from us, and now *we want it back*!" he roared, "Now do as you *promised*, Scribe! As you set down in the very Ink we gave you!"

"Ah, Miss Glass, Mister Glower. You should know better," sighed the Scribe, "The truth is not absolute. It is fluid, subject to context and intention, changing from one moment to the next."

The monstrous figures of Glass and Glower reached out towards the Scribe with twisted, grasping limbs. The Scribe ignored them, turning his attention back to Joseera, and the Font.

"And the truth is," he murmured, "I don't need you."

Without warning, a sudden blast of energy slammed into Glass and Glower, and hurled them effortlessly over the dark reaches of the ruins, towards the river far beyond.

"I don't need any of you." whispered the Scribe.

Thung.

From their huddled position on the floor of the Keep, the Three had watched with terror and amazement as the great golden figures of the Sun Kings advanced steadily towards the Font, each thundering step pulverising the stone beneath and sending a low ring echoing around the ruined walls. Now the sudden commotion at the Font drew their attention, and in horror they saw the Scribe and

Joseera rise into the air, lifted by the terrible flood of power rushing out. The girl seemed possessed, otherworldly, skin of alabaster white shot through with cracks of inky black. Her eyes sank endlessly inwards, to the deep purple-blue of the abyss.

Thung.

Unfaltering and inevitable, the Sun Kings neared the Scribe, no more than one great stride away. The Scribe's head rose, trance-like, jaw wide and drooling mouth, as he took in the three golden figures around him. He lifted his arms slowly up, above his head.
"*Too late! You won't stop me. Now, all of you...*" he called, in an ancient voice that boomed around the ruins. "*GET AWAY!*"
The Scribe flung out his arms, and a wave of thunder followed, rolling out across the platform and beyond, smashing into the Sun Kings like an avalanche. It swept up the Three, and it was all Duma could do to ignore the searing pain of his broken ribs and grab hold of Sofya and Loulouthi, before the blast tumbled them unceremoniously away. It gathered up Fulza, Gaven and Jubal, along with many others who lay dead or unconscious in the wreckage, casting them all onward and outward.

Only Fulza, recovered from the Scribe's assault, managed to resist at all. Catching hold of a jutting piece of wall with one strong hand as he sped past it, he clung on tightly while the rest were flung to the furthest edges of the ruined Keep.
"Joseera!" he cried out desperately, "*Joseera!*"

As the terrible force battered against it, hammering it with flying shards of stone and debris, and threatening to uproot even its great bulk, the Sun King turned to look at its brothers. As the Sun King watched, it saw the gleaming gold light of their bodies begin to swell and darken, turning a thick and baleful purple-blue instead. It raised an arm against the blasting wind, and looked down at its own hand, seeing the golden skin start to crack, to tarnish and blacken.

"We have failed then." said another.

As its own vision darkened, the Sun King looked up into the sky.

"The sun will always rise."

oOo

In the darkness of the ruins at the river's edge, two twisted figures lay quietly, arms stretched out towards each other, just a little out of reach.
"This was ever *dangerous*, my love." whispered the first, softly, "We misjudged him."
"Don't fear, my sweet." replied the other, "We are together, still."

Chapter Thirty-One

The buffeting wind tore at Fulza's skin, and he felt as though it might be stripped from his bones altogether by the screaming gale, but he held fast regardless. Biting dust and chips of rock and stone stung his face and arms, and it was all he could do to keep his eyes open against the wind. He could not see what had happened to Gaven or Jubal, or any of the others. On the platform ahead though, he could still make out Joseera hanging in the air above the Font. The figure next to her seemed different now, somehow changed. Fulza could not be sure if he saw true, squinting into the storm, but it looked as though the Scribe had faded from focus, edges blurring in the air, as dark, smoky tendrils twisted outward and around Joseera. It did not matter though. Whatever was happening, Fulza did not intend to leave Joseera now. He did not intend to fail her again. Grimly, though his limbs burned from holding on, though his skin pricked with tiny needles, Fulza reached out with one mighty hand, and began to drag himself forward. Somewhere behind, even over the raucous howl of the wind, he heard an almighty crash, and a dull metal ringing, but he put it from his mind, focusing all his strength into inching closer to Joseera.

On the platform, the Scribe heard the terrible crash too, and gleefully looked to the source of the noise. Its golden skin now rippled and blistered, a wet, tarry black, one of the Sun Kings had fallen to the rushing force pressing against it. An avalanche of metal pounded into the floor, great weight shattering the stone beneath to powder and causing huge chunks of rock and earth to launch into the air, only to be shredded by the hurricane blasts and hurled lethally outward.

The Scribe laughed. Few would have recognised him now, disfigured by the lodestones and the flow of power through him, as he strengthened his hold upon Joseera, and drew himself closer to the Seri-gae he craved. He entwined the girl in smoky tendrils, whispered and goaded her, guiding and encouraging as she gave in to his will, releasing the force at his bidding.
"Yes, child, good... Let it flow, child, let it come to me!"

Fulza's dogged advance had brought him a few feet closer to the platform. He could barely see anything now, but peered up at the dark shape outlined against the sky he took to be Joseera. He fought to fill his lungs in the rushing air, and shouted hoarsely out to her.
"Joseera! Joseera! Don't give up! Hear me, girl? Don't give up! I'm coming, girl! Don't give up!"

Behind him, another of the Sun Kings stumbled. For a moment the stricken giant hung in the air, gripped by the wind, then it toppled, ripping through the remnants of the Keep's thick walls like paper. The resounding smash rang out over the howling rush of the wind, as the Sun King hammered into the ground beneath, sending spinning shards of stone wheeling into the gale.

Fulza heard the noise and gave a yell of helpless frustration, shouting blindly into the wind.
"Joseera! Hold on, girl! I'm coming!"
The Scribe cast his gaze out at the desperate Savage, and laughed cruelly. Although Fulza had not thought it possible, he felt the blasting gale grow stronger still, tearing at his fingers as if it *wanted* him to leave go. He roared, and dug deep into the little stamina he still had, and his grip held firm. Behind he heard a thunderous

chorus of booming impacts, deep, metal echoes and showering stone.

On his left Fulza watched the Sun King drag its vast bulk through the rubble, scoring deep gouges in the stone as it went. Although its golden hide was split and swollen by the dark blight that afflicted its brothers, its eyes still burned ferociously. With a yawning screech of protesting metal, blasting wind whistling discordantly, the Sun King raised its fist high in the cold morning air
"Wait!" Fulza cried to the giant, screaming out against the wind, "Give her chance! Give her time!"
The great golden head turned painfully, and Fulza heard the Sun King's voice, dry and cracking.

"No time left."

The hand of blackened gold fell.

The wind dropped as suddenly as it had begun, and Fulza lay breathless and exhausted on the ground, feeling the full cost of his exertion. Painfully, he lifted his head in bewilderment. The Sun King had not directed its strike at Joseera and the Font. Instead, its broad hand had fallen at the platform's edge, sheltering Fulza from the hurricane that pinned him down. Great blasts tore at the giant's hide, blistering flakes of metal tearing free as it shook and shuddered under the force, but it held, and Fulza was able to move.

"*Go,*" came the echoing voice again, while the golden skin bubbled and darkened.

Fulza needed no further encouragement. He quickly found his feet, and hurried forward as fast as his battered body could manage. When he reached the great golden hand, he twisted under the long fingers, bracing against them in preparation for the force beyond. Joseera was barely visible now, in a crackling, arcing swirl of energy, wicked forks leaping and jetting forth unpredictably. Leaning forward, powerful legs driving on, he crept closer to the Font.

The Scribe was ready for him, and reached out, wrapping Fulza in a huge wreath of malignant force. Scorching agony leapt through Fulza's body, searing his bones and scalding his flesh, but he did not cry out, and he held his gaze firmly on Joseera.

oOo

From behind the shelter of a broken pillar, the Three looked out at the awful scene beyond. Even here, the rush of wind was deafening, and the Book shouted to be heard above it.
"We have to do something! He'll kill them both, then who knows what?!"
The Sword nodded.
"You're right, Sofya! But what?" he gestured to his broken ribs, her twisted leg, "We're hardly in good shape here ourselves!"
The Heart drew one of her sharp little daggers, and handed it to him.
"What about this, Duma? Can you use this?!"
"Normally, perhaps!" he shook his head, "But how can I throw like this? And against this tempest?!"
The Book rubbed her hands together. "I'll take care of the wind! Loulouthi, can you deal with the rest?!"
"I can, Sofya! I will!"

The Heart drew a deep breath, and reached out her hands, placing them on her friends shoulders. In an instant the wind seemed somehow quieter, and the pain of their wounds was gone. A great calm overtook them, and they felt at peace. The Book and the Sword looked at each other, and nodded.

"Ready, witch?"

The Book lifted her arms and found focus easily, despite the chaos surrounding them. Her hands twisted in the air, and channel of stillness shot forth, tunnelling through the hurricane wind towards its source.

"Now, Duma. Throw!"

With practised ease, now untroubled by injury, the Sword launched the little dagger with a powerful flick of his arm, sending it hurtling straight and swift at its target.

oOo

At the Font, the Scribe could taste victory. The force that flowed through him now was unlike anything he could have imagined, and he savoured its touch, manipulating it with pleasure, marvelling at the waves of torment he poured forth on the prostrate Savage beneath him. The Sun Kings had fallen, barely a challenge against a power such as this, and now the Savage would die a painful death for his interference. Then the Scribe would consume the girl, and-

At the edge of his awareness, the Scribe noticed something odd. A path, a calm avenue of air at his side, defying all reason, and - what was this? Travelling along it, something glitters and spins...

Instinct flaring, the Scribe jerked his head violently back, just in time. The sharp little missile missed his eye, instead opening a deep gash along his cheek. The Scribe cried out, in animal reaction to the pain, and for a moment almost lost control of the terrible power around him. Then, quickly, he gathered himself.

Just for a second, through the flickering light, Fulza thought he had seen Joseera's eyes regain focus, looking down into his, full of pain and fear. Though his voice burned in his throat, and pain almost took his words, still he looked up in hope and called out to her.
"Am-am here, girl! W-won't leave you! Don't give up, girl, don't give up! Joseera, don't give up!"
Through the chaos, their eyes found each other again.

In the whirl of energy that surrounded him, the Scribe felt a flutter of panic. Impossible as it seemed, his hold on the girl was weakening. Despite the incredible rush of Serigae flowing up through the Font, intoxicating and absolute, in his brief moment of inattention the girl had somehow changed something. The power was still there, but now she moved it further from his reach, and with each passing second she drew it further still. Although it ravaged her body and tore at her mind, her resolve seemed to strengthen as the life ebbed from her, as if she would rather die than give in. Then the cold realisation dawned on the Scribe that this was exactly her intention. Just as others had, so very long ago, the girl meant to sacrifice herself. The rush of exhilaration he had felt at the proximity of the ancient power, was replaced by a terrible, burning rage.

She meant to cheat him.

Summoning all of his strength, fuelled and bolstered by his anger, he tore into Joseera, and his voice screamed out in her head.

"How dare you resist me! Ancients command you, child! Give in to me! It is written! It is my *destiny*!"

Wicked claws lashed at Fulza, ripping at his flesh, great weals springing up on his skin. Through the searing air and hail of dust and grit, Fulza saw the Scribe lean in towards Joseera, and although he could not hear the voice, he could just make out the shape of the words that fell from the twisted lips.

"*Give in to me, child, or this Savage dies.*"

Joseera's eyes fixed on Fulza and between them everything else disappeared. She felt his resolve, calm and absolute. She felt his strength, supporting her, holding her up, replenishing her. She felt his love. When she found her voice, it was flat and peaceful, and she spoke just one word.

"No."

The word still hung in the air, when, with an odd rushing absence of sound, the bright energy around the Font disappeared, sucked back into the centre of the thing itself. For a brief moment, the Font stood, plain and unassuming, as if nothing had take place at all. Joseera, no longer held aloft by the swirling power, fell limply from the air. The second before she struck the ground, Fulza's broad and powerful arms caught her and drew her safely to him. Her eyes never left his.

On the other side of the Font, the Scribe stood, grasping the carved handles weakly. His tall figure looked just as it had before, save an emptiness about him now, as if he had been hollowed out. His frail frame wavered, and the old man looked helplessly about him.

"Oh… it's gone… it's gone…"

Around the Keep, something was happening to the vast shapes of the Sun Kings. Their golden skin began to clear and gleam again, their deep eyes returning to a warm glow. Great limbs shifted and creaked, stone rumbling beneath them as they climbed slowly to their feet.

"No! You can't!" sobbed the Scribe, "You can't! It's mine! I felt it! It was mine! It was mi-"
His voice caught abruptly in his throat as though constricted, and his face began to turn a mottled red. Beneath his papery skin, every muscle and sinew drew tight, pale arteries bulged at the surface, split and swelled beneath. The Scribe's thin hands locked tightly to the Font.
"Oh no, p-please... So much... s-so much power..."
Shuddering gasps escaped his bloodless lips as he looked down to where Fulza and Joseera lay.
"*Help me.*"

The Font exploded in light.

From the middle of the platform where the Font had stood, a vast column of spinning force burst forth, shattering the Font itself, and tearing the Scribe's fragile body apart in an instant. It thundered upwards, launching powerfully into the sky like the greatest of geysers. Where it met the clouds, they spun and circled, turning the sky above into a dark, churning sea, cruel and threatening. Fulza threw himself desperately over Joseera to protect her, and screwed up his eyes, blinded by the intense light. Unseeing, he scrambled away, dragging Joseera with him.

At the centre of the whirling storm on the platform, the flow of Seri-gae coursed round and inward, circling and growing uncontrollably. It swelled and fed upon itself, increasing impossibly fast, pulling chunks of the stone platform away into the sky, as still it grew stronger, wider, a vast waterfall turned on its head.

At the broken edges of the ruins, the Three, dazed and bloodied, looked back at the platform from the Keep's battered doors.
The Sword shouted over the deafening noise. "What is this? What's happening?"
"Something has happened to it, the seal is broken, Duma!" the Book yelled back. "There's no control, no way to stop the flow!"
"What do we do?!" cried the Heart.

Ahead, the platform split and shook, as the swirling column broadened and intensified.

"I don't know, Loulouthi, I don't know!" replied the Book. "But look!"
Wild-eyed, she pointed over to the Sun Kings, waving her finger at the etched golden back of the nearest of the giant figures.
"That symbol, Loulouthi, Duma! That symbol! Don't you recognise it?! The chains we wore about our own necks! Look!"

oOo

Outside the city, others heard the terrible roar as the Font crumbled and Seri-gae flooded out, and saw the great tower of energy leaping into the sky, a churning, purple-white tornado. As the clouds darkened above them, people stared awestruck at the incredible sight, then a few began to panic. They cried out in terror and dismay, proclaiming the end, inciting others to flee for their lives. In a few short minutes, there was chaos outside the city walls, a flurry of bodies, screaming and running.

Parvel and Juna stood, clinging tightly to each other, staring up at the terrible vortex rising from beyond the city walls.
"Be safe, Joseera," Juna whispered softly, "Be safe, Gaven. Please, be safe."

oOo

Towering above the tiny figures of Fulza and Joseera below, the Sun Kings looked down, golden faces as implacable, unreadable as ever, while the vast column of energy burst into sky.

"The seal is broken. There are none left who can remake it," said the second. "*It will bleed the land dry. It will consume the world.*"

"*They have brought about destruction.*" said the third.

The first said nothing. Instead he took a step towards the swirling beam.

"*What are you doing, brother?*" asked the second.

The first turned for a moment, and looked back at his brothers.
"*They did not give up. They stood in our path, fragile and futile. They still hoped.*"

"*The folly of the living.*" replied the third. "*They have not seen as we see.*"

The first turned away, looking out across the city, and into the Fold beyond. His gaze fell on a great spreading tree far in the distance, standing lonely on the slopes of the Long Hills. Frail, fresh leaves swayed calmly with a gentle breeze, and somewhere, deep within the cold, metal body of the Sun King, a recollection stirred. The first remembered a tree far larger than the one he looked upon, for in his memory it towered over him as he stood beneath its branches. He remembered the rough feel of the bark against his hands, the soft whisper as the wind crept by, making him shudder and prickling his skin. He remembered the sun, creeping out from behind the clouds, shining, dappled, through the spreading branches. He remembered the colours, and the gentle warmth upon his back.

"We are ghosts." said the first. *"Forgotten how to live."*

He stood before the spinning vortex, spiralling up into the air before him, dark purple tongues of crackling force licking out and sparking against his golden hide. He looked down at the tiny figures below, Fulza still huddled over the Joseera, shielding her from harm. Then he reached out with one great hand, and pushed it forward, into the maelstrom.

The pain he felt was immediate, and surprising. The first almost pulled back in response, more through unfamiliarity than discomfort. He wondered at the dark energy that could make even a frame as cold as his feel such a thing. Then he gathered his resolve, and began to push down, trying to bring his hand to the source of the flow. His metal skin danced with agony made all the harsher by the strangeness of sensation. His joints burned and stabbed, pain forcing a path through any chink or open plate, and the swirling light began to flow around him and into him, crackling through his limbs and blazing in his eyes. Despite his size, the first realised with despair, it was not enough. The flow of energy was too strong.

The pain grew greater still, and a wretched hopelessness grew with it. Then a golden hand clutched his.

One after another, the Sun Kings thrust into the flow, until they stood, together, six great hands clasped in the beam. The pain of the first spread among them all as they pushed against the thunderous energy, together. The dark force screamed, and whirled around them, whipping at their bodies, tearing stone from the earth, lifting the debris and casting it high into the air. Still they stood, and struggled against it. Yet it was not enough.

At the edges of the ruins, three small figures echoed the Sun Kings' movement, hands clasped together, eyes tightly closed. Together they reached out to the giants, giving over what little strength and power they had left to bolster the great spirits within, bracing their will and renewing their resolve. Together they stood, and struggled. Yet it was not enough.

Far below the golden figures, at the base of the storm, Joseera lay in Fulza's arms, sheltered by his broad shoulders. She looked up into the dark, kind eyes sat deep in his hard face.
"Thank you, Fulza."
Joseera smiled, and the light of her smile began to grow, soft and warm, spreading into her eyes and throughout her until Fulza was bathed in it, and it was all he saw.

"*Sunrise.*" said the first.

With a final, rumbling impact, the six great hands fell heavily onto the Font, the base of the whirling column, and in an instant, there was peace.

The dark beam rising into the sky vanished, and the roaring winds ceased, dropping the stones and furniture, beams and rubble they carried. All was quiet in the ruins of the Keep.

Three great figures stood frozen, motionless, hands planted together on the stone between them. The sun danced and sparkled on their golden skin, and beneath them, a Savage knelt, cradling a slight, red-haired girl in his arms.

"Girl?" whispered the Savage, "It's done, girl. Wake up now, it's done. Joseera?"

He didn't look up or respond when voices called out from the ruined doors of the Keep, and he did not notice the Three hurrying across the field of debris towards him, shouting out as they came. He did not notice the great boar, hobbling awkwardly through the scattered rock and wood. Instead the Savage remained still, his eyes fixed on the girl's face as he murmured her name again and again.

"Joseera? Forgive me, girl... Don't leave me, Joseera. Please, don't go."

The girl did not move.

The Savage's eyes widened, and he gasped. Quickly he went to his pack and dug through the contents with furious speed. After a few moments searching, he pulled forth a small bundle, wrapped in cloth. He laid it gently down on the floor, then carefully, gingerly began to unwrap it. Inside lay a curious twisted thing, like the knotted root of an old tree, but rather than a wooden brown it shone a pale golden colour, iridescent.

The Savage looked around, pulling aside pieces of the broken stone, until he found a small, clear patch of earth. Then he scraped at it with his hands, making a rough hollow. When the hole had been dug, he looked down into it uncertainly for a moment. Then he placed the twisted thing down into the dirt, and pushed the earth back into place, filling the hole and patting it down again.

"There." he said softly.

The words had no sooner fallen from his lips than the earth before him shifted. As he watched, a thin, golden stalk pushed itself up through the earth. It stretched skyward, until a tiny leaf unfurled itself at the tip, white-gold and glistening.

After a moment, the Savage smiled.

Epilogue

The city of Bantha stands against the side of a great slope, at the foot of the Long Hills. At the base of the hill, a wide river, called the Pulchren, runs fiercely by, and gives life to the city as it does. Bantha is, in the manner of such places, a strange construction to look upon – architecture, buildings and styles from every age, new and fashionable stood next to the ancient and traditional. Strangest of all though, visitors will tell you, is the wide open space that lies at the centre of the city. An great open square is home to a mighty tree, its leaves a soft golden colour, strong branches spreading wide as the people of the city come to sit, and talk, or rest beneath its shade. And beyond that, a huge statue, bigger than any you have seen, and cast in glittering gold. Three figures, knelt together, hands clasped on the earth.

oOo

The people of Lerncos were hard-working if nothing else, and as such, every family found themselves in a serviceable house well before the first frosts of the new winter arrived. Many had taken the opportunity to expand and improve upon the buildings that had stood there before, and everyone had pitched in to help their neighbours. The village had a fine new inn and tavern, with a grand fireplace that the landlord, Tutty Cooksharp, was particularly proud of, and the village hall was the quite the best that old Jarry had ever seen, or so he said.

As the dim light of the last warm autumn evening began to fade, a broad, gnarled hand lifted the staff it held, and knocked gently with the golden pommel on the little door of a modest house at the village's edge. After a few moments, the door opened, and Parvel Mayweather peered out. He looked the tall visitor up and down, and his face softened.

"Mister Fulza, hello," he said, with a sad smile, "It's good to see you again. But what brings you so far from the city?"
The broad Savage smiled briefly in return, then his expression darkened.
"Your daughter, Parvel Mayweather," came the rumbling voice, "Joseera."
A dozen emotions crossed Parvel's face in the space of a few seconds. He eyed Fulza warily.
"Joseera." he whispered, "What is it? What about her?"

Fulza's wide brow furrowed for a moment, and his gaze fell to the dusty earth at his feet. Then he looked up, eyes shining.

"She's back."